W9-DIL-865

Being Audrey Hepburn

Being Audrey Hepburn

MITCHELL KRIEGMAN

THOMAS DUNNE BOOKS
ST. MARTIN'S GRIFFIN ⚏ NEW YORK

THOMAS DUNNE BOOKS.
An imprint of St. Martin's Press.

BEING AUDREY HEPBURN. Copyright © 2014 by Mitchell Kriegman.
All rights reserved. Printed in the United States of America. For information,
address St. Martin's Press, 175 Fifth Avenue, New York, N.Y. 10010.

www.thomasdunnebooks.com
www.stmartins.com

Designed by Anna Gorovoy

The Library of Congress Cataloging-in-Publication Data is available upon request.

ISBN 978-1-250-00146-7 (hardcover)
ISBN 978-1-250-01349-1 (e-book)

St. Martin's Griffin books may be purchased for educational, business, or
promotional use. For information on bulk purchases, please contact Macmillan
Corporate and Premium Sales Department at 1-800-221-7945, extension 5442,
or write specialmarkets@macmillan.com.

First Edition: September 2014

10   9   8   7   6   5   4   3   2   1

DEDICATED TO VERONICA GENG

I want to still be me when I wake up
one fine morning and have breakfast at Tiffany's.

—HOLLY GOLIGHTLY

Being Audrey Hepburn

It all started with that little black dress.

Yeah, I mean *the* little black dress—the wickedly fabulous, classic, fashion perfection Givenchy that Audrey Hepburn wore to brilliance in the opening scene of *Breakfast at Tiffany's*.

Right in front of me was the dress dreams were made of.

"Let me try it on, please, please, please," I begged Jess.

"No way," she said. "I'll get fired."

Jess was already the special projects assistant at the Metropolitan Museum of Art in New York City, otherwise known as the Met. It was kind of a glorified grunt and gofer position but a real foot in the door at the museum, and like me she was only nineteen. That was just one of her jobs. Jess attended fashion-design school all day, worked the Met at night, and waited tables with me at "the Hole" on weekends.

Determined to design her own line of clothing before she turned twenty-five, she'd always known what she wanted to do—like the way she "came out" in tenth grade and never looked back. Considering she was an absolute genius with fabric, scissors, and a sewing machine and the most responsible, goal-oriented person on the planet, let alone anywhere near where we lived in South End Montclair, New Jersey, I had no doubt she'd pull it off.

"You won't get fired," I pleaded and gave her my saddest, most pathetic, BFF, *puh-leese let me try on the most spectacular dress in existence* face.

"Nobody's here but you and me. It's the least you can do for dragging me out on a sweaty Friday night in July to sort a bunch of broken pottery fragments from the ancient Nile while all the Park Avenue princesses and baby moguls whoop it up downstairs." We could hear the party from the main galleries below: popping corks and clinking champagne glasses, the opulent uppity classes murmuring obscene nothings to one another in their preppy Manhattan tones at another over-the-top celebutante gala.

Jess was the only person in the world besides my Nan who had any idea what a big deal that dress was to me. *Breakfast at Tiffany's* wasn't just my favorite movie ever, it was my jam, my mantra, my addiction, the one thing that got me through all the crap at home.

Unless you live in a cave, I know you've seen it. I don't know if anything more perfect has ever existed on film. The pearls! The tiara! That *dress*! Really, what would you give to live for one day in a world where it would be perfectly normal to wear a little tiny tiara without looking like a runner-up in the Miss Hackensack pageant?

To think that this scrawny girl who came from nothing could become a fabulous socialite with mobsters and writers and photographers and millionaires falling all over themselves for her. New York City in 1961 was cooler and more wonderful than it is today, so full of possibilities. All the men Holly knew turned out to be rats, of course. Or super-rats. Holly was so right. There are so many super-rats out there.

"Please," I whined. "You know how much I love that movie."

"Yeah, I know," said Jess. "That's why I'm letting you *see* the dress."

I gently lifted the dress out of its archival wrapping and held it up. I knew for a fact that Audrey Hepburn and I were almost exactly the same size, 34-20-35, although she always appeared elegant and gamine, where I tended to be more, well . . . scrawny and boyish. My boobs were smaller—I could maybe hit 32-20-33 if I held my breath and thought Katy Perry.

The black satin was rougher than I expected. It had a hip-length slit on the left side and was accompanied by a pair of elbow-length gloves in a tinted plastic bag pinned to the satin padded hanger inside the box.

Unbelievable.

This was the *mystery* dress that everybody swore existed, but almost nobody had ever seen or touched, Givenchy's hand-stitched original design. I wondered if the delicate smell of the fabric was something from the preservation, though I secretly hoped it was a tiny bit of leftover Audrey Hepburn perfume.

"You're such a stalker," Jess whispered. "Be supercareful. That's like a million-dollar dress."

"Actually, 923,187 dollars. The highest auction price ever received for a dress made for a film at the time. And this one might be worth even more." I sighed and held the dream dress up to my body.

She took a deep breath and looked me in the eye.

"Okay," she said. "Try it on. But just for a minute."

2 If you'd told me that, while I caressed the rough satin of Audrey's famous black dress, my life was about to change in a million unimaginable ways, I wouldn't have believed it. Not because I didn't believe that Audrey's dress was magical. Or that I didn't believe in magic. I did, desperately.

In fact, I saw magic around me all the time—in the lives of the famous people I ogled in movies and magazines and online. But magic was for those people, not me. I just couldn't imagine how magic could even find me sitting in the gray Jersey suburbs where I'd lived my whole life.

Five hours before caressing Audrey's precious Givenchy, I stood at ground zero of my totally unmagical life: the greasy South End diner where I waitressed, the Finer Diner, appropriately nicknamed the Hole. I was wearing "eau de short-order grill," the smelly, sweaty perfume of a diner waitress, along with a greasy pink apron. I had just dropped two mugs of coffee and a plate of fried pickles. The zombie shift at the diner was enough to kill you, and I had just finished a double. It wasn't like I had anything else to do.

Making my way home on 21S, one of New Jersey's finest state highways, I thought I might fall into a coma. I turned off at the 4th Avenue exit, struggling to keep my eyes opened, and drove down Bloomfield Avenue to my house, thankful there were no cars outside.

"Hey, sis, you look like shit," Ryan said, startling me as I stumbled through the front door. For a thirteen-year-old, he already had a sewer mouth. But considering the way Mom talked, what could you expect? He gave me a crooked grin and twirled that nasty braided mullet of his. As usual, Ryan was playing World of Warcrack, as Mom called it. The most addictive computer game ever created, where kids with no lives have names like Worgen and are always leveling up.

"Thanks a lot, Ry. Where's Mom?" I asked.

"She went with Courtney to pick up her car. It got towed."

"Again? How long ago?" I contemplated whether to flee and crash at Jess's house.

Car doors slamming and the rusty screech of the screen door gave me the answer—it was too late.

"You don't know crap!" Mom yelled as she barreled through the door. "You can't go through life without a plan." She lit up a cig and headed for the kitchen. She wore her usual pale blue scrubs from the hospital.

"I have a plan! It's just not *your* plan!" screamed Courtney, stomping just a few steps behind, tramping around in her furry boots wearing shredded Daisy Dukes. Her deep-scoop tank was so tight that her breasts looked like they'd pop out any second.

Ryan gazed up at me with that glazed look and went back to slaying warlocks and werewolves. A death stare from Courtney made it clear that, unless I wanted to become the equivalent of roadkill, I had better get out of there. Getting in the middle of a blowout was the last thing I wanted to do anyway. In this situation, either Mom or Courtney could train their sights on me, so I made a beeline for my bedroom.

"Where do you think you're going?" Mom shouted. I froze. Between alcohol and cigs, her voice sounded like she had swallowed a shot glass.

"I just got off work and I smell like bacon," I said as softly as possible. "I have to take a shower." She turned to the cabinet, grabbed her coffee mug, and went to the fridge for some ice cubes. I slinked away.

The walls in our house were so flimsy that even in my bedroom I could hear Courtney clomping across the linoleum floor and Mom rattling the ice cubes in her cup of Gordon's.

It didn't take much to get Mom going at Court. Toenail clippings left on the bathroom floor? A 2:30 A.M. hookup in the driveway? The fact that my older sister was flunking out of junior college because she hadn't attended a class? Or just another bad day of work at the hospital for Mom—all of the above could trigger Argumageddon. I did, however, know how it would end. The same way it always ended.

You would have thought Mom would have been happy she wasn't drunk driving. I guess it didn't help that Courtney had left her car by the side of the road in a stupor for the second time this month. The three-hundred-dollar towing fee had to hurt.

"A plan is something with a future. Responsibility. Not getting shitfaced, smoking weed with your idiot friends, and leaving your car by the side of the road," Mom spit out downstairs. "I can't keep saving your ass all your fucking life."

"Nobody wants you to!" Courtney screamed.

Mom was wrong about Courtney. She *did* have a plan. Her goal was to relieve the world of all its alcohol, one Jell-O shot at a time, in Jersey City's vast array of lowlife nightclubs, while fantasizing she would get picked next season as a finalist on *American Idol* or *The Voice*. Courtney believed she should get her own reality show—hey, everybody has that same dream, right? Once, she made up a whole new family and seriously tried to get a slot on *Mob Wives*. There just aren't enough of those reality shows around for all of us real people to become famous.

Sometimes, it seemed like Courtney was trying to outdo Mom. See, I knew from Nan, my grandmother, that back in her day, Mom was the same as Courtney, only more so. Before MTV discovered New Jersey, Mom was drinking and cruising the seventy-five exits of the Garden State Parkway from Whippany to Seaside Heights. She practically invented shooting beers. She was like the original JWoww, before rehab became a college alternative.

The door slammed, and the vibrations echoed throughout our tiny house. The walls might as well be hospital partitions. That slam was definitely the kitchen door. I listened for the sound of Courtney's junker starting.

Nothing. Shit. That meant get ready for round 2.

Really, in this situation, the best thing to do was to lock myself in the closet. I just needed to stay out of the line of fire; otherwise, I'd be collateral damage.

I was the middle child. Staying out of the way was my specialty. In fact, I was so out of the way, I was nowhere, but that was better than being somewhere in the middle of what was going on at home.

"You're just mad because you're old and you're always going to be alone and nobody cares about you!" Courtney yelled. I guessed Court had come back inside.

There was a pause for crying until Mom finally said something that was hard to hear because it was buried in tissues. "You have no right to talk to me that way . . ." And another pause. "This is my house."

"Nobody cares!" screamed Courtney. The door slammed again, and I waited.

Inside my closet, the sounds coming from downstairs were considerably more muffled. You probably thought I was kidding about the closet.

My closet was my haven, my panic room, my refuge. Mom usually came home from work at 4 P.M. and got her drink on until she passed out on the couch. Once in a while, she'd get super tipsy and silly—singing old Springsteen songs. That was fun. We'd play along until she fell asleep at the kitchen table. But most of the time, she'd get all weepy, and then start hurling ashtrays. She was always angry.

See, Mom never had a "plan" either. After her party years, she never moved away like she told Nan she would. She expected Dad would make money someday, but instead he ditched us and left Mom with a ton of debt.

Eventually she had to make ends meet, so she went back to her maiden name to avoid all the creditors and spent a year in vocational school to become a nurse. We ended up in South End, which isn't exactly Upper Montclair or even Lower Montclair. Lower Montclair, which we're close to, was where all the hip professionals lived. They had three ice cream shops and lots of espresso bars and clothing stores like Anthropologie and American Apparel. In South End, we had the K&G Fashion Superstore and Advanced Auto Parts.

Mom worried 24-7. She worried about the dishes in the sink, about the heating bills, about Courtney stealing her last two cigarettes. Then there was my brother, Ryan. At thirteen, he had racked up so many misdemeanors that the security guards at the courthouse knew him on sight.

And *my* "plan"? Good question.

My life was mapped out. I'd always been the good girl. As much as I'd missed out on a lot of the kind of wild stuff Courtney did (binge drinking, wet T-shirt contests, and generally waking up someplace and having no idea how you got there), I was fine with following the rules. Honestly, I didn't want to put myself out there that much. Too many friends and friends of my sister's ended up pregnant early, drunk, addicted, or dead without ever even getting old. Maybe it was that middle-kid thing (if you consider my younger brother, Ryan, in the category of "kid," rather than, say, devil spawn or homeland terrorist threat). I never had a rebellious phase.

But just because I was quiet didn't mean I had no opinions. In my head I always had a witty retort. I just never had the guts to say anything out loud. I'd mumble to myself or write it down in my journal. No one really knew I had a clue, except Jess. After all, I wasn't sitting home like a shut-in licking orange dust from the last bag of Cheez Doodles or anything. I'd go out weekends just to get out of the house. I drank a little, but I never got in trouble or drew attention to myself.

Mom's plan for me was two years at Essex County Community College to get all my requirements out of the way and then Montclair State University for a MSN or DNP degree. Mom wouldn't have to pay my room and board because they were both close to home. The goal was to become a nurse-practitioner, which was one step below a doctor but a step above being a nurse like Mom. Mom told everybody about her plan for me whenever she introduced me to anyone.

The truth was, I'd agreed and got decent grades just to keep everyone off my back. Courtney even helped me cram for finals because she wanted me to go, too. It took the pressure off of her.

Downstairs, Courtney must have come back inside. She was still screaming, but the words were hard to hear with my closet door closed. They were probably in the living room. But it didn't matter where in the house they were. I knew the words by heart. In fact, I was the only one who knew *why* they fought—even though they didn't.

Underneath it all, Mom and Courtney always argued about the same thing. My sister and my mom were like the same person at different points in time. Like *Back to the Future*, where you traveled forward in time but had to be careful not to run into your future self at the Piggly Wiggly because the space-time continuum would collapse. That space-time collision pretty much happened at my house every day.

Though Courtney was a total bitch to me, I felt for her, because Mom knew everything Courtney was going to do wrong before she even thought of doing it, like she was crawling inside her skin. I think that's why Courtney pushed it to the limit.

Then there was my surprise baby brother, Ryan, who seemed destined to become a complete undermining tool. Dad left a few months before Ryan was born. Funny about that.

When Ryan was little, he burned through babysitters like toilet paper. It didn't matter if they were nice old ladies, perky teenagers, a Navy SEAL or the Cat in the Hat. None of them made a difference, and none of them lasted. Mom used to joke that she felt like the devil recruiting new souls for a three-to-midnight shift in hell. Once Ryan turned twelve, Mom just gave up.

It sounds weird, but I'd been hanging in my closet since I was five. First time was when Dad put his fist through the kitchen wall, which was followed by a barrage of dining room plates Mom hurled at him. Years later, Courtney and Mom's screaming matches sent me into hiding again

I pulled the door tight. It was pretty comfy when I was little, almost like a walk-in, so it's not like I was a total coffin freak. Although these days, I had to squeeze. Even though we didn't have AC, the temp in my closet was pretty cool. Mashing the pillows around me like a nest, I pushed the big turquoise body pillow to the door, blocking the light and their voices.

I grabbed a Coke out of the minifridge. Yes, I had a minifridge in my closet. I won it by selling more wrapping paper and chocolate than anyone in the history of my tenth-grade class. My secret weapon was to hit up old lady Conner down the street for a bundle. She smoked a lot of weed and bought my chocolates so I wouldn't tell anyone. As if I would.

I opened my laptop and thanked God for the Internet. There was always a new Web site to check out. I think the Internet was designed for people like me, who need somewhere to go to forget where they really are.

Within a dozen clicks, I could get lost in the urgent need to know the most important details about all the stuff I couldn't have, didn't need, but couldn't live without. There was an update on the hot young royals at Jezebel, Kate Bosworth's ultrachic cocktail sheath, and red python-print heels at FabSugar, a rundown of who's prematurely aging at TMZ for their "Celebs Without Makeup" feature, a sneak peek at Jason Wu's unbelievable new designs for Fashion Week, and a fleeting look at Page Six, the old standby, where I saw the latest on Taylor Swift. Ugh. Did they pass a law requiring that every celebrity Web site had to have a feature on Taylor Swift's crimped dos and her latest glitter-like-a-princess dress?

Once that was out of my system, I clicked on the DVD in my computer—*Breakfast at Tiffany's*.

As the mournful first chords played over the Paramount logo, I fell into a trance. I was there on the street as the lone cab crept up Fifth Avenue, the melancholy notes of "Moon River" weaving their way through my headphones, deep into my cerebral cortex and through my entire body, like the gas they give you at a dentist's office when your wisdom teeth are removed.

Sinking into the pillows, I melted away to be with Audrey as she stepped out of that yellow 1960 Ford Galaxie taxi wearing the exquisite Givenchy with those extravagant gloves and the four giant strands of pearls. We looked up at the chiseled Tiffany & Co. name above its Fifth Avenue entrance and gazed through the jewelry store window at those miniature chandeliers and floating bracelets, all the while sitting in my closet.

Although I was completely addicted to all of Audrey Hepburn's movies, *Breakfast at Tiffany's* was my total fix.

It was my IV drip bag.

3 Here's the big secret—Audrey Hepburn is the cure for everything.

Dumped by your lifelong crush? *Sabrina*. Want to escape your life and go incognito? *Roman Holiday*. Tired of being a bookworm? *Funny Face*. Crisis of conscience? *The Nun's Story*. Family secrets to cover up? *How to Steal a Million*. Ready for a vacation escapade with a little intrigue in Paris? *Charade*.

A movie cure for every need.

Above them all is *Breakfast at Tiffany's*.

I loved the flat-out glamour of *Breakfast at Tiffany's*, the false eyelashes, the roaring parties, the tiaras and pearls, and the "darlings." I loved that Holly Golightly slept with a satin mask and turquoise earplugs with little tassels. I wished I could pull off a look like that.

Edda van Heemstra, Audrey Kathleen Ruston, Audrey Hepburn-Ruston were some of her names, and each one was an evolution toward the Audrey we grew to love. From hours of obsessive online research in the confines of my closet, I knew she grew up during the Holocaust and World War II and was at one point forced to eat tulip bulbs and bake bread out of grass. If Audrey could do all that during a world war, you'd think that I, Lisbeth Anne Wachowicz, growing up in South End Montclair, New Jersey, could make something out of my life. Although the bread-out-of-grass thing seemed totally out of the question.

Breakfast at Tiffany's was the one-hour-and-fifty-five-minute version of my hopes and dreams and all the lurking dangers inbetween. I'll never forget the first time I ever heard Holly Golightly talk about the mean reds. I immediately realized that there were mean reds around me all the time.

Everybody knew that you got the blues because you were stuck or you were depressed or you were being treated unfairly. But the mean reds were more unsettling, because when you have them, you don't know what you're afraid of, except that something bad was going to happen, and you didn't know who to tell or what to do.

There wasn't a time I can remember when I didn't feel that way. Something bad was always about to happen. Mom and Dad were building to a fight. Dad was itching to leave. Mom was getting plastered, and Courtney was nowhere around. Ryan . . . well, who knew what lurked inside that poor boy's soul? And me, what could I do about it all?

When the mean red panic light inside me flashed, I found myself further and further away from who I was or could hope to be. It all just made me want to put everything on hold, keep to myself, and be quiet as a mouse.

I loved Holly Golightly's Tiffany cure. It wasn't about the merchandise. Even Holly said that—she didn't give a hoot about jewelry. "Diamonds are for old elegant white-haired ladies," she said famously.

Have you been to Tiffany's? I don't mean the mall stores like the ones in Short Hills or Hackensack. Fifth Avenue is the only one that will do. Just walk in sometime and experience its tranquility, harmony, and splendor. You don't have to buy anything. Diamonds aren't just a girl's best friend, they're a sparkling tonic for the soul, like summer rain, gazing at the Milky Way, or snowflakes that land on your tongue.

Tiffany's was a state of mind, exquisitely removed from fear and panic. That's what made it medicinal. When Holly Golightly took me on my first Tiffany's tour, I realized that I'd finally found someone who felt what I felt.

Pretty much since my ninth birthday, I'd been watching *Breakfast at Tiffany's* continuously. That's when Nan gave me my first VHS tape of the movie.

I watched that one nonstop until the tape became hopelessly entangled in our secondhand VCR. The replacement copy lasted longer, but I was limited by family viewing time, which meant I couldn't watch when Ryan was mainlining *SpongeBob* and *Fairly Odd Parents*. Thank God for laptops with DVD drives. My closet became my own personal multiplex, my ticket to a world that I lived in more than this one. And it was really all because of Nan.

Nan was my grandmother, my mom's mom. She was so different from Mom; it was hard to believe they could possibly share the same DNA.

Nan laughed all the time and had a totally wicked-smart sense of humor. Tiny and elegant, everything she wore was from the 1960s. She never left her house without a touch of rouge, lipstick, and her classic double strand of pearls—a look she'd been wearing since her debutante days—though she worried about the punks on the street trying to snatch them.

Oh crap! Nan!

I grabbed my phone and checked the time—5:04. Crap, crap, crap. I was supposed to have been at Nan's at five. Yanking off my headphones, I scrambled out of the closet on my knees and dug through the piles of laundry in my room for my favorite pair of jeans, a blouse, and shoes. I slid my laptop into my bag, tossed the bag over my shoulder, and bounded down the stairs toward the kitchen. How was I going to make an exit without getting stuck?

As I tiptoed into the kitchen, I saw Mom at the table in the breakfast nook, her face puffy and red from crying. No sign of Courtney. I couldn't just ignore her, could I?

"Mom, uh, are you okay?" I asked.

Big mistake. She turned full bore on me.

"You better not turn out like your sister." I nodded my head no.

"Good. There's leftover lasagna. Make us something to eat," she said and walked over to the paper towels, wiping her nose. "I'm too upset."

Shit.

I forced myself to say something.

"I have to go."

"What?" She was inspecting me, in that way of hers, like I was under a microscope. Mom has this way of picking on people's sensitive points. Like in second grade, when I used to invite Sarah Policki, our next-door neighbor, over to play, and we'd ask for a snack, Mom would laugh and say that Sarah looked like she'd had too many snacks already. Just like she made fun of my bony knees. Eventually Sarah stopped coming over. Mom wasn't exactly great for your self-esteem, especially when she was drinking.

I saw the wheels turning in her head. There was still too much fight in her.

"Mom, I'm already late for Nan's." I hated that I sounded like I was begging. She paused for a second, probably debating whether she should strike and go for the kill.

"Nan's waiting, Mom. I've gotta go," I said. Seizing the moment, I pushed open the kitchen door.

"We need to have that talk," Mom yelled after me.

I didn't know and didn't *want* to know what "that talk" was.

But what I did know was that she hadn't found out yet.

You know my "plan"? The whole thing I told you about, the one thing Mom was counting on and Courtney almost as much? The Mama's "good girl going to school at Essex and becoming a nurse-practitioner" plan?

I wasn't going.

I hadn't told Mom or Courtney yet. Mostly because I was chicken. But also because I had no idea what I was going to do instead.

I just knew I wanted out. Out of that house, out of that life, out of New Jersey.

As much as I loved my closet, I couldn't do another four years in there.

"I know, Mom. We'll talk later for sure," I shouted back, already out the door.

"I mean it, Lisbeth," she said. "You can't avoid this forever!"

Maybe not.

But I could try.

I ran out the door and headed toward my car as fast as I could.

4
The Purple Beast wouldn't start.

Pumping the gas pedal, I turned the key—holding it more forcefully this time. I had to show my 1965 Cadillac Coupe de Ville who was boss. The starter whined as it cranked. It whined again and finally turned over. The car roared. The Caddy was Nan's, but the lavender paint job was all mine. Twice the size of a normal car, I knew it was environmentally incorrect, ugly, and ate a hole in my pocket because it took two days' worth of tips to fill the purple monster up with gas every week. But if you asked me, it was worth it. Probably the only cool thing about me. I would have gone insane without it.

Grandpa kept the car in perfect shape all those years, so it usually ran like a dream, even if I forgot to change the oil. The only thing that didn't work was the convertible top and the left-turn signal. Hey, nobody in New Jersey uses turn signals anyway.

I threw it in reverse. The car jerked as I backed out of the driveway, swinging narrowly past Mom's old Corolla and rolling over the trash cans at the bottom near the street. Damn, the car had a mind of its own. Shifting it into drive, I made my way up our street toward Nan's part of town.

Nan lived at a retirement village called Montclair Manor. When I was younger, it sounded to me like a really fancy estate with servants in black uniforms and crisp white aprons, tea and cucumber sandwiches at 3:00 in the afternoon—only it wasn't.

The actual Montclair Manor was a dreary cluster of tiny, tumbledown, smog-gray minihouses surrounding a big parking lot and a community house. It had a lovely view of the Barclay's Vinyl Window plant on Route 495 complete with the factory's toxic aroma.

To hear Nan, you'd think she was living at the Waldorf, but this place was depressing as hell. I don't think she's ever complained about it once. She didn't even complain about the fact that the Montclair Manor community dining room smelled like old people's feet. She never complained about any of the aches and creepy diseases that most old people wanted to discuss. And she never complained once about the fact that I was the only one who visited her. My mom and sister hadn't been there in years. Ryan barely knew she existed.

Mom and Nan didn't see eye to eye. That's the nicest way to put it. I wondered if that was something that ran in our family, like nonexistent boobs. There was totally this history of moms and daughters not getting along.

Montclair Manor was an assisted-living home, which meant that the old people were basically on their own, but there was a nurse named Betty and a couple of staffers who checked on the residents every day to make sure that no one had fallen down or, you know, snuffed out in their sleep. I wouldn't mention it, except it happened—twice last year and three times the year before. Sometimes you got a run where these old people dropped like flies.

A crusty old guy two doors down from Nan died in his ratty plaid recliner while reading a romance novel called *The Blackmailed Heiress.* His name was Sarge, Army Retired. His name wasn't actually "Sarge Army Retired." That's just the way he said it every time, and how Nan and I would refer to him. He was eighty-three and still trimmed what little hair he had left in a crew cut. He would drop down for fifty push-ups every morning.

Poor Sarge must have been cringing in his grave, because every one of those old ladies he worked so hard to impress with his macho push-up routine found out, in excruciating detail, about his girly Harlequin-romance-novel habit. Personally, I thought it was cute. When the aides cleaned out his place, they found tons of paperback romances everywhere, stashed under the bed, in his old army footlocker, and under the kitchen counter. Sort of like my mom with booze. Anyway, I guess he didn't want anyone to know that there was a starry-eyed romantic hiding underneath that tough GI exterior.

Nan knew he was a softie. Sarge had a crush on my Nan; he'd tried to flirt with her in that gruff way of his. All of the old guys there did. They would ask Nan out to dinner at Mama Luigi's or line up to dance with her on Copacabana Night. Her eyes still had a twinkle of enchantment in them. I didn't know how she kept it going in that dreadful place.

Betty the nurse was leaving as I walked up the crumbly path to Nan's house. I tried not to laugh when I saw her. She had to be pushing seventy herself. She wore a push-up bra, a bucket of foundation and blush, and she dyed her hair unnaturally jet-black. It shined like the coat on Black Beauty, the horse. She also must have worn an industrial version of Spanx under her uniform. Who knew how she breathed in that thing or how she worked there when she should have been an inmate herself. It was pretty funny when she walked around all day checking on "the old folks" as she referred to the residents, calling them "old dear" and "ma'am" and speaking very loudly while emphasizing every syllable: "HOW ARE YOUR BOW-ELS? DID YOU HAVE A BOW-EL MOVE-MENT TO-DAY?" Please somebody kill me when I get so old people start asking me about the last time I pooped.

"Nan, I'm here," I yelled. I stepped into the living room and took a deep breath, inhaling the scent of rose oil and Joy perfume, which I loved—Nan's patented antidote to wallowing in your own worries.

"On my way, Lisbeth," Nan said. She was precariously balancing a giant cheesecake on a silver platter from the kitchen. "Grab forks and plates, will you please, dear?"

My phone buzzed. It was Mom. I hit IGNORE and stuck the phone back in my pocket.

I dropped my backpack on the dilapidated gold velvet slipper chair by the front door. Nan's place was the same as always—time-warped and tidy. Most of her furniture dated around the 1960s—an eclectically elegant mix of things from her life with Grandpa and the graceful Park Avenue furnishings she inherited when my great-grandmother and great-grandfather died, way before I was born. The rich burgundy embroidery was now yellowed and the silk draperies were probably older, maybe from the forties—and to-tally oversize for the tiny windows they now framed. But Nan made it all work.

"What is this?" I asked. Nan's eyes twinkled mischievously as she set the giant cheesecake down in front of me on the coffee table.

"I was thinking, if you don't mind, we should skip dinner to-night and go straight to dessert?" Nan was my kind of girl.

I nodded and contemplated the cheesecake, which was smoth-ered in chocolate and caramel and pecans. "It does have nuts on it . . ." I said.

"Yes, and pecans are a good source of protein," Nan added.

"Totally, and you can't beat chocolate for antioxidants!" I said.

"Just what I was thinking!" Nan said, delighted. "It's practically health food."

I gave Nan a hug, and she squeezed me tightly.

You have to understand what it was like to be hugged by Nan. You didn't just hug Nan, you melded with her. It felt like your heart and her heart found each other, all perfectly lined up, and they started to beat together. As she hugged you, you noticed her tiny heartbeats grow stronger and stronger with every beat. It was total bliss.

She was petite, as Nan would say, probably five foot five, maybe shorter. Nan did yoga and Aquacise and tap, plus she went ballroom dancing every Thursday. She was as fit as she could be. Once she actually did a headstand right in the middle of her living room. I could hardly believe it. It's not every day you see an octogenarian upside down.

But lately every time I saw her, it seemed as though she was shrinking a bit. I think that really happens—old people just get smaller because they're so wrinkly. You know like how your shirt looks when you take it out of the dryer after a couple of days?

"May I?" I said, cutting us each slices and delicately placing them on two small china plates, giving the biggest one to Nan. Nan always ate on china, even if it was just moo goo gai pan from Ping

Chong's Chinese. According to Nan, every day she had left on the planet was a special occasion. She certainly made it feel that way. She was leaving the china to me in her will, probably because I was her favorite and the only person in the family who wouldn't pimp it on eBay.

"Dear, do you prefer milk or champagne with your cheesecake?" Nan asked as she headed toward the kitchen. I laughed.

"What are you having?" I asked, grabbing a couple of napkins from the veneer antique sideboard.

"Personally, I think a little rosé champagne couldn't hurt," she said. She brought in two flutes of pink bubbly. "Everybody says wine is medicinal, and drinking champagne is like sipping starlight." Her mischievous grin widened, and she whispered, "I want you to have some of the good stuff." We clinked glasses, and the bubbles went right up my nose. And that's when my phone buzzed.

There was a text: "SOS @ the Met MMB☺"

It was Jess. She was working late at the Metropolitan Museum of Art that week. They were always giving her impossible projects to finish by dawn, like cataloging dirty and dusty dioramas or making hundreds of labels for every single jar, lid, bowl and floral collar that ever existed in the pharaoh's funeral tomb. She impressed them every time, but sometimes she was desperate for help or she'd never get out of there. I don't know how she did it—it was kind of like the worst middle school project ever times a thousand, so not my thing. Lately, Jess had resorted to bribery to get me to come.

I quickly texted her back that I was with Nan.

"Hug Nan for me !! But you need to see this !!"

"Is everything okay?" Nan asked.

"Jess says hi," I told Nan, and she blew back a kiss. "Uh, Nan . . . ," I began.

"Go! Have fun with your friend in the city," she said. She was smiling, waving me to leave and picking up the plates before I could say another word.

"Another hug?"

"Certainly, dear." I didn't know who was squeezing tighter, Nan or me.

Jess was texting me on the way out the door to hurry up.

"What's up ?!" I typed as a pleasant champagne buzz kicked in.

"U won't believe it !! ☺"

5 The forty-five-minute train ride was boring. I searched my phone for texts I hadn't answered. I texted everyone and their dog, but no one texted back.

Mom called, but I didn't pick up. I just couldn't deal with her tonight. I tried to slyly read the story on the back pages of the *People* magazine the lady directly across from me held in front of her. Something about Kim Kardashian on a shopping spree in Beijing. But the lady kept shifting, so it was pretty hard to keep my place.

As she turned the page, she caught me leaning forward and gave me the stink-eye, like I was stealing her gossip news. Everyone around me silently turned and glared at me. I shrugged "sorry," and they went back to what they were doing.

I stared mindlessly out the window at the southern view of highways and wires while the train sped its way to the city. I noticed another dirty scowl from the lady with the *People* magazine and zoned out. What was she so cranky about?

I opened my eyes, surprised I was at Penn Station. I hated falling asleep on the train and waking to find everyone gone and me just sitting there. Crap.

Bumping my way through the closing doors, I sprinted up the stairs to catch the bus to the Met. I checked the time on my phone. I could still make it by eight.

I got off the bus and made my way toward the employee entrance of the Met on the left side of the building.

"Here !!" I texted, but rounding the corner at a sprint, I slammed into a wall of people crowding the sidewalk in front me, so I stepped out into the street. I heard a screech and turned to see a limo skidding to a stop behind me. I jumped.

"Sorry," I said. The limo driver drove by, yelling at me. A real New Yorker would have flipped him the bird. There was a flash of light, and I was startled as cameras flashed everywhere around me. I was wearing my favorite jeans and a plaid boyfriend shirt from American Eagle because I don't have one, so I knew I wasn't the focus of their attention.

Through the blinding flashes, an unbelievable vision of wealth and fashion rose up before me. A perfect Bergdorf-blonde trust-fund baby, wearing a short gold shift dress with a plunging neckline and puff sleeves, posed for the cameras. Was she wearing Roberto Cavalli or even Christian Siriano? No matter, the Met was having a huge gala, and I was standing smack in the middle of a photo op. The perfect blonde was followed by a Tory Burch sequin tunic dress on a girl with the skinniest legs and a six-hundred-dollar haircut. To the right of me, a drop-dead-gorgeous guy rose out of a nearby limo.

He flashed a megawatt smile with this amused twist like he was laughing at everybody for admiring him. He spun around to find someone and turned to look at—*me*. I couldn't pull myself away. My heart slowed, thumping louder and louder. Time seemed to shift into slo-mo. He seemed oddly alone. I was so close, I could see that his eyes were hazel green with gold flecks. He was at least six feet tall, and his dinner jacket fit him as if he were an Emporio Armani model or, better, an underwear model for Abercrombie. I closed my eyes and imagined him in his underwear. When I opened them again, I swear he was still staring right at me.

A long pale leg, and one spectacular stiletto (Louboutin, judging by the red on the bottom) stepped out of the limo, followed by a low-cut V-shaped formal dress exposing almost every part of a lithe, tan young body. Was she wearing Versace? Mr. Underwear-Man reached down and helped her out of the car. It was Dahlia Rothenberg, the princess of all celebutantes, totally famous mostly because she was skinny, blond, notoriously promiscuous, and due to inherit half the real estate in Manhattan.

The cameras went crazy as she posed with Mr. Underwear-Man, then alone. God, I couldn't stop staring at her body. I bet she never ate. Linking her arm in his, they sauntered down the red carpet, smiling and chatting as they moved toward the museum entrance with the other young fashionistas. Dahlia made her way up the museum steps in those sky-high heels with elegant, tiny steps. If it were me, I'd have tripped and fallen already.

I said a little prayer that Mr. Underwear-Man would look back at me. Of course, he didn't. He disappeared inside the museum doors. Turning to leave, I found myself blinded by a bright light that beamed steadily in my eyes. It was the light from a camera crew. A scruffy, unassuming guy held the camera as a slick Ryan Seacrest type in a tux with a microphone searched for people to interview. The cameraman noticed me shielding my eyes and moved the light away, and I could see again. He shrugged an apology, and I nodded thanks.

Ohmygod—Tabitha Eden stepped out of another car! Yes, the Princess of Pop, the fave of teenyboppers everywhere. And despite my being way older than her audience, I LOVED HER! She was wearing a supershort silver dress. Completely awesome, by the way. She was totally going to make FabSugar's best dressed. And she managed to get out of the car looking like the star that she was without pulling a Britney.

Every minute I kept watching made me feel like a lowly tourist in a country of fabulousness, but I couldn't tear myself away. The women were stunning, and the men were all graceful and hand-some. I couldn't imagine being with people like that. I personally didn't know any boys who didn't burp the alphabet. Maybe I could track down my father and ask him to set me up with a million-dollar trust fund, a good trick considering he'd never paid child support. Besides, money alone wasn't enough to hang with this crowd.

Limousines, personal shoppers, and weekends in the Hamptons—these kids were just so *not* like me with their thousand-dollar handbags, designer drugs, and life options. It was sick—just another club that I'd never get into, waiting at the ropes as usual. They had all the wealth and glamour in a world where a lot of people I knew were forced to choose between groceries and rent, where kids graduated college with crippling student loans and no job prospects, and where my greatest opportunity in life was to be a nurse-practitioner. I felt like a troll. You'd never know my world existed while gazing at these beautiful and carefree creatures.

I glanced at my watch and realized I had been standing there for over ten minutes. Jess was probably annoyed already waiting at the back door, but I was sort of stuck. There was no direct route to the other side of the building, which meant I had to either cross the red carpet (um, yeah, that would go over well) or go back across the street to get to the other side.

Being a good girl, I opted for the street and made my way up Fifth Avenue. Another limo (or was it the same guy out of spite?) nearly clipped me as I stepped off the sidewalk. Walking halfway up the block, I crossed back to the museum.

"Where r u ?!" Jess texted

Running across the street, I couldn't stop thinking about the gowns, the shoes, and Mr. Underwear-Man's golden-green eyes. As if I'd ever go to a party like that.

At the door, Jess gave me a quick hug. She looked her usual cool—short Halle Berry hair dyed dark blue tucked behind her ear with a pencil and her museum key card hanging around her neck. She wore five or six chunky necklaces, one made of dozens of weird old antique buttons and a black Ramones T-shirt over a tiered skirt with a sort of iridescent blue lining. It must have been one of her own creations—it was way too cool to be off the rack in our price range.

"What took you so long?" she asked.

"You know, the paparazzi were blocking my entrance as usual," I said.

Jess laughed. "Happens to me all the time, dahling."

"What's going on here tonight?" I asked, images of Mr. Underwear-Man on the museum steps wistfully replaying in my mind.

"It's the Millennial Social Register Gala, sorta like prom for Park Avenue Princesses and Moguls in Training with a few pop stars thrown in to make things interesting," Jess said. "Got to admit, it is one *hell* of a fashion show."

As we walked through the back entrance, Joe, the security guard, buzzed us in as Jess nodded and I waved. Following Jess down a series of hallways and up the stairs to the large, very cold room where she worked, I wished I'd brought my hoodie. Even though it was summer, I was shivering. Jess said that the reason it was so effin' freezing in there all the time was that it helped preserve the artifacts. After ten or twenty minutes, I felt like a frozen turkey—so I guess it worked.

The long metal tables were always covered with whatever project Jess had been tasked with. That night, fragments of an Egyptian sculpture—hundreds, maybe thousands of pieces of noses, ears, faces—were everywhere. Jess was wearing a pair of blue nitrile gloves and threw some my way.

"Jeez, did a tourist go nuts and smash up one of the pharaoh statues?" I asked, putting on the gloves.

"Yeah, didn't you hear?" Jess asked. "It was a big deal—three-thousand years ago." She chuckled.

"Ha, sorry, I'm so clueless."

"This is what's left of Queen Hatshepsut, the great female pharaoh who ruled Egypt during Dynasty Eighteen, approximately 1473 to 1458 B.C. Her son did it. Thutmose the Third. He must have been a total dick. When she died, he destroyed all the images of his mom in existence. Thankfully he missed a few. These are the smashed pieces of the funerary temple."

"Maybe he was pissed about that name . . . Thutmose—that had to really suck in middle school."

"For sure. But, lucky me, I get to bar code and enter each of these little fragments into the collection management system. Fun, huh? And you get to help."

"This will make for a thrilling night," I said. "Why do I let you rope me into this drudgery?"

"I guess you must like me," she answered and gave me a goofy grin.

"Hey, didn't you say there was something I *had* to see?"

"Oh yeah, I have a little surprise for you." With a mischievous look, Jess lifted up a large box from under the table.

"Apparently it was recently logged in on loan from Hubert de Givenchy's private archive, no less," she said. "I came across it in my last plunge into the frozen depths of the Met's Costume Institute archives. I'll have to put it back right away."

She gently opened the box and pulled back the paper. I felt my breath catch short as I realized what was inside.

I could hardly believe it.

6 "It's going to be fine," I said, sliding my arms through the holes above my head. My heart was thumping so hard it felt like it might just pop out of my chest.

"Why didn't I know I had asthma until now?" Jess asked, dropping down onto one of the swivel work chairs. "I'm so stressed I can't breathe."

"You'll live," I said as I carefully avoided sticking my hands through the neck opening.

Being a total Audrey fanatic, I knew from endless Internet searches that this was the dress that almost no one in the history of the world besides Hubert de Givenchy had seen and only one person had ever tried on—Audrey Hepburn. That's because the actual dress Audrey wore in *Breakfast at Tiffany's* didn't exist. It was covertly destroyed under the supervision of the notoriously controlling Queen of Hollywood Costume and Wardrobe, Edith Head, and Audrey herself, at least that's what every fan site on the Internet said. Edith Head was kind of the Wicked Witch of the West when it came to Audrey's wardrobe.

But the dress in *Breakfast at Tiffany's* wasn't the dress Givenchy created for her anyway. Givenchy's original, which had a slit along the left leg and a slightly shorter length, was even more exquisite and dazzling than the one in the movie. Givenchy designed the entire ensemble, adding the perfect accessories to match the gown: a bundle of pearls, a foot-long cigarette holder, and opera gloves. Hard to believe, but in those days Hollywood was prudish about showing a little leg—long before Angelina Jolie's gams came peaking out of her dress at the Oscars. Even though Holly was supposed to be an escort kind of call girl, the studio didn't want her to look like one.

Shimmying the dress over my hips, I was actually thankful, for once, that I didn't have any. To think . . . I had to be the only person to try it on since Audrey Hepburn.

It's a bit of a mystery, but most people assumed that the dress Audrey wore in the opening scenes of the movie was a Givenchy. In fact, the dress was a phony redesigned by Edith Head. The dress I was pulling on, with its weighted hem and opening at the leg, was one of three versions in existence that were all Givenchy originals. Audrey likely wore the hand-stitched version when she was fitted by Givenchy, but a photograph of her wearing the dress has never surfaced.

Edith Head's version did away with the open leg and lengthened and tightened the bottom to deemphasize how "revealing" it was. That's why Audrey had to take such tiny Geisha girl steps, almost waddling to the windows at Tiffany's.

It seemed like there was some kind of agreement between Paramount and Audrey that Edith would destroy the two phony dresses she had made after filming, perhaps to save Givenchy the embarrassment of the bogus dresses floating around that were more sedate and conventional than his original design. It's believed that they were taken apart and burned at the Western Costume Company's cavernous warehouses in Hollywood.

The swoon-worthy dress was sliding down my back, and the black lining felt incredibly smooth against my skin, more like a silk hug than a dress.

Of the three dresses Givenchy created that still existed—all with the exposed hip-length slit down the leg—one, a machine-stitched version, was donated to the Madrid Museum of Costume and is permanently exhibited there. Another was sold at a Christie's auction to an anonymous telephone bidder. That anonymous bidder is suspected to be none other than Posh Spice, who is an Audrey fanatic like me, but with money. They say she has an Audrey room in "Beckingham Palace" that she shares with her soccer hubby. I cringed to think what Audrey would have thought of her dress sitting in a Spice Girl's mansion.

Lastly there was the Audrey-fitted original hand-stitched dress, which was the one I had just slipped on.

"Well, instead of sitting there—you could help?" I said, trying to adjust the shoulders.

"Sure, why shouldn't I make it easier for you to get me fired?" Jess snapped off her blue gloves, stood up, and helped pull the dress down. Turning the hem, she had a surprised expression on her face. "Dude, this hand stitching is awesome."

When she gently drew the zipper up, a tiny gasp escaped her lips.

"Ohmygod, Lisbeth, this dress fits like it was made for you." The gown settled perfectly around my hips with a snugness and a lift I had never felt before.

My cheeks flushed with excitement as I searched for a mirror. Spotting one in the corner, I lifted up the dress, feeling the weights that Givenchy had strategically placed in the hem to ensure the fabric fell perfectly on Audrey's body.

"You need shoes," Jess said.

As she rummaged through her giant bag I pulled on the long black gloves.

"How about these?" she asked, holding up a pair of black patent stilettos like she'd just caught a pop fly as it was about to go over the left field fence.

"Ooh! Gimme!" I said, wondering why Jess would keep a pair of these CFM pumps in her bag.

Jess steadied me as I slipped into the heels. I didn't want to sit down for fear I'd wrinkle the dress, imagining Jess trying to explain to the curator how the most famous dress in the history of all dresses ended up with my ass creases.

Jess's shoes were too big (I wear an 8½, Jess wears a 10), but they were for looks, not for dancing, so I didn't really care. I shuffled the rest of the way to the mirror like a kindergartner in her mother's shoes, my heart floating in anticipation.

I was already hyperventilating when I saw myself for the first time. I seemed long and lean and elegant, and with Jess's shoes, even the length was perfect. It just skimmed the patent shoe—an inch or so off the floor, and the fabric revealed just a tiny bit of my ankle. I could hardly believe my eyes. The black dress was perfection.

"You must be the best friend ever." I glanced back at Jess. I'd never seen such a wide-eyed expression like that in her eyes before.

"I can't believe how perfect you look!" A glaze had come over her eyes, as if she were mesmerized by a hypnotic illusion. "Wait! One more thing!" she said and ran out of the room.

She was gone for thirty seconds—but it could have been an hour for all I knew. I was busy staring at myself in the mirror. Someone entirely new was staring back.

"Sorry we don't have the Audrey tiara." Jess reappeared. "Jackie Kennedy's will just have to do."

"You just happen to have Jackie's tiara hanging around in a drawer?" I was shocked.

"Nah, it's a repro. We have like six of them back there. We use them for private events when the dresses are on display." Jess grabbed a comb and a few clips out of her bag.

"Stop fidgeting and hold still; we might as well do this right." She dragged a stepladder from the side closet to where I stood and carefully placed a polyethylene sheet over my shoulders to protect the dress and began cutting. Though she didn't act like it, I knew she loved digging into my hair, pulling and teasing it into an updo.

"Ouch!" I yelped as she yanked an unmanageable chunk into submission.

"Shhh!"

I wanted to tell her that trying on the dress was enough, that she didn't have to do this, but I didn't think she'd stop anyway.

Jess is the queen of updos, mostly because her mom owns a beauty salon. Every Saturday morning since the time she was eight, her mom would drag her to the beauty shop to crank out hair helmets and elaborate chignons and poufs for the never-ending procession of brides, bridesmaids, mothers of the bride, and various Garden State big-hair fanatics. But I never knew how torturous it could be.

"Does it have to hurt so much?" I pleaded.

Jess pinned the final strands of hair into place, before tightly securing the tiara—directly to my skull, from the feel of it. Then she pulled out a pair of scissors and started cutting my bangs!

"Come on, Jess, now you're getting carried away."

Crap. My last bangs disaster took seven months to grow out to any degree of normalcy. I'd been stuck in the dreaded barrette stage for three months. She made cut after cut.

"Ha! I've been dying to do this for years," she said, clipping maniacally.

Helplessly, I watched five-inch clumps of my agonizingly slow-growing hair float past my eyes and settle on the floor.

She stopped and searched through her giant bag; I stole a quick glance at myself in the mirror—it was flawless.

"Close your eyes. Just one more thing—don't peek."

I obliged, despite the fact that not seeing the dress every possible second was driving me insane. Did she have to stand in front of the mirror the whole time? Jess sprayed my hair with something, most likely the same stuff she uses to keep her own hair defying gravity for fourteen hours a day. It smelled citrusy, like tangerine. I tried to peak around her, but she smacked me on the side of my head like a child.

"Eyes closed—I'm not done yet." I felt her applying eyeliner to my lids, powder to my cheeks, and a gloss to my lips.

"Okay, you can see now," she said as I felt the plastic covering slip away.

I opened my eyes and a wonderful stranger smiled back at me from the mirror. She was beautiful and elegant. The kind of girl I wished I could be. Jess had performed a miracle. My normally mousy-brown hair was transformed; the tiny tiara gave just the right touch of sparkle to the clean and simple yet sky-high updo. My eyes were lined dramatically but delicately with smoky black eyeliner; my cheeks had just a faint blush, my lips a tender gloss.

Enthralled, I couldn't stop gazing at this incredible creature. If only that was who I really was. The dress hugged my body, but, more than that, it gave me curves in places where I knew for a fact there weren't any. It felt like it was made for me, even though the idea was flat-out ridiculous. Did I need further proof that Audrey Hepburn and I were connected in more profound, cosmic ways than I'd ever imagined?

I wondered what Audrey felt the first time she put on the dress. Did she know that it would change her life forever? For the tiniest second in time, wearing the original Givenchy, it felt as if Audrey and I existed together, in that moment, in that dress, like stars crossing.

I spun like a ballerina and couldn't stop marveling at myself in the mirror. The front neckline was deceptively simple, but it made my neck and shoulders look wonderful. Of course, the back of the dress was where things became really interesting, the neckline sort of scooping down to attach to the back of the dress—my shoulders and parts of my back exposed, my pale skin a sharp contrast to the smooth black satin.

"Just awesome. Lisbeth, you look amazing," she whispered.

That Givenchy guy really knew what he was doing when it came to the body of a woman, specifically the body of a woman like Audrey Hepburn. I've read the story online a hundred times . . . how Audrey, a twenty-four-year-old actress with only a few films to her credit, showed up at Givenchy's studio wearing a simple T-shirt, cropped pants, and a touristy gondolier's hat . . . you know, those hats with the blue or red bow dropping to one side. Givenchy, just twenty-six but already famous, thought he was meeting Katharine Hepburn, not Audrey Hepburn. He had never heard of her. He was unimpressed and barely gave her the time of day. But little Audrey waltzed right into Givenchy's backroom. She won him over with her exquisite taste and indomitable spirit, marking the beginning of a successful and very long collaboration between artist and muse.

Givenchy took his cue from Audrey's idea to highlight what other people considered her less than stellar features. He showcased Audrey's rail-thin physique and long neck, making them assets of a new style and fashion. God knows how, but that Givenchy magic was working for me.

If I weren't so conscious of how the dress caressed my hips and shoulders, I would have said I was having an out-of-body experience. I saw the result in Jess's face.

With all the drama I could muster, I put my arm on Jess's shoulder and gazed deep into her eyes and, using my best Audrey Hepburn voice, said, "Well, I'll tell you one thing, Fred darling . . . I'd marry you for your money in a minute. Would you marry me for my money?" I raised my gloved hand to my chin and gave Jess that wounded-fawn look.

Jess's bag and comb tumbled out of her hands to the floor.

"Who are you?!" she asked.

"Golightly," I said, "Holly Golightly. I live downstairs. We met this morning, remember?" I struck a classic pose with my arm raised in a flourish like Audrey in *Breakfast at Tiffany's*. All that was missing was the long black cigarette holder.

"Your accent is perfect," marveled Jess. "You sound exactly like her. *Exactly*. Have you been getting lessons or something?"

"All my life. Every day since I was nine, darling." I let out a small laugh à la Audrey.

"It's mind-blowing, not a trace of Jersey. Come on, did you take speech class?"

"The rine in spine sties minely in the pline!" I said. "Oh, Freddy, you don't think I'm a heartless guttersnipe, do you?"

Jess laughed so hard she flopped back down in the chair, which spun around and around. She couldn't stop laughing, until the phone rang and she picked up the desk receiver.

"Hey Joe, what's happening?" she asked. In a split second, the blood was draining from her face. "Shit!" She slammed down the receiver.

"What is it?"

"My boss came back. He's on his way up right now." Her hand was shaking—I've never seen her that panicked. "I am so totally fired."

7 "We've got to get that dress off you!" Jess yelled.

I pulled off the gloves and stepped out of the too-big shoes, and we both reached for the dress's zipper at the same time.

"Hurry, hurry!" she hissed. "Myers will be here any second." Her fingers brushed mine out of the way. I wondered which would be worse—Mr. Myers, Jess's boss, walking in to see me in the million-dollar *Breakfast at Tiffany's* dress or walking in to find me naked.

Naked would definitely be better.

"The zipper's stuck!" Jess said, and her face went white.

"Let me try." I pushed down—no-go. I pushed down and jumped up at the same time. It wouldn't budge.

"I am so fucked if I lose this job, Lisbeth," she said and gave the zipper a massive yank that practically lifted me off the ground. I couldn't believe that Jess was willing to risk tearing a million-dollar dress apart, but I guess it was her job on the line. She gave the zipper another huge dress-ripping pull, but it didn't budge.

"Fucking fifty-year-old dress," she said. The two of us tried to wiggle the zipper up and down, but it just wouldn't move. No time for soaping or waxing, and there was no way to drag the dress over my head.

"Ohmygod, what if we have to cut me out of this dress?" I said. Jess gave me a nasty you're-not-helping look.

"You have to get out of here." I knew that voice of Jess's. It was her take-charge voice, and you had no choice but to get on board with it.

"Okay, but where do I go? The closet? Your office? Under the table? Just walk by Myers and say 'hello darling' as I pass him in the hall?"

I watched her eyes dart around the room until she zeroed in on the door that led to the main gallery.

"Out there?! No way!" How could she think that was even a possibility?

"The party in the main gallery," she said. "You'll blend right in." She scooped the black stilettos off the floor and shoved them at me. "Put them back on."

"I can't do that. I don't know how ...," I said as I dropped the shoes on the floor and reluctantly stepped into them.

"Do it anyway. I *have* to save my job." As we heard his footsteps in the hall, she grabbed my arm and dragged me to the doorway. I was lucky I didn't break my neck wearing her too-big stilettos—at this point, Jess may have considered that an acceptable plan B.

"I can't walk in these shoes!"

"Just do it!"

She shoved me out the door. "Don't go *anywhere*," Jess commanded. "I'll come get you when Myers is gone."

The door closed solidly behind me. After the panic and heavy breathing, everything was silent.

I looked around.

All dressed up in a Givenchy and nowhere to go.

8 I heard the murmur of martini laughter, the clinking of glasses, and champagne corks popping. I looked at the door I wasn't supposed to wander away from and imagined the gallery downstairs and all the graceful, wealthy young things below.

What the hell.

Shuffling in my big shoes, I edged over to the railing and surveyed the party on the lower level.

A battalion of black-tied waiters and waitresses armed with champagne flutes and hors d'oeuvres weaved among the trust-fund babies. There were so many "familiar" faces rubbing shoulders below—all the people I knew but would never meet—glitterati, diva girls, famed and adorable. Girls size 00 with perfect tans and the latest Gucci, Louis Vuitton and Dolce & Gabbana. We grew up in Jerze reading about them, watching them on TV, and hearing about their endless parties. Jess always joked that those kids had affluenza, an enviable disease that included boredom, alcoholism, apathy, deviant behavior, and an unshakeable sense of entitlement.

Spotting Dahlia and Mr. Underwear-Man by the bar, it hit me why he seemed so familiar. Mr. Underwear-Man was ZK Northcott, oil and gas heir, a collector of vintage motorcycles and would-be actresses. Famous for being a one-date wonder, he'd been with every heiress, hottie, party girl, and up-and-coming movie bimbo from coast to coast. His picture had been taken on the red carpet a thousand times. But he never lingered with any of them long enough to become an item, so they didn't actually write about him much.

That's why I couldn't place him. Dahlia seemed almost out of his league, too heavy for a one-nighter.

"Excuse me, young lady . . ." The gruff voice of a museum guard snapped me out of my trance. It was Joe from Security.

Crap. Double crap. Totally busted, I felt myself start to cry. *I'm sorry I'm wearing a million-dollar dress that I stole,* I wanted to say, like a schoolgirl caught shoplifting. I wanted to confess every bad thing I've ever done. I pondered a hundred excuses to save Jess's job and my ass, but none of them were any good.

"Miss, this area is restricted," Joe said.

He hadn't recognized me. How could that happen? Even though we'd said hello dozens of times, he had no idea who I was.

"You need to go back downstairs to the event," he said curtly. Relief filled my body. Jess was right. I did blend in.

"Oh, I'm terribly sorry . . . officer," I said in my best Audrey voice. "I was just looking for the powder room. Would you mind awfully . . ."

"No problem at all, miss. Down the stairs, first door on the right," Joe replied. His gruffness was gone, and he was actually smiling. Why Audrey was so successful with people became instantly clear to me. Her whole way of talking assumed that the person she was talking to was . . . well, nice, and would prefer to be helpful.

Joe watched me protectively as I stepped delicately down the grand staircase, methodically taking each step so that my giant shoes wouldn't clomp, clomp, clomp on the marble stairs. With every move, the shoes slipped farther from my feet. I prayed I wouldn't go down headfirst.

"New shoes," I said over my shoulder, smiling winsomely to Joe. He smiled back, making sure I made it down safely before he continued on his rounds. I gave him an Audrey wave, stumbling for a second, then recovering, and kept going.

Close call. I must have looked so stupid. I knew Jess had instructed me to stay put, but I couldn't ignore Joe, and she couldn't really blame me for peeking, could she? When would I ever get another chance? Now I would really see if I blended in. But first, I'd have to do something about the clown stilettos that were killing my feet. Then I'd rush right back upstairs—after stalking of course, just a little bit. I couldn't wait to tell everyone at the Hole!

Downstairs, there was a long line at the ladies' room (it's the same everywhere you go, isn't it?). Everyone waiting was decked out and gorgeous. Too many people meant too many questions, so I tramped my way across the back of the main gallery where the action was and went down another empty, darkened hallway, in search of a less popular restroom.

As I walked along the hall, I saw a handsome man in an Armani tux alone, pacing and talking on his cell phone. His hair graying at the temples. Considerably older than the rest of the crowd, he was utterly sophisticated and distinguished. He had that tan that comes from St. Tropez or Martha's Vineyard as opposed to Sizzletan in Parsippany, with its patented fast-acting spray and sweaty bacteria-breeding tanning beds.

He smiled condescendingly as I plodded along, trying to disguise my walk and hoping he wouldn't examine me too closely. I took a sharp turn and score! Another ladies' room. I pushed open the door, and nobody was there. Thank God!

Reaching into the nearest stall, I grabbed a yard of two-ply, wadded it up, and crammed it into the tips of my shoes. I slipped my foot back into the left shoe. Ahh, big improvement. Admiring myself in the mirror, I couldn't believe ten whole minutes had passed since I looked at the dress. As I grabbed for another handful of industrial-grade TP, I heard a soft moan.

Someone was there.

Time to stuff my right shoe and leave. Another moan. It was coming from the last stall on the right. Okay, I needed to get out of that bathroom and up the stairs. I crammed my foot into the shoe for a snug fit and headed for the door.

"Oh shit," a voice said.

Then silence. After a moment, there was vomiting . . . retching, really. Yuck. I waited until she stopped. Damn, I couldn't just leave her there.

"Are you okay?" I tapped gently on the stall door, but it wasn't latched, so the door swung open. Splayed on the tile floor, her head resting on the porcelain basin and her silver dress hiked up around her hips was the Princess of Pop herself, Tabitha Eden. I couldn't help noticing her exposed $175 La Perla thong—next week's *Us Weekly* cover story in one shot.

"Who are you?" she demanded. She was totally intimidating, even though she was superwasted. For the first time in my life, I didn't know if I could say my own name. I was speechless. I couldn't stop looking at the pale circle of fine powder that sprinkled her flawless face, which was concentrated in a ring on the right side of her nose.

"Lisbeth," I said finally with an Audrey Hepburn lilt. I'd never realized how pretty my name was until I said it that way. It sounded like another person's name. Immediately, I cringed that I'd told her my real name. Not the best idea, though she would probably tell me to get lost anyway. Surprisingly, she tried to smile at me, which wasn't easy in her condition. I couldn't believe I was talking to a Page Six pop star!

"Hi." She reached out her hand to shake mine but stopped. "I'm . . . I'm . . . I'm gonna be sick." She turned to vomit in the toilet again. Leaning in, I held her perfect strawberry-blond hair away from her face while she threw up. Could I pull off walking around in a Givenchy dress (*the* Givenchy original) and stiletto heels? Not so sure. Could I help a friend puke her brains out? Totally up my alley.

As she vomited, I counted how many times I'd held a girlfriend's hair while she spewed chunks. Vomiting leveled the playing field. How many girls hadn't found themselves retching up fourteen mango daiquiris in a public bathroom at some time in their lives, right?

She wiped her mouth off. Staring up at me like a homeless

puppy, she tried to say something, but she was puking again and barely turned her head back to the toilet bowl in time. Standing as far away from her as I could, I held her hair. *Please, please, please—no backsplash—please don't puke on me.* I was painfully aware of the fact that I was wearing a stolen, irreplaceable, million-dollar dress, easily within hurling distance of a completely hammered pop sensation. I absolutely could not return Audrey Hepburn's dress to Jess with barf chunks on it.

"Don't you dare take a fucking picture of me," she slurred.

"I wouldn't," I said, surprised at how insulted I felt. Why would she think that? "I don't even have a camera."

"Yeah right, what about your cell phone?" I shrugged, realizing instantly that I didn't have my phone, my driver's license, car keys, or anything that would identify me other than this magic dress, which wasn't mine. "I have people who'd sue you." Tabitha eyed me warily, trying to wipe the puke off her lips. Gently, I handed her another piece of TP.

"I don't have a cell phone."

"You don't have a cell phone?" She seemed confused. "Who doesn't have a cell phone?"

"Well actually, I mean, I have one, just not with me at the moment," I answered as politely as I imagined Audrey might have explained. I also figured that this was definitely not the time to scream to Tabitha that I was a huge fan of her music and her wild fashion sense.

She threw up again—kind of at the end of her run—not much came out, and she rested back against the side of the stall, exhausted. I walked back to the sink and wet a couple of paper towels. Returning, I handed her one for her lips and placed several on the back of her neck.

She softly moaned and gazed up at me. "You're wearing a tiara."

"Yes, that's very observant for someone in your condition," I responded. This made her laugh and totally broke the ice.

"These paper towels feel so good."

"Yes," I said, "towels on the neck cool you off nicely, and, as an added bonus, it won't ruin your makeup."

The bathroom door flew open, and there was the penetrating sound of a gaggle of giggly girls invading our privacy. Discreetly closing our stall door, I locked it, stepping deeper inside with Tabitha as the girls filled up the bathroom.

I put my finger to my lips, and Tabitha drew her feet to her chest in a little ball. We tried not to crack up as we listened to one of the girls pee in the stall next to ours. Listening to someone pee had never been so funny. We held our breath and managed to keep it together for another three minutes, eavesdropping on the random high-heeled socialites peeing and flushing. There was some idle chatter and no good gossip to speak of. Soon they were at the mirror checking their lip gloss. We heard the door open again as they left, and we burst out laughing. It was so ridiculous, we had to catch our breath and force ourselves to settle down.

"God, what am I going to do?" Tabitha said, still almost crying from laughter. "I can't go back out there and face everyone like this."

She really was a mess; I couldn't just leave her there. "Let's see how you look standing," I said, pulling her up to her two wobbly feet and moving toward the sink. I scanned myself in the mirror, hoping I hadn't damaged Audrey's dress.

"Can I get someone for you in the main gallery?" I asked.

"I came alone," Tabitha said.

She avoided making eye contact and sounded so abandoned that it made me feel sorry for her. It was hard to believe that a person as fabulous as Tabitha Eden could ever feel alone.

"If I go out there," she whispered, "the paparazzi will have me on TMZ covered in puke within the hour. And if they don't, one of my 'friends' will call them."

"Darling, you didn't really get any on your dress, and your makeup is fine."

Taking another wet paper towel, I freshened her up a bit while I tried to think of some way to get her discretely out of the museum.

As an aside, I was very proud that I could do a decent "darling." I'd had a lifetime of hearing it, that was for sure. No one in the history of speaking has ever said the word "darling" the way Audrey did. There wasn't anything cloying or pretentious about the way she said it. On Audrey's lips, "darling" was a friendly endearment, plain and simple.

"You *do* have a driver, don't you?" I asked, trying not to giggle in disbelief that anyone was taking my Audrey Hepburn impression seriously.

"Yes, but I'll never make it out the way I came in," Tabitha said, almost crippled with fear.

"Well, I happen to know a back entrance that no one uses. Can you get your driver to meet us there?"

An expression of disbelief crossed her face. She grabbed her diamond-studded phone and thrust it in my direction. "Call Mocha," she said.

"Mocha?"

"He's my driver," she slurred. "You call him."

Taking her phone, I scrolled through her contacts for Mocha. He picked up on the first ring.

"Hello, Mocha? I have, um, your guest here with me. She finds she is terribly tired and would like to avoid any attention. Can you please meet us at the back entrance on Eighty-second Street?"

He agreed, and I gave him directions to the freight doors. I'd been there a couple of times with Jess.

"Well then," I said, "we're all set." I grabbed another damp paper towel from the sink and delicately dabbed at her beautiful face until all traces of the mystery white powder were gone. She closed her eyes and seemed utterly oblivious.

"Do you have any lip gloss?" I asked. She nodded and motioned to a tiny beaded bag on the floor by the toilet. That bag probably cost more than my mom made in a year, and there it was, sitting on the floor of a public toilet.

Fishing out the lip gloss between the makeup and pill bottles, I was struck by how lovely Tabitha was, even in this condition. Her electric-blue eyes went blank as I dabbed the gloss on her lips.

"Good as new," I said. She wobbled and leaned against me, and I realized I might be overoptimistic.

"You don't understand. We'll have to cross the main floor with . . . all of them out there. I don't think I can do it. What if I puke in front of everyone?" She was starting to panic, and her face was looking green again.

"Darling, you *can* do it. I'll put my arm around you, you'll lean against me, and we'll laugh like I'm the funniest person in the whole world." She smiled at the thought. I was so totally Audrey!

There were basic skills a girl learned in every high school in the state of New Jersey. Springing a shitfaced friend from the ladies' room just happened to be at the top of that list. I'd even done it in the high school bathroom. Since I'd always been a supporting player in life, I was really good at it.

"You have a very interesting accent," she said. "Where are you from?"

Audreyville? I wanted to say. But I just avoided the question.

"Come now, enough about me. Mocha is probably waiting at the freight landing right now." I steered her to the door, hoping I could keep up my act.

She leaned heavily on me, wobbling scarily on her stilettos as we headed toward the main gallery. Thank God mine were stuffed with toilet paper, or we'd both be on the floor after the first two steps.

"We can do this," I whispered.

Arm in arm, we left the bathroom and walked down the empty hallway, giggling loudly and laughing our way into the crowd. Absolutely everyone was watching us. We were acting so completely entertained by each other's presence that we couldn't stop to look at anyone because we were actually *really* laughing about our fake laughter.

Me? I had to use every bit of my self-control not to stop in the middle of the gallery floor just to gawk at the gazillionaire boys and girls and scream! But I had a mission to fulfill. And my mind was already floating back toward Jess, wondering if she was trying to find me.

We made sure not to make eye contact, no matter who waved in our direction, stopping for no one until we reached the hallway that took us to the freight entrance and Tabitha's getaway. I was keenly aware of the distinguished man with the graying temples I had seen before talking on his cell phone. He did his best to shadow us as far as he could but became distracted by an attractive young ingenue who pulled at his sleeve and demanded his attention.

I pushed open the unalarmed heavy metal side door, hypercareful of the Givenchy, and dragged a metal stanchion over to hold it as I helped Tabitha down the concrete steps to the car. I looked up for a second, unfortunately staring straight into a security camera. I turned away quickly, praying that Joe was still on his rounds.

As promised, her driver was waiting. When I saw Mocha, it was really tough to keep from dropping my act and talking the way I usually talk. He was the first person I'd seen that night who was like any of the guys I knew—a totally Jersey City, old-school Italian juicehead. He even looked familiar, like a bouncer my sister used to hang out with at one of the clubs Jess and I avoid in Jersey City. Miraculously, there wasn't a photographer in sight.

"I can't believe that worked," Tabitha said. Neither could I, actually. "How on earth did you know where this back entrance was?"

"Oh, you know, a girl always has to know how to make an exit." Was that a line I copped from *Sabrina* or another movie?

Mocha and I helped Tabitha into the car. As I was about to close her door, she grabbed my hand and pulled it to her face.

"You've been so unbelievably cool tonight. Most people would have just fed me more drinks and pushed me in front of the cameras. Those people in there are total liars."

"I'm sure that's not true," I said, though I felt like the worst liar of all. I wondered if she was right about the people upstairs. I bet it was hard to know who to trust in her position. So many hangers-on, you'd never really know who your true friends were. I said silent thanks, lucky to have a friend like Jess.

Crap, Jess! She was probably so mad.

"It *is* true," she said. "I can't trust anybody anymore." She seemed sad and introspective. "Hey, there's an Island Records party next weekend. Are you going?" She brightened. Oh yeah, sure. I went to parties with rock stars all the time. Excuse me while I check my calendar.

"No, I don't think so."

"You have to come! It's for my new release," she said. "I'll put you on the list. What's your cell? I'll text you right now." Can you imagine?

As I gave her my number, I winced. She looked at me quizzically, and I was certain this was the end of my charade.

"Is that a Manhattan number?" she asked. Even in her condition, she knew.

"No. It's a secret number just between us. I like to keep a low profile."

"Smart girl."

She pulled me toward her awkwardly for a drunken hug, which was a tough maneuver not only because she was sitting in the back of a limo but also because I was wearing a fitted floor-length dress, which made it impossible to squat, turn, or bend at the waist. I twisted as gracefully to the side as I could, which sort of crushed my kidney, hoping I didn't burst out of the dress.

We hugged so long, I worried she would pass out on me in that position. But finally, she let me go. It was good to breathe again.

"I really should go back inside," I said. Jess would have blown a gasket if she'd known I'd worn the Givenchy *outside* the museum with a paparazzi-plagued teen phenom. It was totally, completely, awesomely insane.

"See you next weekend!" she said. She gave me the biggest grin, like a little kid who'd found a new friend. Mocha winked at me and swiftly closed Tabitha's car door. I moved back up the steps and yanked the metal stanchion out of the way, hoping I didn't split a seam. As the doors closed, the limousine took off and rounded the corner, out of sight.

Audrey would have been proud.

9 Now the guilt came flooding in. Here I was helping a drug-addled pop singer who had everything, instead of doing what my best friend had asked me to do in her hour of need. I headed for the quickest, surest path back up the stairs. I planned to be standing by the door waiting dutifully for Jess. She would never need to know. If I kept my head down as I passed through the main gallery and didn't gape at all the celebs like I've been dying to all my life, it was doable.

I walked as gracefully as I could, but the toilet paper had compacted so much that Jess's shoes were sliding off my feet again. A group of twentyish girls walked by, including two actresses I swear I knew from *CSI: NY*. They checked me out, nodding and smiling as though they knew me.

"Stunning dress," I heard one remark.

"Do you know her?" another asked.

Each step was like an up-close and personal tour through the lives of the rich and famous. Trying to keep my composure, I counted each breath as I walked until I felt a firm grip on the back of my arm. I tried to move away, and it tightened. I inhaled as much spiritual Audrey as I could and turned.

It was the swanky old guy from the hallway who had been talking on the phone. Why did he keep popping up?

"So, I assume Tabitha made it to her car?" he asked. I eyed him warily. Just the tone of the question was enough to make me wonder. Who was this guy? He was old enough to be Tabitha's father.

He leaned in closer and slipped his arm around my waist and whispered in my ear.

"Tabby needs good friends like you," he said. Okay, I was totally creeped out. "She was absolutely wasted. Lucky for her, I don't think anyone noticed." He was so smooth that I felt completely trapped. He had his arm wrapped around me without expecting the slightest resistance. I tried to shift away, but he held me firmly by the waist, his arm around me *and* the dress. I smiled demurely but didn't say anything.

"The poor girl has been through enough," he added, finally letting me go and lighting a cigarette. He seemed to be thinking about something. "What did she tell you? Has she changed her plans?" he asked.

I didn't answer.

"Typical Tabitha, no idea when it comes to realities. Do remind her. There's a price to pay for this kind of thing. I *am* just trying to help her, really."

What the hell? What did *that* mean? It was hard to imagine Tabitha in any relationship with this guy. Maybe he was one of those super-rats Holly talked about.

"The fact is it affects everything. Better to leave as is for everyone's sake. "

I wondered briefly why he'd chosen to impart this bit of information to me, but I realized that Tabitha and I probably seemed like the best of friends, giggling and hanging on to each other as we walked through the party. He'd been lingering outside the bathroom and watching us as we left. Maybe he thought she called me for help. Unbelievable that he was lighting up a cigarette in the middle of the main gallery as if no one would stop him. And no one did.

"If you don't mind me asking, Mr. . . . ?" I began.

He eyed me suspiciously, surprised that I didn't know who he was. I wish I had never asked.

"Francis. Robert Francis."

"Well, Mr. Francis, why haven't *you* asked her?" I replied, desperately hoping to take the focus away from me.

"We're still not talking," he said. He appeared slightly taken aback and seemed to think that I should know this. "Well, it was nice chatting with you . . . I didn't get your name?"

"A friend," was all I said.

"Well, I'm sure we'll talk again," he said and slipped into the crowd, leaving me standing there, bewildered.

I was starting to feel really sorry for the fabulous Tabitha Eden. What did she have to do with this creepy guy? Maybe she was too busy upchucking in museum toilets to talk about her "plans," whatever they were. A waiter carrying a silver tray filled with champagne flutes approached me.

"Miss? Would you care"—I grabbed one and threw it back, the champagne bubbles going straight to my brain—"for champagne?" he finished saying as I put the glass back down on his tray and grabbed another.

Thankfully, they weren't checking IDs that night.

IO "Holy crap, that's really good!" I said to the waiter. He looked at me funny, and I realized that I had dropped my Audrey accent. I avoided making eye contact. Okay, it was time to blow this Popsicle stand, as Grandpa used to say. I wouldn't be able to keep this up.

"Nice dress," said a smooth, deep voice from behind me. Was I busted? I spun around, unsure.

Smiling at me, with dimples so sexy they were wicked, was none other than ZK Northcott. How was it that a couple of cute little dents in a guy's face, even a face as nice as his, could make him even more appealing? My heart stopped pumping, I swear. His dark, wavy hair was slicked back. I'd bet he just rolled out of bed looking gorgeous. Not like the gorillas I knew who spent as much time (and product) on their hair as the girls. Up close, I could see that his eyes were even more enticing: hazel, caramel-colored with flecks of green and gold. Jeez, talk about genes. He grabbed a bottle of champagne from one of the passing waiters and refilled my glass a third time.

I eyed the line of his jacket against his shoulder and almost swooned. Some guys were just born to wear two-thousand-dollar formal wear. Giorgio Armani would be pleased. I wondered where his date was. Lost, I hoped.

"Everyone wants to know how Tabitha is," he said. What did he say? Who was Tabitha? I couldn't believe he was talking to me. My mind went totally blank. He was gorgeous. For a second I flashed on the fear that he would recognize me from outside on the street when our eyes locked. But of course not. When I went gaga, gazing into his eyes, he didn't even notice me. We settled into an uncomfortable silence because I had no idea how to respond.

I took another sip of champagne, buying time to think, but the bubbles made it harder. Finally I began to sputter, "Well, Tabitha was, well . . ."

"There you are!" ZK turned, and Dahlia Rothenberg inserted herself between us before I could utter another word. Dahlia Rothenberg. Holy shit. She was even more perfect up close than she was in the magazines.

"Yes, how is our dear Tabby?" she asked. "We're all dying to know." She stared right through me as though I were made of tissue paper. I was so over my head, I felt like I'd plunged into the deep end with piranhas and had forgotten how to swim. Time stopped. How long had I been standing there absolutely tongue-tied? No line lifted from *Sabrina* or *Tiffany's* or *Roman Holiday*. No witty retort. A total blank. All I could think of was that ZK was starting to look bored, which seemed the worst possible thing in the world. Each second ticked by excruciatingly.

"Well, I guess dear Tabitha's the center of attention as usual," I finally offered, smiling, hoping this would pass for conversation. It was only the most obvious thing I could think of, but Dahlia and ZK laughed as though I was brilliant. Good grief.

"You know her too well!" ZK said and gave me an amused look. I felt as though he knew I was faking and was congratulating me on my recovery, but it didn't really matter what he was thinking. I was gobsmacked by his gold-flecked eyes.

"Well, you haven't done poorly yourself," Dahlia added, watching ZK watching me, but he barely seemed to notice. As I searched for a witty reply, I saw Joe the security guy leaning over the upper gallery stairs. He was pointing right at me and looking down at— Jess! She'd just reached the bottom stairs of the main gallery.

I was in *so* much trouble. Jess motioned me to come right away. I shrugged helplessly, unsure how to extricate myself.

"Is there something going on over there?" Dahlia asked. She couldn't quite see Jess, and even if she had, a mere museum employee wouldn't register for her.

"Not at all, it just seems as though someone has had too much fun and it's time for them to go home," I said sadly. Jess pulled a waiter over, handed him a note, and pointed in my direction.

"And I'm afraid I will be on my way as well. It's been lovely meeting you," I said and turned from my newfound "friends." But ZK grabbed my arm. First the creeper, now Mr. Underwear-Man . . . these rich people were so grabby.

"I'm curious, have we met before?"

"Darling, I assure you, no one knows me. I'm quite a homebody, actually," I said in my quietest Audrey voice.

"Excuse me," the waiter interrupted. "I believe this is for you."

"Thank you, dear." But before I opened the note, a perky thirty-ish young woman with a blond ponytail and an expensive camera interrupted us.

"Page Six?" she asked.

"I'd rather not," Dahlia started.

"Oh, come now. Take one of the three of us," ZK said. He put one arm around Dahlia and the other around me before I could say a peep. God, he smelled good. Like citrus, musk, and leather—all sex appeal. ZK squeezed me tighter, as if we were old friends. It was so totally absurd that I practically giggled as the camera flashed.

I caught Jess's eye. She was in shock. It took a second to register what I had just done. There was now Page Six photographic evidence of me wearing the Audrey dress. Oh God, I was a total screwup.

"Thank you," the photographer said, looking down at her camera. "Would you mind spelling your name?" Before she looked up, I slipped into the crowd without answering.

ZK, Dahlia, and Page Six were probably wondering who I was and where I came from.

I walked deliberately in Jess's direction, savoring the last few seconds of everything—the champagne, the dress, the sad pop princess, and my too-big shoes, leaving the world of my dreams to begin the unavoidable descent back to my sad, uneventful life.

11 The Hole.

If you wanted to visit my own personal version of hell, it was right off the Jersey Turnpike, exit 14C.

Everybody called it the Hole, except tourists. Our semiofficial motto was, "It's gotta taste better than it looks."

It wasn't the worst job in the world, but it was close.

At 11:08, I was late for my shift. I overslept—if staying up all night and passing out for two and a half hours could be considered oversleeping. It seemed more like undersleeping. But how could I stop thinking about that night? The shimmering dress, vomiting pop stars, and gorgeous baby moguls.

And Page Six. Holy shit, Page Six.

I acted totally horrified that the Page Six reporter snapped my picture, but secretly I was amped. I spent the night at Jess's place; her mom was totally cool as usual. After Jess fell asleep, I googled Page Six on her computer and hit refresh over and over until it posted at 5:43 A.M.

ZK Northcott, Dahlia Rothenberg, and little ole me. *Me.*

It was so Technicolor vivid in my mind that it already didn't feel real anymore. It seemed more like a movie I had seen, a dream I had, or a lost scene from *Breakfast at Tiffany's,* which was why I couldn't wait to see Jess at the Hole that morning to rehash every glorious second of it. I'd promised myself over and over, though, that I'd be considerate of how freaked Jess was.

I dropped off some of my things at the house around 10:30 A.M., tiptoeing in and out as Mom was leaving for work. She seemed pretty hungover, so we barely said hi. Not a word about the calls.

I could see the neon-pink DINER sign perched on top of the dilapidated, art deco train car from a block away. Roaring into the lot, I overshot the parking space a little, screeched on the brakes, and choked the Purple Beast. One tire was up on the parking block, but I grabbed my stuff off the seat and slipped through the front door, trying to blend in as fast as I could.

I'd worked the past two and a half years at the Hole, where the smell of coffee and bacon permanently emanated from the cracked orange Naugahyde booths. There was greasy black gunk in every corner of the floor from decades of half-assed mop jobs. The most expensive thing on the menu was the Jersey T-bone, at $13.85. I'd seen them in the fridge before they were cooked. I wouldn't go near them.

The customers at the Hole were frequently wasted and always cheap. Although we were pretty steady all day long, our busiest time was after 2:30 A.M. That was the zombie shift, right after the bars closed and the shift change at the window factory. It paid more tips. People didn't seem to know how to count change after two in the morning.

The Hole was a convenient place to eat for people who'd rather take their chances with food poisoning than tunnel traffic. It made for a lot of cranky, unhappy customers. Thankfully, the people who worked there were mostly cool.

"You're late," chided Buela, my boss. Her middle-aged body was squashed into an ancient pink waitress uniform, and her unnaturally red hair was teased and sprayed into a pouf, adorned with a silvery clip. Buela's dad, Milton, owned the Hole, and she'd worked there ever since she was twelve.

"One day," she always told us, "I'm going to own this joint." We always nodded enthusiastically and wondered why she'd ever want to.

"Sorry, Buela," I said meekly over my shoulder, not slowing down as I made my way to the employee lockers in the back.

Jess was there, joking with Jake, who was leaning against my locker. His faded jeans hung low on his hips in that way . . . that way that made you want to hook your finger around a belt loop and just reel him in. Jake had smoky-blue eyes and broad shoulders and great arms, which I couldn't help but notice because he was wearing this sky-colored BLUE NOTE RECORDS T-shirt that looked vintage and fit him exactly right.

My heart did a little flip when I saw him. Jake and I had this thing . . . well, we sort of had a thing. I guess it was almost a thing, like an urge to have a thing. I don't exactly know how to describe it.

He'd started working there three months earlier. Light flirting early on had recently turned into heavier stuff. We'd gone out a couple of times but always with people from work. Then the previous week, in a shocker, he kissed me in the walk-in freezer, pressing me against the giant bags of frozen french fries until I was breathless.

Jake Berns was older than me, twenty-three, a musician who had graduated a couple of years ago from Paterson and lived in Hoboken with six roommates, all of them in his band, Rocket Berns, although everyone called then simply the Rockets. Jake fronted the band, played guitar, sang lead, and wrote most of the songs. He was determined to make his mark. They played five or six gigs a week, but basically only made beer money. Jake waited tables at the Hole to keep up. Money was tight because, strangely enough, the music scene in Jersey was astonishingly good, which meant that, in addition to the homegrown talent, bands came from all over to get heard by the record execs who were always trolling the clubs, scouting for the next Bon Jovi or Springsteen. The gigs were prime exposure-wise, so the club owners nickel and dimed the bands to the extreme.

The great thing about Jake was that he knew exactly what he wanted with no backup plan, which was hot as hell—to me anyway. He had complete and utter commitment to his purpose. Not like some people—aka me. Honestly, he was out of my league, but for reasons I didn't understand, he was into me. Maybe it was because I gave him a hard time about being a rock 'n' roll heartthrob, since I figured he was beyond my reach. Honestly, he scared me a little.

Jake was one of the few genuinely cool people I knew. The other one was Jess, of course. Considering I was ready to nod off, I was glad all three of us were on shift that day. I was hoping to grab rewind time with Jess to rehash the previous night in detail.

"Hey you," Jake said. He gave me a sly grin.

"Hey back."

"You look like roadkill," said Jess. She tied on her pink apron and grabbed an order pad. "Did you sleep at all?"

"A couple hours."

Jake shifted just enough away from my locker so I could shove my stuff in.

"How much did your mom freak out?" she asked.

"I don't know. I was only there for a sec."

"She's probably just worried about you," offered Jake and gave me a look with those soul-puppy eyes.

"What'd she want?" Jess prodded.

"Something incredibly important she couldn't remember," I answered, tying on my pink Finer Diner apron. "Just the usual vodkainduced amnesia. She probably doesn't even know she called me a gazillion times. Maybe she was butt dialing."

Jess shot me a painful look. She knew how my mom got. What Jess didn't know was that I had been avoiding Mom way more than usual. There would be a meltdown when she found out I wasn't going to college next fall. I hadn't told Jess either. At some point, I was inevitably headed for a complete and total shitastrophy.

"So Lizzy's a regular party girl, eh?" Jake said. I half-smiled at his warm bad boy eyes. Jake, like everyone I knew, had the *Sopranos* accent that everybody else always made fun of, saying "party" like "potty."

"Yeah, but nothing compared to you and your groupie worshipers," I said. Jake laughed.

Jess and I had made a concerted effort in our last year of high school to drop our accent by getting rid of the *w* and *u* sounds we grew up adding to everything. We also sharpened our r's. But I still let out a "youse" now and then, especially if I'd had a few beers. And whenever Jess stabbed herself with a sewing needle, she gave out the biggest "owwuhwhwwwuhwwwuh"—five whole syllables of ouch. But I think she did that on purpose.

We thought New Yorkers had accents. Even though you didn't hear a trace of it when he was rocking with the band, Jake talked totally Jersey. Kind of like Audrey and me. That was one of the weirdest, most undeniable things about that night at the Met: not one of the guests talked the way my friends and I did. It was like Americans visiting London: everybody speaks English, but nobody speaks your language.

I couldn't help comparing everything to last night. God, I was gonna burst if I didn't get a chance to talk about it. I turned to Jess. She could tell I was about to blurt it all out and shot me a cautionary glance.

"Are you three forming a social club or something?" yelled Buela. "We got customers. You too, lover boy."

Hurrying up front, we saw there was only one guy sitting in the far booth by the window—typical Buela. We traded annoyed looks with one another, but I figured I was the late one, so it'd better be me. I went over politely to see if he wanted to order something.

"Hey, you want a coffee?"

He silently nodded no. Couldn't care less. No problem. So much for the lunch rush. It was going to be a very long day.

I was wrong. During the next five hours, we were hit by so many customers that I felt as if I'd fall over from exhaustion. Which was how I ended up dumping an entire deluxe chili con carne and egg special with homemade cornbread hash and salsa all over myself trying to serve an old truck driver named Buddy at table 6. He was a regular, so Buela was furious. Jake leapt across the diner in a flash, cleaning up my mess.

"You okay?" he asked.

"Super," I said, shaking egg yolk and chunks of chili from my hair. "I'm good. Jake, you don't have to do that."

"No worries, I got this. Take a break." Buela seemed anything but fine with that.

He winked at me and began wiping down the side of the booth, now speckled with hash browns.

"You're the best," I said. Really, I felt as if I was gonna faint if I didn't sit down. Shuffling off to the bathroom to clean up, I did my best not to make eye contact with Buela, who was steaming at the cash register. I barely could keep my eyes open.

I grabbed a Coke in the back for the caffeine and sat down in Buela's office, the only place I could sit down. I took a swig and figured I'd rest my eyes for a second and wished I could crawl into my closet and dream about being Audrey at the Met.

"Hey, I don't think you want to sleep here forever," I heard a voice say. "Buela might start deducting rent from your paycheck."

I opened my eyes and there was Jake, gently shaking me by the shoulders, my head on Buela's desk and a puddle of drool in the shape of a whale. So not cool. I wiped my mouth with the back of my hand and then secretly dried the desk with my other sleeve, hoping Jake wouldn't see. Classy, I know. Jake was smiling, wearing his "dress-up" blue flannel shirt. Our shift must have ended. Shit.

"God. You've changed your shirt. How long have I been sleeping for?" I was so screwed.

"Musta been a killer night," Jake said. He laughed, tossed me a couple aspirins, and handed me a cup of water.

"Yeah, totally killer," I said groggily and swallowed the aspirin.

Jake didn't mind how Jersey he was. We had talked about it. He'd never leave. And me? I didn't know why, but more than ever after last night, it seemed as if I had been dying to get out of there forever. What's that expression about keeping them down on the farm after they've seen Paris? It was something like that.

Jake pulled up a chair and straddled it. "So Lizzy, there's this band called Dalton that's supposed to be total kick-ass playing at Hiram's Junction. I'm checkin' out the drummer for my band. It's a couple miles away. You up for it?"

I gazed into his smoky eyes full of mischief and shook my head no. I didn't even know why.

"Pillow, bed," I mumbled. He leaned toward me. His fresh, clean shirt smelled so good.

"You sure?"

My body trembled a little bit. I knew where this was going. He moved closer and kissed me on the cheek, his lips slowly making a trail toward my mouth. I didn't stop him. I kissed him back, closing my eyes, feeling his breath, the warmth radiating from his lips winding through my body, forgetting where we were until there was a bang on the door to the kitchen.

"Am I counting all these tips myself?" Jess called. "Because if I do, I'm taking the whole show. I can definitely use the cash."

One last breathless kiss, and I pulled myself away from Jake.

"I'm coming, I'm coming." I dragged myself out front. Jake

trailed behind, gently pulling the tie on my apron until it fell off. I snatched it back.

"Behave yourself," I whispered.

We settled up with Jess, and I offered my share to them. Jake, of course, refused to take it. I threw my pink apron into the locker and figured I'd better make the first move or it would look bad.

"G'night, I'm nowhere near cool enough to hang out with you two. Besides, I can't keep my eyes open."

"You're stickin' with that line?" Jake asked with his sweet hang-dog face.

"I gotta check to see if my mom called another hundred times." They both laughed.

"Okay, then listen. There's a gig the day after tomorrow that we're playing and then next weekend—we're rocking a big show-case for lots of A and R guys at Reilly's that you've got to come to, deal?" he asked. He hesitated for a split second before he gave me a chuck on the shoulder. I wanted another kiss. From the look he gave me, he did, too.

"Okay rock 'n' roll Romeo, deal." I chucked him back on the shoulder, which was firm and strong, hard as a rock. As I dragged myself away to my overparked purple monster, I regretted my decision.

I heard Jess console him as they left. "Come on, stud bucket," she said. "You can take me. Maybe we can both get lucky and pick up some chicks." Hearing them laugh, I felt like an idiot. I guess there was no reliving my night of glory with Jess either. I hesitated for a second, but my brain was starting to go fuzzy from sleep deprivation. I checked my phone, just to see if Mom had really called.

Shit.

"Ms u bathroom buddy ! Let's connect b4 the party ! ;) Tabby"

Ohmygod—I had a text from Tabitha Eden, *the* Princess of Pop. She was so wasted; I thought for sure she'd forget.

I imagined how incredible it would be to go to an Island Records release party, the entire industry of rock stars, fashionistas, trust funders, and me hanging with my BFF Tabitha Eden on her own turf. But there was no way I'd get close enough to pass the ropes.

And what if we had gotten busted at the Met? Jess fired. Both of us facing felony charges for hacking a million-dollar dress. Humiliation. Shame. Mug shots on the Internet. And though it ended up being, hands down, the greatest night of my entire life, I would have to be incredibly stupid and boneheaded to ever try and pull off another Audrey charade again, right?

12 *Crap, crap, crap.*
Rounding the corner in the Beast on the way home from work, there it was—red and blue lights flashing, a New Jersey State Trooper squad car in my driveway.

Ohmygod, ohmygod, ohmygod.

My heart bashed at my rib cage. This was it. They'd come to arrest me. They knew about the dress. I tried to breathe, but my lungs felt as though they were being crushed. *Stay calm, stay calm.*

Okay, I didn't actually steal it, right? I didn't leave the premises. So that wasn't stealing. It was borrowing. Not even. Really, I just *relocated* the dress from the archives to the main gallery and back again. Like a curator. Except not.

It's not like I was a klepto, taking a five-finger discount at a jewelry store. Didn't celebrities swipe stuff all the time? No, it wasn't stealing. I didn't steal the dress.

It was way worse. Fraud.

I pretended as if I were someone I'm not. I lied to everyone and let them believe I was *somebody.* I'd spent my whole life imagining what it would be like, full of magic and glamour and tuxedos and sparkle. That night, I'd gotten a taste of "sipping starlight," as Nan called it, though it was for just an hour. It was flat-out glorious, and inevitably I had to pay for it.

The cop car just sat there with its lights flashing but no sound. I assumed they must still be inside. Jess was right. Trying on a one-of-a-kind, million-dollar dress was a boneheaded move.

Oh crap. I walked Tabitha Eden out the service entrance in the back. I *did* leave the Met with the dress. They'd convict me in a second . . . you know, like shoplifting jewelry. Once you leave the store, you're guilty.

A million tiny details of my crime gone wrong flooded my mind. Of course, the Met had dozens of security cameras everywhere. It was a museum filled with valuable things, for chrissakes. I mean, was it okay to grab a six-thousand-year-old pharaohs' necklace made of gold and turquoise and dance around with it on your neck? Duh. No.

Surely they'd tracked every movement I made and had me red-handed, leaving the building in a hot Givenchy.

About six hundred people, including the most famous people in New York City, saw me in the dress, prancing around, laughing, and drinking champagne. How hard would it have been to pick out *that* dress on a security camera, with a tiara in my hair, no less? Security Joe, he must have told them.

It was eerie how the cop car just sat there, lights flashing, no sound. New Jersey's finest. I gunned the gas of my Purple Beast and kept driving past my house.

Jess flashed in my frantic thoughts. She was screwed way more than me. I had let my complete and total obsession with Audrey Hepburn drag her smack into the middle of all this. Jess would get blamed, even though it was my fault. I stomped on the brakes and steered the Beast to the curb.

Oh shit, I was the worst, worst friend ever.

The police were probably combing my room for evidence that very second.

Page Six. Oh, crap. What about Page Six?

I was sure the Page Six photo was up on my laptop. Mom probably saw it, or Courtney or my creep brother. Page Six was photographic evidence, now posted on the Internet for every DA in the state to see. I'd practically turned this all on myself.

In my rearview mirror, I caught a glimpse of Mom as she walked out on the stoop dressed in her worn yellow tracksuit. Her face creased with worry, leaning against the rickety railing, she lowered herself dejectedly to sit on the front step of our house like she was in pain, drawing on a cig.

She was sipping from her usual blue travel mug. Apparently, a houseful of police officers wasn't enough to keep her from the booze. She pulled out her cell phone.

My phone buzzed, and I was terrified it was her.

Instead it was another text from Tabitha.

"Pop up party at the High Line !! Use Tabbycat to get in ;) XOXOXOXO."

Jeez, the life of a party girl never seemed further away.

I stepped on the gas and headed for the only place I could think of.

13 The second she opened the door, I was sobbing so hard it felt as though I might implode.

"Well, this isn't good, is it, dear?" soothed Nan. She squeezed me tightly and ushered me inside. I made my way to the couch on wobbly legs as Nan closed the front door.

Oh God, she knew. The police had probably already been here. I hoped Nan was okay. Should I have gone somewhere else? I was so wound up, I couldn't think straight. Sinking down into the cushions on her worn velvet sofa, I inhaled the soothing essence of my Nan—rose oil and vanilla. She sat next to me, her arm encircling me tightly.

"Dearest, it's probably not as awful as it seems right now."

I sobbed. Nan reached for a box of tissues, and I felt my phone vibrate. I didn't want to look, but I was worried it might be Jess. Were the police at her house, too?

It was Tabitha Eden again.

"R u coming ?!"

Jeez.

"CALL ME !!"

I was pretty positive that America's pop princess wasn't going to want me at that pop-up party once it hit the news that I was a felon, a couture con. I couldn't even think what she'd say.

Of course I'd gotten caught. I've never gotten away with anything in my entire life. Ever. Unlike most of my friends, I'd never shoplifted, I'd never cheated on a test, I'd never snuck into a movie theater, I'd never pinched booze or money or cigarettes from Mom like Courtney always did.

I guessed the good news was that if I got jailed for Givenchy jacking, I wouldn't have to confess to Mom that I wasn't going to college and killing her "my daughter the nurse-practitioner" dream.

A fresh wave of sobs wracked my body. I couldn't think of a single thing about my life that didn't suck. Nan rubbed my back, her voice low and soothing.

"There, there, these things have a way of working themselves out," she said.

Gulping deep breaths, I tried to speak. Nan looked at me with those kind blue eyes and pressed her cool, silky hand to the side of my face. Oh how I wished I could be Nan. All eighty-one years of her. To have her memories would be better than having my life.

"Not to sound disrespectful of your feelings, dear, but I'm a tiny bit surprised you're so distressed about this," said Nan.

"It's a disaster!" I wailed. Of course I was distressed!

"I wouldn't say it's a disaster," soothed Nan. "Ryan will probably just get probation." Wait, what? "That would be the best for everybody."

We were clearly talking about two entirely different crime sprees. An involuntary laugh bubbled up in my throat before I could stop it, like a hiccup. I swallowed, trying to shift gears.

"*Ryan's* in trouble? What'd he do this time?"

"Isn't that what you were upset about?" she asked.

I didn't want to lie to Nan. I *couldn't* lie to Nan.

"I came home from work, and there was a state trooper's car in the driveway," I said cautiously. "I freaked out and drove straight here."

Question avoided. Jess would have strangled me if I told Nan. Which sucked, because I didn't keep anything from Nan.

"Your brother set off the fire alarm at school. And then he joked with some kids he had a gun, but of course he didn't." Nan sighed. "These days, even saying something like that is practically a felony. I don't know what gets into that boy. The sprinklers went off and flooded the gym. They put the whole school on lockdown. It was on the local news. Quite a big stir."

"What was he thinking?" The knot in my gut began to loosen a little; I could almost breathe again. Ryan seemed as if he was going to end up in Rahway before he even got his learner's permit.

"Your mom called here fifteen minutes ago, trying to find you," Nan said. "She thought she saw your car."

Oh great. If Mom called Nan, then she was really upset. They *never* talked.

"How'd she sound?"

"Not well," she said. "She couldn't find Courtney either. She said she feels abandoned."

I groaned.

"Dear, it's not your job to take care of your mother," Nan said. "She can take care of herself."

"I don't want to go home. It's going to be bad," I said, burying my face in her shoulder. I felt like a big blubbering baby, scared and helpless.

"Yes, well it probably is a good idea to wait while she's in that . . . condition." We both knew exactly what she wasn't saying.

"You can always stay here as long as you'd like." She gave me a warm squeeze. "How about milk and cookies, and maybe a medicinal viewing of *Tiffany's*?"

I nodded gratefully, and she gave me one last squeeze before she

eased off the couch and headed into the kitchen. I'd totally dodged a
bullet. Okay, maybe the cops were after Ryan, my delinquent-
threat-to-society brother. But they could have been after me. Next
time, I might not be so lucky.

I closed the drapes, grabbed the *Tiffany's* DVD from its case, and
popped it into the player. A healthy dose of Audrey. Or . . . maybe
not. How guilty would it feel to see that dress again?

Grabbing an afghan from the basket behind the couch, I fast-
forwarded through the outdated previews until I reached the menu
screen so the movie would be ready when Nan returned from the
kitchen.

She elbowed her way through the kitchen doorway, balancing a
giant plate of cookies, napkins, and two large glasses of milk. She
could have worked at the diner.

"Let me help you with that," I said, relieving her of the plate of
cookies and setting them gently on the coffee table. She handed me
a napkin and a glass of milk.

"So what's going to happen to Ryan?" I asked.

"Pretty much like last time. Your mom said Ryan's been suspended. There's a mandatory fine for the false alarm, up to a thousand dollars. He'll probably have to do significant community service
and more therapy, which might do Ryan good, honestly. I love my
grandson, but he needs a wake-up call. When you think about it,
maybe this isn't a bad thing after all."

"Mom's going to lose it over the thousand bucks."

Nan just nodded.

"And the family drama continues," I said.

"You know, Lisbeth, sometimes good things aren't always so great,
and bad things often turn out to be good for you," she said.

I nodded, trying to figure out what she meant, but honestly I'd
never really understood what people were talking about when they
said that kind of thing. Seemed to me it was all pretty black and
white.

We snuggled on the couch together and gathered the afghan

around us. I hit PLAY on the remote and mere seconds later found myself lulled by the opening notes of "Moon River."

Audrey appeared on screen in the Givenchy. The night before, the original of that dress had transformed me into a creature far more glamorous and elegant than I could have ever dreamed of being on my own.

My breath caught in my chest.

Audrey stood there with her little white coffee shop bag . . . that somber, subdued opening always seemed to me like the ending to a movie, not the beginning. For the first time ever, I couldn't watch. I turned away, feeling horrible.

"What is it, dear?" Nan's face filled with concern. "There's something else, isn't there?"

I nodded, terrified and desperate to tell her. Jess would kill me.

"You know whatever trouble you may be in, no matter what kind, you can always come to me."

"I'm here, aren't I?" I said harshly. I don't know why I spoke that way, but I felt as if I was drowning.

"And that's a good thing," Nan said, perplexed.

She patiently waited for me to say something. I closed my eyes and bit my lip, trying to hold back the tears.

"Nan," I said, "what if it *was* me that the cops were after, instead of Ryan? What if they came after *me* tomorrow or next week or next month? What would I do?"

"You've got me worried now, Lisbeth."

My hand felt as though it was moving in slow motion as I reached for the remote and paused the movie. Audrey was frozen on the screen, larger than life, resplendent in her pearls and timeless elegance, staring into the Tiffany's window.

"Nan," I said, my voice shaky and weak. "There's something I have to tell you."

14 Nan was laughing so hard, I worried she'd pass out from lack of oxygen. Seriously, she was practically purple.

"I'm pretty sure you're not going to jail for trying on a dress!" she laughed. "Even a very dazzling, extraordinarily wonderful, famous dress." And she did a little spin as if she were wearing it herself.

"Really? What do you mean?" I was desperate to believe her.

"Well, first of all, I do believe the Met has a vested interest in keeping this quiet. Many of their exhibits are loaned or donated, and the last thing the museum needs is for people to get the idea that their security is lax."

I was dumbfounded. I hadn't even thought of that.

"You and Jess didn't damage the dress or spill anything on it, and it's safe and sound locked up in the vault at the Met, right?" I nodded yes.

"Then, no harm, no foul," she said, her eyes gleaming.

I shrugged. "Right. But what if the security cameras or one of the guests . . . ?"

"The museum staff knows that all sorts of things happen when they open the museum up to party guests. Occasionally some mischief is going to take place." Her eyes sparkled slyly. I couldn't help smiling. I had a feeling I was about to hear a story.

"In fact," she continued, "I seem to remember a little soiree in my debutante days where a certain Kennedy sibling spent a large portion of the evening drinking single malt scotch while wearing a priceless New Borneo Fertility mask."

"Scandalous!" I said.

"As I recall, he did a sort of tribal dance to go with it. What a night!" Her eyes sparkled with mischief and memories. "He was a good dancer, that one. Swept a girl right off her feet."

"You? . . . Really?" I couldn't help but picture Nan doing a wicked tango or snuggled in a corner of the Met with a Kennedy. I wondered which one.

"How hard do you really think the authorities are going to be on you for trying on a little dress? They don't want to know! You're so clever; you've completely fooled them. In fact, they should hire you to curate a show about Audrey if they're smart."

"But Nan, what if they *do* come after me. What should I do?"

"Apologize like mad. Promise to never, ever do it again."

I laughed.

"Enough about that," she said and set off for the kitchen, returning with a bottle of champagne.

"Now let's talk about something far more serious, my dear," she said, pouring us each a glass with a studied look in her eyes. "Tell me everything that happened at the party."

We placed the plate of cookies between us, and I spilled every detail: what it felt like to wear that iconic Givenchy, the champagne, Tabitha splayed on the floor with her underwear showing, the glitz and glamour of the main gallery, flirting with ZK Northcott, my picture on Page Six.

"Page Six!" said Nan. "Oh, I'd love to see that!" I took her over to the small desk in the corner of her living room, cranked up the old desktop that she never used, and quickly searched online for the image. I was already starting to feel lighter.

"Oh, my! There you are!" she exclaimed. "You look exquisite! And happy!" She raised her left eyebrow at me. "Glamour adores you."

"Really? Glamour and me? I would be happy if we could just get along. Are you sure?"

I gazed longingly at the image of me in the Givenchy on the screen one last time, trying to let Nan's words sink in. Wouldn't it be amazing if I could look like that for real? If I could be the girl in that photo? I don't know why—maybe just relief, maybe it had something to do with Nan seeing the Page Six picture and being so proud of me—I felt like crying again. I tried to keep myself together as the two of us returned to the sofa.

Nan clasped my hands in hers and giggled. "Of course, my

advice . . . if you have the opportunity to try on . . . say, the gown from *Gone with the Wind* or Marilyn Monroe's dress from *Gentlemen Prefer Blondes*, you should probably decline."

"Thanks for the tip." We laughed, even though I was a little choked up. She squeezed my hands tightly; my panic over the police car nearly dissipated. "Nan, can I ask you something?"

"Anything, love."

"When I hear you talk about your life in New York before you met Grandpa, it all sounds so glamorous and exciting. I mean, the parties and the dancing and hanging out with the Kennedys and Jackie Bouvier and Frank Sinatra and everything. Don't you miss it? That's all I dream about, living a life like the one you had. I mean, did your family go bankrupt? Was there a scandal? Like, maybe one involving fertility masks?"

"No, no, not at all." Nan laughed.

"It seems so impossible. How could you just give it all up?"

She shrugged her tiny shoulders.

"I fell in love."

"Really? Was he a scoundrel? A cad? Did he take all your money? Did your parents cast you out?"

"No, I went on my own. Happily. Never looked back."

"But how? You had all of New York in the palm of your hand. You could have been or done anything. You knew the Vanderbilts. You knew the Rockefellers and that Mafia guy."

"I knew everybody," she laughed. "They're just people, dear."

"But really rich and famous people. Wasn't Peter Lawford trying to go out with you? And, like, the Duke of Liechtenstein or something? I mean, I loved Grandpa, and he was the greatest guy ever, but how could you give up the life you had to marry a construction worker?"

Nan smiled a faraway smile and glanced over at the old black-and-white photo of her and Grandpa Frank snuggled together in a beach blanket by the ocean, way before I was born, way before my mother was born, even. They looked so content together. So totally at ease in each other's arms. I knew that I'd never felt that way ever.

She looked at me with watery blue eyes and said, "Lisbeth, my sweet, when you truly fall in love, you'll understand." She stifled a tiny sigh.

"I'm sorry," I said, hugging her tightly. "You miss him, don't you?"

"Every day." A bittersweet expression came over her face. "You said it yourself: Grandpa was the greatest guy ever. Something special, that man. Someone to change your life for."

"Can we look at the scrapbook again?" I asked, sliding it out from the side table cabinet before she had a chance to answer.

Flipping through Nan's scrapbook was one of my favorite things to do. Nan's photos were like a drug to me; they made all the darkness go away—all the ingenues and dashing young men, their faces golden with hope and possibility. I didn't know anyone in my family who believed in hope besides Nan.

"Hope is a kick in the teeth," Mom always said. Maybe that was why she never visited. It was just so weird how troubled Mom was, when her parents seemed so perfect and loving.

"Someday, Lisbeth, I expect your own memories will be as exciting to you as mine," said Nan.

"As if," I said, flipping the page. "Now tell me again about the time you fell in love with the jazz drummer at your first debutante ball . . ."

We plunged. The beginning pages were all photos and society-column clippings from before Nan met my granddad. I loved those photos. Nan dressed in pearls and white chiffon for her debutante ball or poised and elegant on the arm of a dapper young man or gracefully posing with my great-grandparents in a crystal ballroom.

And so many dresses.

"You had to have five ball gowns, at least four cocktail dresses, and all the accessories to lunch in and to wear to tea, cute little hats and several pairs of matching gloves," Nan said. "It was really quite something."

"I wish I could see you in just one of these dresses," I said. "You were so beautiful."

"They still fit, you know," she said, "every one."

"You don't still have them, do you?" I'd been in Nan's little apartment a million times, and I'd never seen *any* of these dresses. "Are they here?"

"Not here—there's not enough room. I know it's extravagant, but I couldn't bear to give all of them away. I always thought I'd give the ones I kept to your mother, but she had no interest."

"Where are they?" I realized how urgent I sounded. She laughed, and I did, too.

"I haven't been out there in years. They're packed away in one of those big concrete storage places by the Holland Tunnel entrance. Pay the bill every month."

No way. My heart was racing.

"Oh Nan! Can I please see them?" I begged. "Please, please?"

"Of course! You can *have* them." She laughed. "Or what's left of them. They're all yours if the moths haven't gotten there first. I haven't visited that place in almost twenty years. Dearest, bring me that little music box over there, would you please?"

I crossed the room, fetching a little heart-shaped music box with a crystal lid, and placed it in Nan's lap. As she opened it, the box played "Moon River." We looked at each other and grinned.

"See, I love Audrey *almost* as much as you do."

She slipped a little key tied with a pink ribbon out of the box and gently dropped it in my hand.

"Alpha Building, unit 504."

"Holy shit. I mean, wow. Thank you!" I said, tracing the outline of the key in my palm.

"So are we going to watch this movie or not?" asked Nan.

"We are!" I laughed and reached for the remote.

I hit PLAY and Audrey came to life again. Nan and I snuggled together, holding hands while we watched *Tiffany's*. When it was over, I hugged Nan close once again, thanked her for everything, and said good-bye.

As I made my way to the Beast, my phone buzzed with another text from Tabitha Eden.

"Do u really exist ?!"

I couldn't believe how many times Tabitha had texted me. Honestly, I'd figured she'd get bored when I didn't respond and forget about our bizarre encounter in the Met bathroom that night.

"U better b my +1 this wkend !! ;) don't make me go alone !! >.<"

Alone? How could she possibly be always so alone all the time? At her own party for her new album? It was so weird, I felt bad for her. I was dying to go, but I had to be realistic. I couldn't possibly show up at her record party. Tabitha and her A-list friends were bound to figure out that I wasn't actually the reincarnation of Audrey Hepburn.

Besides, I didn't have a thing to wear, did I?

I gazed at the little key with the pink ribbon and wondered.

15   The instant I left Nan's, I phoned Jess, begging and pleading with her to meet me at the Room-2-Spare Self-Storage.

"Why are we meeting at eleven o'clock at night at some danky storage unit by the Holland Tunnel?" Jess asked.

"I don't want to spoil the surprise," I answered.

A half hour later, we were walking down the main corridor past the lockup. It was so close to the tunnel entrance that you could hear the constant grind of cars and trucks downshifting.

"Okay, just tell me your mother finally murdered your little brother and we're stashing the body in a container that you're shipping to Brazil."

"How did you know?" I laughed as we walked down the dimly lit aisle with the flickering fluorescent light, searching for the elevator.

"Seriously, Lisbeth, stop walking." Jess grabbed my arm. "Why are we here?"

"Because you're my friend *and* a fashion genius."

"And?"

I dangled the key in the air in front of her face. "What would you say to haute couture gowns from the fifties and sixties?"

"Um . . . yes . . . ?"

"I was at Nan's and she told me she's been saving her fancy debutante gowns all these years. And naturally, I thought my favorite fashionista just might want to take a peak."

"No way." Jess's eyes lit up. "Well, what are we waiting for?" She was sprinting down the aisle. "C'mon, c'mon!"

I followed behind her, peering cautiously into each doorway we passed. These storage buildings were serial-killer creepy, just the kind of place where you might have a run-in with a couple of axe murderers.

"Here it is!" shouted Jess. She was holding the elevator door, dancing around like her feet were on fire. "Hurry, hurry."

I followed her into the elevator and pushed the button for the fourth floor, and nothing happened. The elevator smelled like urine. Finally it jerked upward screeching, metal against metal.

The buzzer dinged as we hit the fourth floor and just sat there. It took another twenty seconds for the door to open. I hated when elevators did that; like, instead of opening, the car might dead drop, crashing through the elevator shaft into a bottomless pit where nobody would hear you scream.

The door creaked opened.

Jess sauntered confidently out into the hallway. Nan's storage was only a few units down. Jamming the key into the lock, I couldn't turn it either way. It was stuck.

"Come on," said Jess. "Let me try."

"I'm on it," I said, jiggling the key up and down.

"I'm about to die of anticipation. I can't wait." Jess was hopping up and down. I pulled the key out, stuck it back in, and shimmied it back and forth until I felt the lock give way.

"Taa daa!" I threw open the door.

It was pitch-black.

"There's got to be a light," Jess said.

Even though it was creepy, I groped around in the dark for a few seconds. The switch stabbed me in the palm, and I flipped it on.

In the flickering fluorescent light, we saw a few antique chairs and a mahogany armoire wrapped in plastic. I recognized some of them from Nan and Grandpa's old house before she moved into the manor. There was a floor-length gilded mirror, an antique gold-leaf vanity, and framed portraits of people I didn't recognize leaning against the walls.

"That one looks like you!" Jess said, pointing to a portrait of a young girl.

"Dead relatives, I guess."

"Or maybe Nan as a kid?" Jess asked. It was hard to tell.

"Look at this," I said, digging deeper into the dimly lit room.

A crystal chandelier poked out from the corner of a large wooden crate in the corner, glittering faintly. A plush black chaise, which seemed like it should come accessorized with its own lounging movie star, was wrapped in plastic nearby.

"Why in the world does your Nan keep all this stuff in storage?"

"You've seen my Nan's place at the manor. The weight of that chandelier alone would bring down the ceiling."

"Then why doesn't she just sell it all?" Jess asked.

"She's sentimental, like me," I said. "She probably doesn't want to part with any of it."

"Just don't let your Nan turn out to be one of those old ladies who eat cat food and ramen noodles, and when they die you find out they have eight million dollars stuffed in a mattress."

"I'm pretty sure her primary food group is cheesecake. But next time I visit, I'll check her mattress." I was nervous with anticipation. "So where are the dresses?"

Jess dragged a plastic-covered inlaid sectional table out of the way and was digging around in the back.

"Oh . . . my . . . God!" she said. I scurried around the table and a few other crates to see. At the very back, stacked against the wall, were more than a dozen heirloom storage boxes, plus a couple of big plastic bins marked SHOES and HANDBAGS.

Jess pulled a box off the stack and tossed it to me. I carefully lifted the lid. Inside, wrapped up in a see-through plastic clothing bag, was a gorgeous sky-blue taffeta gown. Jess unzipped the bag and lifted the dress from the box. It appeared as vibrant and spotless as if it were new. I went to touch it, but she stopped me.

"Are your hands clean?" she demanded. Spoken like a true museum nerd.

"Yes, Mom," I said, holding my hands up for her to see. I lifted the hem and we both examined the fabric as the magnificent dress fanned out before us.

"This is couture," Jess said breathlessly. "*Vintage* couture. I'd say this dress is probably worth thousands."

My heart was pounding as I dragged down another box. Inside was a silvery-gray tweed Chez Ninon suit with a pink collar.

"I've never heard of this one." I handed it over to Jess, her eyes wild and excited.

"Wow. This is exactly the kind of suit Jackie Kennedy wore. You know, everybody thinks that Jackie was wearing a Chanel suit on the day that JFK was shot. It was actually a Chez Ninon line-by-line copy of a Chanel made with Coco Chanel's approval, because Kennedy's father didn't want Jackie to appear to be wearing snooty French clothes. As if everyone didn't think Chez Ninon was French. Of course, the jacket is a little shapeless and the skirt hits the knee. That's the way they made them in those days."

We tore through the boxes like kids on Christmas morning. There were suits from Lilli Ann, Chanel, Nina Ricci, and even Irene. There was a midnight-black beaded art deco evening bag, gowns made by every designer you've ever heard of and some only Jess knew. I held up a gorgeous black organza cocktail dress while Jess inspected a red chiffon gown.

"Oh my God," she squealed. "This is a red Valentino. Red! Do you know what a big deal this is? And there's a green one, too."

"Whoa, look at that plunging neckline." Good ole Nan. She was the real thing to pull off a dress like that one.

"Look at this boning." Jess pointed it out on a gold brocade gown. "I mean, who needs to breathe?" The designer in Jess couldn't be suppressed. With every dress she touched, she couldn't help commenting on how fashion had changed over the years.

"That History of Twentieth-Century Fashion class at FIT is really coming in handy," I joked. She hardly heard me.

"You know, I have a pile of Chanel buttons I found in the garbage on Fifth Ave. after work one day that would be perfect for this," she said, holding up a dark red Chanel dress.

I couldn't stand it anymore. I stripped down to my underwear and pulled on an emerald-green cocktail dress with a fitted bodice and a full skirt.

"What are you doing?" Jess asked. "Be careful!" She helped me slip into the green wonder, and her eyes lit up as she zipped me into the gown.

"You look fantastic. It's weird, but your body is made for these kinds of dresses." She inspected the dress from every angle, turning over the hem and the sleeves. "Your Nan is a couple of inches shorter than you are, but you're on the short-waisted side, so all your tallness is in your legs."

"Huh?"

"It just means that the dresses will be a little shorter on you than they were on her, but bodice and hip-wise, you're pretty close to the same size. Of course, her boobs are bigger than yours."

"Everybody's are, but thanks for reminding me," I said.

"That's what I'm here for," she cracked.

"Short's good, right?"

"Yeah, more contemporary," Jess said. I spun around in the gorgeous emerald-green cocktail dress before the floor-length mirror, and even though we were standing in a concrete closet, I might as well have been in the grand ballroom at the Waldorf Astoria. I felt like I'd traveled back in time to a world where all the rules were different, where I was no longer bound by my mom, my hometown, and my limited prospects.

I couldn't wait to see the rest and reached for the bins containing shoes and jewelry, pulling out everything I could get my hands on. The shoes, I confess, were sort of a letdown. There were a couple of cute pairs of flats, but most of the heels were pretty boring and very dusty.

One smallish box left.

Inside—the jewelry, oh, the jewelry—a jaded Juliana rhinestone necklace, jeweled drop earrings, enameled bracelets, and sparkling flower brooches. I felt giddy when I spotted the last item at the bottom of the box—a velvet sack with a drawstring. I opened it and pulled out a tiny rhinestone tiara. So totally Audrey.

It was like finding buried treasure.

My mind raced, thinking what it would be like to be the kind of person who wore dresses like these; the people I'd know, the parties I'd attend, a life filled with glamorous possibilities.

I would give anything to have Nan's social abilities, her sly intelligence and humor. My own upbringing was so hopeless. Being raised by wolves would have been better than Mom and Courtney. I'd give anything to live the way Nan had, with enough elegance and poise to float through New York society as "one of them."

Jess placed the jade Juliana necklace around my neck, hooking it in the back, its breathtaking teardrop gemstones sparkling even in the dim light. That's when it struck me.

"Do you think you could, you know, *update* these?" I asked.

"What? No way, they're art!" Jess said, replacing the lid on the jewelry container. "They shouldn't be altered; they should be preserved. Nan should donate these to a museum. Maybe the Met, maybe the Smithsonian. Most of them are pristine. It would be criminal to alter them."

"But they're fashion. They're meant to be worn," I said firmly. "Their *destiny* is to be worn. Preferably, some place fabulous. Like, say, a recording-industry party."

Jess was silent; her jaw hardened and her eyes glowered.

"Dude, are you insane? We are lucky, LUCKY, that we got away with the whole Audrey thing without getting caught. You know what happens if somebody figures that out? I'm still waiting to see if Joe reviews the security camera footage. I'm hoping they record over them every night, or I get fired. Fired! And both of us get hauled off to jail. End of story."

"Nan doesn't think we'd actually do any jail time," I offered.

"Oh. My. God!!!! Seriously? You told Nan? What part of 'we can't tell anybody about this, *ever*' was unclear?"

"Calm down. The police were at my house—not for me—for Ryan, and I freaked. Nan asked, and you know I can't lie to Nan. She won't tell anyone. She thought it was funny."

Jess shook her head and exhaled sharply with disappointment. "You've got to be effin' kidding me. I can't believe you're planning to risk my job just to go to another cocktail round with the trust-fund crowd. To be Tabitha Eden's *groupie*."

"It's not about Tabitha. And we're not talking about the Audrey dress. It won't have anything to do with the museum."

"Don't be stupid," she said. "You don't think that when this whole charade blows up in your face and they start asking questions, they won't trace it right back to Page Six, the Met, and that gala?" I hadn't thought about that.

"Don't be mad at me," I said. "You're the one who's always saying I should find something to be excited about."

"I meant a career! Shit, even a hobby. Not risking public humiliation, unemployment, and jail to pull an Audrey Hepburn con job on a bunch of socialites and your sad little pop star." Jess sat down on the chaise lounge, looking annoyed. "And what would you gain if you pulled this off?"

I paused.

"I don't know."

"Dude, I think it's cool and everything, but where does it go? Do you want to become some kind of professional poser at parties for a career?"

She was right. I didn't have a plan or goal—other than to get to that record party to see what it would be like to hang out with Tabitha Eden for one more night. I craved one more sip of starlight. But how much of a plan did Cinderella have when she went to the ball at the prince's castle, anyway?

"I'm sorry, Jess. I'm just miserable," I said. "I feel like my life is hurtling down a mountain at a thousand miles an hour and the destination is all wrong. Last night at the Met in Audrey's dress, something happened. I know I was a complete fraud, but there was a spark of something inside me that I just can't let go of. It wasn't just the dress that fit me perfectly; it was the whole feeling that there was this other person inside me. It's different for you. You've always known what you were meant to be. But I've been clueless until now. Last night I could feel it. I could taste it. But if you don't help me, I'll never be able to touch it. I don't know how, but I feel like it could change my life forever."

A sad, puzzled expression crossed Jess's eyes.

"You know it's not like you can just put on a dress and waltz into some world you don't belong in," she said. "Don't you think they'll check up on you and wonder who you are? Where you came from? What you're doing there? These are blue bloods. They hang with blue bloods."

I didn't know what to say. It was too painful to think about being stuck where I was. I closed my eyes. I didn't want to cry. When I opened my eyes, Jess had picked up the Dior and was holding it up to her body, looking in the mirror. She inspected a tattered piece of the hem.

"We probably found these dresses just in time," she said.

"Yeah, nothing lasts forever," I added wistfully, watching her turn the Dior inside out, running her fingers along the stitching.

"My profs would consider your suggestion blasphemy," she said. "Taking a pair of scissors to a vintage Dior or reworking a Cassini is crazy."

"Aw, come on, we don't have to treat these dresses as history. It's the perfect combo of everything you know and what you want to do," I said. "Besides, the dresses are mine. Nan gave them to me."

I hated that I sounded like a child saying that, but I could see her mind was working a million miles a minute.

"That's breaking a lot of rules," Jess said.

"Yeah, we don't want to break any rules," I said. Hidden in the corner of her mouth was a budding smile dying to come out, and I knew I had a chance.

"Well, I guess everyone gets to do some idiotic thing before going to college."

"You're the best friend ever," I said, throwing my arms around her and squeezing her tightly, trying to ignore that she'd just said the word "college."

"Don't you forget it," she said.

"It'll be our little project," I added. "We'll call it Being Audrey Hepburn."

She should have said no, but she didn't.

16 I needed a secret identity.

"Lisbeth Dulac." I figured that would work. It was Nan's maiden name, so it seemed like less of a lie, better than picking a random name out of a phone book.

Sliding the closet door closed, I retreated to the privacy of my tiny childhood refuge. Tabitha's record party was three days away, and I needed more than just luck and Nan's old dresses.

Phase 1, Jess and I agreed, was to create a Facebook page. It was the quickest way to invent a present and a past, something that could be googled, proving that the new "me" existed. I wasn't a tech wiz, but, like everybody, I grew up on Facebook and knew a thing or two.

I chose May 4, Audrey's birthday, and a birth year three years before my actual one and then opened a new account with a bogus e-mail, but my fingers froze on the keyboard when it was time to start filling in the details. I didn't have a clue how many languages Lisbeth Dulac spoke, what her favorite music was, or what high school she attended.

Sinking into the pillows, I tried to get my head around the situation. Every piece of information I entered could be the one that blew my cover and exposed me as a fakester. It made my brain ache trying to think about it. The soft hum of the minifridge lulled me, making it impossible to keep my eyes from closing.

The sound of Nan's music box playing "Moon River" was swimming round and round in my head until I awoke, realizing the song was actually the muffled sound of my phone ringing buried beneath the pillows. Groggy, I answered and figured it was Jess calling. She'd help me figure this out.

"Hey, wuz up?"

". . . Lisbeth?"

I froze. Whose voice was that? Crap.

"Lisbeth? Is that you?"

My God. Tabitha.

I powered off my phone and dropped it on the floor like it was red hot. I panicked. Shit.

Then I thought, *My voice message.*

Crap. If she called back and heard my normal, goofy, homegirl message, the whole plan was cooked. I had to move faster than Tabitha's little manicured fingers on her jewel-encrusted phone.

Powering my phone back on, I went to the phone settings, voice mail greeting and selected default—then sunk back into the pillows, watching, waiting, heart beating. My thoughts raced. Maybe it wasn't her after all.

Clearly there was at least one problem with living a fantasy life—it made me paranoid as hell.

The phone lit up, playing "Moon River" in my hands. I let it ring through, and allowed myself to breathe.

For a split second, I actually considered forgetting the whole scheme. I wasn't the kind of girl that lied, even on normal stuff. When I told a lie, I got this queasy, fluttering feeling in my stomach like there was a little trapped creature down there who couldn't get out.

Even when the little beast calmed down, the second I thought about the lie again, the creature began bouncing around. So I just didn't lie that much—except to Mom about college, I guess. That wasn't so much a lie as an omission.

Checking the phone, I saw that Tabitha hadn't bothered to leave a message. Was she losing interest?

I worried how long Page Six would keep my photo posted, so I dragged it from the Web page to the desktop. I cropped out ZK and Dahlia and created a perfectly good FB picture. But what about the other details?

For sure, everybody lied on Facebook. My sister, Courtney, had a friend, Stephanie, who claimed that a gossip Web site guy was paying her to go to his parties—free bottles of tequila, limo rides, three-course meals, swag bags, and nobody cared if she had an ID. All she had to do was tweet how hot the parties were. It turned out it was just her building an excuse for her flaky, alcohol-soaked behavior. Blatant embellishing was the norm for how good you were doing, how great the party was, and how drunk everyone got.

My phone buzzed, and I looked at the screen.

"Hey you ! ;)"

Shit. I'd have to say something. What would Audrey do, I wondered. What if Audrey had grown up in the age of digital distraction?

Audrey knew all her faults and figured out how to make them work for her. She had an inventory of things she disliked about herself—bumpy nose, eyes that were too wide apart, chest too flat—I could relate to that and more. But she developed her own sense of style and found her own look—the updo, gigantic sunglasses, a simple, elegant wardrobe of classics.

Audrey Hepburn created Audrey—like Cinderella without a fairy godmother. I wanted to be my own fairy godmother, too, given that I hadn't seen anyone with a golden wand my entire life.

"CALL ME !! TEXT ME !!"

I imagined Audrey on Facebook. No, she'd never do that. But maybe a blog? A blog could be my magic wand, helping me create something out of nothing.

I envisioned flamboyant opining's on fashion and life. I imagined blog entries while traveling with my beloved Nan. I could post from anywhere around the world without ever leaving home.

"Jst called. . . Was that u ??" Tabitha wasn't giving up this time.

Like it or not, it was a moment of truth. Either move forward and renew contact or pack it in. Screwing up my courage, I texted back.

"I've been traveling. Jst boarding my flight now. I'll be back in time 2 see you @ your party."

"Can't wait !! ;)" I added.

There was no turning back now. I had to remind myself to breathe.

Okay, I thought, *just make some choices and get this done.*

I discovered there were dozens of ways to blog anonymously, so I created a page where I posted the links to a few worthy causes that Audrey would have supported, a party calendar from Guest of a Guest, and a few of my favorite New York stores that I'd never be able to buy anything from. It still seemed pretty empty; I had so little to work with.

The Page Six Web lift was perfect for "about me," but the blog needed a title and some kind of image. I thought back to the night Jess and I unlocked Nan's storage area, remembering all the dresses we saw, the paintings and the jewelry. I dug in my bag, found Nan's tiny rhinestone tiara, and marveled at it.

It said everything. I took a picture of the tiara with my phone and placed it at the top of my blog page.

Using Bodoni Seventy-Two font, the one they used for the titles in *Breakfast at Tiffany's*, I typed the name of my blog above the tiara. Shades of Limelight—it just came to me. It's from one of my favorite Audrey quotes.

For the first time, I was putting myself out there, exposing myself to some of the limelight . . . just not too much, I hoped.

"Kk see u soon ;)" Tabitha texted.

I started to text back but figured in first class they were already serving me cocktails.

So I had a new identity and a blog—but did I have anything to say? Strong opinions were the key to Audrey Hepburn's success.

Now if only I had some.

17 I felt like an operative for the CIA preparing to go deep cover.

The next phase of the Being Audrey project was to build a photo history of me appearing at superswanky events wearing Jess's redo of Nan's fabulous gowns.

There were only two problems, of course. The first was that my status as a New Jersey diner waitress didn't exactly land me on the guest list of the city's coolest parties. Solution? I'd just have to crash.

The second was that the press had no reason whatsoever to take pictures of me. Because, you know, I was nobody. So I was going to have to basically photobomb a bunch of trust funders and celebrities. I had a feeling that wasn't quite as easy as it sounded.

Okay, three problems. What if I got caught? I'd be dragged out of the party and humiliated in front of the very people I had been trying to impress. The worst part, the part I feared most, was that my whole adventure would go up in flames before I'd even started. Solution? None.

Jess had arranged with a girl from one of her classes who worked as an assistant at a PR firm to get us into a Bar3 party as gossip bloggers. We ditched work at the Hole, which was no small sacrifice, considering we both needed the tips.

The first event was one of those sponsored parties for a new vodka made from really expensive designer potatoes in the Hamptons. No kidding. This was the kind of event where they paid a celebrity wrangler to populate the room with young movie stars and press-hungry celebstitutes and a few "real housewives," plus all the gossip bloggers and reporter types they could beg, borrow, or bribe. This sort of party would be slumming for Tabitha and her crowd, so I wasn't worried about running into her.

Inside, we flashed press IDs that we literally made on Jess's printer and laminated an hour before. Jess was dressed in one of her slightly punk'd pixie getups and I wore the most bland and unremarkable outfit I could dig out of my closet. My black skirt, black flats, and white button-down blouse practically guaranteed I'd be invisible in the sea of New Yorkers. No one would notice me until I changed into tonight's glorious ensemble.

We ducked into the bathroom, and Jess lifted the remade Dior out of the huge shoulder bag she always carries. The dress was outrageous. With a fitted bodice and a full tulle skirt, it was stunning. I was so excited I could hardly stand still. Jess didn't do a lot to the dress, but her modifications were really fresh. It was kind of like the way rappers cop a riff from a classic song you know by heart and turn it into something so cool and original you couldn't wait to get on the dance floor. Jess did the same thing, except with timeless couture.

It hadn't been easy to get Jess going. I swear, I thought she was going to burst into tears when she made the first cut. I kept telling her, it's not like she did anything but shorten it a bit and remove a little of the boning in the bodice to keep it from impaling me, a brutal side effect of my being so short-waisted. But Jess was completely freaked out about doing even that. If there hadn't been a bit of damage to the hem already, I might never have gotten her over the hump. Of course, after that first adjustment, she was totally hooked.

In one of the bathroom stalls, I slipped into the dress while Jess stood guard. She insisted on a final touch-up, adding a little color to my eyes and lips. I half-expected her to spit on her finger and clean my face like Mom used to do when I was little.

Once dressed, we wished each other luck and discretely parted company. Making my way into the center of the party, I tried to get my nerve up to intrude on a few choice subjects. As a backup, Jess got ready to snap candids from the sidelines. If the police dragged me away, she'd get those, too, and sell them to *The Post* for bail.

I walked around the party for fifteen minutes, eyeballing various photographers, checking out who they were covering, and trying to work up the nerve to do something.

Bingo. One photographer had lined up two horse-faced banker types, which I figured would be an easy place to start. Old guys never turned down a young girl. I inserted myself between them, linking my arms in theirs as the photographer snapped away. My heart was beating as quickly as a hummingbird from the outright deception of it all, but at least there was one more photo of my alter ego. One of the old guys grabbed my ass, by the way.

Jess steered me over to a lineup of six debutantes who I assumed had wandered in from the hotel next door. They seemed so out of place, chatting away with deep Southern accents, wearing the old-fashioned deb look, long white gloves and all. I stepped into Jess's shot and posed just as the flash went off, acting as if we were long-lost sorority sisters or something. My modified Dior in a sea of hillbilly debutantes.

Slipping away, I downed a flute of champagne from a waiter and photobombed another quick four shots, hanging out mostly in the background as if I was laughing or talking to someone. I wound my way to Jess, who was lingering by the bar to take a breather. She gave me a thumbs-up.

"The Dior really popped against all those traditional styles. It's going to be a cool shot for my portfolio," Jess said.

"Glad to oblige, my dear, but maybe we should leave before someone realizes I'm a total fake."

"You're probably right," she said, "but get me a drink before we go? I've got to pee."

"Sure thing and thanks for sharing." I waved to the bartender for more champagne while mentally critiquing my performance. I was feeling pretty self-satisfied when a good-looking man sidled up to the bar in a black suit with a lavender shirt.

"Oh, how awful," he said to no one in particular. He was assessing the same giggling gush of debutantes I had photobombed earlier. "A tsunami, don't you think?" And to my terror, he turned as if he were talking to me.

"Pardon?" I asked. But I was really thinking: *Oh my god, that's Isak Guerrere.*

Isak Guerrere, the handsome, uberfamous fashion designer who had owned and lost his own line many times and had become single-name famous for being Isak more than anything else. That and his fashion reality show, which I watched religiously. His rugged good looks made you wish he wasn't gay. But the makeup defining his cheekbones and his jellied hair confirmed beyond a doubt that he was.

"I said, those debs are an utter *disaster,* a fashion tsunami, don't you think?" His piercing eyes were unabashedly taking in every inch of me, my hair, my dress, my shoes. No detail eluded his glance. To say I felt like a deer caught in the headlights is an understatement. Fearing panic, I pushed my brain to say something, anything.

"Perhaps it's a reenactment of a decisive moment in fashion history?" I offered, feigning nonchalance, crossing my fingers under the bar, hoping that would suffice.

"Ah yes, but fashion history is always subject to revision," he said, smiling.

Returning from the bathroom, Jess froze in her tracks when she saw who I was talking to. Her eyes looked like they were going to pop right out of their sockets.

"Speaking of which, what are you wearing, if you don't mind my asking?"

I almost choked on my champagne.

"Manners, manners, my apologies. I'm Isak Guerrere."

"Of course," I said, recovering. "I'm a huge fan of the design you created for Natalie Portman for the Golden Globes. Pure Genius." See? Six years of obsessing over celebrity blogs wasn't all for nothing.

"Really? Well, thank you, that was one of my favorites," he said offhandedly. "And you would be?"

"Lisbeth Dulac, it's a pleasure to meet you." It felt more like playing a part in a play than a lie. *Think Audrey. Think Audrey.*

"Dulac," he said, as though he were attempting to place the name. Obviously, that wasn't going to happen. "Lisbeth Dulac," he said, taking my hands in both of his, "do let us look at what you're wearing." I wanted to bolt, but the way he held my hands made me feel trapped.

"Vintage, Dior. Or is it?" His expression serious, his eyes wild.

Up close, his jellied hair made him look crazy, like a mad scientist. I did my best to be bright and pretty despite his scrutiny.

"Your dress is giving me a fashgasm," he said. It was such a goofy thing to say that I couldn't stop myself from giggling. Isak seemed slightly offended.

"Laugh if you like, but your dress is incredibly foolhardy, mildly blasphemous but stunning. And the designer would be?" he demanded.

Moving in closer to him, I whispered, "I hope you'll understand that I can't reveal the designer." He eyed me suspiciously.

"It's your secret?" He feigned shock but seemed intrigued and satisfied—for the moment.

"Yes, I appreciate your discretion."

"Completely unique and perfectly fitted," he whispered, "as exceptional as the wearer." Isak flagged a waiter with a tray of champagne glasses.

"A toast," he said, "to my very stylish new friend."

I beamed. Jess was going to *die* when she heard what Isak had said about her dress.

"Thank you," I said, bullet dodged.

Champagne flowed, and soon my worries bubbled away. Isak and I were laughing like the best of friends.

"Now tell me, Lisbeth, two things you've done recently that you've never done before," he asked. He seemed so taken with me. Jess discretely snapped pictures from a distance.

"Well, I've met a wonderful fashion designer, named Isak," I said.

"Thanks for the plug. That's one, and two . . . ?"

"Well, let me see. Oh, I started a blog." I immediately regretted saying so.

"Indeed! Its name?"

"Oh, I'm embarrassed. It's really nothing," I said, meaning every single word of it.

"Come now."

"Shades of Limelight, but I've only just started," I said, feeling totally self-conscious.

"I'm sure it's wonderful. I love the quote. It cuts both ways, clever girl," he said. A little smile turned at the corner of his mouth. My heart sank, fearing I had exposed myself more than I should have.

Jess signaled we should leave. She probably could tell I was worried.

"Well, Isak dear, I can see we could chat forever," I said, rising from the bar, "but it's time for me to leave. I hope you don't mind." I didn't realize how much I had been drinking until I stood up.

"I do mind quite a lot, but it's been charming," he said, standing and taking my hand. "I trust I will see you again soon?"

"I hope so," I said and did my very best to exit gracefully without stumbling on my heels.

That night, Jess and I practically peed ourselves laughing as we clicked through the photos on her camera, reliving every glorious second of the adventure. Had we really gotten away with it so easily? Jess's first redo was so spectacular that none other than Isak

Guerrere had taken notice. I didn't mention anything about the blog. I didn't want her to worry.

The next night we planned to return to the scene of the crime—the Met.

A nagging part of me worried we were pushing our luck.

18   I couldn't help mulling over in my mind the conversation with Isak. Every moment of our encounter was delicious. Although I faked every bit of my savoir faire, I had done so quite successfully. There seemed to be some value in that, as if I had stitched together a life and personality in real time as I talked to him. I had acted as if I were *somebody*, a person with a point of view and personality. Isak seemed to be genuinely interested in what I had to say.

I was also somebody with opinions, but they were buried down where no one would hear or see them. Now I had a reason to drag them out of the dark pockets of my mind and bring them into the light. Specifically, the "limelight."

Spilling the beans to Isak Guerrere, of all people, meant that I'd have to actually make a few entries on my fledgling blog if I was going to make this work.

In order to comfort myself and get going, I imagined bravely talking to Isak as if my opinion mattered. I opened up the blog page and began writing my first full entry.

"Standing pigeon-toed in a new dress and posing with your head tilted at a 45 degree angle doesn't hack it anymore," I wrote. "If you want to find the heart of fashion, you need to start small—one detail at a time, one stitch followed by the next. It's as much about removing the clutter as finding the next fashion design."

I took a deep breath to read and reread what I had written. Satisfied, I continued.

"The film director Steven Soderbergh once said, The making of any art is just problem solving. You have to eliminate the versions that aren't any good. Then you see what you have left." I wasn't sure where I had heard that quote, but at least I wasn't quoting Chanel, like every other fashion blog.

"Fashion is certainly more than dressing your Barbie. It's one choice at a time, step by step." I thought for a moment before continuing.

"A button, a shoe, a glove that fits just right—that's what this blog will be about. It's about examining fashion from the ground up, detail by detail, appreciating the art and craftsmanship that goes into perfecting each item. Little by little, I'll build from there to show you, my dear reader, that anyone can go from nothing to something and sustain your soul in all shades of limelight."

Phew, it almost sounded pithy.

Laying out Jess's modified Dior as well as a few items from Nan's treasure trove, I clicked my little digital camera, photographing a few of the wonderful buttons Jess had added, the hem she had modified, the corner of the collar, the wonderful hand stitching inside.

I shot everything out against white, so that the photo frame was invisible on the blog page. I wanted just the bare, stark essentials. I ended with another quote I remembered from that fashion neophyte, Winnie the Pooh.

"Sometimes, the smallest things take up the most room in your heart."

I took a deep breath and went back and double-checked everything. Filling in the "about me" link, I wrote:

Hello. Starting a new blog is like starting a relationship. In the beginning, it's fresh, promising, and new. I hope for both our sakes it stays that way. I pledge to be a good chum and post frequently and share a few designs from my friend, Designer X, a secret well kept who is fated to shine.

This was the beginning. Next stop—the Met.

19 Crashing another event at the Met was not our first choice. It was only because we couldn't find anything else on the social calendar that we had any chance of getting into. Jess was still worried about Mr. Myers. There was nothing else going on in the museum that night, so the chances were slim that he'd show at an event like this. Mr. Myers wasn't exactly a socialite.

Save the Cheetah Night was the name of the event. I hadn't seen too many cheetahs lately, so they were definitely scarce. Although poverty also seemed like a worthy cause, I'd read there was compassion fatigue in the "what jewels should I wear tonight" set, so I guessed cheetahs were a tad easier to feel sorry for.

I was wearing the sky-blue silk taffeta gown, the very first one we'd found in Nan's storage unit. Jess replaced a limp satin ribbon sash with a funky hand-beaded band and thinned out the tulle under the skirt, among other alterations. It was drop-dead gorgeous.

Slipping through a service entrance near the cafeteria, I sidestepped the beefy *Men in Black* security guys and snuck into the main gala without being noticed.

The anxious little beast in my belly was squirming around like crazy. Everywhere, I saw security cameras and guards. What if my presence jogged the memory of one of the security people or gave some detective the last clue he or she needed to put the whole escapade together? I took deep breaths.

Adam Levine from Maroon 5, who I consider a total sex god, was standing with a reporter and photographer from *Us Weekly*. The reporter was actually waiting for Adam and a couple other guys from the group to pose for a picture, so I just moseyed right up to them.

Seriously. I think that Nan's taffeta gown gave me superpowers or something. Just before the photographer snapped the picture, I jumped in between them as if I'd started the freaking band myself. Adam sort of cracked up, posing with a funny grin on his face and putting his arm around my waist, just as the photographer snapped the picture.

"Wonderful, darling," I said in my best Audrey voice as I

twirled to face Adam, my back to the reporter before he could ask my name. I was shaking, but I channeled Holly Golightly and her "life is a continuous cocktail party" attitude.

"And how is the secret album coming along?" I whispered.

He seemed taken by surprise, quite clearly wondering who the hell I was and how I knew that he was working on a new album—just a total lame guess—aren't they all working on one?

"Insane, actually, we just finished."

"Lovely, can't wait to hear it," I said, smiling at the other band members as I sauntered off, my body tingling from my toes to my updo with a brazen sort of confidence I'd never felt before.

I couldn't believe it, little me, a nobody from South End mingling with fancy-schmancy rock and rollers. Who'd have thought? I spied Jess on the balcony with her camera—she gave me a thumbs-up.

Ah, confidence . . . I can do this, I thought, until someone tapped me on the shoulder.

"I know what you're up to," he said, and I wanted to die.

I turned slowly to give myself a few extra milliseconds to formulate an excuse or find a getaway.

He wore a sharply styled black leather jacket. His face was sort of familiar, but I didn't know why. My eyes met his. His wry smile gave the impression he knew me. Was that a good smile or an evil one? I couldn't tell. His lively brown eyes were inquisitive and striking against the backdrop of his tousled auburn hair, and he was holding a video camera.

"Excuse me, I don't believe we've met?" I asked with false bravado.

"Not formally, but I've seen you before," he said. "Where was it, do you know?"

Panicked, I scanned his eyes, searching for intent. Was he the cameraman outside the Met that first night who turned the camera light away from me? Did he already know I was the same skinny girl in jeans gawking at all the celebrities on the red carpet outside?

I went full-on Audrey to distract him. It was my only option.

"Darling, I don't think we've had the pleasure, which is unfortunate . . ." His burnished brown eyes connected with mine, and I froze. He examined me with such intensity that I blinked.

"Unfortunate?" he asked.

Oh jeez, how was I going to finish that sentence? What was I even trying to say? He was just a nosy cameraman . . . I had to get out of there.

"It's unfortunate because I'm late to meet someone," I said, scanning the room for an escape route. "Please excuse me." I turned to leave.

"Wait," he said, thrusting his hand in my direction. "Chase Reynold, Lux TV." I smiled and offered my hand reluctantly.

"So nice to meet you, Chase Reynold, Lux TV," I said. "Funny last name, Lux TV." Now it was his turn to be flustered.

"Actually it's just my production company. I had to put something on the camera. I'm a fashion shooter. I feed footage to Web sites, cover Fashion Week, parties, that kind of thing. Here's my card in case you want more, uh, coverage." He gave a quick glance up at the balcony where Jess was standing. She gave me a quizzical look, wondering what was going on.

"Well, that's very interesting, but I really must be going."

He laughed. "I've seen this before," he said. "Always making an entrance, then slipping away. Trying to control your image."

"Uh yes, you're absolutely right," I said. "A girl has to preserve her privacy, don't you think? I appreciate your confidentiality. Now if you don't mind . . ."

My heart pounded ferociously as I walked to the bar. I asked for a glass of champagne and sipped it quickly. I stalled and then pretended to wave at someone and moved toward the exit. It was so lame and fakey. I certainly wasn't fooling anyone but myself. I scanned the balcony for Jess, but she was gone. Chase Lux made me nervous. We needed to get out of there, fast.

"Miss Dulac, it's so marvelous to see you again."

I jumped, surprised to hear my fake name spoken by anyone. Turning, I found my new pal, Isak Guerrere.

"Aren't you the girl about town? But you shouldn't be hiding in the corner, pet, especially when you're wearing yet another stunning party frock! Avoiding one of your many admirers, I assume?"

"What a pleasure it is to see you," I said. I already loved Isak. He made me feel drop-dead gorgeous in the way only a gay designer could.

Giving me the once over, he twirled me like a ballerina as he touched the gown at my waist. "Certainly original fabric, but pristine. Another startling redux by . . . what did you say the designer's name was?"

I giggled. "Isak, darling, you know I'm sworn to secrecy." I took another sip of my drink, noticed the Lux guy move away, and felt comfortable again.

My phone rang, and I lifted it from my clutch without thinking. "Hello, darling."

"Lizzy, that you?" Shit. It was Jake. "You're talkin' kinda funny."

My heart jumped, I hadn't talked to Jake in three days. I'd missed him the night before at the diner because Jess and I ditched work, and there was another one of his shows the night after.

"Listen, Lizzy, after our shift do you want to—"

I panicked and hung up on him.

"Poor boy," said Isak. How he could tell, I don't know. I gave a tentative smile. But I felt like crap. I didn't want to treat Jake like that, but I'd just spent the last hour doing my most convincing Audrey to an audience of reporters, celebrities, fashionistas, and one of the most famous fashion designers in the country, which meant if I uttered one more word in front of Isak, it would have blown my cover.

"Well, I'm very happy to see you here tonight," Isak said, breaking the awkward silence. "These events can be so tedious." He seemed oddly weary, as though party going was boring for him. I guess new meat like me was good for a change. "Perhaps another drink?"

Jess reappeared on the balcony, alarmed and motioning for us to leave.

"Isak, darling, you're so wonderful, but our timing is inopportune. I'm on my way out," I said as calmly as I could manage.

"So soon? Such a shame," he said, shaking his head. "Whatever will I do without you? I do hope that I'll find you again at that event for your friend . . ." Before he could finish, the glare of a camera light was on us.

"Mr. Guerrere, can I get a quick shot of you two?" Chase Whatever was back with a self-satisfied expression, his eyes locking on mine.

My first instinct was to bolt. But it would appear suspicious if I did. So I snuggled right up to Isak and posed. How long could one photo take?

Chase laughed.

What had I done?

He leaned forward and whispered, "Uh, this is video. It's okay for you to move." He'd said "shot"——didn't that mean photo? I felt my face flush red.

"Awfully sorry," I said.

"In fact, movement is preferable," Chase advised. Isak rolled his eyes. My palms began sweating, and my pulse pounded in my ears. Where was Jess? How could I get out of this? I knew I could pose for a camera shot—but video? I had never even YouTubed. This was absolutely out of my league.

"I'm sorry, I can't," I whispered to Isak. "It was delightful to see you again, but I really must go." The sad little beast inside was crying for help. But Isak firmly grasped my arm, never breaking eye contact with the camera.

"Not so fast, cupcake," he said. "Stand, smile, and look gorgeous while I drone on about tonight's worthy cause. You'll be fine."

I had two options: give in to my terror and run or stay and risk passing out. I decided there really wasn't a choice. I prayed Jess could hold on.

"Of course," I said, taking a deep breath to calm myself, trying very hard not to think about the video camera. I'd seen celebrities stand there as the cameras rolled, appearing relaxed and poised, and I grew determined to stand up straight and smile like someone who belonged there instead of what I really was—a Holly Golightly imposter in a fifty-year-old dress.

"So, Mr. Guerrere, you're here at the Cheetah Conservation benefit. I know you're a big wildlife supporter. What should we know about tonight's event?" Chase asked.

Chase seemed to know that if he gave Isak a softball question, he would run with it. Isak, ham that he was, launched into a speech that sounded as if he were reading from a brochure. All the right words were there: "natural heritage," "holistic approach," "outreach," and "race for survival." He even had an anecdote about Jane Goodall.

I started to see spots in front of my eyes and realized I must be hyperventilating. But somewhere between willing myself to smile and hoping I wouldn't faint, something magical happened. I found myself staring right down the lens of the camera, and, astonishingly, I felt warm all over. I actually loved standing there.

Then it was over, as quickly as it began. The warmth of the light went away, and the magic of that moment was gone.

Out of the corner of my eye, I spotted Jess, up on the balcony. Her back was turned, and she was talking to someone. As she shifted, I realized what her panic was about. Her boss, Mr. Myers, was standing inches away, yelling right in her face. Shit.

"Thanks, Isak," Chase said.

I instinctively looked down at my bare wrist to check my imaginary watch. "I am . . . very . . . late. Terribly sorry, Isak darling." Isak and I exchanged air kisses, a first for me. It was just as goofy as it appeared in the movies and felt ridiculous.

"Chase, dear, it was so nice to meet you," I said.

"We'll meet again soon. I'm sure of that," he said.

I tried not to worry what he meant when he said that.

I glanced up and spotted Jess out of the corner of my eye. Myers was gone, and she was frantically waving her arms at me like some sort of psychotic airport-runway worker. She seemed as if she might burst into tears at any moment.

It was time to go.

20 Jess threw herself on my bed, her arms spread out like she wanted to be crucified. "I'm such an idiot," she said.

"Come on, Jess, was it really that bad?" We'd been sitting in my bedroom all afternoon. I'd run out of arguments to make her feel better. Although we'd been gloriously successful in our debut with Nan's dresses, she was quitting. No more Being Audrey.

"I got so carried away with your crazy project, I forgot what I'm supposed to be doing," she said, burying her face in the pillows. I didn't know what to say, so I sat on the edge of the bed and worried.

Apparently, Mr. Myers caught Jess taking photos of me in the museum. Normally that wasn't a big deal—museum visitors could take pictures all the time as long as they didn't use flash or put their camera on a tripod—*except in certain areas.* The party was in one of the contemporary galleries, and that was one of the *except in certain areas* you couldn't take pictures in. Of course, not everyone knew that photography was strictly forbidden in the contemporary galleries, so usually a guard just asked you to refrain. But Jess knew because she worked there. Only she forgot because she was taking pictures of me.

Myers didn't fire her, but he came close. Worse, he screamed at her in front of everyone.

When we were leaving the Met, her face was so flushed and embarrassed I thought she would fall apart crying in front of everyone, and Jess never cries. She also never makes mistakes at work—she felt totally exposed—and I could understand why. It probably hadn't helped that I was downstairs playing ingenue with Isak and Chase.

"Myers hates me!" she said. I could barely hear her voice muffled in the pillow. Weird reversal. Jess was always more daring than me. But unexpectedly, I was on this strange track where I was willing to risk everything. Unlike Jess, I didn't really want to keep all those things I was risking. My life might go down in flames, but it wasn't a life I wanted to have anyway.

Working toward a career that made sense to everyone, Jess was supported by her family at every turn, while I was doomed to be a nurse-practitioner, which might be a perfectly good profession, just not for me.

She stood up, crossed the room, and began digging in her monster bag—tossing out a pair of textured thigh highs, a professional sewing kit, an entire library of rumpled paperback books, pliers, balled-up dollar bills, and a complete Allen wrench set. She could have pulled out a live rabbit, and I wouldn't have been surprised. She kept digging.

"What are you looking for?"

"Shhh," she said, furiously burrowing around the secret pockets of her massive bag. "Arrrggggg!!!!" She turned the whole thing upside down, and the remaining contents came pouring out all over the bed—coins rolled across the floor, and everything else went everywhere.

"There it is," she groaned, like she'd finally located a lost child. She snatched the Hershey's Cookies 'n' Creme bar off the bed, ripped the wrapping off, and maniacally bit into it. Not a pretty sight, especially when you consider that Jess spent a whole lot of will power trying not to feed her sugar jones. Inside Jess's skinny, pixielike body, there was a portly, chubby-cheeked Italian girl just dying to get her hands on a meatball sub.

She wiped her mouth. "God, I need a cannoli."

Jessica Giovanna Pagliazzi was Jess's full christening name. In the old-world Italian tradition, Jess's nonna lived with her—along with a revolving collection of assorted cousins and distant relatives who frequently visited from the old country.

Her dad owned a takeout pizzeria and deli. The whole family worked there at one point or another. Every meal at home was a feast, and there was always room for one more at the table. Jess loved her nonna, but she was a massive food pusher of everything Neapolitan—chicken cacciatore, steak pizzaiola, manicotti, lasagna, and her seven-thousand-calorie macaroni and mayonnaise salad.

"You look tired. Eat something!" she'd say. "Bella, you're too skinny, *mangia!* You seem sad today. *Mangia, mangia!*" With all that delicious food and the constant pressure to eat, Jess developed a weight problem. It was practically unavoidable.

If I'd lived with Jess's family, I probably would have been chubby, too—all my mom ever had in the house was vodka, ramen noodles, and cigarettes, so I never had that concern. Jess went through years of idiotic elementary school ridicule, and despite four summers at fat camp (which Jess paid for herself out of babysitting money because her family all thought her weight was just fine), everyone still called her Chubby Cheeks.

Nothing worked until the tenth grade, when Jess just decided to give her life a massive makeover. She changed everything by sheer force of will: exercised like a maniac and never touched pasta again. Then she came out to her entire family at a Sunday dinner, got her belly button pierced and her first tattoo.

My stupid obsession had pushed her back over the edge.

"Jess, we don't have to do this." I couldn't believe I was saying those words. Could I do this by myself? No. Did I really mean what I was saying? Barely. But Jess was my best friend in the world, and there was no way I was going to pressure her to continue risking her real future for my fantasy life. "Really. If this is going to—"

"Shhh," she mumbled, her mouth full of chocolate. I sat back down on the bed and waited, wondering if she would stop stuffing her face long enough to breathe.

"Oh God, that's better," she said, wiping her mouth off with her hoodie sleeve.

"I'm really sorry," I said. "I've been selfish."

An odd smile crossed Jess's face.

"Myers has never liked me. You know he didn't hire me. The head intern did, and she's gone. He's been trying to find a reason to fire me ever since she left."

"Why?"

Jess looked at me like the answer was obvious and I was totally naive. She swallowed and paused as if she were trying to figure out what she wanted to say.

"Lizzy," Jess began, "I'm really sorry . . ."

I knew instantly that I didn't want to hear the rest, but I was determined not to pout or weep, at least not until Jess went home.

"I can't do this anymore. I have to think about my future."

But what about my future? I thought.

"I understand," I said, despite myself. I did. Really. But I was crushed. I didn't know why I'd thought it was going to work anyway. Nothing ever did.

I couldn't just sit there, so I went over to the computer and clicked around. Jess knew I was heartbroken. She squeezed onto the desk chair with me, both of us feeling bad. A part of me wanted her to hurry up and leave so I could crawl back into my closet and cry.

I tabbed through my usual random gossip sites and blogs, feeling completely numb.

"I should probably get going," she said after a few moments.

"Okay," I said.

"Holy shit. Look at that—TMZ posted a picture of you in the blue dress with Adam Levine. They must have gotten it from *Us Weekly*!" She pushed her fingers across the computer track pad.

"I guess."

"That dress is actually pretty awesome, and you look incredible."

She double clicked the dress to magnify her handiwork and check out the details.

My heart leapt and then plunged. There would be no more dresses. No more parties. No more Adam Levine. I glanced up. She was right about the dress, but it seemed way less awesome than it had ten minutes before, when it actually meant something.

Jess clicked through to the next page, "Look, they have you tagged in another photo—you and that shitfaced 'queen of pop.'" She clicked to enlarge, and there I was, arm in arm with Tabitha Eden, our heads thrown back in what appeared to be a raucous giggle.

My heart stopped when I realized how clearly the picture showed the *Breakfast at Tiffany's* Givenchy. Someone had gotten another angle on the pop princess and me that night, as we were sneaking toward the back door. I could tell Jess was fixated on it, too. After her fresh encounter with Mr. Myers, I guessed that her memories of that night weren't quite as glorious as mine.

"Whatcha looking at, losers?" Jess and I spun around at the same time.

Courtney, my sister, stood behind us in knee-high white boots, distressed jeans, a crop top, hot pink accessories, and a nasty smirk on her face.

I snapped my laptop shut.

"Porn?" Courtney asked, laughing. She sat down on my bed and lit up a cigarette. Like this day wasn't already shitty enough.

21 "What are you doing here, Court? I thought you and Mom agreed to stay away from each other for a while."

Courtney tossed her hair back and laughed. I knew her entire library of moves—the hair whip, the hip wiggle when she sat down, her exaggerated fish lips, all the stuff she did with her cigarettes—all calculated to get boys to look at her. They were so ingrained into her psyche that she couldn't stop herself from doing them even when there were no boys around.

"Yeah, Mom has been up my ass lately," Courtney said.

"Lately is an understatement," I said. She examined her cigarette and spat out a piece of something. It was gross. Still, it was better to wait for Courtney to leave, like a storm passing, than to confront her.

"Yeah, she's such a cow." I could tell Jess was dying to leave but was staying out of loyalty. She hated Courtney more than I did. But Courtney was my older sister. She could be mean, but I couldn't totally hate her.

"So what are you girls doing in here? Cyberstalking some of your high school buddies?"

"We graduated, remember?" I said. "Aren't you worried about hanging around? Mom should be back soon with Ryan." I had no idea if that was true or not, but I'd say anything to get rid of her.

"You should start checking out the hot nursing dudes over at Essex County for next year," she said. "Of course, not *you*, Jess."

Lesbian joke. How original.

I couldn't figure out why Courtney was lingering. From the way she was dressed, I could tell she was planning a big night out. I stopped talking, hoping Courtney would just leave if there was a long uncomfortable silence.

"Listen, brat," Courtney said after a few excruciating moments. "I need some cash."

So that was the deal. She'd probably already rifled through all of mom's hiding places, turned the living room couch cushions upside down, and come up empty-handed. A couple of new packs of cigarettes, mom's brand, stuck out of her bag. Probably all she could find. I'd buy her off in a second, but I didn't have anything more than my PATH SmartLink card, a Metrocard, and maybe thirty-five cents.

"Here's twenty. It's all we've got," Jess said, rummaging through her things and pulling out a crumpled bill.

"What are you doing?" I asked.

"Just take it and stop bothering us," Jess said, thrusting the twenty at her.

Courtney was as surprised as I was, but she took the money. She stood up to leave. "Keep your trap shut to Mom that I was here, understand?" I hated that I nodded yes.

Jess and I waited until we heard her junker start up and tear off.

"You totally didn't have to do that. I'll pay you back," I said. But Jess wasn't even listening. She had opened up my laptop and was clicking through all the photos on TMZ.

"I should kill that bitch."

"My sister's not worth it . . ."

"No, I mean Tabitha Eden."

"What?"

"Check this out—she looks like she's about to vomit on my pumps." Jess laughed. I did, too. Jess clicked over to the Guest of a Guest blog and instantly found a picture of me in the Dior, arm in arm with Isak Guerrere. She began reading intently.

"Wow, they called you 'Isak Guerrere's fashionable companion.' You know, I should have done more with the Dior, I think. I could have pushed it further. I was intimidated."

If only we hadn't gone back to the Met, she would have been fine with all this. The Met was a big mistake.

Jess scrolled through the Web sites, trolling for pictures, and for some reason I flashed on a story I had read about Audrey when she was cast in *Sabrina*. The Queen of Wardrobe, Edith Head, dressed everybody who was anybody: Elizabeth Taylor, Grace Kelly, Marilyn. She controlled the fashion and appearance of those Hollywood actresses even when they attended the Oscars. But for *Sabrina*, the director, Billy Wilder, wanted Audrey to wear something different, something French. So he went behind Edith Head's back and asked the wife of the head of Paramount Pictures in Paris for help. She introduced Audrey to Hubert de Givenchy.

Audrey asked for a strapless evening dress, modified to hide the hollows behind her collarbone. The lovely dress that Givenchy created for her—a strapless bodice with a voluminous embroidered skirt—made Sabrina the belle of the ball and established Audrey's look for the rest of her career.

Edith Head famously received an Oscar for Audrey's dress in *Sabrina* without ever crediting Hubert de Givenchy, the designer of that crucial piece of wardrobe. Years later, when a biographer outed her, Edith snapped back, "I lied. So what? If I bought a sweater at Bullock's Wilshire, do I have to give them credit, too?"

But Givenchy was no mere department store designer, and Audrey remained loyal to him until she died. "In a certain way," Audrey is famously quoted, "one can say that Hubert de Givenchy created me over the years."

"Oh. My. God. There you are, walking and talking," Jess laughed. She clicked on a video, and there I was with Isak from the night before.

Who was that? I mean, it was *me*—a beaming, graceful, Technicolor me. I appeared so at ease, as though standing in front of a camera arm in arm with a famous designer was something I did all the time.

Jess was watching me as I watched. "You might want to close your mouth a little or bugs might fly down your throat," Jess advised, lifting my jaw.

"I'm in shock."

Bright lights, stunning dress, famous designer, winsome smile . . . for a second I felt warm all over again, just like I did in front of the camera.

Jess clicked through the video to a party Web site.

"Whoa! What's this?" she said. There were photos of me on the party page. No name, just my picture and a question mark.

"You're just a mystery inside a riddle wrapped in a remade Dior," Jess joked.

"How many pictures is that?" I asked.

"There are eight pictures of you, including Audrey's Givenchy," said Jess. "But I don't think we should use that one on that blog of yours."

"You know about my blog? I was going to tell you," I said, embarrassed.

"It's pretty hard to avoid a fashion blog that Isak Guerrere comments on from the first post. I think every young designer in the country has a Google Alert on that one."

"What?"

"You didn't see?" Jess asked as she clicked over to Shades of Limelight. "He loves you."

There it was: Isak's ringing endorsement of everything I said and already one-thousand-plus hits and followers.

"I thought it was pretty good, too. I especially like the Designer X part. Hmm, wonder who she could be . . . ?" she said, smiling.

"Listen, the Met is off-limits," Jess added. "I can't afford to give Myers a chance to fire me. I want to keep my job, all my jobs, until I get my line going or at least finish school. I'll hang in with you on this. If you're going to become famous, someone's got to dress you. And I don't want to miss it."

"You'll be my Givenchy!" I said.

"That makes you Audrey," she countered.

Not quite, but I was on my way.

22 I had no idea what I was dreaming that night, but woven into the soundtrack of my dream was a version of "Moon River" that sounded like a mash-up with the theme from *Hellraiser II*. It creeped me out so much I snapped awake, sitting up with my eyes open.

My cell phone was ringing. Who would call at . . . what time was it? The clock said 5:49 A.M. Shit. I thumbed ANSWER, put the phone to my ear, and fell back on my pillow.

"You up?"

"Jake!?" I croaked.

"Hey Lizzy. Good morning at ya!"

"Uh, good morning . . . ?" I tried to reboot my brain.

"Yeah, don't you think?" He sounded a little slurry.

"Think what? I kind of just woke up, Jake. I don't start thinking until much, much later." He laughed.

"You're a hoot, Lizzy. Look out your window. Awesome sunrise, right?" I glanced at the clock by my bed.

"Jake, it's five forty-nine. No, now it's five fifty."

"Come on, Lizzy," Jake said. "Just take a look out your window."

"Okay, fine . . . if you really want me to." I dragged myself out of bed, stumbling my way to the window, and looked out. The sun was just rising, and the purple night was giving way to a pink and yellow sky over our sad, sleepy neighborhood.

"Yep, the sun is coming up. I can confirm that, Jake." I looked down, and there in the dawning light was Jake with his cell phone, jumping up and down and waving to me like some kind of nut. I'd never seen Jake that wacky before, and I couldn't help laughing.

"Hello, crazy person." I made a little wave to him as he stood on my lawn.

"I was going to throw stones at your window, but I've got a mean fastball, ya know. Did I tell you I was the pitcher on the high school team?"

"I guess I missed that one in the Rocket Berns Wikipedia entry, but thanks for sharing."

"Well, I just didn't want to break your window."

"Oh . . . kay. Well, thank you for not breaking my window." It was pretty comical standing there, especially since we were still talking on our cell phones.

"So want to come out and get a cuppa coffee?" Jake asked.

"Are you kidding? It's like five a.m.," I looked back at my alarm clock. "Actually just turned five fifty-two, but who's counting?"

"Best time for coffee, really, when you think about it," he countered. "Besides, Lizzy, I've got to tell you, I've been up all night thinkin' about you."

I blinked a couple of times, unsure that I heard him correctly, and took a deep breath.

"I'm sure you've got better things to think about than me . . . are you high?"

"Come on, Lizzy, believe me. Look, I'm standing on my head!"

"Yeah, right."

But sure enough, out there on the tiny front lawn of my house, none other than hot rocker Jake Berns was doing a pretty decent handstand, all the stuff in his pockets falling out. He fell down after a while and got back up again.

I put down my cell phone and opened my window.

"Okay. Stop that," I whispered. "Somebody might see you. I'll be down in a sec."

Yanking on a pair of jeans under my oversized sleep shirt, I hunted around the room for a bra and slipped on a clean white T from my dresser. But I startled myself when I looked in the mirror.

Last night's updo had turned my hair into a bird's nest, and there were still traces of shimmer at the corners of my eyes from my eye shadow. I debated whether to wrestle my hair into a ponytail or go full-on *Cosmo* girl and just rock the bedhead. I opted for the latter. I wiped away as much shimmer as I could, swished my mouth with mouthwash, and snuck down the stairs, slipping through the front door and closing it quietly behind me.

We pulled away in Jake's slightly beat-up 1976 BMW 2000, which was no ordinary rock and roller's ride. Jake was a car freak; he always had five cars parked in front of his house in various stages of repair. There was the band van—the whole thing painted like the American flag, of course; an old military jeep that was always on cinder blocks; a '61 Impala with holes in the floor where your feet were supposed to be, like a Fred Flintstone car; and his brother's Saturn, which was always breaking down.

The BMW, a hipster mobile, was the only thing he loved as much as music. He rebuilt it from scratch, and I knew for a fact he never took it out unless he was trying to impress. I was impressed and nervous.

The streetlights were still on, even though the sun had come up, as Jake drove us through the still-empty streets of South End Montclair.

"Okay, so you were up all night doing what? Or should I ask?" I said.

"I told you," he said with that sideways smile of his, "thinking of you." Jake was wearing one of his vintage flannels. He seemed pleased with himself but a little tired. His right hand dropped down from the steering wheel and slid close to mine.

"Okay, so what *else* were you doing?" I asked, trying to keep up the conversation, and abruptly moved my hand into my lap. After a moment, he put his hand back on the steering wheel. This was really strange. I wasn't used to anyone paying this much attention to me, let alone a heartbreaker like Jake.

I've always had trouble even sitting next to a guy who liked me. Usually I've felt like I'm about six years old and that I'm going to throw up any second or say something stupid I'll regret. I'm pathetic that way, which didn't mean I wasn't interested. I just never got past that unbearable feeling of terror when boys flirted with me, unless you counted that creep Maxwell Duryea, who was really more of a stalker, though I did go out with him once.

"The Rockets had a private gig in Tuxedo Park until three A.M., which we totally rocked. It was swank—you shoulda been there. Tons of managers, celebs, music folks. We just got back about an hour ago. Can you believe the effin' van broke down twice!"

Jake drove up to Cupcakes Galore and More, the local pastry dive. We ordered two regulars and a bagel, and then Jake insisted on ordering an "everything cupcake" like it was his birthday or something, which was about the last thing I wanted to see this early in the morning. But he seemed pretty hungry.

"Didn't eat much? Or is the rock 'n' roll Romeo a little hungover?" I asked. His head shook slowly side to side as a wide grin came across his face. There was one thick strand of black hair that fell across his face that I adored.

"Naw, just hungry." I took a napkin and wiped a little of the icing away from his cheek. "Okay, and a little hungover," he said, laughing. "So what have you and Jess been up to? I haven't seen you guys at work for days. Plotting to take over the world?"

I hoped so, but there was no way I could talk to Jake about it.

"No, our shift got changed."

"That true?" he asked. No, but I wanted to change the subject. "And what was the deal with you hanging up on me last night?" he asked.

"Oh that was you?" I asked, knowing full well what the answer was, worried he'd get mad.

"And how come you didn't call me back?"

"I'm sorry. Weren't you playing last night?" I asked.

"Yeah, exactly . . ." Shit. I was supposed to be there, wasn't I? He paused for a second. There was a serious expression on his face, and I started to worry what was coming next.

"Listen, Lisbeth, this is about the fifth time since we started, you know, hanging out . . . that I've asked you to come see my band, and you always seem to be busy. And see, I thought there was, you know, something good happening between us. But I guess . . . I could be wrong?"

There probably wasn't another female in the entire Garden State who wouldn't jump at a chance to go out with Jake Berns and see his band play. I'll admit I was clueless the first couple of times—not playing hard to get—I just couldn't believe it was true and knew I'd probably make a fool of myself. Nobody like Jake Berns ever noticed me before.

"I just . . . got tied up in this fashion project I'm doing with Jess." God, I'd probably be screwing up my courage, dragging Jess to the front of the stage of every one of Jake's gigs, if this conversation had happened before my week of Dior and Givenchy and Page Six. I just had to see how Being Audrey would go first.

"You know, I wanted to have coffee because I didn't want you to think I was just some guy at the diner who kissed you next to the frozen peas."

"They were french fries," I said.

"So you remember?"

"The french fries? Yeah, they were freezing my butt."

Jake smiled, and I wanted to kiss him right then and there in the middle of Cupcakes Galore with all the sleepy coffee drinkers sitting around. His eyes met mine, and I wondered if maybe he was thinking the same thing, too.

"So . . ." He slid his hand across the table to hold mine. His fingers intertwined with my fingers. I took a breath, struggling to handle the attention, trying not to run away. His hand was strong and a little calloused, probably because of the guitar playing. I locked my fingers around his. It would be so easy to get swept away.

"Lizzy, I'm sure there's a lot of stuff happening to you. I'm sure everyone thinks you're cool. I mean, you're one of those girls who secretly keep the world from falling apart. Everybody knows that."

"Oh really . . ." I said, rolling my eyes but thinking, *Who could say lines like that?* I knew he was a songwriter, but really? He said it in a way that was so understated, so Jake.

"You're laying low now, but you're gonna break out and be awesome. I can tell," he continued. "I was there once. I'm a good judge of that kind of thing. I want to be there with you."

"Yeah, like you were once the shy retiring type?"

"Totally."

"As if." I couldn't help laughing. I wondered if I sounded goofy.

"I know you won't believe this, but I was shy in high school. I played the tuba in the Paterson High band. I was a total dork. Cool kids do *not* play the tuba. The closest I came to rock and roll was when I did Elvis imitations for my mom and dad, shaking my hips at cocktail parties. Totally embarrassing."

I could imagine that—he must have been so cute.

"I tried to join the choir," he continued, "but they said I was too introverted and tone-deaf."

"So when did you become Jake Berns, rock and roll god?" I asked.

"My older brother was the cool guy. Everyone hung out at his place, and he used to be a pretty good guitarist. The girls were all over him. He worked at a car-repair place and let me help out, although it was kind of illegal. But little hands can get into all sorts of good places when you're repairing a car. I was working on a front-end brake replacement when Zeke, an old drunk guy who worked there, tripped the jack and the whole four-by-four came crashing down on me and totally fucked up my leg. I was lucky to be alive. And that's what did it."

"A broken leg?"

"Yeah, it bent at a forty-five-degree angle to the rest of my body."

"Yuck."

"I had nothing to do but lie there in a body cast for God knows how long and teach myself how to play my brother's guitar. Thinking back on it, I needed that break from the usual routine. What seems like a bad accident turns out pretty well when it's your moment. It's happening to you, Lizzy. I can feel it."

"Are you saying you're clairvoyant and there's a broken leg in my future?"

He rolled his eyes, "No, I'm just trying to say be ready. You're going to make something great happen. I know it. I have a special sense for these things."

"Lisbeth Anne Wachowicz saves the world!"

"Come on, smart-ass, let's get out of here." Jake grabbed my hand as we got up and then paid at the register. As we walked to the car holding hands, my heart beat faster and faster.

"You're not recruiting for groupies are you?" I joked nervously, leaning against my side of the car, waiting for him to unlock the door. I happened to know perfectly well that Jake's band already had all the groupies they'd ever need. What is it about guitars that instantly made a guy five times hotter?

"Groupies? Not really my thing," he said as he opened my door.

I moved to get inside, but his body blocked me. He leaned in to kiss me, his arm sliding behind my back, pulling me close, pressing his lips into mine, soft and slow. I closed my eyes and just gave in, kissing him, too. He turned his hip bones against mine, the car hard behind my back, and I felt like I was melting from the inside.

I pulled away to catch my breath.

"We're in public, Jake Berns," I said, still breathing hard. He dropped his head, staring at the ground, a little embarrassed yet unbelievably sexy.

We climbed into the car. I took a few deep breaths, and it occurred to me that maybe I was afraid to see his band, because if I did, I might totally lose myself and fall hopelessly in love with Jake Berns.

"So, I stole Dalton's drummer and he's playing with us tonight. A ton of A and R guys are coming. It's gonna be huge. I don't care about the last gig you missed, but you've *got* to come to this one."

Okay, here's what I was thinking. First of all, Tabitha Eden hadn't texted me in two days. Maybe she was a flake or maybe she thought I was off jet-setting with Nan. I had absolutely no idea where her party was going to be or if I was actually invited. And it was supposed to be tonight. I'd promised myself I'd do this Being Audrey thing, but in that moment, sitting with Jake, it felt pretty ridiculous. I kept thinking of Jess saying how foolish the whole idea was. It would definitely be stupid to put Jake off for something that might never happen. Maybe, I figured, I should try to get over being all nervous and shy around him. I didn't want to end up sitting at home with Mom and Ryan. Why did Jake's big gig and Tabitha's party have to happen on the same night anyway?

"So? Tonight—you coming?" he asked, playfully looking at me with his smoky-blue eyes. "I've got something special I've been working on that I want you to hear. First time the band's going to play it. I think it's going to be our first single."

How could I say no?

23

I'd gotten the text three hours earlier and called Jess right away—only it wasn't from Tabitha. It was from ZK Northcott, Mr. Underwear-Man himself.

"Let's make it a surprise!" ZK texted. It was the only line I could focus on.

Well, that and "record release event."

What was the big secret? A surprise for Tabitha? I couldn't imagine why ZK Northcott wanted to have drinks with me. I did know that I was practically giddy about the idea of walking into Tabitha Eden's record party on ZK's arm. And he had my phone number. Interesting.

I wondered if ZK would wear a tuxedo. My mind wandered, picturing him greeting me, giving me a corsage. That was stupid—of course he wouldn't. It wasn't prom.

"I would love too ;)" I texted back.

Oh my God. Was this actually going to happen? Grabbing my bag out of the Beast, I headed inside for my shift at the Hole, the most un-Audrey place I knew.

A wall of smell hit me the second I walked through the door—used grease, Pine-Sol, and liquid cheese. It occurred to me that the venues favored by New York's rich and alluring were always lightly scented with lipstick and orchids. Or maybe it was hundred-dollar bills.

It wasn't liquid cheese, that's for sure.

After my two fabulous photobombing fashion appearances, the dreariness of the Hole had never been so acute. Every second I was there leached a little of the light from my soul. Like sequins sucked into a DustBuster.

Shoving my stuff into my locker, I grabbed my pink apron and tied it on. For once, Jess was late instead of me. Ten minutes after our shift had started, she came bounding through the door, dragging an oversize garment bag behind her.

"You finished it!" I exclaimed as I dropped table 14's order off at the window.

Jess motioned for me to keep a lid on it.

"This dress is freaking spectacular," she whispered. "The best one yet."

My skin tingled as I followed her into the kitchen; I was dying to see it. "Should be smashing, my de-ah," Jess said, limp wristed. "The junior railroad baron will *adore* you in this dress."

"Junior oil baron," I corrected.

"Wikipedia much?" she laughed.

"I already knew that, but I did look up a few of the people I may happen to run into at these things. You know, so I have some idea who I'm dealing with. I don't want to sound like a total moron."

"Good thinking." She hung the garment bag on the coatrack next to the employee lockers and grabbed her apron and tied it on. I yanked the zipper down to get a peek.

"We got customers out here!" Buela yelled from the cash register.

"Come on, let's not piss her off," Jess said.

I zipped it back up and walked to the front, glancing back at the garment bag longingly.

As I took an order from table 12, it dawned on me. Jake wasn't there. Fuck. I had no idea what I was going to say when he showed up. I should have explained the whole thing to him that morning over coffee. Would he have laughed at me? Why was I trying to hide it from him?

Jess and I were superefficient on the floor, hoping to get ahead and go back and check out the dress. But business was slow and slow nights sucked because you ended up watching every tick of the clock and making happy talk with Buela. I offhandedly asked her about Jake, and she said that he had asked for a later shift because he had stuff to do for his gig tonight.

Maybe I won't have to tell him before I leave, I thought. *I am so totally chicken.* As soon as my last table settled up, Jess and I went to the back.

Grabbing the garment bag, I followed Jess to the ladies' room and hung it on one of the bathroom stalls. Tugging down the zipper, I lifted the dress from the bag and squealed with excitement.

Jess was right. This dress was the best one yet, a jade-green homage to Valentino. She had taken all the scraps left over from working on Nan's other gowns and pieced them into a diamond-shaped matrix of color and texture, recalling not only the hues but also the opulence of peacock feathers. The inset had been fitted into the center of the bodice like a bib, drawing the eye to the heart of the dress. A slip of sheer silk in matching jade had been cut on the bias and stitched over the shortened skirt to create movement. It was breathtaking, the perfect balance of delicacy and strength.

"It's . . . stunning," I breathed, yanking off my clothes and stepping into it quickly. Jess just nodded agreement as she fussed with the zipper.

"Thank God you don't have any boobs; this bodice is pretty snug as it is." She grinned at my reflection in the mirror.

"I'll ignore that comment," I said. As she zipped up the dress, I felt an exciting surge run through me. She pulled a tiny clutch adorned with feathers out of the bottom of the garment bag.

"I did a purse for you with peacock feathers. I couldn't resist," she said, and I swear it felt like Christmas.

"Oh, Jess, it's perfect."

"It has a secret pocket in the lining for your ID," she said. "That way, you can tell ZK you forgot it and preserve your secret identity, but if you need it coming home or whatever, you'll have it."

"You're way ahead of me," I said.

Opening the little peacock clutch, I gasped the second I realized that Jess had lined it with some of the green satin left over from the Valentino.

"Waste not, want not," she said. "Or maybe it's waste not, don't have to fork over cash for lining fabric. Something like that."

I set the clutch back down inside the garment bag; I didn't want to accidentally splash water or get makeup on it or anything. It was almost too perfect to touch. Jess was watching me in the mirror.

"You do clean up nicely," she said. "Oh shit, I was in such a hurry to get the dress done, I forgot all about jewelry."

"No worries," I said and reached over to my bag. "I actually brought this funky jade pendant on a tiny gold chain. I took one of the loose pieces from Nan's treasure chest and placed it on my one gold chain."

As I put the necklace on, Jess stood back to check me over.

"That really works," she said. "It's so delicate, I wouldn't have thought to put it with that dress, but it absolutely makes the whole ensemble."

"Thanks."

"You really do have an eye for style," she said.

I hugged her. I don't know why tears started rolling down my cheeks. Or why I thought that was about the nicest thing anybody had ever said to me. I didn't want to cry, it was just that it meant a lot coming from Jess. The whole thing started to feel so momentous, like I was on the precipice of something big, like I might actually have a shot at this vague idea of the life I wanted, even though I couldn't begin to explain what it was. If it weren't for Jess and Nan, I *never* would have gotten this close.

Jess pulled back, grabbed a tissue, and dabbed my eyes.

"Come on, you'd don't want your face all red and puffy."

"Thanks, Jess," I said, trying to stop. "Thanks for everything."

She grinned and tapped her watch. "We're on a schedule here—get moving."

Spreading my makeup over the countertop, I gave myself a little birdbath in the sink to get the fry smell off. I needed to leave in like ten minutes, or I'd never make it to the city in time.

Another problem was my hair. It was too gross to wear down, and I swear if ZK got close enough, he'd smell the grilled cheese sandwiches. Wearing it up and spraying the hell out of it was the only solution, so Jess twisted my hair into an updo as I applied eye makeup.

False eyelashes, the application of which I spent a good chunk of the day trying to master, were the eighth wonder of the world. Thank God for YouTube is all I could say. Two minutes later, and I was instantly glamorous. Audrey would absolutely approve. Barely blushed cheeks, muted red lips, and I was ready to roll.

"Shit. Shoes?" I had totally forgotten. My Converse sneakers were not going to cut it.

"I hope these will do?" Jess said, dangling a pair of heels on the end of her finger as if she had read my mind.

"Louboutins!" I squealed. I couldn't help it.

"Scored them on eBay. Had to repair the heel. They'll only work for a night or two."

"Almost as good as a glass slipper," I said, bending over to put them on. Shoes had begun to be a bit of a challenge. Jess and I had gone to her favorite thrift store at St. Luke's Church in Hell's Kitchen and found a pair of very cool snakeskin stilettos with these funky crystals and some strappy sandals that she embellished with tiny strands of pearls and a pair of mismatched but coordinated brooches, but we couldn't find anything formal.

The great thing about the Louboutins was that they were invisible. Stylish and current enough not to out me as a poseur, but so go-with-everything neutral that no one would remember them from one event to the next.

I stood as far back as I could in the Hole's speckled and ancient ladies' room mirror, until my back was almost right up against the peeling pink wall. The stunning green of the dress looked wondrous, even in the flickering fluorescent lights.

"You ready?" Jess asked.

The two of us gathered up my stuff and shoved it back into her bag. I gave Jess a quick hug before we headed out the door.

"You're the best," I said, giving her a peck on the cheek.

"Aren't I, though?" Jess laughed, almost blushing. "Call me later. I want every detail."

I snuck out the back way and walked across the parking lot to my awaiting Purple Beast.

"Whoa. Lizzy, is that you?" Jake Berns in all his flanneled glory was leaning against his car waiting for me. "I figured I'd get here early to make sure you knew the way to Reilly's tonight. Look at you—all this to see my band? You look like a dream."

His eyes twinkled in the moonlight.

"Crap, I meant to tell you."

Realization darkened his expression.

"Ah," he said, lowering his eyes, "that's not for me."

"I'm so sorry, I just have this other . . . it's this thing . . . I promised to go and . . ." The words kept rushing out and none of them sounded good.

"Who? Who did you promise?"

"A . . . friend. No, not the kind you're thinking. I want to see your band, I swear I—"

"You're dressed like that for a friend?" he interrupted. "Didn't you promise me?"

I had no idea what to say.

"Damn." He dropped his arms at his side and hung his head.

"I'm sorry. I really am. I'll leave as soon as I can. I won't stay late. It's just something I have to check out for myself, and then I'll leave. I promise." The last word echoed in silence.

He kicked around the gravel and dirt at his feet, but he didn't say anything.

I ran for it, across the parking lot to my car, and didn't look back because I didn't want to see the expression on his face.

24 I parked the Beast at a riverside lot and walked the four blocks to the Soho House. The closer I walked, the denser the crowd became with paparazzi, celebrity stalkers, and other gawkers. I wondered how I would get in. Gathering my courage, I plunged.

The beefy doorman stood in my way and informed me that this was a "members only" joint. Which meant he knew that I wasn't.

How could he tell? Or did they say that to everyone? Was it because I was wandering around looking absolutely clueless? Shit, I hoped ZK put me on the guest list somewhere. Then I realized that he didn't even know my last name.

"I'm a guest of ZK Northcott," I said, beginning to feel a panic that I might have come all this way and not even get in.

"Wait here," the doorman said and stepped back, speaking into his walkie-talkie.

It was called the Soho House, but it wasn't in Soho, which was that part of Manhattan that was like the biggest, most expensive shopping mall imaginable and took up twenty-six square city blocks. A café sandwich there costs more than a steak in Jersey. The Soho House is actually in the Meatpacking District, where they used to pack raw meat for the aforementioned steak but don't anymore. These days, they mostly pack trendy, six-figure-salaried twenty- and thirtysomething Manhattanites—which was meat of a certain type, I suppose. These trendsetters and trendettes tend to rendezvous in restaurants at 10 P.M. for dinner and end up at exclusive rooftop hotel bars and party into the early hours of the morning.

A gorgeous girl with a severe blond bob, a red wrap dress, and stiletto heels was marching my way. She carried an iPad, which seemed odd considering how she was dressed until I realized that she was a high-tech clipboard Nazi, Mistress of the Door and Keeper of the Holy Guest List. I mustered up my best Audrey and made the first move.

"Pardon me. I'm meeting ZK Northcott, has he arrived?"

"And you are?"

"Lisbeth. I'm a guest of ZK's." I'd already mentioned his last name once, and I didn't want to sound like a name-dropper suck-up, like, *oh yeah, ZK and I go way back.* I felt pretty fakey anyway calling him by his first name, er, initials. I hoped she couldn't hear my knees knocking together.

Her fingers swiped through the iPad pages, and I could see the rejection buzzer in her eyes that was set to go off any moment, tick-tick-ticking, resulting in the most cringe-worthy five words: *I don't see your name.*

"Lisbeth Dulac?" It took me half a beat to remember my new last name.

"Um, yes," I muttered.

She leaned in close to me and whispered, "Your dress is awe-inspiring."

"No way?" Jess's design work had scored another victory. "I mean, thank you . . . darling," I corrected. I had to watch out for my normal me-speak.

I'd practiced my "darlings" for this very occasion, watching all of Audrey's movies to match her cadence as closely as possible. I'd step-framed *Breakfast at Tiffany's* to listen to every single instance where she'd said "darling," which, by the way, is exactly forty-four. But I found myself spouting "darlings" without even thinking about it.

I had called my sister Courtney "darling" the night before by accident, and she looked at me like I was possessed. And when I "darlinged" Buddy, one of the regulars at the diner, he laughed and said, "Sure thing, honey cakes."

"Miss Dulac, if you don't mind, I must ask . . ." Uh-oh. Here's the part where she would say: *Aren't you a lowly waitress from South End Montclair masquerading as well-to-do trust-fund baby?*

"Aren't you . . ." Her voice was getting all squealy and schoolgirl, which was totally weird considering her stiletto heels and shiny red lipstick. "Aren't you the Limelight blogger?"

My God. A fan. I couldn't believe it.

"Why, yes . . . c'est moi," I said, finally finding some use for those great grades in high school French.

"Oh my God! I absolutely adore your blog," she said. "I've been reading you for ages." This struck me as hilarious, as I'd actually only been blogging for about a week and a half.

"I was so impressed with Isak Guerrere's comments. He just loves you!"

"Yes, of course, Isak is such a dear," I said, trying to sound blasé.

"You have such a great look," she gushed.

"Thank you." I couldn't help but beam. I actually had a look! She went on and on, and I started to notice people staring at us. I guess she did too and pulled it back a notch.

She leaned close to me and whispered, "I should have known it was you when I saw your dress."

"Darling, you are much too kind." I really wanted to hug her and jump up and down. But I figured this wasn't quite the place for it.

"Well, Miss Dulac, I'm sure you have more interesting things to do tonight." She gave me a wink, and it took me a heartbeat to realize that she was probably referring to the famously handsome ZK Northcott.

I panicked for a second when it occurred to me that she might ask for my ID or something. Stuffed in the lining of my peacock feather bag was my regular old New Jersey driver's license and my fake ID, which wasn't any better, because it was just Courtney's old license. Both of them pegged me as that far-less-than-fabulous girl from South End Montclair.

"Mr. Northcott is waiting for you in the Billiards Room. Please come this way." She turned and I followed. Humiliation averted. I guess getting carded was something they only did on my side of the river. Drinking restrictions must be optional in a place like the Soho House.

We took the elevator to the fifth floor. The multifloored Soho House was like a giant layered cake with each layer more fabulous than the one below. I'd read about this place on TMZ and even taken a virtual tour on their Web site: drawing rooms, billiard rooms, private dining rooms, and apparently a whole spa, all topped off by a breathtaking rooftop pool, which all the gossip blogs said was the hottest place to be. Capping it all—only if you belonged, of course—were handsomely designed hotel rooms, with egg-shaped bathtubs where members could stay with their guests. Which, I guessed, was helpful if you were ever too wasted to drive home or had other things in mind.

We entered a stunningly appointed room filled with warm light and dark wood walls, highlighted by brass fixtures, marble-topped tables, velvet drapes, and chandeliers.

Lots of suits and heels crowded around the bar. It was low-key while being upscale at the same time. On my way in, I saw Alicia Keys laughing and drinking a mojito while playing pool and suppressed my urge to snap an Instagram pic with my phone. I was bowled over by the glamour of it all—every girl in the room was drop-dead gorgeous, even the waiters and waitresses were good-looking.

"Finally, the mysterious Lisbeth Dulac has arrived!" ZK rose from his leather wingback chair. He kissed me on both cheeks, and my skin almost sizzled where his lips lingered on my face. Really, I could get used to the whole kiss-kiss thing, too.

"You're stunning tonight," ZK said, lowering his eyes, and I thought about how much nicer that sounded than the "Yo Lizzy, you look hot" that guys said on the other side of the bridge. I couldn't believe I was actually sitting and talking with ZK Northcott, aka Mr. Underwear-Man.

A waiter arrived instantly.

"I'm drinking greyhounds tonight. May I offer you one?" ZK asked. I had no idea what a greyhound was, but I figured out right away that it wasn't a dog or a bus. I smiled and said yes. It had to be alcohol, and I needed some to calm my nerves.

My eyes wandered from his caramel-colored eyes to his full lips to his sturdy jawline, down to his shirt that was opened just enough beneath his perfectly cut navy blue jacket. I forced myself to stop there. Phew.

He regarded me with those amused eyes of his, and I smiled back. If I wasn't standing right there, just a few inches away, I'd swear that no guy this flawless actually existed outside of an Abercrombie catalog. And yet there he was. No backlighting or airbrushing or hair-blowing fan necessary.

"I feel like we see each other everywhere, but we never get to talk," he said, moving a little closer, his head tilted down, without breaking eye contact.

It struck me as a funny thing to say since we'd only just met once, a little over a week ago. But my heart thumped wildly anyway.

"Who knows?" I laughed. "Maybe we would have nothing to say."

"That can't possibly be true," he said. "Tabitha talks about you nonstop. You've made quite an impression on her, and I'm dying to know more about you."

"Why, there's nothing to say, darling. I'm just a free spirit."

"Even a free spirit has to come from somewhere." ZK smiled. I could see he was going to be persistent.

"I'd much rather hear about you," I insisted, oddly at ease. Somehow Being Audrey made it easier for me to talk to someone like ZK, while I was so apprehensive trying to be myself around Jake.

"What's left to say that hasn't been said already? I'm a Northcott." He laughed. "There's probably not a single person in this room that doesn't know my entire family history, good, bad, and wretched."

"And is your *personal* history wretched as well?" I asked. He laughed.

"Well let's just say I've been notoriously thrown out of a variety of elite high schools and Ivy League colleges for various instances of inappropriate and lewd behavior, a tradition of my own making, which I hope to continue into the future and bequeath to my children."

"Impressive," I said. "And is that all there is to ZK Northcott?"

"Pretty much. You might say I was born with a silver spoon up my ass and I've never gotten over it."

"That must be a painful burden to bear," I said as deadpan as possible.

"Yes, very."

"Well, I think you're doing a fine job of handling it," I said, and we both cracked up. The waiter arrived with our greyhounds, which tasted pretty much like a screwdriver with some supertart grapefruit juice instead of the usual Tropicana I was used to. Freshly squeezed, I assumed.

"Now it's your turn," he said, raising an eyebrow.

"It's quite tedious, dear."

"Bore me."

I'd decided that staying close to the truth would be the easiest way to keep myself out of trouble. I had enough difficulty remembering my new pretend last name without adding any fake relatives or pets into the mix.

"Well, I have an ailing mother who travels a lot and is never at home, a wildly irresponsible sister I never see, and a brother who is *always* in trouble."

"Ah, your brother sounds like a man after my own heart."

"Yes, I'm sure you could tutor him in the finer points. And then there's my dear Nan who drinks champagne and eats cheesecake all day. See? Nothing quite as exciting as your life."

"There must be more. Is that all you'll tell me?" he teased.

"For now."

"You are very . . . intriguing," he said as he put his arm across the back of my chair and leaned in closer. Glasses of grapefruit juice and vodka were arriving and disappearing quickly, and I swear it seemed as if we were flirting. How I could be chatting up one of the most handsome eligible men in New York City was astonishing. But I was determined to keep my wits about me.

"I'm delighted that you wanted to meet for drinks, ZK," I said, "but I'm a little curious as to the reason. Truthfully, we've barely met." The last thing I wanted to do was to kill the vibe, but ZK was moving too fast. I needed to have some understanding of what he had in mind and why he texted me.

ZK sat back in his chair, unbuttoning his jacket, and turned thoughtfully, thinking for a moment. "Beyond the fact that you're absolutely lovely?" he asked.

I smiled, taking in his amused eyes. He seemed so boyish at times.

"I've been trying to help Tabitha out. The girl is such a mess and there are so many poseurs and hangers-on in the music business."

Tell me about it. I knew a little something about that subject.

"I want to make sure she doesn't get hurt," he added.

"That's kind," I said.

"Tabby's had an especially hard time. I'm sure you know about her mother . . . ? Tragic woman, actually, incapable of handling her own affairs or Tabitha's from the time Tabby was a toddler. Very little stability in her life, I'm afraid. Someone had to step in. Lots of men coming and going—lots of stepfathers. Her mother has been in rehab so often that she met two of her last husbands there. One was the manager of Blondie, the Cars, and all of those seventies groups. Then there was an Italian duke who actually had a fiefdom in some remote corner of Italy—Bomarzo, I think. And last year her mother married this new quite wealthy but seriously ill fellow. Who knows how long that might last; he happens to be a founder of Soho House. Or the So-So House as we call it. This place is so over, isn't it?"

Really? I'd just gotten here and it was already out of fashion?

"Tabby and I grew up together, the same schools with the same friends. We've all known each other for so long that it's like a club— which makes everyone extremely tedious, by the way. I feel like I'm playing tennis with the same people over and over again." He laughed and I did, too, although I didn't have a clue what it was like playing tennis with anyone. "But, curiously, none of us knows you."

I nodded, as though I understood perfectly.

"You're a mystery girl."

"But isn't every girl?"

"Not to me," he said, never taking his eyes off mine. "New York is just a tiny bubble, all the same people everywhere you go. You, Lisbeth Dulac, are a red gown at a black-and-white ball."

I felt like we had somehow moved even closer to each other,

kissing distance. I felt little sparks flying between us, as ZK's eyes met mine, and I wondered if it was unmistakable to him as well or if I was just crushing. I could have sat there gazing at him forever.

"Which black-and-white ball?" interrupted a slender blonde approaching at my side. I immediately recognized Dahlia Rothenberg. ZK and I instinctively pulled away from each other.

She was gorgeous. Opulent. Oh, and of course ZK's date at the Met that night. Where had she come from? Had she been listening to us joking and laughing?

Surprise barely registered in ZK's face, and he smoothly rose to kiss her on each cheek. "Dahlia, you're looking radiant."

It was true, she did. Radiant was the perfect word. Like the sun. It must have been exhilarating to be the center of the solar system. She wore an elegant, buttery strapless gown, her pale skin shimmery and translucent. I couldn't help but wonder how she got it that way. Probably diamond-dust facials or snacking on the stem cells of small children.

"Where's Tabitha? Vomiting in a corner somewhere?" Dahlia asked and put her arm in ZK's as if she were staking a claim.

"Don't be so harsh," said ZK. "You know she's under a lot of pressure."

"Yes," she said. "It must be emotionally taxing to be a singer when you can't actually sing." I felt a sudden urge to defend Tabitha, her music was totally Top 40. Besides, weren't they all old friends?

"I think she has a wonderful voice," I said. ZK and Dahlia smiled conspiratorially. Dahlia seemed to suppress an urge to laugh.

"Well, that's one word for it," she replied. A squeal rose up from behind me, and I turned.

"Lisbeth, you made it!" Tabitha Eden jumped up and down excitedly in her sky-high stilettos, like a sorority girl hopped up on strawberry daiquiris.

"Ah, our little Tabby has arrived," Dahlia said, her voice dripping with feigned enthusiasm.

Tabitha rushed over and hugged me tightly, as though she was my oldest best friend. And in a way she was; I had been thinking about her for what seemed like an eternity.

"I'm so glad you're here!" she squealed. She was polished and perfect, every inch the celebrity in her pale-blue minidress.

"Darling, I'd never miss it!" I said.

"Love your dress," Tabitha gushed.

"Thank you, you look gorgeous," I said.

"Come with me." Tabitha linked her arm in mine, pulling me along, nodding to ZK but barely trading glances with Dahlia.

My head spun with the thrill of it all—the glamour of the party, my new bestie pop princess, my blog fan downstairs, laughing with ZK, the fact that the chic city life I'd always aspired to was actually happening all around me in vivid, panoramic color. If Jess were there, I'd have asked her to pinch me.

I tried to catch ZK's eye as I was swept away, wondering if he'd felt the little sparks I had. But he was otherwise occupied, engrossed in an intense conversation with la Rothenberg.

25 The elevator doors opened right out onto the famous Soho House rooftop, and Tabitha was greeted with a roar of recognition from the hordes of party people there to celebrate her new release.

What a scene! The pool, in the center of the rooftop, was small, but it seemed like the clubbers didn't mind—nobody was swimming laps anyway. A DJ was spinning; cigarette smoke and probably lots of other kinds of smoke swirled around us. The sounds of laughter and revelry spilled off the rooftop into the New York City night. The beat was irresistible and unrelenting. Two watermelon-ginger cocktails miraculously appeared in our hands, and the DJ high up on a platform at the far end of the pool nodded to Tabitha and began his rap in a melodious Jamaican lilt.

A group of exquisitely dressed Italians were laughing so loudly that it even competed with the music.

I spun 360—listening to the body-shaking beats ricochet around the pool and off the buildings surrounding us, looking at all the beautiful people, and breathing in the sensuous summer night air. I wanted to let every single sensation sink into my skin. I couldn't remember ever being as excited about anything as I was in that moment. It was hard to keep from shrieking and screaming for joy, but I figured that would have given me away as a total newb.

"That new single is going to be a smash, Tabby," said a skinny British guy with jutting cheekbones and sparkling blue eyes. He had to practically shout even though we were all standing next to one another. "I didn't realize you were such a brilliant composer," he added with a broad grin.

"Oh Balty. You're such a tool." Tabitha laughed good-humoredly, but Balty (what kind of name was Balty?) wasn't paying attention. He stared right at me, making it unequivocally clear what he had in mind.

"Ahem, Balty, the girl you're undressing with your eyes is my friend and she has a name—Lisbeth. Lisbeth, this is Balty Birkenhead. Don't let him lay a hand on you."

"I'll keep an eye on him," I said, smiling. "So nice to meet you."

"The pleasure is mine!" he said. "I confess, Lisbeth, I couldn't take my eyes off of you from the second you walked in the door. That's some dress." Balty grinned mischievously.

"Stunning," added a tiny intense woman behind him. She had close-cropped dark red hair and was wearing a simple black sheath.

"Why, thank you," I said.

"Your name is so familiar. Have I met you before?" she asked.

"She's the Shades of Limelight girl," Tabitha volunteered. I was?

"Of course!" the redhead responded. "The girls on my staff read that blog all the time. It seems to have developed a following out of nowhere." She thrust her hand out to shake mine. "Florence, but you can call me Flo."

It was surprising how viral my blog had gone. I guess on the Internet, no one knew you were from Jersey.

"Please take my card," she said, handing me a square red and black card that matched her hair and dress. "I specialize in fashion and Internet marketing. I'd love to work with you. I'm sure we could procure a number of key endorsements for you and solicit the best aggregators. Our ad placement is quite impressive, if I do say so myself."

"Why, thank you," I said. Aggregators? I didn't have a clue, but I saved her card in my little clutch anyway.

"Tabby, she's absolutely precious," Flo remarked, as though I wasn't there.

"Isn't she?" Tabitha laughed. "Come on, Lisbeth, we have to keep moving or these two will start drooling over you. Ta-ta for now!"

Tabitha dragged me off through the crowd, turning to whisper in my ear. "Balty's family owns half the newspapers in London, Murdoch's biggest rival. The redhead is his sister; she runs the whole online operation, which has already surpassed the core business."

Tabitha steered me in and out of conversations all over the rooftop, and I was impressed with how adept she was at working the crowd. I'd never seen anything like it. She was some kind of social savant, sharing little inside jokes or dishing about a friend in common or the best place to eat spaghettini alla vongole in Portofino. She managed to laugh at every lame joke, riding a wave of conviviality.

"Tabitha, a quick sound bite on the new album?" Tabitha and I turned to find Chase, the video guy. He gave me a snarky "told you so" smirk and lifted his camera. I moved to step away as the interview began, but Tabitha grabbed my hand and held tight.

"Sure!" Tabitha said, all sparkly and showbiz as she entered the spotlight, dragging me along. "I'm here with my best friend, Lisbeth Dulac, famous blogger and fashion critic . . ." I tried not to look astonished.

While the tape rolled, I realized I was uncomfortable being in

Chase's orbit. I had a bad feeling about him. I did my best not to make eye contact. Looking around through the lights, I was surprised to see ZK watching me. He raised his glass, toasting me from the other side of the pool, and I smiled back. Had he noticed that spark after all?

". . . Is that true, Ms. Dulac?" Chase was asking. How many minutes had passed?

I felt Tabitha tug on my hand, dragging me out of my ZK-induced daze. I saw the camera and Chase's face in front of me. Chase followed my gaze and saw ZK and gave me a knowing smirk.

"Yes," I answered, bewildered, not having a clue what the question was. Chase terminated the interview. Tabitha giggled.

"Told you I'd see you again," Chase said so that only I could hear as Tabitha dragged me along. I felt totally confused.

"No worries," she said. "It's always hard to concentrate when you have an admirer watching you." She laughed and instantly another watermelon-ginger cocktail appeared in our hands. The drinks kept coming. Tabitha threw them back like sodas as we moved our way through the rooftop crowd.

"Everyone loves you," she gushed, her eyes closing as she talked. After five or so drinks, if my count was correct, she seemed dangerously unsteady. Who wouldn't?

I drew her into a shadowy corner. The girl just didn't know how to "regulate her alcoholic intake" as we said back home. Why weren't her girlfriends looking out for her? Speaking of which, where *were* her girlfriends? Where I came from, if a hottie like Tabitha started acting shaky, the guidos closed in like vultures. A girl depends on her peeps to keep her safe. I figured if I could just get her out of the action for a second, she might be able to catch her breath.

"I'm so happy you came, I've been so out of it, I realized I hadn't texted you the details, sometimes I get totally spaced. I was worried you wouldn't come," she said, throwing back her head and looking exhausted. "This party would be such a drag if you weren't here."

Her voice was so slurry and she just rambled, so I didn't really absorb what she was saying. I just wanted her to feel better. "You have such lovely friends, Tabitha, and they all adore you," I said. "I'm sure you would have been fine. After all, it's your party."

"It's so *not* true; you don't understand." Wobbling on her high heels, she leaned close into me and whispered, "I didn't want this party. I didn't want to even record the album." She slid back into the corner and seemed to become smaller. This girl definitely needed a two-drink max.

"So . . . why were you talking to them anyway?" she asked, her face an expression of pure petulance and paranoia. I tried to grapple with her margarita mood shift.

"Talking to who?"

"You know, Dahlia and ZK. He's okay, but she's a terror."

I surveyed the party. What was Tabitha asking? The deck was getting so crowded I couldn't believe how many hip-hoppers, music-biz insiders, ingenues, and party boys were there. I tried to focus, but the watermelon cocktails clouded my brain, too. Weren't ZK and Dahlia *her* friends? Hadn't she asked ZK to check me out? Otherwise, why did ZK know to text me?

"Poor Tabitha—we're looking out for her." Wasn't that what he'd said? ZK, Dahlia, and Tabitha had all seemed like such good friends, although I agreed Dahlia seemed pretty scary.

"How do you even know them?" Tabitha asked, like a spoiled brat trying to hide her hurt feelings. Maybe she was more smashed than I'd thought. None of it made much sense.

"Don't worry, darling," I said in my most reassuring Audrey accent. "I ran into them at an event ages ago, and quite coincidently they were here when I came in. I hardly know them at all." She glanced up at me with that same disoriented expression I recalled from the Met bathroom floor. Tabitha was so odd. She morphed from superconfident pop queen to abandoned child in seconds.

"Were you talking about me?" She seemed genuinely concerned.

"Actually no, we were talking about me!" I laughed because,

unbelievably, it was true. "One thing you can always be sure of, darling," I said, taking her hand in mine, "I never gossip about my friends."

Tabitha's eyes brightened, and it occurred to me that maybe she'd been worrying about ZK and Dahlia since we rode up the elevator together and just hadn't had the nerve to say anything about it.

"Oh my God, what's he doing?" someone near us yelled. There was a commotion across from the DJ at the center of the pool. We tried to see what was going on. A gorgeous-looking guy bounced playfully on the end of the diving board, stripping off his shirt. He had one of those uberperfect hairless bodies, and I couldn't help but wonder if he waxed, or threaded, or blasted his follicles with some industrial-grade laser.

"Isn't he a spokesperson for Power?" a woman standing next to us asked. She was wearing thigh-high boots and practically drooling over the guy.

"You're right!" her too-pretty-to-be-straight companion agreed. "By the way, is Power a cologne or an energy drink? I forget."

The new spokesman for whatever tossed his shirt into the crowd and dropped his pants. The entire party gasped. He had not a scrap of underwear whatsoever. Not even a thong or *anything* other than his anatomical parts, if you know what I mean. At least we knew he wasn't a spokesman for underwear. The security guards rushed him, and he dove a perfect half pike into the pool to a round of applause.

"Come on," Tabitha said, reenergized. "Follow me." As security fished the flasher out, we scooted along the poolside behind a group of stuffy Wall Street warriors who were smoking cigars and observing the action. Tabitha gave me a mischievous grin.

"Watch this," she said and hip checked some random guy. He didn't know what hit him. Cell phone, Armani suit, keys to his Porsche (I assumed)—all in the pool. Another guy almost fell in and regained his balance until somebody off balance elbowed him, got pissed, and pushed another dude, who grabbed a lady standing next to him. She teetered on her high heels until both of them fell into the water.

Soon it was sheer mayhem as everyone pushed everybody else into the pool. Tabitha grinned, delighted. She grabbed my hand, and we slipped down the stairs to the Drawing Room, giggling the whole way, hearing screams and laughter from above.

"Let's hide here for a while," said Tabitha as she flopped onto a red velvet love seat. "Cozy, right?"

I checked out our little refuge and the rest of the room. The wall of concert speakers on the small stage seemed out of place with the plush sofas, armchairs, and soft lighting. Tabitha's band, Coma Romance, was on stage, finishing their sound check. I didn't know if Tabitha was a promotional genius or just a kook, but her prank brought the entire pool crowd downstairs. They crammed into the small space like lemmings.

Coma Romance's lead guitarist, Max Ferme, looking very emo, shuffled up to us.

"Tabby, we're ready to rock," he said in an emotionless monotone as if playing in a Top 40 band was the most boring thing in the world. I knew the names of all of the guys in Tabitha's band by heart, having seen every one of her videos about a million times. Max was the one who always seemed totally bored no matter how hard they rocked. He seemed even more low-key in person.

"Do I have to?" Tabitha whined.

Max rolled his eyes.

"I'm about to get swallowed up, Lisbeth," Tabitha whispered. "I don't want to wait so long to see you next time." She paused, suddenly worried. I thought she might break into tears. Then, just as quickly, her mood brightened. "Come shopping with me next week, okay?"

"Shopping? Ah, of course, I'd love to," I said. Yeah right. Couldn't wait to use my maxed-out two-hundred-dollar-limit prepay.

"Really? That's so cool!" Tabitha squealed. "I know just the place—this new store on Fifth . . ." She stopped, frozen midsentence.

"That was quite a stunt you pulled on the rooftop, Tabitha," an authoritative voice said. Staring down at us was the old guy in the Armani from that first night at the Met, Robert Francis.

"Hello Robert," she responded, looking uncomfortable. He leaned in to give her a kiss. She closed her eyes and turned her cheek in a formal manner to accept it as if she were taking bad-tasting cough syrup.

"Nice to see you again as well, Miss Dulac." He leaned forward to kiss me, too. In high school Health and Home Economics, they had skipped right over social kissing and gone directly to condoms and STDs, so I had no idea why accepting a peck from someone I disliked was good manners. But following Tabitha's lead, I turned my cheek.

Tabitha stared at me oddly, and I realized she didn't know that I had encountered Mr. Armani after helping her escape through the freight exit at the Met. More troubling was that he acted as though he expected me to say or do something. What did he want? Was I supposed to blab to Tabitha about the "plans," which I knew nothing about? I put on my happy face and ignored him, completely clueless what to do next.

After a couple of excruciatingly long moments of the two of us fervently praying he would go away, Robert Francis politely wished Tabitha good luck with the new album and departed. We both breathed a sigh of relief.

"You know Robert, too?" Tabitha asked, regarding me with suspicion.

"Not really. I met him shortly after I encountered you in the . . . well, bathroom." I figured there was nothing to lose by being honest. Reminding her that the first time we met her head was in a toilet had to count for something. "He simply asked how you were."

"That's a laugh. And that was all?"

"Pretty much." I wondered if I should in fact ask her about her "plans," whatever they were.

"Figures."

"Who is he?" I asked.

"My keeper, my prison warden. It's a long story," she said. "But I'm not worried about him anymore. Mother's coming back soon, and she's going to make him go away."

"Your mother? Where is she?" I asked. "I'd love to meet her . . ."

"Tab, love, we have to begin," Max interrupted. He was holding a headset mic with an earbud out to Tabitha. Who knows how long he had been standing there with his hangdog face? The band appeared ready to go, and the crowd was growing rowdy for a bunch of rich kids in fancy clothes.

Tabitha let out a dreary groan, grabbed the mic from Max, and headed for the stage, yelling over her shoulder, "I'll explain everything when we go shopping! Can't wait!"

The band kicked into a club beat, and not a minute later she strutted across the stage, dancing and singing.

Surprisingly, people kept saying hello or nodding to me as they passed by, as though I were actually part of this crowd. Maybe they'd noticed me hanging out with Tabitha. Maybe it was the dress. Either way, mission accomplished.

I felt like I'd successfully passed in a world that seemed utterly unattainable to me only a week before. Every single moment so far had been more interesting and exciting than any moment I'd spent in South End Montclair.

I scanned the room, taking in the dancing crowd. They loved my BFF Tabitha Eden, the Princess of Pop. My eyes found ZK, who was watching me from across the room again. He acknowledged my glance and made his way toward me through the crowd.

He circled around and slid in close behind. "How do you manage to get everyone talking about you?" he said in my ear. "You're the 'it' girl of the evening." His voice sent delightful shivers down my spine.

"I'm just here to support Tabitha's brilliant new release. And you?" Was Tabitha paranoid about ZK and should I be suspicious? It was all too much to understand, and besides he was so delicious to look at.

"Me too," he said. "Thank goodness for lip-synching, right?"

Really? Wasn't Tabitha actually singing? I strained to get a better view. The band was playing for real, but it was all so loud, I couldn't tell. Tabitha danced around the stage like a crazy girl, never standing still long enough for me to see if she was actually singing.

"Next Saturday is the Schnabel opening," ZK said over the music. "If you aren't already going, would you give me the pleasure of your company?" Inside my head, I think my brain exploded. He wasn't actually asking *me*, was he? I'd have gone anywhere with ZK, a Costco opening or a monster truck rally, as if he'd ever do that kind of thing, even to a Schnabel opening, whatever that was.

There was just one problem. "What about . . . ?"

"Dahlia?" He glanced over to Dahlia, who was languidly laughing, surrounded by no less than five drop-dead-gorgeous Euro types, French or Italian, all with perfectly styled clothes and fashionable stubble. She was gesturing, touching each suitor eagerly waiting for her attention. I guess what they said about her in the gossip Web sites was true.

"Dahlia is a force of nature," ZK said. "She has other amusements to preoccupy her." I didn't have a clue what he meant. But everything that had happened was a whirlwind; what I saw, heard, felt, and wore. Was it real or had I been dreaming?

I let myself linger on ZK for just a second longer, thinking about the way he had been watching me most of the night. He was gorgeous, rich, and well connected. I was nobody. It would be pure insanity to think that he and I could ever end up together. There was no way. I'd never be able to keep Audrey going long enough to make it work.

I saw Dahlia walking our way, and I figured it was time to go, better not to get my hopes up and spend too long at the ball.

"I'll text you the details tomorrow," ZK said. I nodded yes and gazed one more time into his amused eyes, wondering what he was really thinking.

If I ever wanted to preserve my memories of this charmed fantasy fling, I needed to drop out of sight immediately. I had already stayed way, way later than I'd ever expected to.

Crap. Crap. Crap.

I'd forgotten about Jake.

26

"Are you still @ club ? XOXO ME."
I waited for Jake to answer.
Nothing.

Crap.

As I hit the summer night air outside the Soho House, I felt woozy. Watermelon and ginger sounded so harmless at the time, plus all those greyhounds before with ZK. I had reached my daily requirement of vitamin C for sure . . . tequila maybe more than required.

Limos were still lining up as a new shift of parties and scenes were beginning. Where had I parked the Purple Beast? The river parking lot. Right, that seemed ridiculously far away. And where was Reilly's? I'd never been there before, although I knew it was on the strip near the diner. I was sure I could find it somehow. Maybe springing for a taxi would be the safest thing. Checking in my peacock-feathered clutch, I fished out all of fifteen dollars and eighty-six cents—barely enough to get my car out of the lot, let alone all the way to Jersey in a cab. Was Jake even still there?

"Please don't b mad @ me :(" I texted.

"Hello, fashionable companion," a voice behind me said.

I turned to see Isak Guerrere, my newest, bestest friend.

"Isak, it's so nice to see you," I said, concerned I might be a little tipsy.

"You as well, my dear. And look at you: you're wearing another wonderful dress by your favorite designer who is not me!"

I smiled. "That's true. I'm sorry to say."

"What genius designed this fabulous frock? Valentino, of course, but refreshed, almost sassy. Extraordinary," he said.

I gave him a disproving look.

"I know, I know. Designer X is a secret. But I'm the one you should be telling *all* your secrets to!" he said. If only I could. "At the very least, you have to introduce this Designer X to me. I insist!"

"I promise," I said.

"Well, you can make up for it by having a drink with me at the bar. I hear your friend, Tabitha Eden, is playing in the Drawing Room tonight . . . What do they call her? The Princess of Pop? Everyone is royalty these days!"

"Regretfully, dear Isak, I am quite late and must be going." I made a sad face.

"*Quelle dommage,*" Isak said. "Just another disturbing pattern in our relationship. You always seem to be leaving as you see me. Is it the jellied hair? I know. It's an acquired taste," he said with a sparkle in his eye.

My phone buzzed—Jake? I grabbed a peek. No, it was Jess.

"Howzit going ?! I'm dying to know !! :)"

I sighed. Jake had forgotten by now, probably celebrating with his friends.

"Not the news you wanted to hear, I assume," Isak said. I tried to hide my disappointment.

"No, it's fine, Isak. I'm sorry to be such poor company, probably a few too many watermelon and gingers. I'd be careful of those if I were you."

"Point taken. May I help you to your car?"

I hesitated.

"Well, then a taxi?"

"No, Isak, thank you," I said. "I think . . . I think I'll walk."

"Oh my, how will you ever forgive me?"

"Pardon?"

"Right this way," he said, grabbing me by the arm. "Please

forgive me for suggesting that you take a lowly taxicab to what must be an important romantic rendezvous. I know that look . . ."

I was startled as Isak pulled an earsplitting two-fingered whistle.

"It's okay, Isak, darling. You're so nice, but I . . ." A limousine drove up and Isak opened the door. I stopped yammering. There was a lovely little man in the front seat wearing a chauffeur's cap.

"Allow me to provide my limo to safely carry you to your rendezvous," he said. He must have seen my jaw drop.

"Don't worry, you won't have to talk to Rudy. He talks too much anyway." Rudy, the chauffeur, rolled his eyes and gave me a little wave.

"But I'm not even sure where I'm going . . ." I stuttered, astonished.

"Ah, an adventure! Wherever it is, Rudy will find it. He's a GPS jockey, could have been one of Santa's reindeer—actually, maybe he was." Rudy shrugged good-naturedly. I started to get in, stopped, and turned to give Isak the biggest kiss and hug ever. He looked totally astonished.

"Remind me to offer you my limo more often," he said. "Have fun, sweetie."

As Isak closed the door behind me, I sunk down into the luxurious black seats, imagining what it would be like if this were my normal everyday mode of travel. Not having actually attended prom, I'd never been inside a limo and was glad I had saved all my excitement for this moment.

"And where might we be going, miss?" Rudy inquired gently, not wanting to disturb my reverie.

"Oh, call me Lisbeth. Well, it's this bar; it's a club, really— called Reilly's? It's in Jersey, near Montclair. I hope that's okay? Is that too far? Do you have any idea how to find it? I'm sorry—I don't know where it is. I know that's odd, but you see . . ." Rudy was losing interest as I rambled, and I was losing my Audrey, so I stopped.

"I know exactly the place," Rudy said after a pause. "My boyfriend and I love that bar. Best karaoke in Jersey every Wednesday night at midnight."

"Really?" Up-and-coming rock and rollers and gay karaoke nights, who knew?

"Please sit back and relax. I'll take care of everything," Rudy said as the car accelerated onto the Westside Highway.

"Thanks Rudy." I couldn't believe my luck.

"B there soon. Don't be mad :(I really wanna c u ! XOXO ME." But before I could hit SEND, my phone was buzzing like crazy.

"MUST TALK NOW." Mom? Texting?

There were two more texts in rapid succession.

"WHERE ARE YOU?"

"I NEED YOU HOME."

Mothers should not be allowed to text, I thought, *especially mine.* But I wondered what the urgency was. Maybe she was just pissed that I'd barely been home in the last week and that, when I had been, it was only to change my clothes and get some sleep.

The other possibility was that she had figured out that I wasn't going to college. Either way, it was a whole lot better not to respond right away. As a kid, it had taken me a long time to learn that it was safer to let the storm blow over a bit rather than rushing right into a hurricane.

"GET YOUR ASS BACK HERE," she texted.

Oh God. I closed my eyes and tried not to think.

"Lisbeth, we're here," Rudy said in a quiet voice. I opened my eyes and noticed we had stopped. I wondered how long I had been sleeping.

"We arrived a moment ago," he said as if reading my mind.

"Oh. Thanks Rudy, is it . . . ?"

"Still open?" Rudy answered before I could ask. "Yes, but I do think the band is leaving. There's a van backing up near the service entrance."

"Red, white, and blue?" I asked.

"Yes."

"Then I'd better go," I said, wondering if Jake had already left ahead of the band.

"Would you prefer I wait?"

"No, no. You've been too kind already. I'll find my way from here," I said as Rudy hopped out of the car and opened my door.

"You're certain?" Rudy asked. "The neighborhood is okay, but . . ."

"Yes, thank you. And by the way, you can tell Isak he's wrong. You absolutely do not talk too much. In fact, you're perfect." Rudy smiled, made a little bow, stepped back into the car, and drove away.

"Nice limo. Is that from your 'friend'?"

I turned to see Jake standing a few feet away near the entrance to Reilly's. Stragglers were leaving, happily boozed and laughing it up. He looked washed out.

"Yes, Isak. But he's just a——"

"That's okay. Don't explain." Jake was pissed off, but I could see he was trying to keep his cool. Maybe the gig didn't go well. Maybe he was tired of my excuses. I searched my mind for something to say.

"I'm here, aren't I?"

"Yeah, good timing. The band finished playing an hour and a half ago." Jake closed his eyes, and it seemed like he was trying to make a decision. He stared down at his boots.

"Well, how'd it go?" I asked, trying to change the subject.

"Good actually." He warmed up a little, begrudgingly. "An A and R rep showed up. Offered us a deal."

"Really?" I asked, inching closer. "That's so great!" I was going to run up to him and smother him in hugs and kisses and say I really did want to wear this dress for him and I would next time, but this woman came out of the bar and walked up behind him.

Lingering with her well-manicured hand hanging on his shoulder, she didn't see me at first. "Hey Jake, should we have one more for the road?" she asked. I noted the plural pronoun. She wasn't your ordinary garden-variety groupie, either. From her top-of-the-line True Religions to her red high-heeled cowboy boots and blond tresses, everything about her screamed big bucks.

"Sure, Monica, I'll be right there. Give me a minute," he said. That's when she noticed me, gave me a quizzical look like she felt sorry for me, and went inside.

Shit. I guess I was later than I'd thought.

"So it went *really* well," I said and tried not to get emotional. "I'll be going. See you at the Hole."

"Wait."

I stopped and turned.

"I know what you're thinking," he said.

"Yeah? It's okay, Jake. I wasn't here. I can't blame you. I really should go."

"Lizzy, listen, I'm trying to tell you . . ." But I kept walking and he stopped talking.

I pictured him running after me.

But he didn't.

27 "Still up ?!"
I texted Jess and waited.
The wind was blowing down North Pine Street. I was trying not to get all weepy, wishing I had done something differently. Anything. Wishing Jake understood or I had told him to begin with. Now it was too late. I had no right to be jealous. I hoped it was the wind that was making my eyes tear up. I couldn't stop thinking about him, seeing that cowgirl lingering behind him. The sad way she looked at me.

When I heard footsteps behind me, I panicked and picked up my pace. On the uneven sidewalk, I felt my ankle twist. Shit, Jess was right about the Louboutin heel not lasting. I kept walking anyway, not wanting to stop for a snapped heel. I turned on my phone light to make sure whoever was behind me knew I was ready.

The footsteps came closer and then faded. I glanced back. No one was there.

The wind whistled around me, giving me the creeps. Why hadn't Jess texted me back already? I absolutely could *not* go home in this dress.

"Knock knock :)" I texted and waited.

I tried to think about what ZK and Tabitha were doing now. Not walking on a dead-end street in the dark, I bet. This fantasy project of mine felt pretty pathetic at one o'clock in the morning. The evening had been miraculous and all. But here I was, all alone with nowhere to go.

My phone buzzed.

"Of course I'm up! It's only 1 AM 0.o" Jess texted.

"Ok if I crash ?! :)" I asked.

"Duh !! I've bn waitin ! Come to my house & tell all !! ☺"

I dialed Hometown Call-a-Cab, figuring there was enough money in my little peacock-feathered clutch to get to Jess's house. Once inside the cab, I slipped off my shoes. The taxi cost exactly fifteen dollars. I hoped he wasn't expecting a tip. I figured eighty-six cents wouldn't be interpreted as a compliment.

I let myself in Jess's back door. I'd had her key since the seventh grade in case of . . . well, emergencies. Climbing the creaky stairs to her room, I tried to make sure I didn't wake her mom.

Jess was sitting cross-legged on her bed with the orange Cassini in pieces across the bedspread. I gasped.

"No worries. If I can take 'em apart, I can put 'em back together again," she said, smiling. "I never stop being amazed at what goes on inside the clothes. Breaking down these dresses is better than all the courses at FIT. I just had to open one up completely to see how it was structured. They sure knew how to rock a cocktail." She put down her seam ripper and looked up at me with expectation.

"So? Spill it! From the beginning!"

I propped myself up against some pillows and began replaying everything in detail, from the clipboard Nazi who loved my blog to meeting ZK, from the gorgeous clothes everywhere, the jewelry, and the rooftop pool to Tabitha's crazy, erratic behavior and every single word that Isak Guerrere said about Jess's dress. Telling it all to Jess, I realized how unreal and remarkable it was.

"Do you think Isak Guerrere actually liked the dress? You sure he isn't just being nice?" she asked.

"He *is* nice, very nice. And yes, I think he really loves all the dresses. I'm pretty sure he used the word 'genius,'" I said. "He's even envious I don't wear *his* designs." Jess beamed with satisfaction, and she seemed totally excited about the possibilities. This was the first time I could ever remember Jess actually caring about what anybody else thought of her or what she'd done.

"They know you as Designer X from my blog."

"Oh, I like that," Jess said. "Lisbeth, you must be pretty incredible in action," she said. Although she'd seen me at charity events before, it definitely seemed so much more remarkable that I had hung out with the whole famous gang at the Soho House.

"They're actually buying you as one of their own. It's so weird."

"The scariest thing is this Dahlia Rothenberg chick. She's really nasty about Tabitha and talks behind her back like she's dirt. And she looks at me as though she'd like to rip me apart—if it wouldn't damage her perfect nails. I don't know if she's on to me or she just hates me for some other reason."

"Are you getting too many looks from ZK?"

"I guess," I said, studying the edge of one of the pillows.

"So, what's next?" she asked, neatly placing the dissembled dress in pieces on her desk by the window.

"Well, ZK invited me to this opening thing next week. By the way, what's a Schnabel? Is it a drink like schnapps?"

"Julian Schnabel—he's an artist," she said.

"Oh cool, an art opening. And get this—Tabitha says she wants to go shopping. Can you imagine what that girl buys? Has to be some serious cash."

"What?"

"Yeah, she wants me to go shopping on Fifth Avenue with her," I said, uncertain why she'd responded so strangely.

"Do you hear yourself?" she asked. "What on earth are you talking about?" Jess seemed appalled.

"What do you mean?" I asked tentatively.

"Lisbeth, what are you going to do? You're broke."

"I don't really need any money. I'm not going to buy anything. Hey, last night I went out and drank and ate and then there was the limo. I forgot to tell you about that . . ." But Jess was reacting oddly, and I didn't want to go into all that stuff about seeing Jake with the swag cowgirl.

"School will be coming up in a month," Jess said. "You haven't talked about it once, let alone made any plans to get ready."

"That's because I'm not going to school."

"What?!" The way Jess scowled at me—you would have thought I had confessed to robbing a bank or committing murder.

"It would be the end of all of my possibilities," I said. "The end of my life." It felt terrible to say it out loud like that. But there was relief in saying it.

"Does your mom know?"

"Are you kidding?"

"Jeez." Jess turned away from me, peering out the window into the darkness. It was so dark you couldn't even see the moon. I felt bad. Not just because I'd been lying all that time to her and everyone about college, but I knew that Jess would be disappointed in me. Despite her enthusiasm for reworking the dresses and the fun of sneaking into those events, she had been clear: she regarded it all as a prank. All along, I knew she thought my Audrey dream was shallow.

"Well then, what *are* you going to do?" She wouldn't look at me, but we could see each other's reflection in the window.

I shrugged. I didn't know.

"Are you going to throw away a lifetime of responsibility, of actually being someone, to become one of *them* when you're not really

one of them anyway?" Jess asked. "You know, when they finish par-
tying, they go home——to trust funds and Park Avenue apartments
and vacations in Saint Bart's and indulgent rich parents who let
them do anything, even when they completely fuck up."

"It's different for you——you know who you are. I never have," I
said. "I want to be somebody, too. I just don't know how."

"Wow. I was afraid you'd get lost in this game and believe that it
was real," Jess said.

"It *is* real to me," I said.

She shook her head slowly, astonished.

"I know," I said sadly. "It's not really like the Lisbeth everyone
thinks they know around here."

"I've got to get some sleep," Jess said abruptly and began putting away her sewing tools. Then she stopped and sat next to me on
the bed.

"Well, I have something I haven't told you, too," she began. "I
found a tiny studio in Chinatown I can afford and I quit the Hole."
I was stunned.

"No way!"

"It literally just happened."

"Why didn't you tell me?"

"It wasn't even a plan, not right away anyway. But I checked out
this ad on a whim, and when I saw this place, I knew I had to do it.
I'm moving in next week."

"Why does it have to be so sudden?"

"It just happened that way, believe me. I was going to ask you to
help me move."

"Sure," I said too quickly. I wanted to sound positive, but I didn't
feel that way. I always seemed to be a step behind. Whenever I
would get close to what I wanted, something would change, and my
goals would seem impossibly far away once again. Jess looked at me
like she was worried I might tear up. I was worried, too.

"I've done a bunch more of the dresses, just so you know," she
said. "I had a few ideas I wanted to try out. Here, look." She walked

to her closet and opened the accordion doors. Inside was a rainbow array of four more dresses already finished, modified, some radically, from Nan's treasure trove. I flipped between the dresses.

"Jess, they're so wonderful." My Designer X was truly amazing. Looking at the dresses, you realized that she was just beginning to tap her talent.

"Yeah, this design 'exercise' has been good. I didn't have the courage to develop my own line, at least not this fast. But I've gotten a lot of confidence working with these dresses, and I'm thinking about it now. I could do way more," she said. "And you gave that to me, Lisbeth. You've been an inspiration."

"Yeah, sure . . . really?"

"Yeah. Come on, we can talk in the morning. Let's get some sleep." She threw me one of her Sonic Youth T-shirts.

I headed into the bathroom to take down my hair and scrub my face. Jess kept a toothbrush for me in the medicine cabinet; I grabbed it and hunted around for the minty toothpaste I liked. The cinnamon kind that Jess's family favored just burned my lips.

I stopped and examined my face in the mirror. I didn't look like Audrey Hepburn at all, just plain, ordinary Lisbeth Anne Wachowicz.

"I hate to be the bearer of bad news," Jess said from the other room. "Your mom called my mom last night trying to track you down, and my mom promised to send you back right after breakfast."

I closed my eyes and tried to breathe.

"You have to go home sometime," Jess said.

28

Delaying the inevitable, I hung out at Jess's house as long as I reasonably could.

Ever since Jess told me that my mom had phoned her mom, my brain imagined every dire scenario, trying hopelessly to anticipate what I was walking into. It's one of the freaky things about being the kid of someone who throws plates and bottles around the house—you can't help imagining the worst—because it happens and you've seen it.

Leaving the green strapless Valentino from last night in Jess's closet with the other dresses, I borrowed a tank top and clean underwear and grabbed my jeans from the day before.

Turning down the street toward my house, I figured: shower, eat something, try to stay calm, and prepare to talk to Mom when she comes home. It was two in the afternoon, and I assumed no one would be there until three thirty—only I was wrong. Mom's car was in the driveway.

That was unusual. She never took time off from the hospital, and they never gave her any. I took a deep breath and opened the screen door.

"Well, look who's here. Howdy, stranger," she said from the kitchen, lighting a cigarette. There were a few bags of groceries on the kitchen table. I dropped my backpack and started helping her put them away.

"Is something wrong with your phone?" she asked, taking a drag of her cigarette.

"No, Mom, I've just been busy, you know, with Jess and at the diner." I took the four packages of frozen corn, opened up the freezer, and found myself staring at the stacks of half-eaten ice cream containers and the hundred-year-old frozen hot dogs. "How come you're home so early?" I asked.

"At the court-ordered therapist's office for Ryan," she said and handed me the milk to put away. I noticed that she was rubbing her arm.

"You know the whole family was supposed to be there. The school-board attorney made it a condition of your brother's release. I didn't expect your sister," she said, taking another drag on her cig. "But I expected you."

"I'm sorry, Mom. I didn't know," I said, wondering why those words hurt so much and why I felt so bad that I had let her down.

"Well, how *would* you know if you don't answer your fucking phone? I even texted you," she said. I felt her pushing toward a buildup. "I called everywhere; Nan didn't know where you were." I wondered if Nan was worried. Crap.

She grabbed her usual coffee mug by the sink. The bottle of Gordon's would be next. Then Ryan walked in. He stood in the kitchen doorway. I hadn't seen Ryan for a while. He seemed taller and his hair was longer, especially in the back. Mom must have cut his mullet for the therapist meeting. The run of freckles across his nose had faded, but he had the same crooked grin.

"Hey, sis, did you hear?"

"Hear what, Ry?"

"I'm clinically depressed. Pretty cool, huh?" He had a smug expression on his face. Instead of being repentant for all the trouble he caused, he seemed to be thriving on the attention.

"Well you seem pretty happy about being depressed."

"Funny, sis, I get it." Mom sat down at the table, and, oddly, I smelled coffee. She hadn't walked over to the liquor cabinet. She had poured herself coffee.

"Make me some Eggos, Mom," Ryan demanded. How did he think he'd get away with that? But Mom was silent. Normally she'd have snapped at him by now. He seemed to have some edge on her, maybe the therapist told her to be nice to him.

"Do it yourself, Ry, I need to talk to your sister," Mom said quietly.

"But I always burn them," he said with a tiny wicked smirk.

"I'll make them," I volunteered and opened up the freezer. I figured it couldn't hurt to drag this out as long as possible to avoid whatever it was that Mom wanted to talk to me about. Putting the waffles in the toaster oven, I noticed Mom's hand shaking slightly as she held her cigarette. Something was going on with her, but I couldn't tell what.

"So, who said you were depressed, Ry?" I asked.

"The head doctor. He said I need more stability at home," Ryan said, smugly pleased now that he was the focus and everyone had to worry about him. I guessed that Mom had gotten reamed at the therapist's office.

The timer rang on the toaster oven, and then I buttered the waffles and handed them over to Ryan. He sat down across from Mom at the table.

"Ryan, I told you I need to talk to your sister," she said. Ryan seemed unfazed, like he wasn't afraid of provoking her.

"But I want to hear," he said. He was totally pushing it. Mom looked up from her coffee at Ryan. I thought she was going to leap across the table and choke him.

"Get the fuck out of here," she said quietly and went back to her coffee.

Ryan hustled up, so I guessed there was a limit to how far Mom would accommodate him. He grabbed his waffles and nodded with that shit-eating grin of his as he left.

"You missed the school orientation," she said. "Hand me my lighter, will you?"

"Really?" I passed the Bic and she lit another cigarette.

"They sent this letter." She fished a piece of folded paper out of the pile of papers on the kitchen table and slid it over to me.

"Mom, it's addressed to me—it's my mail," I said.

"It isn't if you don't pick it up."

I took my time reading the letter. It wasn't anything new, really. I had been to one of the orientations before. It wasn't like I didn't know what dorm I was going to live in or where the classes were. The school was only five miles away. But the fact that she was opening my mail meant that she had some kind of clue. That couldn't be good.

"I don't have to go to that orientation," I said matter-of-factly. "It's optional. I went to the first one instead when we signed up."

"Is there something going on you want to tell me?" she asked, exhaling the smoke as she spoke. She rubbed her arm again as if it were sore and straightened her sleeve. Mom was on the hunt. That was her way when she suspected something.

"Don't go off the rails on me, Lisbeth," she said, looking me in the eye. "You're the only dependable one left."

"I know, Mom," I said, not having the slightest clue how I'd ever be able to talk to her about what was really going on.

"I'm going to need you around more," she said, sternly.

God, I hope not, I couldn't help thinking.

She knew something was up, but she hadn't put her finger on it—yet.

29

I arrived at Montclair Manor without calling, and when minutes passed and Nan hadn't opened the door, I started to panic. What if she had fallen or had a heart attack?

Peering through the side windows, I couldn't find a sign of her anywhere. She wasn't in the back either. I knocked on every door and window. As I decided to head for Nurse Betty's office, Nan's door opened and there she was, dressed in a fluffy lavender bathrobe, her cheeks rosy, her silver hair pulled into a chic knot.

"Nan, you're okay!" I said.

"Of course, dear, I was just taking a bubble bath." She stretched her arms out to hug me. "Like liquid Prozac, isn't it?"

We entered, and I wondered how on earth I had stayed away from Nan's apartment for so long.

"It's so lovely to see you," she said from her bedroom as she changed into her clothes.

"I'm sorry. I didn't mean to interrupt your bath."

"Oh, not a problem. I'm quite shriveled up and wrinkled as it is," she said with a laugh. "Although the sea salts were soothing."

I heard the distinctive snap of her Chanel compact, the one she still had from the sixties that she continuously refilled herself.

Don't ask why, but to me that little click had the definitive sound of luxury. It always summoned the smiling, elegant image of Nan.

She entered the room all bright and shiny, with a light blush highlighting her cheeks, an absolute minimum of makeup, totally put together in seconds. I marveled at how she did that.

"And to what do I owe this wonderful impromptu visit?"

"Missing your cheesecake?" I said sheepishly.

"Well, unfortunately there's no cheesecake in the house," she said with a sad look. "But today's special is chocolate heaven cake. I hope that will do?" Her eyes twinkled.

"That sounds even better," I replied. "And I could help with the whipped cream."

"Splendid idea," she said.

We both slipped into her miniscule kitchen that was hardly big enough for one. As I whisked the cream in a metal mixing bowl, I inhaled her perfume and immediately felt at ease.

"You know, Nan, there was an oil painting in your storage area of a little girl. Is that you?" I asked.

"I doubt it, dear, that was probably my mother."

"Really? But she looks so much like you," I said.

"Everyone said that, and I always thought it was funny because I knew my mother as a very stuffy old woman. She wasn't really involved with us children and although she was a suffragist, she kept it very hush-hush. She was a snooty upper-crust society lady, given to secret cigarettes."

"Well, you're not stuffy."

"I certainly hope not!" she said as she dolloped endless spoonfuls of whipped cream onto her homemade chocolate cake. "Come, let's eat! I have something to show you!"

We squeezed through the kitchen and sat in the living room. There on the table was a new scrapbook I had never seen before.

"I've been working on a little project," she said. She handed me the cake knife. "Would you please do the honors?" Sitting next to me, she opened the scrapbook to the first page. There I was, in the Audrey Givenchy on Page Six.

"What is this?" I asked as I put down the cake knife and began turning the pages. Page after page contained clippings and photographs, some from the Web, some from newspapers and magazines, including *Us Weekly*.

"You knew about these?" I gasped. "Why didn't you say anything?"

"I assumed you'd tell me all about it at some point," she said, smoothing a strand of hair behind my ear. "It seemed like such a grand adventure. I didn't want to spoil your fun. But I couldn't help collecting every bit of it." She was beaming with pride.

It startled me that I was actually the girl in these pictures. My charade was a complete fiction, but laying them out like that, collectively, seemed so real. I was impressed at how perfectly she had prepared each photo. Museum-quality work, Jess would have said.

"I even bought a printer and started using the computer." She pointed proudly to her ancient desktop, where there was a nice new printer and mouse pad.

"Oh Nan . . ." As I hugged her, I closed my eyes and felt tears welling up.

"At first, I didn't know what to think. I recognized the dresses, though I was completely shocked at what you'd done to them," she said.

"I know. Jess was worried about that. But aren't they incredible?" I said, grabbing a tissue and wiping the tears from my cheeks.

Nan nodded. "I was mostly surprised that you'd cut and changed them so dramatically. But the reworking was indeed impressive. Your friend Jess is quite brilliant. It made me realize that those dresses weren't meant to stay in a storage box. They were meant to play a part of some romantic adventure. They were meant to be worn *dancing*."

"That's what I told Jess!" I said. "She didn't want to alter them, but then the first one was such a hit that she's created a whole look."

We flipped back through the clippings in the scrapbook, and I gave Nan details on every dress, where I wore it and who I met. I spilled everything about Being Audrey. I worried at first that she'd be disappointed in me for pretending to be something I wasn't, but her expression grew more interested and astonished as I shared every delicious detail.

"You are so absolutely stunning in these dresses," she added.

"It's all Jess. She did an incredible job on them, really," I said.

"Stop, Lisbeth." She held my chin up and gazed deeply into my eyes. "Look at me. You are *beautiful*. You always have been. I often wondered why you didn't see that. And it's important that you know now. You are smart, clever, original, and beautiful. It's the most wonderful combination, and I am *proud* of you."

We hugged that Nan heart-melding hug, and it was such a relief to be with her, to know that she loved me and understood.

"Of course, I worry that I've filled your head with too many stories about how wonderful the old days were."

"But Nan, they are the most amazing stories," I said, feeling a bit defensive.

"Well, it's good to see you making your own memories and not only living off of mine. Now you'll have your own to look back on and cherish. That's why I wanted you to have this scrapbook."

I was so moved, I didn't know how to thank her. My eyes found hers, and she gave me such a warm look I almost broke down and started crying again, but I wanted to keep it together.

"I still have a hard time believing that the trust funders accepted me so readily," I said, recovering. I cut each of us a slice of cake.

"I'm not," said Nan, taking a forkful of chocolate. "You're intelligent and vivacious, and that's appealing to any social group. Besides, it's all about money with these people, and if you appear to have money or they *think* you have money, then they are intrigued. Otherwise, how could you be with *them* if you didn't have money?"

"You don't think it's lame that I've been just acting like Audrey?"

"You may have started that way, but at this point I think it's something more," she said. "Even Audrey Hepburn was pretending to be Audrey—until she was, that is. When Audrey started out, much like you, she was operating solely on her charm, wits, spirit, and personal style. She never quite felt like she belonged; she was never fully prepared for what she was about to do next. She just jumped right in and hoped for the best. Eventually, she became the kind of woman we all assumed she was from the very beginning."

"But Audrey did *something*. She danced, she acted," I said. "My friends, Jess, Jake, they know what they want to do with their lives. They know who they want to be. I'm playacting. Do you think there's a way I can turn my passion into something?"

"Well, you're going to college, sweetie, that will help, won't it?"

My eyes dropped and I nodded, hoping she didn't take too much note of my response.

Nan took my fingers in her smooth, cool hands. "Be true to yourself, Lisbeth. It doesn't matter that you've used Audrey Hepburn as a starting point. The most important thing is where you end up, and that you use this experience to become the best *Lisbeth* you can be."

"Oh Nan, it sounds so possible when you say it." Throwing my arms around her neck, I hugged her again. I needed so many hugs.

Feeling better, I scooped a gob of whip cream frosting with my finger, popping it into my mouth.

"I want to give you something," Nan said, rising from the couch thoughtfully and walking to the sideboard. She opened one of the lower drawers.

She was holding a bracelet I had never seen before—a simple platinum band. She hesitated a moment, looking at it in her hand, then returned to the couch.

"This is from my days back then. It's a gift from one of the 'boys,' and I want you to have it."

"Nan, it's lovely," I said.

"And remember," Nan said, jutting her jaw forward and stroking her chin—her version of a movie mobster—"one day I may come to you for a favor." Her voice was an octave lower and raspy, an almost perfect Don Corleone impression. I couldn't stop laughing.

"What exactly is this?" I asked.

"It's a talisman for protection, inscribed by an old boyfriend of mine," she added. "It will go fabulously with those dresses, and maybe it will keep you safe."

I turned the bracelet in my hands. It was elegant, just like Nan. Inside, there was an inscription in Latin: TUAM TUTAM TENEBO, SAMMY G. I marveled at how stylish and mysterious it was.

"Be careful, Lisbeth," Nan added. "As Sammy used to say, 'a liar's mouth can be full of truth, but he's still a liar.' Be careful who you trust."

As the platinum band slipped effortlessly around my wrist, I marveled at its soft beauty.

"By the way, dear, I think you should know—your mother has seen the photos, too."

30

"Why does everything I do for you involve lots of repetitive physical work?" I asked Jess as we pushed her steamer trunk up the five flights of stairs to her new digs in Chinatown.

The scent of decomposing fruit, roasted chestnuts, and fresh fish intermingled with stale frying oil, the heated exhaust of industrial fans, and the cigarette smoke of the Asian men working in the market downstairs: Chinatown was one of those parts of New York that you could pick out blindfolded by the pungent smells alone. All those odors floated up through Jess's new neighborhood.

Jess had packed her mom's station wagon with all her worldly possessions—three battered trunks filled with her own designs, as well as fabrics and salvaged clothes that represented years of flea market and church store scavenging. She also had two sewing machines, including a serger that she bought at a yard sale, three dress forms, and a cool antique sewing box filled with the tattered marble composition books she used as journals.

It was Jess's big move. In return for my moving skills, she promised to help me get my Purple Beast out of the Hudson Street parking lot. I needed to borrow some money to do it. I hadn't been back for three days, and I was sure my beast missed me, although the parking guys were probably wondering by now if someone had left a body in the trunk.

I actually liked lugging stuff around with Jess for a while. It seemed so normal after the last few days of high drama. The situation at home with Ryan and Mom was intense. The Hole wasn't the same without Jess, and it was awkward around Jake. I felt like he was avoiding me, not that I could blame him.

Hauling dress forms and sewing machines up five flights of stairs was good distraction therapy, and Jess's apartment was awesome.

Okay, it didn't look awesome; in fact, it looked downright crappy. The building, 507 East Broadway, was home to a former sweatshop, after all. Jess said that, only a few years ago, there used to be sixty-three people per floor in the buildings around here. From the window in the stairwell, you could spy a sweatshop that was still in operation, where women were bent over sewing machines making cheap polyester clothes on the sixth floor of the building across the street. Even in Jess's converted space, you could see the lines on the floor where the walls that divided the room into tiny sections used to be.

But as grim as it was, the raw space was awesome because of what it represented—the city, a place of her own, freedom. Jess would make it ubercool. With lots of raw brick walls, no windows except one in the bathroom, and a big skylight—it was the perfect interior design challenge for Jess's imagination. Jess said that it was fitting that her first apartment was a sweatshop; it suited her sense of industry.

The last thing we carried up the stairs was Jess's futon mattress, which we threw against the back wall beneath the skylight.

"Graduating high school meant nothing, you going to college first meant nothing, your first girlfriend meant nothing, but the first apartment in the city all your own—that's a big deal between friends," I said as I flopped down on the mattress.

Jess dropped down beside me.

"Jessica Giovanna Pagliazzi, you have my official admiration, envy, and undying resentment."

"Yeah, pretty crazy, huh?" Jess said, leaning back against the wall.

"Someday I hope I'll do it, too," I said.

"So does your mom know yet?"

"That I'm dressing up in Nan's Chanels and crashing galas at the Met?"

"No, that you're not going to college."

"Oh, that." I took a deep breath. "She's snooping around. She knows something is going on. I've got to get out of there before it blows up. Ryan is way too weird. He's always baiting Mom, and she might have to homeschool him if they don't take him off suspension. But why she hasn't shut him down is even stranger."

"Are you sure you don't want to go to school after all? I mean, you could change your mind, right?"

"I guess. I don't know. I can't bear to live at home," I said. "I wish I had more options."

"Have you seen Jake?"

"I saw him at work. I can tell he's moved on, and I don't even know what to say to him. I've got to get out of there."

"You know, you can actually get out any time," Jess said.

"Yeah, sure." I couldn't help staring at her like she was nuts.

"You could get a place of your own if you really wanted to."

"I couldn't even afford a deposit, but it's a nice thought," I said.

"Well, you could stay here," Jess offered. "I mean, you'll have to pay rent after a while—when you get a job. Hell, there are plenty of restaurants and diners in Manhattan with lots better tips than the Hole."

"Really? I wish I could . . ." I leaned back against the wall. "I don't know. I just feel so adrift about everything."

I was going ask Jess if she thought she'd come home much. But before I could say anything, she leaned toward me, and, honestly, why I didn't see it coming is beyond me.

My eyes caught hers as she paused for a second a fraction away from my lips. It wasn't indecision; I could tell she wanted to give me the chance to know what was about to happen. I felt her warm breath brush my cheek and then slowly our lips touched. Her breath took mine away. I closed my eyes as I felt her fingertips on my face, in my hair, pulling me nearer, and I thought about how many times we were close enough to do this but never did. It was something that had occurred to me dozens of times, but we never talked about.

When Jess came out in the tenth grade, I was the last one to know. She never confided in me, so when I found out from all of our friends, I walked right up to her in study hall and told her that it was totally cool with me that she was gay, but if she ever didn't tell me something important like that, we were through.

"I was afraid," Jess said at the time, "that if I told you, we wouldn't be friends anymore."

That's what I was thinking while we kissed—not surprised that we were kissing but wondering why we had never kissed before. How long we kissed I couldn't tell you, but when it was over, I just sat there for the longest time, breathless.

"Kissing is such a strange thing," I felt compelled to say for some reason. "I don't know about you, but I tend to avoid people's spit, I mean . . ."

"It's okay," Jess said. "I just wanted to do that. We're cool."

"But I don't . . ."

"You don't have to. It's all right," Jess said.

"Was that something you thought about for a while or just did?"

"Thought about lots of times and don't know why, just did, now."

"Oh," I said, and just sat there. "A lot of times?"

"Yeah," she said, and we both laughed.

"Wow, so that's what it's like."

"Kinda." Jess stood up, breaking the moment. "Well, I guess, we better get your car." She put her hand out to help me off the futon.

"Yeah, we should," I said, feeling disoriented as she helped me up and somehow disappointed that we weren't going to talk about it more.

"Right, and I better get to class," Jess said. "Let's get the Beast out of hock, and you can drop me off at FIT on your way home."

"Yeah, sure."

Jess opened the closet and grabbed a Chanel jacket that she had reworked to make the waist more shapely. Then she plucked out a pair of jeans on a hanger.

"I scored some True Religions that were on loan to the school for a photo shoot that I *have* to return first thing Monday. I'm pretty sure they're your size. You'll be quite the fashionable shoppette," she said, smiling. "I threw in some shoes I've been working on, too."

I grabbed our backpacks as Jess locked up, wishing we were still on her mattress sitting together, talking. We walked down the stairs, and she stopped like there was something she forgot.

"Hey listen," Jess said. "I mean it. If you need a place in the city and want to keep your stuff here, like the dresses, I can still work on them. And if you do, you don't have to . . ."

"No. Sure. I get it. I'm fine," I said, not knowing what I really felt, wondering if I ever would.

"Good. And hey, you know, I'm getting my own line together, and I need your help. I'm going to do this thing, a show, my term project at FIT. It's going to be pretty fierce, but I can't do it without you."

"Sure."

"Maybe you can get some of your fancy friends to come?"

Yeah, I thought, *me and my fancy friends.*

31 I stared at the text on my phone for most of my morning shift at the Hole. "Whr shd Mocha pick u up ?! :)"

Tabitha, the Princess of Pop, beckoned. I had never felt more like Cinderella than that day at the Hole—the bad side of being Cinderella—the part where she's on her hands and knees in the fireplace, cleaning out the cinders and ashes that were her namesake. Buela was in a terrible mood. I had missed two shifts, and it felt like she was punishing me. I spent an hour and a half of the morning refilling all the caked-up ketchup and mustard bottles.

I spied Jake on the other side of the diner. He purposely turned the other way and wouldn't meet my eye. I tried to talk to him twice in the freezer when I ran into him, but he only nodded. I couldn't help remembering his unexpected kisses. Before, he would have helped me with the ketchup bottles, but not this time. We seemed worlds apart.

Then there was the new girl, Crystal. She was totally put together in that Jersey way, with heavy makeup, cosmetically perfect teeth, plucked eyebrows, spray-bronzed skin, thick accent, and a great bod. I grew up respecting girls like Crystal because, contrary to popular belief, they aren't necessarily promiscuous, no matter how they dress, and they are smart and tough.

Crystal took all of Jess's shifts and was scoping everybody out. High on her list was Jake. She was already hip to the fact that there was something between us—just because he wouldn't look at me. My phone buzzed again.

"Can't wait 2 see you darling ;) what time is Mocha comin ?"

My shift ended at 1:30 P.M. How could I turn down a Fifth Avenue shopping spree with the fabulous Tabitha Eden? I already had the modified couture combo in the garment bag that Jess had given me. It's not like I would ever get to wear that anywhere else.

"2:30 ?" I texted back.

For years I'd surfed the endless pictures of Paris and Nicky, Kim and Kourtney, the Olsen twins, and everyone else dressed in their latest as they balanced an avalanche of shopping bags from Jeffrey's, Chanel, Lanvin, Alice and Olivia, and others on Rodeo Drive, Fifth Avenue, or Oxford Street. The ritual of the celeb shopping trip was as much about what you wore as what you bought. This could be my only chance to see what it was like.

Buela had her eye on me, so I had to look busy. I kept moving, covering my tables, cleaning, and finding little projects like restacking the to-go containers behind the counter. My phone buzzed.

"Soooo where ?" Tabitha texted.

Since Jess's East Broadway address was too downscale and I hadn't yet found that friendly Manhattan doorman I might talk into fronting for me, my first thought was a hotel lobby, something on the Upper East Side. If I could find an address near a hotel, I could step out as Mocha arrived.

I watched the last few moments tick by on the diner clock. At 1:30 P.M. sharp, I punched out my time card and grabbed the garment bag from the locker. Buela gave me the evil eye for being quick to leave, but I kept going.

The Mark Hotel on Seventy-seventh and Madison was described on its Web site as "situated in the heart of Manhattan's most elegant neighborhood." I figured that would do and texted Tabitha.

"16 E 77 ST."

That address was just a few doors down from the Mark according to Google Maps. I reached the hotel a half hour early and slipped through the lobby, ducking into the bar restroom, where I changed in one of the bathroom stalls.

Unzipping the garment bag, I discovered that Jess had left me a surprise. She had transformed a pair of Nan's Ferragamo flats from the 60s, overdyeing them in a deep, lush red and adding a small heel to match. The shoes were stunning and perfect for what I was wearing.

After a touch-up in the mirror, I emerged with my remixed Chanel and True Religions, ready for an afternoon of rampant consumerism, even if it would be only window-shopping for me. I figured there was plenty of time to be on the street and grab Mocha before he began ringing doorbells. I walked over to the Concierge to check my garment bag with my old clothes but as I took my ticket, I saw Mocha through the massive picture windows walking up to the townhouse door early.

I ran quickly to the car, hoping he'd follow. "Mocha, darling! Over here!" I yelled. But he had already pushed the buzzer. He turned, confused. If someone was home, they would be coming down, and soon it would be difficult to explain.

"My apologies, Miss Dulac," Mocha said and hustled back to the limo to open the door.

"It's my Nan. I don't want to wake her," I said. "She doesn't quite handle the stairs the way she used to." As I entered the limo, I almost fainted when I slid inside.

Tabitha, sitting comfortably in the back corner, had watched the whole thing.

"You're here!" I said, barely able to disguise my confusion.

"Will she be okay?" she asked.

"Who?" I asked, sitting, hoping we could leave immediately.

"Your Nan," she replied.

"Oh, Nan! Yes, of course . . . we have a nurse . . . yes . . . ole Betty, must be as old as Nan. She'll be fine . . . but this is her day off. Anyway, it's all fine." I wasn't sure I even knew what I was saying anymore.

Tabitha wore a blush cashmere cardigan over matching silk shorts and white Louboutins, all highlighted by the glittering rose cuff on her wrist—Tiffany's latest metal "discovery"—RUBEDO. We're talking seventy-five-hundred smackers for that kind of bling. I know how much it cost because they advertise it like crazy on the Tiffany's Web site. In her arms, she was holding a white slipper of a dog that perfectly matched her shoes that I recognized from her publicity shots: Galileo, a Pomeranian.

As we drove away, I stole a glance back at the townhouse entrance, where a very annoyed elderly man opened his door to no one at all.

"Is there a problem?" she asked.

"Oh, no, everything's fine," I said and wondered if I had blown it. Tabitha seemed subdued. I realized I sounded heartless about Nan, even though everything was utterly fabricated.

"I hope you don't mind," Tabitha said quietly. "We need to go somewhere first."

Galileo barked.

That didn't sound good.

32 Tabitha was silent. There was definitely a bad vibe in the limo, which made my mind race and my stomach ache. I was the most weak-willed poseur ever. I started to panic. Was Tabitha experiencing one of her mood swings?

"You know, darling," I said, summoning my inner Audrey, "if you need to go somewhere and it's not convenient, we could shop later."

"I'd rather not," she said. Her tone of voice reminded me of the time in the bathroom when she demanded to know who I was, severe and regal despite her dress being up around her ears. It occurred to me that she was most arrogant when she had something to hide.

"I have to go to the studio first."

"The recording studio?" I asked.

"Yes, I've been avoiding it," she answered. "But I need to tell you something." I folded my hands in my lap and tried to remain composed and calm. "I need someone there with me, and I wasn't sure you'd come along if I told you first."

I tried to think of some way to respond. There was a long pause before she spoke again.

"You might as well know the night you showed up, I had taken a shitload of pills. I was trying to kill myself," she continued. "That would have been a great TMZ story, right?" She seemed as if she might fall apart. The image of her beaded purse on the bathroom floor flashed through my mind. I remembered fishing for lip gloss and finding all those bottles of pills.

"I'm sorry, I didn't know . . ."

"It should have worked. I did some blow, too, but it made me throw up."

I became keenly aware of Mocha in the front seat. The glass partition was closed, but couldn't he be listening? How much did he know?

"Then you showed up out of nowhere," she said. "I had the pills. I would have taken more, but you were there and you helped me. No one else would have."

I felt bad for her, and at the same time I felt like a total liar.

"I know who you really are," she said, and I froze, suspended, unable to breathe, waiting for what might come next. "You're an angel. Someone somewhere wanted me to survive, and I know with you here now, I will."

I let out an audible sigh, exhaling sharply despite my desire to be unobtrusive.

"I don't understand," I said, trying to take the focus off me. "Why did you feel you needed to do such a thing to yourself? You have everything," I added quietly, "to live for." Tabitha rolled her eyes, annoyed, like it was the dumbest thing to say.

"Because I hate every single thing about my life," she said, her eyes tearing up, trying to hold it back. She turned and stared out the window again. "You probably can't understand because you don't live your life pretending to be someone you're not."

My brain felt like a piece of paper that someone had ripped in half. If anybody in this car was a phony, we all know who would get the prize. The contradictions were too great. Galileo licked the tears off Tabitha's face.

"I feel like such a fake," she said.

"Your fans don't seem to feel that way," I remarked. Including me, I wanted to add.

Tabitha shook her head and practically snorted in disgust. "I was counting on Mother to put a stop to this, but now I have to go back into the studio to record another album. They won't let me stop, even though I told them I wouldn't tour. I totally freaked out on stage last time."

"What *do* you want to do?" I asked.

Tabitha made a sad laugh. "I wanted to go to veterinarian school and work in an animal shelter." I worried she might burst into tears again. "I like animals." No way.

I squeezed her hand. "So why didn't you?"

"Are you kidding? They weren't about to let me become an unglamorous vet in this family. They'd have to get Donna Karan to design my veterinarian scrubs."

She was so grim that I wasn't sure if she was kidding. "Tabitha Eden: celebrity veterinarian," I said. Tabitha laughed. "Well, why can't you do what you want now?"

"You'd be surprised what I can't do. Too many people decide what I get to do. I feel awful. Ever since I can remember, I've always felt awful. I know one second I'm fine, smiling, and then I can barely say hello. Like I'm not even a person, and everyone in the room knows. One minute, I can see myself in the mirror, and the next, the mirror shatters and I'm gone, and there's no way to get myself back. And I think, maybe everyone is that way, but I know they're not. You're the only one I know who doesn't seem to be weirded out around me."

I tried to think of what I could say, but we heard Mocha over the intercom. "Excuse me, Miss Eden, we're here."

Tabitha nodded and turned to face me.

"Lisbeth, you're my angel. You appeared out of nowhere to rescue me. You have to help me." Her eyes said everything—sadness, desperation, and the tiniest hope that I could change her life. Boy, did she have the wrong girl.

"I'll do whatever I can," I answered.

33 Max, Tabitha's guitarist, stood outside the studio entrance smoking a cigarette, bored as usual.

"Are they pissed?" Tabitha asked, wiping away the last of her tears as we made our way inside.

"Why? Because you've kept them waiting two and a half hours? Nah, they have their toys to play with."

As we entered together, Galileo leapt from Tabitha's arms and ran ahead. The receptionist, bookish in black-rimmed glasses with multicolored tattoos on her arms and neck, introduced herself as Brit.

"Hello, Miss Eden, you're in studio A today," she said. "Can I get you a Pellegrino, cappuccino, lemonade, or . . . ?"

"I'll take a lemonade with tequila," Tabitha answered without stopping as she pushed open the studio door. I guess when life gave Tabitha lemons, she couldn't help grabbing the tequila and salt.

Upon entering studio A, we were met by a massive wall of sound—bright, bubbly pop with a driving shake-your-body bottom beat. I knew the patented Tabitha Eden signature sound, and it felt like entering a club. I wanted to dance, but the music stopped abruptly as Tabitha entered.

"The Princess of Pop has arrived!" said a guy, younger than me, as we walked in. He seemed like an intern but wasn't acting like one. He had dark curly hair and the kind of beard a guy grows when he can't grow one. He seemed to be a mix of Latino and Jewish. His warm welcome put me instantly at ease. Galileo barked at him.

"Hey Bennie, this is my friend Lisbeth," Tabitha said. "Bennie and his partner, Dr. K, are the geniuses behind every hit song I've ever made. The best producers money can buy. Hard to believe for a twerp, right?"

"You're too kind, Tabby," Bennie said, mildly amused. "Nice to meet you, Lisbeth. Welcome to the madness."

Brit entered with Tabitha's drink and placed it on the table in front of her. She grabbed it and took a long draw.

"Kind of early for the tequila gargle?" Bennie chided.

"It's for my voice," she said and gave him a defensive scowl. "Don't give me shit just because you're too young to buy alcohol legally." She noticed me watching and became a little self-conscious.

"You don't want to let her drink alone, do you?" Bennie asked. "Hey, Brit, get my girlfriend Lisbeth a drink, too."

"No thanks," I said, grabbing a bottle of water off the bar for myself. "I'm good."

"Cool, then come on. While Tabitha warms up, I'll introduce you to *da* crew," Bennie said, crossing his arms in a mock rapper's pose. I couldn't help laughing.

Designed like a small amphitheater, the studio had a massive soundboard in the middle with automated sliders, buttons, and blinking LEDs, and at the bottom was a big glass room for musicians and singers. As we descended the levels to the main area, I noticed the framed gold and platinum CDs on the wall, four of them Tabitha's.

"This is where we make the hits," Bennie chuckled. "Straight-up hits and nothing but hits." He walked me right up to the enclosed glass room. Inside, there was a piano, guitars, and microphones. Three backup singers sat around music stands in the corner. There was a big black girl; a skinny white girl with lots of tats, angel bites, and other piercings; and a short Latina with her hair beaded and braided. They were laughing and singing, but we couldn't hear them.

"Those girls inside the fishbowl are our secret weapon—the backup babes, especially Oleta; she's our gospel diva," Bennie said. "They make us all look good. They give us white folks soul." Bennie tapped the window, and the three girls waved back. Oleta threw him a kiss.

The main room was strewn with lots of coffee cups and Chinese food containers. It was pretty clear that everyone had been working for quite some time while waiting for the Princess of Pop. There were laptops plugged into the main board and mini keyboards everywhere. Every few minutes, we would hear a bouncy beat or a mean riff being played, but everything was on a computer or prerecorded in some way. As far as I could tell, no one was playing an actual instrument. I guessed Max was only there for emergencies.

Tuning and adjusting the sliders and knobs on the enormous soundboard in the middle of the room was this superserious guy, tall and thin, wearing red Converse sneakers, light-gray jeans, a gray shirt, and a pencil-thin black tie.

"Come on, guys, let's finalize your kicks and synths so I can run the premix," he demanded. "I've got another session after this." The three engineers working with him scuttled about.

"And this is my partner, Dr. K," Bennie said. "He's not as nice as I am. Or as talented or as handsome."

"I can see that," I said and giggled. Dr. K rolled his eyes and managed a tepid smile.

"Come on, Bennie," he said. "Let's do this."

"Thanks for the tour," I said. "I don't want to get in the way. I'll find my way back up to the couches and chairs at the top." He did a funny bow as I left.

Tabitha was walking down as I made my way up. I stopped and gave her a hug, but she was already in her tough-ass mode and didn't seem to need it. She joined Dr. K at the big soundboard. He gave her a set of headphones and seemed to be teaching her the song that they had already written and produced the tracks for.

"It won't work," I overheard her say. And then a few moments later, "That's not what I want to do."

They seemed to be arguing over the song. Dr. K would try to convince her, and although there was a give-and-take, from my vantage point, she seemed to always get her way. Bennie occasionally joined in to mediate and keep everyone cool.

Up top near the entrance, I sat down next to Max, who appeared to be nodding off. Right behind us was a craft-services table on the back wall, loaded down with fresh fruit, sandwiches, cookies, a full bar, and enough sweets to stock Dylan's Candy Bar for a week. Seriously, there was more food than at my house and almost as much alcohol.

"Okay, this is what I'll do," I heard Tabitha say as they seemed finally to have reached an agreement. Tabitha stood up, and Bennie escorted her to a booth inside the glass room separate from the backup girls. As the mics were turned on, I could hear Tabitha say hi to the girls. They were all very accommodating and sweet, treating her as if she was part of their sorority.

On Dr. K's cue, Tabitha sidled up to the microphone, the way I've seen her do in a dozen music videos, and started to sing. But her voice was thin, even slightly off-key. Not the full-throttle vocals that I've listened to. I mean, I knew kids in my high school choir and had seen many others on YouTube who could sing better. Dr. K stopped her and asked her to try it again.

I peeled the label off my water bottle bit by bit as Dr. K asked her to try again and again, my image of Tabitha Eden, the big-voiced power singer who hit the money notes with phrasing and emotion, crumbling before my eyes.

"So you've never actually had the pleasure of hearing Tabitha sing?" Max asked behind me. He wasn't asleep after all and must have seen how taken aback I was. I didn't know what to say.

"It's not really any worse than the others . . . Katy or Kesha," he said. "Or Fergie, for that matter. Ever watched those YouTube vids of Britney with her onstage mic turned on? I was her lead guitarist on that tour."

"So how does it . . . get better?" I asked, glad that we were outside Tabitha's earshot.

"Auto-Tune—it's like plastic surgery for music, and Bennie usually has some magic synths he comes up with that make it better. But even the good singers would never be able to dance in concert without Auto-Tune."

Tabitha glanced back at me, and I smiled as if everything was great.

"But then if everyone does it, why does she feel so bad about it?" I asked him.

"She shouldn't. Auto-Tune is like an effect that enables her to sing. She just hates the biz. I mean, they drive her hard, but I think they're worried if she stops she'll go off the deep end. And then she's a brand, everyone's making so much money, why stop?"

"Hold on, Tabitha," said Bennie. "I've got a new synth I want you to try." Bennie patched his laptop into the main console, and Dr. K pushed a few buttons. Tabitha nodded and began to sing, but this time it had an even richer texture and was much closer to the voice that I knew from her recordings.

Dr. K brought in the backup singers on the following take. Seemingly out of nowhere, Oleta burst into a rising gospel countermelody and the music came alive with soul, giving the song a feeling it didn't have otherwise. She provided the emotional force that drove the melody, and she knew just exactly how to rock it with her voice, even cracking on the beat. The room was awash in sound—bubbly, infectious, maddeningly danceable, and suddenly soulful. Even Max couldn't help tapping his feet. Then it stopped and started all over again.

Dr. K seemed like the crazy perfectionist, and Bennie, the wild creative genius. He had a new idea every second. It was as if they were all playing chess with riffs, beats, and synths—no real instruments, no real voices beside the backup. In the end, the song would have Tabitha's name all over it. People like me would assume it was all her.

As Tabitha removed her headset and came back into the main room, Brit, the receptionist, left Tabitha another tequila.

"Hey guys, don't you have enough from me?" she asked after a long swallow.

"We need another double," Dr. K said. Tabitha gave him her saddest pout. "Come on, Tabby, we want a hit, baby. Whatcha gotta do today that's more important?" Bennie pleaded. Tabitha threw back the rest of her tequila lemonade.

"Lisbeth and I are supposed to go shopping," she said, as if it was the most serious thing in the world. Bennie laughed. "She's spend-ing the money before we've even made it!"

"Oh, cut it out, you little twerp. If you had any balls, you would come with us and I'd buy you some real clothes, instead of that Old Navy shit you wear. But we'd have to spend some of your vast roy-alty income, and we all know you're too cheap for that."

"Owned," Dr. K said and laughed for the first time all day.

"Okay, okay, I know when I've met my match. We'll double it with Alieya," Bennie said and the short Latina backup girl waved. Tabitha seemed to have no problem having someone else ghost per-form her vocals. "But I'll make a deal with you. If Lisbeth is here next time, I *will* shop with you," Bennie added, giving a smile that I knew was just for me.

"So, can we go?" she asked, on the verge of annoyance. Bennie and the Doc traded glances.

"Sure," Bennie said, "get out of here."

"Ka-ching," Max said. "Another shiny pop performance, a su-percool song, and surefire hit." That seemed perfectly true as far as I was concerned.

"I'll be sure to let the boss know," Doc said, returning to his soundboard.

"Yeah? Well be sure to let him know this, too . . ." Tabitha said, holding her middle finger up. Everyone nodded knowingly.

As Tabitha prepared to leave, Bennie bounded up the stairs and handed me his card.

"Hey Lisbeth, here's my number. I know you'll dig me," Bennie added.

I couldn't help being a little embarrassed.

Tabitha was motioning me from the studio exit to hurry up.

"Shopping time!" she screamed in the fullest voice she had used all session.

34 "La Perla first, the one in SoHo," Tabitha instructed Mocha as soon as we jumped into the limo. "I always seem to be losing my underwear." She giggled. Mocha turned the limo into the traffic and headed toward SoHo.

"The key, darling," I said, "is to keep them on until you get home."

"Yeah, I really should try that, or maybe stuff them in my purse. But sometimes I just don't have time." She shrugged as though she were talking about losing a pair of gloves, a scarf, or sunglasses. Mocha cracked a grin in the rearview mirror. So chauffeurs do hear everything.

"So, you don't hate me?" Tabitha asked, stretching out into the corner of the limo.

"Why on earth would I?" I wondered how much of Tabitha's insecurity I could take, considering there was my own insecurity to deal with. "That was impressive and wonderful."

"Britney's no different, believe me. I sang with her once, and she can't carry a tune in a bucket."

"Ah, yes, that's what Max said."

"Oh. Really?" she said, eyebrows raised. "Well, I guess he should know."

I hoped I hadn't put Max in a bad spot.

"Dear, I'm impressed that you can work with those very talented musicians. The process is mind-boggling," I said, worried that my Audrey sounded a tad old-fashioned.

Tabitha shrugged. The dark cloud that had made her so anxious had lifted now that the studio recording was behind us.

Taking La Perla by storm, Tabitha dropped six thousand dollars on underwear as if she was buying breath mints at the drugstore. I couldn't help but wonder how many mortgage payments my mom would have made with her underwear money.

Walking the aisles, I found a pair of boy shorts that were stretch tulle for $140. I assumed that these magic panties, in addition to conveying visible benefits on the wearer, bestowed confidence, romance, and sensuality, something that I could probably use.

"When was the last time you bought lingerie?" Tabitha asked. I hadn't noticed her step behind me.

"Me? I don't really keep track," I said. Yeah, once at T.J.Maxx, and once Jess and I went to a sample sale—did those count?

"Well, why don't you buy some?"

"I keep my underwear," I said, giving her a disdainful glance and hoping that would put the discussion to rest.

"Tell me the truth, Lisbeth, are you a prude?"

"What? No!" Stunned, it took me a moment to realize that I had become a puzzle for Tabitha to unravel. Being scrutinized, I knew, wouldn't be good for my inner Audrey.

"Well, you live with your grandmother and a nurse. That's kind of old-lady-like," she said.

"Nan is such a dear. It's not like that. She . . . ," I began and trailed off, flustered.

"And you don't seem to get out much," she added. Hey, I'd gone out more times in the last three weeks than I had in my entire life. That did in fact sound kind of spinsterish. *Think Audrey, think Audrey.* At that moment, I saw the two salespeople talking to each other and looking our way. I wondered if we weren't lingering in the lingerie a bit too long. I prayed they would interrupt us.

"I just believe that one should be private and discrete when one is promiscuous," I said finally. "Unlike some people we know."

"Oh, I don't know who you're talking about." Tabitha laughed. "But you know, I don't just buy them for some guy . . . I mean, a little sexy underwear makes me feel confident and alive. Hey aren't you going to that art opening with ZK? So . . . ?" I wouldn't have thought that everyone knew that little piece of information.

My mind was trying to formulate a pithy response when, thankfully, one of the two sales girls approached us. I was still holding the lace shorts and put them down instantly, a reflex born of window-shopping with Jess in stores where we could never afford anything.

"Miss Eden?" the young woman began. "Sorry to intrude, but La Perla would love to gift your companion and wondered if this item might be preferred. Of course, you're free to take anything in the store."

"No, I couldn't," I said, hoping my eyes weren't bugging out. I had never heard the words "free to take anything in the store" before.

"Why not?" Tabitha said. "I certainly spend enough here."

"Any friend of Ms. Eden's . . ." the store clerk began, and in moments I was holding a pretty little white La Perla shopping bag as we exited onto the street.

"Now we'll have to get you a man to go with those," Tabitha said, pleased with herself as we left the store.

Our next stop was Manhattan's Meatpacking District, which typically gets described in the fashion blogs I read as the "Disney World of couture" with so many outposts of fashion labels such as Stella McCartney, Jeffrey, Alexander McQueen, Yigal Azrouël, and tons more, all within a four-block area.

Down the street, we hit a cool boutique where the cheapest thing on the shelves was a plain white cotton T-shirt for $400. Maybe the fabric increased your cup size, or your IQ.

Then we arrived at the DVF store—and I loved it! All the clothes in the store were sorted by color. There were washes of gold, pink, and fuchsia everywhere—the entire place was a work of art, another Diane von Furstenberg masterpiece.

Most of all, it was startling to see how nice all the salespeople were. Whenever Jess and I would go there, the staff was always short-tempered. They seemed to know immediately that we weren't going to buy anything. And if they wanted to be mean, they'd have security follow us. It's amazing how a limo outside and a famous name on a plastic card can get you so much extra service. Tabitha loaded up at both boutiques, and Mocha tossed the bags in the trunk.

More than once, I registered a suspicious sidelong glance from Tabitha. It had literally slipped my mind that Tabitha might actually expect me to *buy* something. It was a bit like not drinking at the bar when everyone else is smashed. And who wants to drink alone? I worried how long I could keep this up.

Returning to the comfy limo, Mocha drove us uptown, and Tabitha shared some of her shopping history with me.

"I've had a stylist and a personal shopper at Barneys since I was ten—Valerie," she said. "I'm excited you're going to meet her. When I was little, I would see her more than I saw my mother. I just never seemed to have enough clothes, so I went to see her a lot." Despite the sad undercurrent, she seemed oddly lighthearted about it all.

I laughed along, but truthfully I'd never even seen Tabitha wear anything more than once. I'd never seen her photographed in the same dress. Her sense of need was clearly different from that of most people on the planet.

"So if your mother wasn't around, who took care of you when you were little?"

"Me and my charge card," she said and let out an awkward laugh. "My mother had this big breakdown after my stepfather left. That was like three husbands ago. She was in rehab a really long time, and she made Robert my guardian until I was eighteen and put him in charge of my trust. All the doctors and lawyers made her do it. Then Robert made himself my business manager. Everything has to be signed by him. He controls all the money. It's been the worst thing."

Tabitha fell silent and gazed out the window. I had a thousand questions, but I didn't want her to start tearing up again. So I stayed quiet for the rest of the ride.

At Barneys, Valerie was ready for us. She had already laid out a collection for Tabitha, and for me as well. The attractive dark-haired woman in her fifties had a Mediterranean complexion. She was somehow both sophisticated and matronly. Utterly attentive, she exuded warmth and understanding while constantly fingering her tortoiseshell glasses on a chain. It was easy to see why Tabitha was so fond of her.

Valerie's assistant, Erica, brought us flutes of champagne as we staged our own little dressing-room fashion show. It reminded me of the times Jess and I invaded her mother's closet and tried on all her mom's dresses, only now we were in Barneys and these dresses cost a fortune. After a glass or two of bubbly, we were both loosening up.

"Ooh, that's stunning on you," Tabitha said to me, eyeing a pale-blue, off-the-shoulder gown that Valerie insisted would be perfect with my skin color.

"Thank you," I said, grabbing a glance at the price tag. For $2,400, it *should* be stunning. At Tabitha's insistence, I tried on everything Valerie had for me: elegant wide-legged pants, a body-skimming silver dress, and blue suede stilettos. I couldn't help but do the math in the dressing room while Valerie's assistant returned with more champagne. I had just tried on $37,000's worth of clothes.

As I modeled a beaded blue chiffon blouse with exquisite ruching in the dressing room, Tabitha noticed my bracelet. Before I knew it, she was holding my wrist up to the light, examining it.

"How unusual," she said, twisting it on my wrist. "Understated but dazzling. Is it platinum?"

"Yes." I had forgotten about Nan's bracelet. I was already used to wearing it.

"It's so mysterious . . . just like you, Lisbeth," she said, smiling.

"Honestly, dear, I don't try to be," I replied.

"I know. You just are," she said and gave me a hug. I was growing to like Tabitha, despite the strangeness of her mood swings and insecurity. Somehow, she unequivocally accepted me for whoever I was. Like a child, she seemed naive to ulterior motives. We had truly developed a friendship. The mysteries about her mom, her loneliness, made me want to take care of her.

Valerie was over-the-top with enthusiasm for a lilac dress that she had given Tabitha to try on, but I had my doubts. When Tabitha came out wearing it, I could see that it was totally wrong for her. It wasn't that she couldn't wear the color, it just wasn't her shade. It's interesting to me how often people don't know their colors. I guess I had consumed enough champagne and was comfortable enough around Tabitha that my guard was down. For some reason, I started blurting out my opinion on everything.

"It's a lovely dress, but perhaps you should reconsider whether it's right for you," I said, assuming I was out of earshot of Valerie. Tabitha looked at me with surprise. It seemed as though she was disturbed that anyone could doubt Valerie, which would explain some of the less-sophisticated choices Tabitha wore in the photos on the gossip blogs.

"What do you mean?" After another sip of champagne, I figured I might as well go for it. "Lilac isn't really your color, and the dress cuts you right across the bust, a very unflattering silhouette," I concluded. When an alarmed look crossed Tabitha's face, I realized that Valerie was standing right behind me, and I regretted my words immediately.

I turned to Valerie to apologize. "I am *terribly* sorry. I'm sure you know better," I said and braced myself for a dressing down. Valerie seemed to be trying to regroup. It dawned on me that if Tabitha had a personal shopper since she was ten, and her mother hadn't been around, she may not have thought about her look independently for a long time. Valerie was her only support, her trusted advisor, and I certainly hadn't intended to interfere. I watched as Valerie put on her cherished glasses and examined the dress again.

"She's right, Tabitha," Valerie said after a moment. "I'm not sure why I never saw that before." Tabitha brightened. "Your friend Lisbeth is quite astute," she continued. "Do you have any other suggestions?"

"Well, do you mind me adding?" I waited for the nod from Valerie. "You might try mixing and matching a bit more, like this Dolce and Gabbana blouse with this piece," I said, grabbing a vintage skirt from a nearby table that was part of a window display they were putting together. I couldn't believe I was acting like such an expert. It was so much fun to get my hands on these clothes and play with them.

"It's nice to see you with such an intelligent and sensitive friend," Valerie said to Tabitha. "And she has such a terrific sense of design." Tabitha glowed instinctively, as if she had been singled out herself.

"You do have the most incredible taste," Tabitha said, relieved that Valerie had given me the seal of approval. "You just see stuff and put it together. No wonder your fashion blog is so incredible."

"Fashion blog?" Valerie asked.

"Yes, Valerie, Lisbeth is that Shades of Limelight blog," Tabitha said. "Isak Guerrere loves it."

"I'm sorry, I haven't heard of that one, but I have to admit I'm a bit of a Luddite," she said. "I will *definitely* look it up."

"Thank you," I said.

"And I'll make a note to the marketing department to send you some samples to review," she said and scribbled herself a note. "You never know, they may even ask you to consult for us."

Consult? Me? Hmmm, I could only hope.

Moments later, Tabitha strutted in front of the mirror in a jade-green romper with knee-high boots. "So, which ones are you getting?" she asked, looking at her hips in the mirror. "You absolutely *have* to get the silver dress. I'm not letting you leave the store without it."

"I'm not sure," I said, trying to think of any excuse she might believe other than "I only have thirty-seven dollars in my purse, and my credit cards couldn't pay for this even if they weren't maxed out." My skin flushed, embarrassed that window-shopping wasn't going to cut it any longer.

"And you absolutely *have* to have those shoes."

When Valerie returned for Tabitha's clothes, Tabitha said simply, "I'll take them all, except the lilac dress of course," and gave me a nod.

Then Valerie turned to me, awaiting my choices. I was tongue-tied. They expected an answer.

"Lisbeth will take the silver dress and the leopard heels," Tabitha jumped in.

Valerie quickly whisked the dress and shoes out of my dressing room and took them to the counter. Tabitha changed back into her clothes, and we walked over to the counter to pay.

How would I get out of this? I struggled for the barest hint of a plan. I put my bag on the counter and began digging through it and was struck with an idea.

"It was here a moment ago," I said, just loud enough that Tabitha could hear. Then I gave Tabitha a desperate look. "Shoot," I said, rifling through my bag. "It's gone!" Valerie wasn't sure what was happening. But she registered my alarm. "I can't find my wallet!" I said.

"Did you misplace it somewhere here?" Valerie asked.

"I wouldn't think so," I said, feigning distress. "I'm sure I had it earlier." I was getting so worked up, even I thought I might manage to burst out in tears.

"Are you okay?" Tabitha asked.

"Do you think it could have been stolen?" Valerie asked.

"I just don't know," I said. "It's not about the money or the cards. It's that the wallet was a gift." Meanwhile, I had been digging in my bag so long, I couldn't help actually coming across my actual wallet, but I kept that to myself.

"Well, let me call Security immediately," Valerie said. She turned to pick up a phone nearby.

"I'm so embarrassed. I don't want to inconvenience anyone," I said. "I was certain I took it this morning, but maybe when I changed handbags? Or did I drop it at the studio? No need to bother Security."

"I'll call Mocha now to check with the studio," Tabitha said.

"It's not a problem, dear. Security will be here in a moment. Meanwhile, Erica . . . ? Please check everywhere," Valerie said, and Erica, her assistant, began assiduously checking every corner of the dressing area for a wallet she'd never find.

"Perhaps it would be best if you wouldn't mind holding these, and I'll just come back later."

"Absolutely," Valerie said. Ah, finally, my plan worked. No harm, no foul.

"No, no, don't worry," Tabitha insisted matter-of-factly. "Just add her things to my tab." Ugh, that was considerably worse.

"Oh no, you shouldn't," I said, yanking the shoes and the silver dress away from the counter.

Tabitha shrugged. "It's really no big deal." Valerie reached out her hands for the dress and shoes. I felt like a deer caught in the headlights. After a few agonizing seconds, I handed them over. It was so unfair—two against one.

"I promise to pay you back," I said and bit my tongue, literally, wishing I could swallow those words as soon as they left my mouth. Only someone without money worries about her friend buying her something when she doesn't have the cash to pay for it. Wealthy people simply don't worry about such things. I had outed myself. What a mess. Tabitha regarded me with concern. I didn't see a way out of this. I summoned my saddest face, hoping to distract her.

"Lisbeth, it's okay. I'm sure we'll find your wallet," she said. "And if I can't buy my friends something, what good is all the money? I'm sure you'll return the favor someday," she said.

"Valerie, ring them up."

"You simply don't have to," I said.

"Don't be silly," Tabitha said, "it's nothing."

It's not nothing, I thought. *It's five thousand dollars.*

35 With my wallet charade behind me, Tabitha and I could both relax. Tabitha seemed to forget my faux pas immediately, no longer self-conscious that I wasn't buying anything. Now she could get down to seriously splashing the cash on Fifth Ave.

During this shopathon with Tabitha, I discovered an aspect of shopping I never knew existed—shoptailing—the art of shopping while partaking of numerous cocktails. Forget *Breakfast at Tiffany's*— think *Champagne at Versace*. Barneys was just the beginning. Leave it to Tabitha to discover how willing merchants were to ply their clients with champagne and martinis to lubricate their shopping desires. And we're not talking about your standard Jersey drunken mall crawl. Tabitha threw herself into such a frenzy of buying and drinking that surely she would wake up from a shopping coma at some point wondering why she bought all of this stuff. On the other hand, her closet was likely already overflowing with tons of purchases that she wouldn't have a clue where or why she bought.

I smiled and declined to imbibe. Besides, I had found a better way to get high. As we waltzed through Fendi and Cartier, then Prada and Gucci, I stopped worrying about my worthless credit card. I couldn't even buy what the shopgirls were wearing, but I could steal pure nirvana under the bright lights of Fifth Avenue's impressive shops.

I sauntered through the artfully displayed stacks of clothing, each item an example of the world's most incredible designers and craftspeople. The entire history of Western civilization sewn into every stitch, polished into every jewel, filling up every room.

I put on an air, poised and aloof like a discerning collector who deigned not stoop to purchase. These were places "where nothing bad could happen to you," as Audrey said in *Breakfast at Tiffany's*, the sure cure for the mean reds, the evil yellows, the blues, and everything else that made you pull out your hair. Even the haughty mannequins seemed like approving gatekeepers.

Judging by these stores, the world was an intelligent, exquisitely tasteful place, with no detail too small to refine. Here, designers and craftspeople infused mere everyday garments—a shirt, a skirt, a pair of flats—with creativity and perfection. While my friend Tabitha bought the store wholesale and pounded back the cocktails, I floated in therapeutic retail bliss. No one knew my wallet was empty but me.

The D&G Fifth Avenue store was a wonder. Shop clerks arranged even the hangers an equal distance apart. I learned from Jess how bold and wonderfully structured their clothes were, and I had also posted a little blog entry on their silk Le Smoking blouse. A pair of beige stiletto peep-toes shot through with chocolate brown and gold piping fascinated me. With all of my Designer X couture, shoes were the missing element we were still looking for.

Tabitha noticed the store manager talking to her staff as we were preparing to leave. A slightly older woman, better dressed, joined them. They were chatting away in hushed tones.

"Lisbeth, this is so weird," she said. "But I think they're talking about you." Immediately, I became paranoid.

"Why on earth would they?" I said, pretending nonchalance.

Tabitha giggled. She found this amusing, I assumed, because usually they would be talking about her—after all, she was the celebrity.

"I think they think you're reviewing their store," she whispered.

"Why? I mean, how could they . . . ?"

"You don't have any idea, do you? Don't you realize your pix have been reposted everywhere? My fans even ask about you, and they're like twelve." She smiled so broadly, I could tell that she felt the association with my blog gave her special props. If anyone knew what a schlumpy nobody from South End I was, they'd change their mind instantly.

"Well, that's perfectly flattering, but I never intended to make such a splash," I said.

"It doesn't hurt that there are shots of us together on the Web, I assume," she added.

As the older woman walked over to us, I couldn't help noticing her shoes. She wore leopard-print, sky-high stilettos, but her stride was as firm as if she were wearing army boots.

"Pardon me?" she said. "I hope I'm not being presumptive, but would you be Lisbeth Dulac?"

"Of course she is," Tabitha blurted out. She was tipsy as all get-out.

"Well, I'm the head of Dolce and Gabbana in-store marketing. We're just enormous fans of your blog." She waited for me to answer, but I stood in stunned silence. In retrospect, I realized that she interpreted my silence as being haughty.

"Well," she said after a moment that seemed to last forever, "we would like to provide you with a few samples of our new line of handbags." With a finger snap, she signaled the store manager waiting attentively in the background, and instantly an army of store clerks brought out six shopping bags filled with the very latest D&G handbags.

As I stood there speechless, everyone was waiting for me to say something. Tabitha gave me a little kick, and I blinked.

"I know a critic of your integrity may not accept gifts," the woman continued, undaunted, as if she were presenting to a CEO of some important organization, "so naturally we will be glad to have them picked up after you have had a chance to peruse them."

"Why, thank you," I managed to stutter out. She seemed greatly relieved that I had broken my silence.

"That's absolutely wonderful," she said and held out a little black and gold D&G card. "If you have any questions or ever feel as if you might like to keep any of the bags, please don't hesitate to call on me. Can we help you out to your car?"

As the army of store clerks swept us and our loot out of the store, I noticed the woman in the leopard stilettos glancing back at her store manager, who nodded emphatically as she hung up the phone. It seemed an odd thing at that moment. I don't know why, but I wondered who they could be calling. We spun through the revolving doors, having no idea what was waiting for us outside.

For maybe two seconds, it felt as if we were in the middle of a TMZ video. Ten or more burly leather-jacketed men with cameras poured out of cars as they skidded to the curb, shouting and snapping pictures of us like sharks devouring guppies. At first, I felt excited that everyone was making such a fuss, but that changed quickly. As the mob of paparazzi attacked, we found ourselves in the equivalent of a slow-motion car wreck.

"Chill out. Guys, chill out," Tabitha said calmly. So many more of them were taking pictures of her. I guessed she was used to it. I wondered where Mocha was.

"Hey, Tabitha, how have you been?" one shouted as if he actually knew her.

"Sing for us, Tabitha," another said.

"Give me a break," she said.

A crowd of tourists gathered and through the flashes of light I saw Chase with a crew standing outside Harry Winston, across the street. Would he swoop down on us, too? After all, he was one of them. As I saw Mocha aggressively working his way through the thick crowd, I held one of the D&G bags in front of my face.

"Hey, Tabby, who's your new girlfriend?" one guy asked, and I wondered what that meant. A camera flash went off almost point-blank in my eyes, and I began to panic.

"Back off!" I heard her say. I worried Tabitha would slug some-one in a drunken rage. We were jostled, mauled, and surrounded. There was no way out. Being photographed seemed beside the point. It flew through my mind that the stiletto-heeled marketing director had contrived this entire sequence to get these photographs, regard-less of whether I reviewed her bags or not.

"We're just doing our job, Miss Eden," someone shouted. In the darkening light, the flashes were dizzying, like a strobe, and I was losing my balance.

As one of the beefiest of photographers walked right up to me with his camera poised to flash, I grabbed one of the D&G bags to shield my eyes. He gripped my arm, pulled the bag away, and shoved his camera up to my face. The flash stunned me, and I stumbled. I saw the sidewalk before I crashed.

But nothing happened.

When I opened my eyes, I found myself looking at Chase. He was holding me up. In the chaos, I hadn't even seen him slip in. He unceremoniously set me on my feet, as one of his crew held a giant white card, those big sheets of foam board they carry for video shoots, to protect us and give us room to recover.

The paparazzo tried to squeeze around, but Mocha had finally broken through and was standing guard. He seemed ready to throw a punch. Chase stepped in front of Tabitha and me as they removed the card.

"Dude, you're ruining the shot," one of the men said.

"This is my interview," Chase said, and though he was a pipsqueak compared to the hefty photographers, he didn't seem like he was bluffing.

"Who the hell are you?" another photographer asked as Mocha started shooing away the rest of them.

"Love you, Tabitha," the beefy guy said as he left. As if. Chase and his crew began gathering their gear.

"Thanks, Chase," I said, embarrassed, trying to pull myself together.

"I've seen you before," Tabitha asked suspiciously.

"I'm a fashion shooter for Lux." Chase gave me a conspiratorial wink. "I just wanted to make sure you guys were all right. I've got to get back to a shoot across the street."

His phone buzzed.

"Shit. Here now?" He looked up, and I saw the stunned expression on his face and what he was looking at—Dahlia Rothenberg and her entourage approaching.

Dahlia wore a tight beige skirt with towering heels and a see-through blouse under a YSL boyfriend jacket—it screamed money, power broker, and sex in the same breath. There was a makeup person trying to catch up behind her. As she made long, elegant strides our way, I could see the curl of her wicked smile. I wanted to run.

"Lisbeth, nice to see you," she said, swooping in, her eyes all daggers. "Slumming with our little Tabby?"

Chase leapt to make amends. "My apologies, Miss Rothenberg. We had just set up for you when we saw . . ." But Dahlia walked right past him.

"It's nice to see you're finally getting a touch of class, Tabby, trying to buy something with taste instead of wearing those slutsuits you usually wear." Mysteriously silent, Tabitha seemed easily intimidated by Dahlia. Then again, Dahlia rendered everyone speechless, and you could see the satisfaction on her face. We had just been through this crazy situation, yet she managed to make us feel apologetic. For reasons unclear to me, I felt uncharacteristically obligated to stand up for all of us.

I took a deep breath and did my best to channel Holly Golightly at her most flamboyant. "I'm so sorry, Dahlia," I began. "We've just had the most ghastly time at Dolce and Gabbana, not a bit 'dolce,' I'm afraid." Then, dipping into Holly Golightly's goofy French, "The entire mise-en-scène was *très fou,* but nothing more *fou* than this little paparazzi disaster. Please accept our apologies for the delay."

Dahlia was stunned. Either she was aghast at my backbone, offended by my mangled French, or thought I was plain crazy. But who cares? When you have nothing to lose, you have everything to gain, I guess. After all, I was just a Jersey girl. I recognized that our little Fifth Avenue confrontation was essentially the same trash talk that went down in the girls' locker room at Montclair High, only we were wearing better clothes.

Dahlia took the longest time glaring at me, hoping I'd sizzle to vapor, I suppose. If I hadn't just rambled on in the silliest way, I assume, I would have. But on this strangest of days, I had something I don't think I've ever had before—audacity. *Why the effin' not?* I thought. I wanted to make the sign of the horns and dance around her sorry ass like some football player who's made it to the end zone.

"Well, thank you, Lisbeth," she said finally, regaining her composure. "Chase, come along. I only have a few moments now, or we'll have to reschedule." She spun around and walked back toward Harry Winston, awkwardly waiting to cross the street with Chase following obediently behind her.

Tabitha seemed dazed as we piled into the limo and headed "home" to East Seventy-seventh Street. We sunk back into the black leather seats, and she looked at me with a sense of admiration, it seemed. I felt for a moment like the older sister I never had. As Mocha pulled up to the Mark, I stopped worrying about my fake address and told him to let me off by the lobby. He deposited the Dolce & Gabbana handbags inside with the young hotel doorman's help. Tabitha hardly noticed me leave—she was pretty hung over anyway.

There I sat in the middle of the Mark Hotel lobby with all those bags and not a clue where I should go or what I should do. I felt only disgust for the D&G marketing woman and these handbags that were likely worth thousands of dollars. I considered hocking them on eBay. I remembered the little black and gold card in my purse, and the tiniest thought occurred to me. I rose, and the attentive doorman sprinted over immediately.

"Can I be of service?" he asked.

"Would you retrieve an item I checked?" I asked, handing him the ticket from the concierge. "And also if you wouldn't mind, please call the number on this card and have them collect these bags? I'd be so grateful."

"Certainly," he said.

I smiled in thanks and he tipped his hat.

I stepped through the doors onto the street with my tiny white La Perla bag and my clothing bag and headed home feeling like a million dollars.

36

Once in the eleventh grade, I attended an art opening at my high school in South End Montclair. They hung paintings and drawings all the way up to the ceiling in the main entranceway of the school for a night. I think they even served juice and Coke. The kids who were good at drawing were buzzing with self-importance. Some of them were pretty talented.

This one guy made these dot paintings that were almost like opti-
cal illusions, sort of ethereal visions of heaven that he called
Change, Loss, Memory and AIDs. Then there was this girl who spe-
cialized in photographs of roadkill, mostly deer and rabbits. Sometimes she'd frame the actual flattened creature next to the
photograph. I'm not sure what that statement was supposed to
mean, but it started smelling pretty funky after a while. That's
what I used to consider an art opening.

Wrong.

Actually, I had never really been to an art opening before. Think
fashion, celebs, glamour—a "Schnabel opening," at the Mary
Boone Gallery in Chelsea, was more like a Hollywood premiere.

El Schnabel, as ZK referred to him, would be the larger-than-
life artist Julian Schnabel, as I discovered in a Guest of a Guest
post. The bearded, barrel-chested, sixty-something art provocateur
was famous for painting with broken pottery on giant canvases and
making art-savvy movies that never quite made it to the Clearview
Clairidge Cinema near me. Fashion-wise, he attended art openings
in his jammies and slippers, wearing yellow-tinted sunglasses,
looking like a homeless bum out squandering his lottery winnings.
He was also ZK's godfather.

ZK effortlessly swept us through the throngs standing outside,
who stared at us like deer in the headlights of an onrushing
sixteen-wheeler of boho-chic wealth and status. Art openings were
challenging for even the most dedicated celebrity stalkers because
the superstar art attendees tended to be better disguised and more
clandestine. We brushed past the Olsen twins, those trench-coated
spies from the Kingdom of Anorexia.

Holding on to ZK's arm, I felt content to be completely swept up
in his graceful motion as he expertly navigated the gallery overflowing with guests.

Inside, boldfaced names were sprinkled generously throughout
the crushing crowd. My heart skipped as I brushed past James Franco
wearing a knitted hipster beanie and holding a plastic cup of white

wine. Even Courtney Love struggled to get to the main gallery. She wore a strapless white Vivienne Westwood dress that she had crammed herself into, looking like she would spontaneously combust, and railed at a security guard for not giving her better access.

I noticed that ZK seemed to make eye contact with a few key individuals as we moved forward. Some seemed to be security and some didn't, but his eye contact miraculously parted the waves of people, enabling us to smoothly enter the very center of the gallery without pausing for a second. He had so much grace and bearing, everyone seemed to make way for him.

We came upon a thin old guy in bleached-white skinny pants and a white shirt that matched his shock of white hair. He seemed familiar, but I couldn't place him at first. ZK offered a quick bow, and the man smiled approvingly, then nodded hello to me before we plunged farther into the exclusive back room.

"What an interesting-looking man," I said. "He looks like an old version of that Talking Heads guy," I whispered in ZK's ear.

"That is the Talking Heads guy," ZK chuckled.

"Oh," I said, feeling instantly embarrassed.

How would I keep up with ZK? Despite Tabitha's wealth and fabulous music career, she wasn't particularly sophisticated. ZK, on the other hand, was utterly well educated and connected. He was a consummate player, moving in and out of every strata of high society. I simply didn't have the background to play on his level.

My phone buzzed, and I took a quick glimpse to see who it was. Mom. I ignored it, turned off the phone, and buried it in my purse.

We reached the room within the room within the gallery. This space wasn't actually part of the show. The walls were covered with huge canvasses and works of art of all kinds. It was so small it almost felt like someone's office. It was *the* most exclusive place you could be in that moment. ZK and I were standing close enough to kiss. I took time to breathe him in, having dreamed of being this close to him ever since I saw him outside the Met, which now seemed like a lifetime ago. He smelled delicious, like apples and wine.

"You know, you're bewildering," he said with that self-amused expression of his. "In some ways, you seem far older than your years, and in other ways, you seem as if you've been in hiding your whole life."

"Can't I be both?" I asked.

He grinned and took my chin in his hand, lifting my head until I was looking into his eyes. I trembled, wondering if he would kiss me right there in front of everyone and what I would do if he did. A shrill cackle broke our moment, rising above all the chatter in the room. It was immediately recognizable as the icy laugh of Dahlia Rothenberg.

She wore a Hervé Léger bandage dress so sleek and minimal that it was hard to call it a dress. What does it feel like to be almost naked among so many people? Her admirers didn't mind. Men flocked around her as she talked, the center of attention. I hoped to duck her scrutiny, but within seconds her eyebrows arched as she observed ZK and me standing arm in arm. I felt myself shrinking from her penetrating glare.

"Mr. Northcott!" someone yelled from across the room, mercifully diverting us. An attractive young man with an open face, ringed by Renaissance curls of brown hair, waved us over. I gladly followed ZK away from Dahlia's intense stare. The two men greeted each other with a big hug.

"Good to see you, Mr. Schnabel," ZK said. This was odd. Where was El Schnabel, the PJ-wearing master painter? This Mr. Schnabel was well dressed and elegant and too young to be a godfather. His eyes lit up as he saw me.

"And this must be the lovely Lisbeth Dulac," he said. "ZK has told me so much about you." I couldn't help feeling a bit confused as he bent down for a hand kiss, barely suppressing a schoolboy giggle. ZK smiled broadly, hardly able to hold back his laughter.

"Do tell," I said, withdrawing my hand. "What would you two find so humorous?"

"Maybe you were expecting someone older and perhaps wider?" the young man with the Roman curls asked, self-amused. I hesitantly nodded agreement.

"That would be my father," he said gleefully. "I guess it would have gone over better if I had worn my PJs?"

"Sorry Lisbeth," ZK said. "It's an old joke of ours."

"Allow me to introduce myself," the man said with a flourish. "Vito Schnabel. ZK and I have been best friends since Saint Ann's in Brooklyn . . . playing hooky, getting high, and sneaking into a thousand crazy parties and openings, and . . . what can I say, making silly jokes."

"Of course," I said and managed to smile.

"Will you forgive us?" ZK said, putting his arm snuggly around me in a way that felt delicious.

"So are you a fan of my father's work or is ZK just showing you off?" Vito asked, but then stopped abruptly and elbowed ZK.

"Um, Dahlia is . . . here."

She was already upon us, looking as if she was about to crush the little plastic wine cup in her hand.

"Dahlia, it's . . . so good to see you," ZK began, dropping his arm from my waist. But Dahlia ignored him and turned her laser focus on me.

"You've been such a bad little mouse," she said in a quiet voice that only I could hear. I could see in her eyes that she hadn't forgiven me from the day before at Dolce & Gabbana. I struggled to sustain my poise. She leaned closer.

"Social climbing by nicking my boy?"

She waited for a response, but I didn't have one.

"No clever quip this time? I'm not surprised. You're out of your league," she said and briefly glanced back at ZK. "He'll be bored and unfaithful by the end of the evening."

She turned to leave, and ZK grabbed her arm.

"Dahlia, be reasonable," he said.

"ZK, I am always prepared to be reasonable when the situation demands," she answered, then threw her cup of red wine across his shirt and casually walked away.

"Oops," she said over her shoulder, smiling.

37 Swooping in, Vito whisked me away before I could say anything to ZK, who had scurried after Dahlia.

"There's something I have to show you," he said. I tried to track ZK as Vito escorted me across the room. "Have you seen Terence Koh's white cock? It's quite famous."

"Pardon, I'm sorry, what did you say?"

He had walked me across the room. "Look."

Gazing up, I saw mounted high on the brick wall the shape of a giant rooster outlined in neon tubing. I turned to catch a glance of ZK, but he was gone.

"Watch, it lights up!" he said, flipping a switch, and the rooster hummed, flickered, and flashed on, casting a white glow down on us. The joke was less than stellar even under the best of circumstances. To his credit, Vito seemed to know it was lame, but was intent on distracting me.

Vito's cell phone buzzed. As he answered, I knew it was ZK.

"Yes, no problem," Vito said. "Yes, she's fine." He closed his phone.

"Is he all right?" I asked.

"Of course! ZK is a pro. He's had wine thrown in his face by the best."

Why was that so not reassuring?

"He'd like us to meet him at the after party at my father's house. He's on his way there now. For a change of clothes," he added.

Everyone was leaving, anyway. The visitors to the inner sanctum of Mary Boone Gallery were decamping en masse. Vito and I became part of an army of chic revelers, plastic cups of wine in hand, awaiting a limo to make our way downtown.

As our limo stopped at the giant Pepto-Bismol-colored building known as Palazzo Chupi, Vito told me the history of the old perfume factory that his father had bought and transformed into a palace, part art studio and part condo with a triplex penthouse. It was a giant Italian-looking pink building built on top of another building.

"This is my father's Moby Dick, if Moby Dick was pink," Vito said, laughing.

"Everyone thinks Dad lost money on it, but they're wrong," he added, as if I doubted him. I had never heard of it before. All I knew was that if Barbie had a Dreamhouse in Italy, it would look like this.

As soon as we passed through the nondescript wooden doors, we entered a world of visual extravagance. The ceiling was double height, and the walls were rough-hewn clapboard. My heels clacked against the black-and-white ceramic tiles, and there was a floor-to-ceiling painting splashed with bright reds, yellows, and blues. I wished Jess could see it so she could explain what it all meant. We took the elevator up to the top floor.

Entering his father's penthouse, the huge fourteen-foot walls progressed from turquoise green to a faded mint and finally a wash of fuchsia. Against these colorful walls, the enormous art appeared even more intense. The paintings were just unbelievably large.

The size of the place made me feel very small and, without ZK, very alone. I didn't feel brave anymore. As nice as Vito was, I didn't actually know anyone here, and I wasn't sure I wanted to stay. The image of ZK running after Dahlia lingered in my mind. With a promise to find ZK, Vito, too, was gone.

Taking a glass of champagne from a waiter, I toasted my dubious achievement of living my dreams by pretending to be someone I wasn't and felt a little better. I gazed over downtown Manhattan from the grand black-and-white tiled rooftop terrace. There were sweeping views of the Hudson River, where a lighted barge made its slow way down to the Statue of Liberty. To the north, I took in the illuminated architecture that made New York City seem like a fairyland at night.

Celebrities I had seen on the blogs streamed in: Susan Sarandon, Sofia Coppola and her boyfriend, Naomi Campbell, Sean Penn, Scarlett Johansson, and Courtney Love spilling out of her dress, looking like the oldest swinger ever. Everyone crammed onto the gorgeous terrace with its solid pink wall and magnificent views.

I heard a high-pitched squeal that resembled my name and turned to see Tabitha running my way. I was so happy to see her. We hugged.

"How's the big date?" she asked. I couldn't help looking disappointed.

"Dahlia threw a fit?" she said. "Classic. Dahlia rules ZK. Didn't you know?"

"No, I didn't quite," I said, although I was lying. I had seen them together before, and of course I let myself believe that something was possible, despite the obvious. I felt foolish.

"You know ZK doesn't have any real money." *Really? Neither do I,* was all I could think. Sometimes when you hear something bad about someone you're crushing on, it makes you want them more. Besides, wasn't he more accessible to me if he didn't have money?

"His father is one of those Madoff Millionaires, and they used to be one of the wealthiest families in America. That's why he doesn't stay around very long. He only goes where the money is," Tabitha added. Well he was certainly making a mistake with me.

"Yes, well, I suppose," I said, trying to sound above it all as if I understood, but wishing ZK would show up soon and tell me something that would give me hope again.

Drinks appeared, and as we talked I realized that Tabitha and I had grown comfortable together. Incredible when you think that the only person I'd stayed close to my entire life was Jess. Catching up with Tabitha was good, until her expression turned serious.

"I need to talk to you privately," she said, giving a quick glance around. Her mood had shifted, and she seemed troubled. Grabbing my hand, she walked me across the terrace to a turquoise and pink alcove that was filled with one giant painting. The French words *"je ne"* were roughly painted in black across massive blue and white brushstrokes on a color-washed canvas followed by another word: *"rien."* Tabitha was all seriousness now, not a trace of the bubbly Pop Princess.

"My mother's husband just passed away—just the latest. Mother seems to have a knack for choosing husbands that drop dead."

"I'm so sorry to hear that."

"It's okay. I only met him once. He was incredibly wealthy, as if my mother needed more money. Unfortunately, she postponed her trip again," she said. "And I have to do something about my situation. I hate asking you to do this."

I nodded. *Do what?* I had a sinking feeling about this. My eyes wandered to the canvas behind her. *"Je ne ... rien"*—something about those words seemed familiar.

"Will you talk to him? He said he'd meet with you."

I dug deep into my memory of high school French. *"Je ne ... rien"*—"I do . . . not." I do not . . . what?

"Talk to who?" I asked, distracted.

"Robert, of course," she said. "I'm just asking as a friend. Robert has said he'll talk to you about my demands. I think he's willing to step aside."

"Shouldn't you hire a lawyer or something?" I asked.

"Never mind," Tabitha said. "You don't have to." She seemed to be on the verge of tears again.

"I'm sorry, Tabitha. I didn't mean to be insensitive."

"You don't realize that when you showed up, my life changed." She grabbed my hand and squeezed it tightly. I guess that was true for both of us. "I don't trust anyone else."

I felt so bad for her. I wanted to make her feel better. I hugged her, and somehow it reminded me of the days when Courtney and I were close. When we were little, she was a tough older sister who was always protective of me. But those days were long gone.

"I've never had a friend like you before," she said, tears filling her eyes, "someone substantial, someone independent."

I hugged her. I knew I should feel proud that she looked up to me as an example. Yet I knew that if Tabitha ever found out that I had lied to her from the first instant we met, it was certain she would feel betrayed and hate me more than all the people she feared. And if she realized I was a nobody fake from South End Montclair, she'd be disgusted.

But even if we lived worlds apart, I knew that feeling of desperation and having nowhere to turn. I gazed up at the painting as we hugged, and I realized the word that was missing. "*Je ne regrette rien,*" which means, "I don't regret anything at all." The words were from a famous Edith Piaf song. I knew the song because Mrs. Lederer, my high school French teacher, would play it over and over for us.

"I'll talk to him," I said. Tabitha turned away, wiping the tears from her face.

"You're sure?"

"Absolutely, darling. I'll help you any way I can." I felt as if there was nothing else I could say.

"Thank you, Lisbeth. You're the only one I could turn to. Everyone except you is such a total liar."

"Yes, of course," I mumbled in a daze. If she told me how wonderful I was one more time, I'd vomit. I felt like a total and complete fraud because, let's face it, I was.

"Okay, I'll text you the address tomorrow."

"Tomorrow?"

I tried not to panic.

"Is that too soon?"

"No, it's fine."

"Great! Well, let's go find ZK and get another drink," she said, instantly brightening. She was in her bubbly-party-girl mode again.

Across the terrace, ZK was wearily heading our way. Despite my better thoughts, I wanted to hold him. I wanted to tell him everything.

38

"Lisbeth, would you mind if I had a word with you?" ZK asked. His impeccable white shirt had been replaced by another identical impeccable white shirt. Looking more handsome than ever against the turquoise and pink alcove wall behind him, he still seemed exhausted.

"See you two," Tabitha said. "Don't mess with my girl, ZK." He nodded.

"Be careful," she whispered to me before leaving.

ZK and I sat close on the love seat, watching the party unfold. He was quiet.

I peered inside my purse and turned my cell phone back on. It buzzed repeatedly. I saw that all the messages were from Mom, six of them.

Sitting under the painting with the cryptic French words, *"Je ne rien."* I felt very *rien* at the moment. The lively partygoers with their outbursts of spontaneous laughter contrasted severely with our subdued and utter silence.

Seriousness pooled in his hazel eyes. No matter, he was still pleasing to look at. Searching for any imperfection, I found none. There was no blemish, no freckles, only a tiny scar above his left brow, but even that seemed perfect.

"I should have known better," he said, tugging at the cuff of his sleeve, adjusting it, pulling at his jacket and readjusting it as he spoke.

"You mean being with me tonight?" I asked.

"No." He seemed annoyed at the thought. I'm certain he saw the skeptical expression on my face. He went back to adjusting his cuff and then his jacket sleeve until it was perfect.

"I meant getting involved with her to begin with."

"Why? She's elegant, obviously intelligent, and . . ."

"Quite wealthy," he finished my sentence. "I do admire her. She knows what she wants and gets it. I'm just not that way."

"Which part?" I asked.

"Let's see, you choose: her wealth, getting what she wants, and my utter lack of ambition."

"Phew, that's a long list to choose from," I said, and he laughed, flashing that million-dollar smile for a split second.

"Well, I think we should start with my utter lack of ambition," he said. "That's the most intractable problem."

"Why did you run after her?"

"To tell her again what I've told her before."

"And that was?"

"That we're finished. She never believes me."

Well, given a chance, I would raise my hand to be a member of the club that would never let him go.

"I'm so sick of living here. This city is old news," he said. "I had an offer to move to L.A. I should have taken it."

"Really? You'd leave everyone you know in New York?" I asked.

"Lisbeth, I live in a tiny fishbowl where everybody knows everything about my family, my love life, my net worth. You've managed to stay off the radar. I envy you." Try living most of your life in South End.

"So, Dahlia is a more formidable 'force of nature' than you expected?"

"I'm sorry I thought I could handle her," he said. "The problem is Dahlia thinks like a man. She thinks she can have whoever she wants whenever she wants." ZK exhaled, exasperated, and I noticed something I hadn't noticed before.

There was a haunted aspect to his eyes that struck me as lonely. Could the most dashing and sought-after bachelor in Manhattan feel that alone? On the couch, our fingertips made the briefest of contact, and flickers of warmth sparked beneath my skin. Startled, I drew away. ZK's pleading eyes met mine. We both felt it. That much was clear. But I also felt wary and over my head.

"It's okay," I said. "You don't have to put yourself through this for me."

"Don't say that," he said, looking orphaned. I moved my hand toward his, and he held it gently. His soft hands felt warm; I sighed, hoping it wasn't noticeable.

"You know what's funny?" he asked.

"Nothing appears funny at the moment, do tell," I answered. The night had turned so completely serious, not my Audrey fantasy at all, and I felt hugely guilty. I was play-acting, and this guy, who seemed above and beyond me, was spilling his heart out, having sacrificed a relationship with one of the wealthiest, most dazzling women in America. A relationship that perhaps he and his family needed.

"The funny thing is that the person who will be most disappointed is my father."

"Really? Has he been vicariously living off your love life?" ZK gave me the most confused expression. "I was just making a joke," I said biting my lip, "maybe not a good one."

"If you knew my father, you'd know how utterly serious and demanding he is. My father expected a bit more of me."

"Expectations are overwhelming," I said. "I had a mother like that." Oh great, now I was speaking about my mother in the past tense. I must have become light-headed with all the stress.

For a moment, he became extraordinarily serious, as if he were calculating something in his head. I thought he might be tempted to tell me the secret I already knew, about his family's recent troubles. I couldn't imagine the shame he felt in being the son of the man who squandered one of America's greatest family fortunes. But I assumed it hung over his head the way my mom's drinking and South End hung over mine.

My mother had expected me to become a nurse-practitioner; ZK's family tasked him to restore the billions his father lost in a Ponzi scheme. Not the same but similar.

His eyes dropped down to our hands, our fingers entwined, and the seriousness lifted. He noticed Nan's bracelet pooled at my wrist.

"What an interesting bracelet," he remarked. "May I?"

"I suppose," I said, then slipped it off and handed it to him, feeling inexplicably naked.

"*Tuam tutam tenebo*," he read. Jeez, of course he could read Latin.

God, I hope he doesn't ask me what it means, I'll look like an idiot, I thought, realizing I never asked Nan what the inscription meant.

" 'I will keep you safe,' but who is Sammy G?"

"A rap star?" I said, making another joke. "It was my Nan's. I see your Latin isn't rusty," I added, hoping to cover for my abject ignorance.

"My Latin teacher literally beat us with a ruler until we learned every word of our lessons," he said and returned my bracelet. I slipped it back over my wrist. I was surprised at how exposed I felt without it.

ZK rose from the love seat. "My apologies, Lisbeth, for a night of drama. You're more than generous not to be screaming at me right now," he said. "Allow me to get you a drink and we can discuss more pressing issues, like why El Schnabel hasn't made an appearance at his own opening party in his own penthouse. People must be having fun somewhere . . . let's find them."

I rose to go with him but thought better of it.

"I'd love to, ZK, but I think I better go home," I said, not believing my own words.

"Ah, now I'm really flying solo. Can't I convince you otherwise?" There really wasn't a choice.

"Well, at least allow me to arrange a taxi for you."

We silently walked to the elevator and rode down to the first floor. Outside, standing at the curb, he didn't seem to know whether to hold my hand or not. I didn't know what I wanted either.

A cab stopped at the curb, and at the last second ZK turned to me, my face gazing up into his golden-flecked eyes. He gently brushed an eyelash from my face and, catching me unprepared, kissed me, our lips pressing together, his arm sweeping around me, pulling me in with sudden urgency, making me want to open my mouth and close my eyes, my whole body molded around him. His kiss was so focused and intense that my fingers clutched for something to hold on to—his jacket, his hands holding my face, his hair.

"Hey buddy," the cab driver said, "why don't you guys put it in the cab. So I can finish my shift." We were still on the street.

ZK released me, but he held my hand tightly, preventing me from entering the cab.

"You're certain I can't rescue this night and charm you endlessly?"

"You already have," I said, catching my breath, "but I have to go." I stepped inside the taxi, gathering myself, still tasting him on my lips.

After all, I thought as the taxi pulled away, I have a super-rat to meet tomorrow.

39 What do you wear to a meeting with a super-rat?

I couldn't help but go all out with a scarf over my head, some giant sunglasses, and Jess's redux of a vintage Burberry trench we had snagged at St. Anne's Thrift for twelve dollars; it felt very *Charade*.

When I woke up at Jess's Chinatown flat that morning, Jess helped me put the whole look together. The trench coat didn't come with a belt, which is why it was so cheap. Jess shortened the coat a bit and made a new belt out of this very cool pink fabric that she had lying around, and I was ready for my rendezvous.

Coming up the stairs of the subway exit, I made my way through the people on the crowded uptown sidewalk, clutching my purse, aware of how much my trench coat with the bright pink sash stood out from the army of New Yorkers wearing shades of black and gray.

I had two more voice mail messages from my mother, and I was planning to call her back until she texted me.

"I NEED YOU HOME NOW!" As I read those words, my urge to call vanished. She would have to wait.

Tabitha had sent me simple instructions where to go.

"St. Regis Hotel King Cole Bar ;) 11:30."

As I reached the red-carpeted stairs at the entrance of the St. Regis, I didn't know how well I would fare with Robert Francis, but I did know my look was a hit. Two women had stopped me in the subway station and on the street to tell me how much they loved my coat. I felt as if I should have started taking orders for the Designer X line.

The exceedingly polite doorman told me where to find the King Cole Bar and motioned me inside. Crossing the lobby, with its frescoed ceiling and elaborate marble staircase, gold-framed mirrors, and stunning terrazzo, was like stepping back in time.

Drawing my trench coat tightly around me, hugging my purse, I entered the King Cole Bar. A fairy-tale mural of King Cole, serenaded by three fiddlers, covered an entire wall behind the bar.

I lowered my oversize glasses and peered around the room.

"Hello, Lisbeth," an older man's voice said from the table behind me. I turned to see Mr. Armani—Robert Francis—standing at his banquette behind me.

"Oh hello, sorry I didn't notice you when I came in," I said as politely as I could manage.

"Come join me," he said, holding up a glass of champagne. "I promise not to bite." He put out his hand and directed me to the chair. He couldn't keep a smirk from creeping into the corners of his mouth.

"Thank you," I said and quietly stepped into the banquette.

"You look stunning as usual," he said. "What an original knack you have. You've remarkably established yourself as the new girl on the rise in such a short time and certainly garnered my attention. Quite an accomplishment."

He wore a deep-gray suit with a yellow tie and a pocket square, his salt-and-pepper hair neatly trimmed. Up close in the sunlight, he seemed older. I couldn't help noticing his hands, their perfectly manicured nails delicate, almost vampirish. Robert Francis had a Dracula sophistication about him, I thought, a superficial elegance with a threat lurking beneath.

"It's nice to be able to spend time with you," he said.

"I didn't really think this would be a social call," I replied. He reclined in his seat, spreading his arms across the banquette, that devious smirk barely suppressed.

"Oh? What were you expecting? Some furtive encounter filled with threats and demands?" he asked. "The trench coat, by the way, is quite wonderful and original. Your so-called Designer X?"

I nodded.

"Clever marketing, that," he added. "The Limelight blog, as well. However do you keep so much going on?"

I wanted to respond that it wasn't that much going on, just me tapping in a blog entry or two before bedtime. And that the clever marketing was just my name for my friend who was a gifted, unheard-of designer and had worked hard for everything she had ever done and that no one I grew up with ever sat in an expensive hotel like this drinking champagne at 11:30 A.M. But I didn't say a thing.

"You've been here before, of course?" he asked, eyeing me unnervingly. I nodded yes, though I'd never been there in my life.

"It's my favorite hotel, an absolute time capsule, you know, built by John Jacob Astor the Fourth in the Gilded Age. If Astor came back, he would feel perfectly at home. Everything is exactly as he left it, including the butlers in white tie and tails scurrying about upstairs like little well-dressed mice. Astor himself collected the thousands of leather-bound books on the shelves over a hundred years ago, and not a volume has been moved since his tragic death."

"Tragic?" I asked, trying to calculate how many times I had met this odd man. I realized that each of his appearances had been more discomforting than the one before.

"Indeed, don't you know your history, young lady?" he admonished. "He died in the sinking of the *Titanic*. It was one of the great ill-fated romances of all time."

"No, I didn't know." I was intrigued to see how enthusiastic he was to talk to me. Not at all how he had behaved before. The hotel, this banquette, was clearly where he spent a lot of time. He enjoyed whatever game he was playing.

"Well, eight years after the Saint Regis opened, Astor divorced his wife and married his secret lover, a lovely schoolgirl named Madeleine. She was actually a year younger than his son. Although these things happen all the time, it caused such a huge uproar that Astor fled with his young wife on an extended yearlong honeymoon through Egypt and the Middle East and the Orient to ride out the controversy. But after seven months, the lovely child bride became pregnant. Considering the state of child care in the Mideast, he decided to return to the States immediately. His misfortune is that he booked passage on the maiden voyage of the RMS *Titanic*."

"I take it they didn't survive?"

"Yes and no. As the ship was sinking, Astor helped his young pregnant wife and her dog Kitty through the cabin window into the last lifeboat."

"Funny name for a dog, Kitty," I said. "Mrs. Astor must have had an interesting sense of humor."

"I suppose," he answered, seeming annoyed at a detail he considered minor.

"And what happened to Mr. Astor?"

"He found a deck chair, lit a cigar, and perished as the ship went down. Now that's the movie that James Cameron should have made. *That's* a romance. But Hollywood prefers to spin tales about a pauper instead. The ninety-nine percent, I believe your generation calls it."

"That's quite a story, Mr. Francis."

"Please call me Robert," he said, immensely pleased with himself. I took a deep breath and gathered my courage to bring our conversation to the point. Being the fly in his spiderweb was exhausting.

"Well . . . *Robert*, I appreciate the vivid history lesson, but I'd prefer to discuss what I came here for," I said. "Tabitha has asked that you step aside and allow her to control her own affairs."

"Ah, a girl who gets to the point! Do relax, dear Lisbeth. Nothing bad is going to happen here. I'm sure the ghost of John Jacob Astor the Fourth would protect an attractive young woman such as yourself in his hotel," he said, self-satisfied. "Have a sip of champagne. Are you hungry? Can I order you a something to eat?"

"No thank you," I said, feeling oddly helpless.

He reached for his champagne glass, revealing a sleek platinum cufflink, and took a leisurely sip.

"Very well, where to begin . . ." As he placed his champagne glass on the table, a Cheshire Cat grin crept into the corners of his mouth. "Clearly you don't know your friend Tabitha very well or you would know that her mother is not in good health."

"I have heard that actually," I felt compelled to say, growing irritated at his condescension. I took a sip of champagne to calm myself.

"Her mother, Eva, came into quite a large fortune when her first husband died, and ever since she has drugged and boozed her way through Europe and Asia and South America, leaving poor Tabby alone and bereft with no one to care for her. In the process, Eva has remarried time and again with disastrous results. Now with the passing of her recent husband, she will likely inherit an even larger fortune. But she is an unreliable and selfish woman with no mothering instinct whatsoever. I've done my best to protect Tabitha's trust while developing her natural singing and dancing talents. Spent quite a bundle on getting her the best of everything. You've met them."

I wondered how he knew I had visited Tabitha's recording studio. Was Robert the "boss" they reported to?

"We vastly overpay her people. That teenager, Bennie Larocco or whatever his name is, is an absolute annoyance, always asking for a bigger cut of royalties. At the same time, Tabby's become quite a superstar, exceeding family expectations."

"Yes, I believe I do know most of that." I was trying not to give him the satisfaction of appearing threatened. "So, if you *are* her benefactor and protector, as you say, why is Tabitha upset with you?"

"An excellent question, to which I do not actually have an answer," he said, lightly stroking the top of his own champagne glass with his fingertip, over and over, until it seemed intentionally inappropriate.

"Her therapist tells me that being abandoned by your mother at such a tender age can be very traumatic. As a result, she has a huge amount of anger, and she projects that anger onto the people who love and care for her because she can do so safely. Her mother is nowhere around and too fragile. Hence I have become a convenient target. I simply want to help her."

He stopped and lit a cigarette. It was remarkable how he felt entitled to smoke anywhere. I expected the waiter, another customer, frankly *anyone* to object, but no one said a thing. He held his cigarette between his thumb and forefinger like one of those concentration camp commandants in a movie.

"I'm curious, Lisbeth," he said, smoke drifting from his lips, "why you didn't tell Tabitha we were acquainted from that night at the Met?"

I had been afraid he would bring that up.

"Why were you waiting outside the bathroom?" I replied.

"Because we were all worried about her. She's tried before, you know."

He knew? The air went out of me, but I tried to keep my poise. I was feeling more and more baffled. If he knew, then why did he allow her to be alone in the bathroom?

"I tried to stop her from getting the prescription," he said, as if reading my mind, "but was unfortunately unsuccessful. Needless to say, I've excommunicated that doctor." From his expression, I knew he sensed my confusion.

"Dear Lisbeth, this all boils down to one thing," he said, tapping the ash from his cigarette onto a bread plate. "Who are you going to believe?"

"Tabitha, of course. She's my friend," I said. "Why should I believe you?"

He raised one of his aristocratic eyebrows. "Because I'm her uncle, of course," he said, taking another draw on his cigarette. Was he her uncle, really? Her protector, her business manager, her super-rat, a creep, and everything rolled into one? Something didn't feel right. And he was so offhand about it all.

I remembered Nan's words from her friend Sammy G . . . "a liar's mouth can be full of truth, but he's still a liar." Who should I believe, Tabitha or Robert Francis? I had no way of determining the truth about Robert Francis, but in my gut I knew his intentions couldn't be good.

"Well, Tabitha said that you wanted to speak with me about her situation. That's why I'm here," I stated.

"Actually, that's not quite accurate. I arranged this meeting to have the opportunity to speak with *you*," he said, his gray eyes narrowing. "You're young and lovely, an impressive new friend with enormous business potential, and Tabitha listens to you. The business possibilities alone would have attracted my attention. I'm not sure where you met Tabitha or how you knew she was in that bathroom that night, but I find you riveting and I thought we should meet under . . . well, more favorable circumstances."

Robert's eyes held me locked in some kind of trance until I managed to pull myself away. I stared down at the table, counting the silverware, hoping to regain my composure.

"I don't know what you want from me," I said. Nothing but my trench coat had turned out as I planned.

"How about a toast to people not being as they seem?" he said.

"You know, sometimes the bad people aren't so bad and the good people aren't anywhere as good as they think they are," he added. My hand trembled as our glasses touched.

"I am entirely willing to discuss Tabitha's situation, once I've gotten to know you better," he said. "I suggest you join me at the party I'm having next Friday evening." He took a cream-colored envelope out of his coat pocket and handed it to me.

"Tabitha has already agreed to come. I hope you don't mind that I asked her in advance. I promise you, it will be quite pleasant."

I held the invitation, its creamy paper thick and luscious between my fingertips. Embossed in a delicate gold script were two words: PENTHOUSE A.

"It's been a pleasure, Lisbeth," he said, rising, a smirk like he'd flashed before returning to his face. I was surprised at the sudden end of our conversation. I stood self-consciously.

"I'll consider the invitation, of course," I said, feeling dismissed.

"Yes, of course," he said. "I hope to see you soon."

I pulled up my scarf and put on my shades and left the hotel, walking several blocks to be sure no one could see me before I headed down the stairs to the nearest subway stop.

Checking my purse, I saw the invitation and the screen of my phone glow and realized it had been buzzing with calls and text messages.

They were all from Courtney.

40 "Where the fuck have you been?" Courtney screamed as I walked in through the back screen door.

Wearing a baggy gray T-shirt that was three sizes too big and sweatpants, Courtney was bending over the stove. No makeup, no tube top, no fuzzy boots. She was cooking smiley-face pancakes as Ryan poured buckets of syrup on a stack on the table.

"Hey, sis, you're just in time for dinner," Ryan said.

"Don't you answer anyone's texts anymore?" Courtney barked.

"I don't remember you answering every text I've ever sent," I said over my shoulder as I headed upstairs to my room. I was relieved Mom wasn't in the kitchen. I threw my stuff on the bed.

"We need to talk now!" Courtney yelled after me, sounding exactly like Mom.

"I'm changing my clothes," I yelled back from the top of the stairs. Grabbing a T-shirt, some underwear, and my comfiest pair of jeans, I headed into the bathroom and turned the shower up as hot as I could stand.

I hated being home.

Twenty minutes later, my hair was washed and the weirdness of Robert Francis was fading. As I brushed out the tangles, I realized something was odd. Courtney was making pancakes for Ryan. Courtney hated Ryan almost as much as she hated me, and she was making him pancakes for dinner. Mom wouldn't like that.

Dropping my damp towel in the hamper, I walked down the upstairs hallway, searching for signs of Mom. Was she hungover? I hated going into Mom's room. You never knew what you were going to find. Peeking cautiously into her darkened bedroom, I could see that her sheets were all tangled and a mess as usual, but no Mom. I made my way downstairs.

"So what's going on?" I asked Courtney.

"Ryan, enough syrup, eat your pancakes," she instructed.

"Why pancakes?" I asked.

"There's nothing else in this fucking house to eat."

"Mom hasn't been shopping?" I asked.

"Where have you been for the last four days?"

"What difference does it make? And why are you suddenly acting all Supernanny with Ry?" I asked.

All the color drained from her face. It seemed like Courtney didn't know what to say. "Just get your ass to the hospital. Mom has cancer."

I didn't remember driving to the hospital or parking my car or saying my name. All I could think about was the endless times that I had avoided her calls, deleted her texts, or turned off my phone so I wouldn't have to talk to her. I was always afraid she would ask me about school, so I ignored her when maybe she wanted to tell me about . . . I couldn't even say the word to myself.

I sat in the waiting room feeling more alone than I had ever felt in my whole life. I was afraid to call Jess and ashamed to call Nan. They both knew what I had been doing for the last four days. Mom had been in the hospital for three days.

The large beige waiting room was filled with rows of mauve chairs and ferns. Fox News blared from the TV perched in the corner of the ceiling. I was the only one there, and it felt like torture. I remember wondering if the ferns were real or if someone actually watered them. There were well-used stacks of magazines and a stand filled with brochures covering everything from chronic bed-wetting to hepatitis B.

After a while, I couldn't remember what I was waiting for. Had the receptionist said a doctor would be with me soon? I couldn't recall. But I recognized some of the nurses walking by, who whispered when they saw me. They knew my mom. I wondered how they felt. Was she as nasty to them as she was to us? I was certain my mother had told them all that I was going to school to become a nurse-practitioner. They probably still thought that was true.

My mind flashed back to the last time I saw Mom, when Ryan was acting like such a wiseass. I kept remembering her rubbing her arm and sliding down the sleeves of her blouse. It seemed obvious now. *She must have had tests,* I thought. *She already knew she had cancer.*

"Don't go off the rails," she had said. "You're the only dependable one left." In my head, I couldn't stop hearing her say that over and over.

My mind was in a fog. I felt like I had to do something. I decided to ask to see my mother as soon as possible, but as I stood up a doctor approached me before I could say anything.

"Lisbeth Wachowicz?"

"Yes?"

"You mother is being evaluated for hepatocellular carcinoma," said the doctor. He seemed barely five years older than me. Had his mother wanted him to go to medical school? Did he want to become a doctor? Was he glad he did? His name was stitched into his starched white coat, Dr. Kenneth Newton. He was tall and skinny as a rail and wore black-framed eyeglasses.

"In English, please?" I asked. He pushed his glasses up the bridge of his nose and paused a moment.

"Liver cancer. We know she has severe cirrhosis of the liver and we're trying to rule out cancer," he said.

"From drinking?"

"Ten years or more of heavy drinking can cause the cirrhosis to form, but there are a number of factors such as how much a person drinks, what they drink, how their body handles alcohol, their underlying medical condition, medical history, genetics. Women who are heavy drinkers are at a higher risk than men."

"So, yes?"

"Yes," he responded grimly.

"But she's been drinking forever. What happened? Why now?"

"Your mother was on her second shift when she became disoriented and confused," he said. "We have a number of safeguards here, and I pulled her in for testing. The liver detoxifies your body, and if the liver isn't functioning correctly, toxins can be released into your bloodstream. It's usually the high ammonia levels that cause confusion and behavior changes," he said. "That's what we tested her for."

Jeez, I guess going to med school pays off.

"Is she in pain?"

"No, actually there are no nerve endings in the liver itself," he said. "Once we normalize her blood levels, she'll be her old self again, up to a point."

Was that a good or bad thing? I wondered.

"Listen," he said. "I know this is tough, but your mom has a lot of friends here. There isn't a nurse or doctor at this hospital that at some point or another your mother hasn't helped."

As he spoke, I saw some of the nurses gathered at reception, and it seemed as though they were listening and nodding to what Dr. Newton had to say. The woman he was describing didn't sound like anyone I knew.

"You're talking about my mother?"

"Yes, Ella headed up the patient-advocacy task force that focused on seniors and has always given one hundred percent to every doctor and patient on the ward," he said. This was from the woman who never visited her own aging mother.

"Do you actually *know* my mom?" I asked.

"Yes," he replied in the same calm tone as he had started. "Ella was probably the first person I met here. She runs the orientation program for all new doctors. It is a *privilege* to take care of her. Let me put it this way: if I were sick, I would want your mom to take care of me."

"You guys . . . *like* her?" I asked, wondering what he made of my astonishment.

"I can only speak for her at work. At home she may have behaved very differently. It's clear now your mother was a very-high-functioning alcoholic. That may have had serious ramifications for you at home, and we have counseling that we can make available to you and your family, but as for the hospital, she couldn't be in better hands."

"Can I see her?"

He signaled the nurses, who were already waiting to take me to her room.

As I walked away from him, I nodded thanks.

I already liked Dr. Newton. I had never known as much about

my mother as in that short talk with him. No one had ever laid it on the line in such a matter-of-fact way. I realized that these doctors and nurses knew her better than I did.

"Right this way, hon," the nurse said. She had a gristled voice like Mom and was wearing the same pale-blue scrubs Mom wore home every day. I noticed the name Brynner stitched into her uniform. I remembered Mom talking about her. I wondered if they had ever gone out drinking together.

With a hiss, the pneumatic doors opened. Gurneys glimmered in a line down the corridor. As we passed the nurses' station, almost everyone stopped to watch us walk by. I don't know why, but it made me feel like crying.

In my mother's room, I couldn't stop myself. My chest was shaking uncontrollably. I couldn't hold back the tears. Mom was lying with her eyes closed on her back, a tube in her nose, a finger heart-rate monitor, a catheter in her arm, and a tube in her wrist hooked up to all kinds of machinery.

"Mom?" I said, trying to focus myself. She didn't move, though I could see that she was breathing.

"She's sleeping," Nurse Brynner said.

"Can I . . . can I just sit here for a while?" I asked.

"Of course, hon, you go ahead. I'll come back in a few." As Nurse Brynner left, I turned to Mom, and it all burst out of me. I sobbed relentlessly.

"I'm sorry," I said. "I'm sorry about your calls. I'm sorry about school. I'm so sorry that I let you down."

All the while, Mom just lay there, her chest moving up and down with the machinery. The hums, beeps, and clicks were the only sounds as the medical equipment tracked her vital signs, more in sync with my mother than I ever was.

41 Nan and I hugged for so long I lost my sense of time. When I lifted my head, there was only darkness outside her window. It chilled me to think of Mom sleeping in the hospital with tubes coming out of everywhere.

"They love her so much," I said. "I could see it in their eyes. They knew about her drinking, but they still loved her." I felt weepy again. So did Nan, her soft little hand holding mine in an iron grip.

"I always knew she had it in her," Nan said, shaking her head. "But with me she was so angry, and her drinking made everything impossible." She wiped a tear from her cheek.

"It's wonderful she's with friends," Nan said, firmly patting my hand and straightening herself on the couch. Nan had tried to visit three days earlier when they admitted Mom, but Mom wouldn't see her. I couldn't even process how that must have felt to Nan.

"Are you okay?"

"Don't worry about me," she said. "Your mom and I will be close again some day. I'm sure we will. As you know, things can be very difficult between mothers and daughters."

"Do you want to talk about it at all? I mean, what happened between you and Mom? You don't have to," I said.

Nan regarded me in silent sadness.

"You have been my shoulder to cry on for so long, you can cry on mine, too."

"I don't know," Nan said, trailing off into her own thoughts. We sat there for a while, holding hands, stuck in the sadness of it all, until I felt Nan stir. "I guess we were unlucky," she began. "There is a history in our family of rebellious daughters. I certainly know that. But the time just ran away from us. And we grew further and further away from each other." *Just like me and Mom,* I thought.

"Did you ever try to stop her from drinking?" I asked.

"Of course, and unfortunately that was another unlucky

part." Nan looked so sad as she said those words. For the first time, she seemed old to me. I knew she was old, of course, but I never thought about her that way until she started talking about Mom.

"What did you do?" I asked, hoping I wasn't pushing too hard. But with Mom in the hospital, I wanted to know.

"You know, it's not like on those reality shows they have on the television about intervention where nine times out of ten they seem to succeed," she said. "I've read quite a lot about it. Many times, the percentages aren't really very good."

"So you and Grandpa actually did a full-on intervention?"

"Yes. And, well, the danger in an intervention is what you'd expect. If it fails, everything can become much worse. I remember the therapist advising that there could be a 'subsequent period of strained communication,' as he called it, and that we shouldn't lose hope." Nan gripped my hand and looked me in the eye. "In our case, that subsequent period of strained communication has lasted for twenty-three years." I saw a tear slide down her cheek. "I try to hope," she said. Nan stood up and went to the kitchen to collect herself. It was too much for her.

"Some tea, Lisbeth?" she asked, her tiny voice still weepy. I nodded yes. She returned a moment later with a tea setting on a silver platter, placing the tray down on the table.

"So Lisbeth," she said, pouring me a cup, "I want to know what is going on with you. Where have you been, what have you been doing? What is your plan?"

There it was, the dreaded word "plan," always looming over me like a guillotine, but I couldn't pretend anymore. Not to Nan. Not even to Mom.

"I'm not going to college," I said. "Not for nursing. Not yet anyway." I waited for a reaction of disappointment to come over her face. But Nan was too cool for that.

"Really," she said. It wasn't a question, although it was. "Well, what *are* you going to do?"

"I don't know, but I want to try to get a job in fashion," I said.

"Really?" This time it was definitely a question.

"You think I'm silly," I said.

"Well, you know I follow your blog. And what do you call that other thing? A Tumblr?"

"You do?"

"I was a bit bewildered to see my maiden name, ahem," Nan said, giving me a sly glance. I winced. "But then I saw you had thousands of followers and you have quite a lot of wonderful things to say and I agreed with it all!" she said. "I don't know how you have time for so many entries. And such lovely photographs, by the way. Do you have a concrete idea how you're going to work in the fashion business?"

I shrugged. I really didn't have the slightest idea. Don't ask how or why, but Nan's question brought to mind the woman Tabitha introduced me to at her record party. Flo Birkenhead, that tiny intense woman with the close-cropped red hair who talked about ad placement, endorsements, and aggregators. I hoped I still had her card. I had heard of people making money on their blogs and Tumblr sites.

"Okay, well, we will have to come up with something, won't we?"

I nodded, wondering how I could possibly have anything resembling a career.

"In the meantime, we have work to do," Nan said with a sense of determination that startled me. "Even if your mother won't talk to me, we have to make a plan that will work for everyone."

42 Penthouse A.

I still had the thick cream-colored invitation in my purse. Dr. Newton wanted to run more tests, so Mom was still tucked away in her hospital room. But like King Kong ready to break his chains and roar, Mom was starting to go nuts. I heard she pleaded with her nurse friends, to "rip these fucking catheters out" and let her go back to work. For obvious reasons, they couldn't. Plus, she was probably in detox withdrawal from stopping her alcohol consumption cold turkey, and I guess there were a few liability issues to work out. At least she was with people who could handle her better than Courtney or I could.

Before Nan and I could start our plan, I had to clean up a few pieces of business. I contacted Flo to have a chat about my blog and was happy she remembered me. As I expected, she was all business and promised to make a market analysis of Limelight and get back to me.

"I'm very interested in helping you build your brand," she remarked. Me? A brand? Fingers crossed.

I was concerned about facing Tabitha. I felt like I had failed her; there was no other way to think about it. Robert's intentions were disturbing, and I had no idea how Tabitha would feel about that, considering the results she had hoped for. Which is why it was so curious to receive her text.

"Come 2 my house 2 get ready b4 penthouse party ! ;)"

She was going, for real? I couldn't fathom the relationship she had with her business manager-slash-trustee-slash-uncle.

"C u @ 9 ? It's bn 2 lng bathroom buddy !! :*(" That didn't sound like someone who was angry with me.

"ZK sez hi. He'll be there. ;)"

The mention of those initials sent quivers down my spine as I remembered our kiss.

Once off the PATH train, I headed downtown to Jess's place, rang the buzzer, and ran upstairs.

"What the hell?" I heard a voice say from inside the apartment as I reached the door. And then a moment later, "Why didn't you tell me she was coming?"

"Hey Lizzy," Jess said, standing in the doorway. She was smiling as always, her pixie hair frazzled, the blue dye fading turquoise.

Five sewing pins were sticking out of the collar of her work shirt and a swatch of fabric dangled from her hand. We hugged, careful to avoid the pins.

"Aren't you going to introduce me?" the girl behind her said with annoyance. Jess looked amused, as if she expected the question.

"Hey Lizzy, meet my girlfriend, Sarrah. She's been helping me with some fittings."

Sarrah had long, shock-red hair, recently dyed from what I could tell. She was wearing overalls and had lots of freckles on her face and arms, like some kind of trippy farm girl. She was very pretty but seemed unhappy.

"Hi." She thrust out her hand to me. "I've heard all about you," she said with a hint of displeasure. I noticed a tattoo in goth letters on her wrist that said BITTER SWEET.

"Good to meet you, Sarrah," I said. I had met Jess's girlfriends before, and they almost always had rough edges, which seemed to amuse Jess. Without fail, Jess's girlfriends resented me, but this time I also felt a twinge of resentment, wanting Jess all to myself. I needed to talk to her about Mom, the crazy encounter at the St. Regis, and ZK and ask her if she'd seen Jake, but there wouldn't be a way with Sarrah there.

"How's your mom?" Jess asked. I guessed the moms had talked.

"Good, as far as I know. They still haven't finished testing." Sarrah was standing right beside Jess, clearly planning to listen to everything we said like some kind of twisted chaperone. Jess shot me a knowing look.

"Hey, I just came by to pick up a dress if it's okay." Not really true, but it was the best excuse I could manage at the moment.

Sarrah was flat-out staring at me.

"Sure, let's take a look," Jess said. "Hey Sarrah, I would love some more hot water for my tea?" She held up her mug. Sarrah broke out of her daze, nodded, and trundled off obediently to the kitchen.

"She's cute," I said. "How long?"

"Three days," Jess said. "Won't last three more." I tried to keep from laughing.

"Hey!" Sarrah yelled from the tiny kitchen across the room, and we both flinched. "Where do we keep the tea?" Jess rolled her eyes.

"I'll be right back," Jess whispered.

I took the opportunity to dash to the closet ahead of Jess. I couldn't help noticing there were four newly modified vintage dresses, each one more wonderful and a bit wilder than the next. They weren't there two days earlier.

There was another dress, as well. It didn't seem like one of Nan's but still had a retro flavor while at the same time being totally fresh and eye-catching. Longer in the back than in the front, it had a patterned black chiffon fabric with white leaves falling like snow clusters mostly at the top. The black overskirt was bouncy and light with only a few white leaves randomly placed, dissolving into pure black. The black underskirt was tight and sexy.

Along the hem, playful light-gray embroidery caught my eye. On closer examination, I realized they were words. Turning the hem in my fingers, I read them.

As we talk the words fall away. They fly like seeds in the wind, clinging to the hem of your dress before they disappear.

The words made the dress a secret message. Was it from Jess's journal? It was startling and provocative, just what you'd expect from Designer X.

"So you like it," Jess said confidently. I turned. She must have been watching me.

"Like it? It's mind-blowing." I felt the air go out of me. Jess was so talented, I felt like I was bathing in her brilliance.

"I'm getting tired of the asymmetric hem length; I might change that. Try it on," she offered, lifting the dress out of the closet. "It should fit."

"Are you sure?" I asked, noticing Sarrah watching us from the kitchen.

"It's for my show. I made it with your measurements."

I stripped down to my underwear and slipped on the tight skirt and overskirt and then the blouse.

"It needs to be a tad tighter at the waist," she said, staring into the full-length mirror propped against the wall.

"Jess, I think it's perfect."

"Then wear it tonight."

"What? Really? It's one of a kind; it's your original..." I stammered.

"They all are," she said. "Do me a favor, Lizzy, wear it. I'm sure you're going somewhere fantastic tonight. That dress deserves to escape this closet and be worn. What did you used to say? Its *destiny* is to be worn?"

I smiled while Sarrah, holding a tea bag, watching us from the kitchen, seethed.

43 The doorman greeted me at Tabitha's building on North Moore Street in Tribeca. He was just a few years older than me and had that unshaven-Euro-model look. His uniform must have been designed by Comme des Garçons. Fanciest doorman I'd ever seen, no joke. He was a perfect fantasy. After all, who wouldn't want a good-looking guy who is always nice and opens doors, hails cabs, and carries heavy packages for you?

"Please let me help you with your bag," he said. I only had a garment bag with the latest Designer X creation inside. It seemed a little silly, but I acquiesced, feeling very indulged. He pushed the PENTHOUSE button as I entered the elevator.

I heard Tabitha's familiar high-pitched squeal as the door opened.

"You're here!"

She was standing in a comfy pink bathrobe with her hair up in a towel, Galileo yapping at her feet. It was good to see her again, and I appreciated how happy she was to see me. Walking into her penthouse apartment, I was totally awed.

The Princess of Pop truly had pop-star-worthy digs. The cherrywood floors and staircase were so deeply lacquered I could see my reflection as I walked in. There was a high-tech kitchen that was so pristine that it seemed impossible Tabitha had ever boiled water in it. The floor-to-ceiling bookshelves complete with a library ladder on rails was utterly impressive. Tabitha's collection of leather-bound literature was remarkable, though I doubted there was a book on those shelves that had ever been touched. The living room had a view of New York City on three sides.

"Hurry," she said as she skipped barefoot up the spiral staircase at the back of the living room. "Come up to my bedroom and help me pick out what to wear."

I followed. The second floor was even more sensational. Calling it a bedroom seemed a poor way of describing the place. There was a large built-in mahogany desk, a plump couch, upholstered chairs, an antique wooden coffee table, and a sleek designer bed that seemed to be floating on air, all of which faced onto an open terrace with views of all of Lower Manhattan. You could even see the Statue of Liberty.

"In here!" Tabitha called. I wondered where she could be.

She poked her head out of a doorway "Hello? Come on, I need help." I followed her and found myself in an enormous walk-in closet.

I know from closets. Even with tons of hangers, clothes, and shoes, this was significantly more than a closet. Nothing like the smushed-in cozy closet I had at home. All the bedrooms in my house could fit in there. This was a closet you could get lost in for days.

It reminded me of the showroom where we tried on clothes at Barneys. At the center of the room was a gorgeous French walnut armoire with a full-length mirror.

"What do you think of this?" Tabitha said, posing in a black

leather halter and black harem pants, looking like an upscale relative of JWoww's. She could tell from my expression that it wasn't
my favorite. "Okay, okay, give me a second." She ducked back behind the armoire.

"So, how are you?" I asked, wondering where we stood relative
to my meeting with Robert.

"Great!" she said from behind the armoire before popping her
head back out. "Thanks to you!"

"Me?"

"What about this?" She was wearing a nude-colored, skin-tight,
studded tank dress and some strappy sandals. It was very close to
being naked.

"Well, that's an interesting dress. I like the sandals," I said.

"I don't like it either," she replied, frowning, and ducked back
into her vast racks of clothes. I contemplated the rows and rows
of shoes. This walk-in was the final resting place of so many of
Tabitha's cocktailing shopping sprees. You could dress an army of
pop stars from this one closet.

"I don't know what you said to RF, but it certainly worked," she
said.

"Really?" I asked.

Tabitha popped back out in her underwear.

"Robert said he's willing to start the process. And my mom is
coming, so we're going to meet in the Hamptons. You have to join
us. We'll celebrate!"

The Hamptons? For me, the Hamptons were a bigger fantasy
than I dared ever dream of, even bigger than New York City. After
all, in Jersey we have the Jersey Shore, the McMansions of Brigan-
tine and the old historical houses of Cape May, but nothing compared to what I had heard about the Hamptons. I hadn't fully
comprehended that summering in the Hamptons was a likely requirement for a Park Avenue Princess or a SoHo Darling.

"We desperately need a little getaway, and I want you to meet
my mother."

"I have a few obligations," I said. "So I can't say for sure." *My* mother for one. Then there was the fact that I still had no means of supporting myself and Jess's show. Although Jess didn't have an exact date, we wanted to time her show at FIT to Fashion Week at the end of the summer. How much she would need me before, we hadn't discussed. We both knew she could stage the show herself. Getting people there was the problem. She would kill me if I didn't make that happen for her.

"Well you'll have to let me know. You should definitely come," she said.

"Thank you for asking. That's quite nice of you."

"I hear you've contacted Flo. She's coming to stay with me, too," Tabitha said as she pulled on a skirt. "You certainly know how to get around."

"I'm just not quite sure if there's anything she can do," I said. "But she's so lovely, and it's just a small hobby of mine." Tabitha made a half smile as if she didn't believe me, and I thought it better to change the subject.

"So Robert is giving you what you want? Are you surprised?"

"Not really. You talked to him, right?" she said, hidden from view.

"But Tabitha, we didn't really talk about very much."

Tabitha popped back out again. "Oh really? It didn't seem that way to Robert," she said. She was half-dressed in a sheer black-and-white dress and tights. The kind of thing Lindsay Lohan might wear at her tackiest. Tabitha noted my expression.

"I don't really like this, do you?" I didn't even have to answer.

"Damn, I just don't have anything to wear." She ducked behind the mirror. "I just bought these." She thrust out a pair of black and nude heels. "What do you think I should wear with them?"

Clearly she wasn't in the mood for a serious talk. I scanned the closet. I plucked a black silk shirt with spiky beaded sleeves and sorted through the hangers and endless dresses until I found a short black mini.

"Try this," I said. She took the two hangers, ducking behind the armoire again.

"By the way, RF said you were absolutely stellar and impressive," she said as she dressed. "He said he admires you." She reappeared, her strawberry-blonde hair falling in luxurious waves over the black silk shirt.

"What do you think?"

"Beautiful. Absolutely beautiful."

"Good. We're all ready to go," she said and noticed for the first time what I was wearing. "Wait, aren't you getting dressed? What's in the bag?"

44

Robert greeted us at the door, and you'd think I was his long lost daughter. He was holding Morris, a tiny shih tzu that all the girls cooed over as they passed by. The apartment was magnificent with floor-to-ceiling windows and enormous unobstructed views of the Hudson. There was a huge skylight over the oversize dining room, and if it ever got dark enough in New York City, I'd bet you could see the stars from there.

"Allow me to give you the tour," Robert offered as Tabitha and I followed him from room to room. It was jarring how quickly Tabitha's mood had shifted again. She and Robert seemed fine with each other. I didn't know what to make of it.

Partygoers were everywhere, young girls lounging on the couches picking at hors d'oeuvres and sipping sugary pink martinis, men smoking cigars and playing billiards.

On the rooftop garden, guests reveled beneath the towering Empire State Building, which loomed overhead and seemed close enough to be next door, its upper stories glowing red, white, and blue. But everyone seemed so used to it they didn't notice. Ho hum, another dazzling skyline, another gorgeous view. I found myself in awe of it all.

There were huge paintings in all the rooms like the ones I'd seen at Palazzo Chupi and in the Mary Boone Gallery, and the place was packed. Music blasted from invisible speakers in each room, young girls danced and writhed to the beat, and bars were set up at every corner. Though it was only 9:30, the crowd already seemed to have imbibed significantly more than usual.

Scattered throughout the apartment were attractive, refined, slightly woozy young women. Interspersed were noticeably older men, some of them Robert's age and even older, chatting and flirting.

I turned to Tabitha to remark on the intense number of young girls, but she was gone. Only Robert was there, holding Morris and surveying the scene like Dracula presiding over his subjects. I almost expected to see his fangs come out.

Back inside, I wondered if ZK was actually here or if Tabitha simply said so to lure me.

"May I offer you something to drink?" a waiter summoned by Robert asked, carrying a tray of the sugary pink cocktails. I sipped one, wondering how I let myself be convinced to come to Robert Francis's penthouse. An antique clock sitting on the fireplace mantel reminded me that I'd forgotten again to call in sick to work that night. Work. Jake. It all seemed so far away. I flashed on Mom, Courtney, and Ryan.

"I'm flattered that you actually came to my little gathering," Robert said, waking me from my trance. "I didn't think you would, considering our last meeting." I felt curiously silent, and he seemed not to mind that I wasn't responding. I remember trying to come up with something witty to say.

"You look absolutely stunning. Wearing a new Designer X creation, I see. I wouldn't expect anything less. I hope you'll introduce me to your designer at some point. I'd love to invest. Perhaps a show this fall? We should talk about that right away. Come, let me show you the rest of the penthouse."

I sipped on the foaming pink confection, feeling oddly light-headed and thinking how I might excuse myself to find Tabitha. I wanted to sit down. I wouldn't put it past Sleazebag Mr. Armani to add something narcotic to these pink drinks. It took a moment to realize that the short tour had ended. We were in an enormous room with vaulted ceilings, a large mirrored armoire at one end, and a bed at the other.

Scooting across the floor, Morris jumped up on a footstool at the bottom of the bed and barked as if expecting something. Robert said a few words I couldn't quite understand and offered me a flute of champagne, which I groggily accepted. As I tried to make sense of where I was, a light crossed the room and reflected in the mirror. I saw an immense tiled bathroom and Robert's silhouette entering the light.

"I'll be right back," he said, and I remembered wondering, *Right back from where? To where? What was I doing here? Why was I in his bedroom?* I thought about the St. Regis and the story of Jacob Astor and his schoolgirl wife. I felt like I was going to be sick.

I staggered, and Morris yelped at me. The incessant barking gave me an instant headache. I could see him yapping at himself in the mirror. I wanted to just fall on the bed and go to sleep, but in my reflection I saw myself in Jess's new dress and felt the urge to get out of there.

I burst out of the bedroom and ran past the partygoers, who barely noticed me, until I reached the terrace and the summer night air, breathing in and out as deeply as I could, until I felt a little better. I found a bar and drank two glasses of water to clear my head.

Still groggy, I sought out a room filled with partygoers and sat on an armchair in the corner to rest. I resisted the desire to close my eyes for fear I'd fall asleep, and decided to keep moving. I needed a bathroom to throw water on my face. I must have turned around without knowing and found myself a few steps away from the bedroom I had run away from moments ago.

The door opened, and there was Robert in his bathrobe, smoking a cigarette and holding Morris. I stepped back in the shadows so he wouldn't see me, and I watched as he took a girl, my age, just like me, gently by the elbow into his room. He paused for a moment, scanning the hallway until his eyes met mine.

He nodded, a slight smile on his lips, and dragged the door closed behind him.

45

I wanted a cup of coffee, but I settled for an espresso at the espresso station by one of the bars. The bitter shot of caffeine did the trick, and I felt awake and a tad wired.

I scanned the room for Tabitha. I texted her twice, without response. Walking quickly through the penthouse, I couldn't find anyone I recognized. That was okay. I just wanted to go home anyway.

In the elevator, I tried to make sense of what had just happened when the doors opened one floor below. Incredibly there was Tabitha with this ubercute boy, and I mean *boy*. He might have been sixteen. Where on earth did she find him in this party of creepy old men?

"Lisbeth!" Tabitha screamed, squealing as usual. She dragged me out of the elevator before the doors closed.

"This is Liam," she said. "He's in one of those new boy bands."

"We're really famous on YouTube, actually," he said, shaking his head and smiling. He had a nice, soft Irish accent.

"Maybe with eight-year-olds," Tabitha said and kissed him. I was happy to see her having fun for a change. I didn't understand what had happened with Robert Francis, but Tabitha seemed liberated. Totally smashed, too.

"Let's go back to the party," she said excitedly.

"I'm afraid I've had my fill of pink martinis," I began, trying to regain some of my Hepburn poise. I wanted to crawl home to New

Jersey, unless I could figure out how to crash at Jess's house without Sarrah throwing a fit. But I realized Tabitha wasn't listening. She and her boy toy were snogging right in front of me.

"Darling, I'm going home," I said, turning to press the elevator again. Tabitha drunkenly pulled away from Liam long enough to register that I was leaving, and together they dragged me from the elevator. Linking their arms in mine, they marched me down the hallway.

"I'm not talking about the old-man party upstairs," she said. "There's a much better one down the hall."

"Really, I'm exhausted."

"It'll be fun," she said. "And ZK is here somewhere."

We entered yet another gorgeous apartment with younger people, a completely different vibe from upstairs. A cluster of girls were chatting in the common room, samba music was playing throughout, the lights were low—overall a much cooler scene. There were couples coming in and out of a room in the back.

"Remember me?" ZK's soft familiar voice asked from just behind me. I turned, and he offered me a glass of champagne. I nodded gratefully. Tabitha winked at me as she led Liam off somewhere.

"For someone so lovely, wearing such an exquisite dress, you seem oddly disturbed," he said. "Everything okay?"

I didn't know how I'd talk about it, where I would even begin. So I managed a small smile and a weary nod.

"Well, I'm grateful for another opportunity to entertain you. Come," he said, reaching for my hand. "It's time for me to dazzle you with my wit and good looks." I followed him through the apartment. "Besides, I need a good-luck charm," he added.

As we passed from room to room, I heard a shrill cackle, and I knew instantly that Dahlia was somewhere nearby. I glanced around and saw her in the den off the side of the main room. She was smoking a cigar and shooting pool with yet another brace of handsome men. She sunk her shot, and they all laughed, toasting whiskies. I had hoped she was sufficiently preoccupied to miss our crossing, but I was wrong.

Her head turned with laser precision, catching my glance. Her fierce gaze seemed utterly aware of what I was doing and where I was going and whose hand I was holding, mocking me as if saying, *you won't get away with it.* Then she went back to her crowd, laughing and joking as though she had never left their company. It chilled me.

ZK led me into a room that was heavy with smoke and dark except for a bright light hovering over a poker table. We took our seats near the end of the table. There was a big haphazard pile of cash in the middle.

One by one, the gents all stood as I arrived, introducing themselves: Brad, Hugh, Ian, Baird, and names like that, one blue-eyed trust-fund type after the next, all incredibly handsome. They already had summer-in-the-Hamptons tans and were built like they were on the rowing team somewhere. I bet they had jackets in their closets with Harvard, Yale, and Princeton logos on them. They sat and resumed their high-stakes poker game.

"Okay, everybody show 'em," the dealer said. Four of the five players turned over their hands, but the last guy, Brad, was teasing each card, turning them over one at a time, "slowrolling" they call it, while everyone sat and watched. I knew a little bit about poker from Nan, who taught me how to play when I was seven. Brad had a very good hand, an ace high flush, so he was rubbing it in and being a major jerk. "A gracious winner," Nan used to say, "never slowrolls."

"Flush!" Brad yelled, and took a big puff of his cigar as he scraped up the pile of money. The other players groaned and bowed their heads.

ZK anted up, and the next dealer dealt him in. I peeked over at his hand. He was on his way to a high straight, but not by much. He smiled when he noticed I was watching his cards and everyone else's for that matter. He drew a two of spades and folded after a few minutes. The same guy, Brad, won again with a fist pump, and everyone mumbled under their breath.

Twenty minutes later, these boys were losing huge amounts of money to each other, mostly to Brad, who couldn't resist declaring that he was on a roll every time he won a hand.

I wished Nan were there. "Nothing is more charming than an elegant lady who plays poker," she would say, and she should know. Nan could always clean up on "casino night" at Montclair Manor if she wanted. She used to count the cards so that she *didn't* win all of the time. I've sat with Nan and watched her fold a perfectly good hand to let some other old biddy get the pot.

The deal moved to the next player, who dealt ZK another hand, two down. The cards were lousy—a queen of diamonds and a ten of spades—"rags" Nan used to call them. But when they dealt ZK a card up, it was an ace of spades. Everyone else showed poor cards, except of course Brad. He had an ace of diamonds showing. I knew from playing with Nan that the chances of two aces up were slim and would probably unnerve the other players. But ZK was smart enough to know that he didn't have much of a hand, so he was ready to fold. But I wanted to see what would happen if everyone thought he had a good hand, just to find out.

"Hold," I whispered in his ear.

"What? But it's . . ."

"Just ante and hold," I whispered again. He gave me a sly questioning look, but turned to the guy dealing and said he'd hold and anted up. Everyone perked up, especially the big winner, Brad, who also had an ace. I knew he wouldn't fold as long as he thought he was still on a winning streak.

After a few more cards, ZK's hand appeared decent if you didn't know that there wasn't anything good in the down-turned cards. Because Brad and ZK kept anteing up, the pot grew steadily bigger. Brad was hanging in, even though his table cards were terrible. I couldn't imagine he had any kind of hand.

Finally it was time for the players to make one more bet.

"Double down," I whispered. "Make it big." ZK examined my face to see if I was serious, and then shoved half of his cash into the pile.

"I call," he said. A couple of guys dropped out right away. Then everyone grew quiet waiting for Big Man Brad to make his move. He puffed and puffed on his cigar, and after debating for a few moments, he folded. ZK took the pot, which had to be a couple of thousand by my reckoning. I threw ZK's cards in the pile before anyone could ask to see them. ZK was laughing and shaking his head as he raked it in.

"Brilliant, you really know how to play," he whispered under his breath. I guess I've always been a better faker than I thought.

"Why don't you play a round?" ZK asked.

"I never carry cash," I whispered, my new excuse for not having any money. He laughed.

"No problem. I'll stake you. Come on—let's switch seats." He stood up, offered me his chair, and slid out a wad of hundreds. I wondered how he had the cash to play with this crowd. Or for that matter, stake me, considering what Tabitha had said about his status as a Madoff Millionaire.

"Hey boys, get ready, ZK's brought a ringer to the table," Big Brad said, giving me a wink as he shuffled the deck. Everyone laughed.

"How about I split my winnings with you?" I said to ZK quietly.

Brad, Hugh, Ian, and Baird overheard me and found the idea to be completely uproarious.

"Lucky guy, ZK, she's going to split her winnings with you!" chortled Brad. I noticed he was wearing a twenty-thousand-dollar Patek Philippe watch. He really was a show-off. I decided to play innocent, as I knew Audrey would.

"Now, if you boys don't mind explaining, what's a good hand again?" I asked. ZK raised an eyebrow, as the boys interrupted each other trying to tell me how to play the game.

An hour later, I had won four hands in a row, although I had to split the pot on a game of seven-card high-low. Brad had dropped twenty or twenty-five thousand, and ZK and I were up about seventeen thousand. My Nan knew how to hold 'em and fold 'em, and she taught me well. The trust-fund boys were no longer laughing.

"Darlings, you have been too kind to me," I said. "Thank you for showing me the game. Apologies for my beginner's luck, but I'm quite exhausted. So if you'll permit me, I'll retire for the evening."

ZK scooped up our winnings with a satisfied grin. There was lots of mumbling around the table until Brad grew more vocal.

"Come on, ZK," he said, "she has to give us a chance to win our money back."

"You should be glad she's quitting now," ZK said. "If she stays at the table, you might just leave here tonight in a different tax bracket." He slid his arm around my waist, which sent a shiver down my back, and escorted me from the table.

46

We walked outside to the terrace and leaned on the marble banisters, glancing out over the city.

"Are you cold?" he asked, smoothly removing his jacket and placing it over my shoulders.

"Thank you," I said.

"It almost goes with your dress."

I laughed and slipped my hand into the crook of his arm.

"Where did you learn to play like that?" he asked.

"My Nan." I smiled, thinking that she'd love to hear all about my poker-playing prowess. "She's a debutante card shark. I'm just a good student."

He slid out the wad of bills in his pocket and handed it to me.

"No, I couldn't—it was your money," I said, trying to be cool about it, although I hadn't picked up a paycheck in weeks. Tabitha said he didn't have any *real money*. So what kind of money did he have? Just a couple thousand in pocket change for poker?

"You should keep the winnings."

He peeled off a few hundred-dollar bills.

"This covers my stake; the rest is yours."

"Thank you, but we did say fifty-fifty, right?" I cut the wad of money by half and handed it back. He hesitated for a second. "If you don't take it, I won't be your good-luck charm next time," I added.

"Yeah, well, you've got way more than luck going on," he said and pocketed the cash. I stuffed the remaining $8,500 in my tiny cocktail purse as though it was a common occurrence.

In that half-empty moment I secretly observed ZK. Although he was standing right beside me, a blank expression crossed his eyes, and he seemed like a forlorn little boy.

I thought back to all the times I had seen him since that evening at the Met when I was outside the fishbowl looking in, a mere onlooker. I remembered even then, there was a moment where he was alone and detached as the cameras flashed around him. I remembered other moments like that; those tiny instances where he let his guard down, where his fabulousness evaporated and he was more boy than man, as if he were just hoping to find a way from one empty moment to the next. I knew that feeling. His solitude made me want to hold him, care for him, and love him more.

We stood there, the city a twinkling galaxy of lights. Our legs touched innocently, but I didn't move, and neither did he. It seemed to snap him out of his moment.

"Come on, let's toast your success," ZK said.

"As long as it's not a pink martini, you're on," I replied. He didn't seem to know what I was talking about, but I wondered if he was aware what went on in the penthouse upstairs.

We headed to the bar. ZK snatched a bottle of Macallan 18 and two glasses, ignoring the bartender's annoyed look. He poured us each a single malt, dropping one cube in both glasses and swirling it around.

"Here's to the mysterious Lisbeth Dulac," he said. "You know, I've never met a woman like you." I felt suddenly shy as we clinked glasses.

"You'll be coming to the Hamptons with Tabitha, won't you?" he asked.

"It depends, I guess." Apparently the Hamptons was on everyone's agenda.

"Well, I'll be there," he said. "Somehow I can't imagine not seeing you for the rest of the summer."

The terrace was dotted with plants and small trees in terracotta containers. I dropped down onto the cushy outdoor sofa, sipping my whiskey, and ZK sat next to me, his knee touching mine. He wrapped his arms around me, pulling me onto his lap. I put my arms around his neck, aching for the warmth of his body, inhaling his scent, listening to the sound of his breathing. He gazed into my eyes, moving toward me a millimeter at a time until, at last, his lips, soft and strong, touched mine.

In that moment there was nothing but ZK and me, the lights of the city, and the dark abyss of the night. I couldn't help thinking that this was where I was meant to be.

47 On the PATH train back to Jersey, I squeezed in among the shopping-bag-toting, Starbucks-sipping, iPod-listening masses, grateful for a little downtime.

Thumbing the keyboard on my phone, I lined up five new entries promoting Designer X's new line of "secret dresses" and hinted at big news to come. I had downloaded the app that allowed me to post to my blog from anywhere, and now I could shoot pictures on the fly anytime I saw something I liked and post them immediately. When I logged on to my Tumblr, I was blown away that there were so many followers. I featured pictures of last night's Designer X masterpiece on my blog, including close-ups of the lyrical embroidery. Isak commented almost immediately, raising the count of my followers numerically.

"When do we get to meet Designer X!" he demanded in a later comment, and literally 237 followers cheered him on in a chorus. "X! X! X! X! X! X! X!" one person chanted, and then others repeated and reblogged, driving up traffic on the Web site exponentially.

I hugged my pocketbook and vagabond bag close to me. I wasn't about to let that $8,500 slip out of my grasp—$8,555 to be exact. I had big plans for that money, and I wanted to get started on them.

I guided the Purple Beast from the PATH station's commuter parking lot directly home. I had a text from Courtney saying she was dropping out of school next semester. That bummed me out because I knew Ryan hadn't finished his year of middle school. None of us were staying in school, which would definitely pain Mom if she knew.

I hadn't heard much from Courtney about Mom's condition for a while, so I was surprised when I walked in the screen door and saw Mom sitting at the kitchen table, smoking a cigarette, and sorting through the bills just as before. I was relieved that things were back to normal until I realized it wasn't Mom. It was Courtney.

Shoulders slumped, Courtney looked so much like Mom it was unnerving. I felt terrible for her. Her biggest nightmare was true— she was becoming mom.

As I put down my bags, she gazed up at me, her face pained and worried, as if she knew what I was thinking. She still wore the sweatpants and oversize T tied at the waist. I don't think she had changed in days. She tapped her cigarette in the ashtray the same way Mom used to and arranged the bills in rows as Mom used to do; Jersey Power and Light, Comcast Cable, Montclair Propane and Gas, and all the others.

Like a fly caught on flypaper whose fate was sealed, she seemed caught up in something bigger, unable to stop it all from happening.

"Do you know how many fucking bills we can't afford to pay?" she asked.

Ryan was playing Warcrack in the living room, and I could hear the computer-generated cries of creatures being vaporized and destroyed. The place was a wreck. Some things never changed. I sat down beside her.

"I'm going to go back to work for Harris, at the bar," she said, rearranging the bills on the table. "Luckily Mom's got coverage at the hospital as long as they keep her there. But I don't know how she's going to make any money when she gets out." She tilted back in the chair on just two chair legs just like Mom used to and gave me a helpless look.

"Mom just can't take care of us anymore, Lizzy," she said, tearing up as the chair legs came down again. "We're on our own." She was going to cry. Me too. We hugged.

"I've checked the bank accounts," Courtney said through the tears. "There's hardly any money for these bills. And if I start working at the bar again, what's going to happen to Ryan?"

We looked across to the living room, both of us thinking about Ryan, even though he didn't seem to notice or care.

"He's already a head case," she said. "There's this letter from the school district. He's supposed to go to summer school if he wants to move up to the next grade. He could get sent to juvie if he doesn't."

After we exhausted our tears, we sat for a little while in silence.

"Well, I've got a plan," I said. She looked at me like I was crazy.

"Yeah sure," she said and reverted to her standard "you don't know shit" expression she has given me since the day I was born.

"You'll see," I said. "This is going to work out. It's bad now, but a lot of times good comes out ..."

"... When bad things happen," she said before I could. "I know that BS from Nan, and it's for suckers ..." She stopped herself because that was what Mom would have said. "I'm sorry, Lizzy, you're the only one who thinks things can change. You're the only one in the family who still believes in hope. I just don't think it's going to happen." Courtney took another drag on her cigarette and let out the smoke in one long weary breath.

"What did they say about Mom?" I asked.

"They don't know. She was going through really bad withdrawal symptoms. I don't think they're DTs, but they have her sedated. She was shaking and all that shit. I think there are some hopeful signs on the liver tests, but the cold-turkey is killing her."

"The drinking is killing her," I said.

"When do you start college?" she asked, her eyes narrowing in on me.

"I'm not going," I said and waited for the look of alarm on her face. When it registered, I though she might throw something at me.

"Don't even say that," she said, astonished. "Mom will freak."

"I have another plan," I said.

"The Hole?" she asked with astonishment. "Word is you're toast there. Have you even been to work for the last week? I have no idea how you pay for all the stuff you do."

"I'm getting a job in fashion."

"How are you qualified for that? Something with your dyke friend?"

"That's not your problem. I'm going to figure it out." I'd wilt if she lit into me, so I slipped ten crisp one hundred dollar bills from my purse and placed them on the table. I thought she was going to fall out of her chair.

"Did you rob an ATM?"

"Hopefully this is enough to cover the bills for now. Let's figure out how we're going to get Ryan to summer school, but first things first," I said and headed for the kitchen cupboards.

In the cupboard above the stove, I found four half-gallon bottles of Gordon's. Checking the cabinet below the silverware, I found three more. Then I went to the freezer and found three bottles of some other generic vodka I'd never heard of and put those on the table.

"What are you doing?" Courtney asked.

"Help me," I said. Courtney thought a second, put out her cigarette, and got up and went right for Mom's stash in the laundry room—four bottles of Captain Morgan's rum and a bottle of Southern Comfort.

"What are you guys doing?" Ryan asked. He must have heard the bottles clanking, and it was the one thing that made him stop playing his game.

"Come on, Ryan, help us," I said.

In a few moments, we were all combing the house for Mom's booze like some perverse treasure hunt. The bottles were everywhere—in the garage behind the paint cans, forgotten bottles under Mom's bed, an unopened case in her closet, half empties under the La-Z-Boy, and another shoved way back behind the towels in the bathroom cabinet. I think it was kind of blowing Ryan's mind, because he knew Mom drank a lot, but this was totally off the charts.

We gathered them from the kitchen table, all thirty-one of them, and started taking them outside, lining them up in the driveway.

"Now what?" Ryan asked as he placed the last three bottles in a row.

I walked over to the first half gallon of Gordon's, picked it up, and threw it down as hard as I could against the cement by the garage door, smashing the bottle to pieces, the vodka pouring out, running down the driveway. I picked up another bottle and smashed that one, too.

Ryan and Courtney looked at me as if I had lost my mind. Then Courtney picked up a couple of bottles and slammed them against the sidewalk so hard we all had to jump out of the way to avoid the glass.

The three of us took turns screaming as we decimated the bottles that had wrecked our mom and our lives. The running rum, vodka, and Southern Comfort mixed together made a sickly alcohol smell like sugar and wood stain as it rose up from the pavement. As grim as it was, we all started to laugh.

I've never loved my sister and brother as much as I did that very moment—the three of us standing in a pile of glass, the stench of alcohol running down the driveway and into the gutter. If the neighbors were watching, they would have thought we were insane.

Courtney got a couple of brooms, and we swept the glass into a garbage can while Ry sprayed down the driveway with the garden hose. Hundreds of dollars of alcohol down the gutter.

We all sat on the curb and watched as the sun began to set.

"That was fun and everything," Courtney said, calming down, "but what the fuck are we going to do about all the other shit?"

"Like I said, I have a plan." I got up and walked back inside. "Let's take a look at those bills for a starter."

Courtney and I began tallying up everything, and it was clear that, as she became sick, Mom had stopped keeping it together. All that ammonia in her blood, I guessed. Some bills hadn't been paid in three months. Ryan ran into the room, interrupting us.

"Hey, there's a taxi outside," Ryan said, running into the room. "And some old lady is getting out." Just then, the screen door opened.

"Sorry I'm late, Lisbeth. I hadn't realized it would be such an ordeal to check myself out of the old-biddy home," Nan said as she entered, dropping her overnight bag on a chair.

She was as bright and vibrant as I'd ever seen her. "Betty nearly had a heart attack. I thought they'd have to finally institutionalize her."

Courtney regarded Nan with bewilderment.

"Hello, Courtney," Nan said and threw open her arms.

"Hi, Nan," Courtney said sheepishly. She seemed like she might cry, but instead went running to get one of those special heart-melding Nan hugs.

"Ry, say hi to Nan," I said. He had already retreated to the living room, where he was thumbing the controller of his game.

"Just a minute, I'm in the middle of a raid," he said.

"Excuse me, young man?" Nan walked over to the television set.

"Oh hi," Ryan finally said and went back to his game. Nan walked around to the other side of the television set.

"Hmm. Let's see how this works." She ducked down and ripped the television cord out of the wall.

"Hey, that's my game!" Ry was in shock.

"Well perhaps you can play some more after we get this house in shape. Let's start with your mother's room so I have a place to sleep tonight." Nan grabbed Ryan by the wrist with her iron grip and led him to the stairway. Courtney's eyes widened and turned to me, stunned. I shrugged.

"Hey, Nan," she said, "can I give you a hand?"

"Why certainly, dear." Nan gave me a wink as they all started up the stairs. I began to follow, but she stopped me.

"You go along to the hospital, dear," she said. "I know you have some important things to attend to."

48 The hospital was quiet that evening when I arrived. They had moved Mom to a different unit, so it took a little while to find her. But even the volunteer at the information desk seemed to know that I was Ella Wachowicz's daughter, so they took me back as soon as they could.

As I passed the nurse's station, all the nurses and the orderlies and doctors were watching me. A few nodded hello.

When I reached Mom's room, Nurse Brynner was coming out the door.

"Your mom is going to be so happy to see you," she said in her gravelly voice.

"How is she?" I asked.

"I have to let Doctor Newton give you the update," she said. "But he's off duty at the moment."

"I meant, how is she doing? You know . . ."

"I know. I've quit now, too," she said. She held her hand up to show me. It was trembling. "Maybe it's just all the coffee I'm drinking so I don't feel it. But I promised her she wouldn't have to do this alone. It's not as bad for me; I've still got a husband at home."

God, I was determined not to cry.

"That's okay, dear. You go and make your mother happy," she said, managing a grin. "I'll be back in a little while to give her a sedative." As she left, I took a deep breath and walked in. Mom was sitting up; all the catheters and monitors had been removed and she was reading the newspaper.

"Hi, Mom," I said. She gave me a glare as if she had never seen me before. I knew that look. It wasn't good. I sat down quietly and waited. She didn't say anything for the first few moments. Already her face seemed less bloated and the splotchy redness was gone, but she appeared gray and weary.

"So what's the story with college?"

I closed my eyes, summoning my courage. "I'm not going," I said.

She put down her paper and glared at me like she wanted to leap out of bed and strangle me. I could tell she was trying to keep from getting angry. Her whole body was tense.

"It's the *plan*," she said.

"I know, Mom, I . . ."

"I don't know what's going to happen to me," she said, not letting me get a word in. "They're keeping me here, and I don't even know if anyone will let me work again." Her eyes glistened, like there might be tears. But she was too tough to let it show. I could see that she couldn't stand being weepy. She turned away to quietly wipe her eyes. For the first time, she seemed vulnerable.

"Have they said that to you?"

"Are you kidding? Now that they know, they'll never hire me back. Why? Are you suddenly an expert?" she demanded.

"Mom, they have to let you work. As long as you go into a program like AA and you get better, they can't fire you." I wanted to hold her hand or hug her. I started to move closer but wasn't sure she'd let me.

"Where did you get that?" Her belligerence resurfaced.

I sat back.

"I was talking to Nan. She's at the house," I said, knowing the impact.

"What?!"

"Yep, a regular staff sergeant, she's whipping the house in shape for when you get home and getting Ryan to finish summer school. Courtney's helping."

That made Mom go silent. We sat there for what seemed like ages.

Mom kept shaking her head in small little nods, staring off into space. She was so tired that her eyes closed a couple of times. Everything seemed to weigh on her, and I realized I had no idea what was going through her mind.

"Yeah, Nan tried to call a couple of times," she added finally.

"Did you talk to her?"

"No," she answered, as if my question was absurd.

"Well, it's time you guys start talking again because I can't be there." I waited for that to sink in. "You need her help."

"And where are you going to be?" Mom asked, but I didn't have a chance to answer because Nurse Brynner came in.

"Ella, isn't it great to have your lovely daughter visit?" she said as she adjusted her pillows and settled her bed. Mom sat silent as a stone. "Don't mind your mother's grumpy face," Nurse Brynner added. "It's just stuck that way. She's really happy you're here."

I could imagine these two tough old battle-axes sitting around shooting the shit about everyone.

Mom was silent as her friend handed her a cup of water and some pills, which I assumed were sedatives. I slid over to the side table, where Mom couldn't see me, and slipped out my envelope of poker winnings. I peeled off twenty one-hundred-dollar bills and put them in her pocketbook, hoping that in some small way it would make up for whatever money she had wasted on my college tuition.

As I got ready to leave, Mom was falling asleep.

"We're not done talking about this, Lisbeth," she said, struggling to keep her eyes open.

"I know, Mom. You rest. I'll be back soon."

49

Fried pickles, bacon grease, and cheese. Those were the first smells that hit me as I walked in the door at the Hole. Everyone was so busy that no one noticed me. It was like one of those scenes from the movies where you attend your own funeral. It was easy to see that the Finer Diner was moving along perfectly well without me, almost as if I had been erased and was never there.

"Two cows with bacon and cheddar, table eleven," I heard Buela say from the kitchen and ring that annoying little bell. Cheddar? That was new to the menu. I saw Jake pick up the order, and I felt my heart sink, wondering if he'd even talk to me this time.

He was wearing one of his skinny Ts and loose-fitting jeans with no belt and the little white apron the guys got to wear instead of the pink one. I hated to admit it, because it's just so weird, but something about a guy in an apron turned me on.

Crystal was all hot in her tied-up work shirt, shredded Daisy Dukes, pink apron, and heels. Who could possibly wear heels while working in a diner? Me, I'd face plant into a plate of corned-beef hash in no time. But Crystal handled it with ease. It hurt to watch as she came by and leaned on Jake's shoulder in that familiar way I used to.

"What are you doing here?" Buela asked. I hadn't seen her come up behind me.

"Oh hi, Buela," I said. "I'm sorry I haven't been in. I came in to tell you that I have to quit, because my mom . . ."

"You can't quit," she said. "I fired you two weeks ago."

"Really? I didn't know I . . ."

"Save your breath. I don't want to hear about it," she said, heading back to the kitchen. "Your last check is in your locker. Take your things and leave. And don't think you're taking your pink apron. That stays here." As if anyone would want to have one of those greasy pink aprons. Maybe somewhere they were much-sought-after authentic diners-of-America souvenirs. I passed Buela's office and the freezer room, and then I ran into Jake. I wasn't sure he'd say anything to me, so I tried not to make eye contact.

"Hey Lizzy," he said softly.

"Hey Jake," I said turning, afraid my knees might buckle if my eyes met his.

"I heard about your mom," he said.

"She's going to be okay. Thanks for asking."

"And you? How have you been?" Something about the softness in his voice, the way the words flowed, made me look up.

"Good," I said. Our eyes met. I had a lot to say, like how I loved that strand of black hair that he didn't seem to be able to tame and the way his T-shirt hung on his shoulders, that I wondered if we could start all over again, but Jake's smoky-blue eyes grew serious, and I worried what he might be thinking so I didn't say all that.

"We've missed you around here," he said.

"I don't think so," I said and managed to smile. "Seems like everyone is doing just fine without me, but I'm glad to see you again."

"Yeah." Then he got quiet, hanging his head, looking down at his feet as he always did when there was something serious he was thinking about. I was thinking, too, trying to find the right way to say that I was sorry for what happened and couldn't we be friends.

"About last time . . ." we both blurted out, speaking at the same time, fumbling over each other's words.

"You go ahead," I said.

"No you, sorry, I didn't mean . . ." and he trailed off.

"I'm the one that's sorry," I said finally. "I'm sorry I missed your gig. I'm sorry I came too late. I'm sorry we're not friends, I miss being your friend. I miss you and me and Jess hanging out at the diner, but I guess Jess isn't here anyway . . ."

I spied Crystal checking us out from the restaurant.

"Hey, I know you've moved on, and I just want you to know we're cool, right? Are we? I mean, we were friends, right?"

"Friends?" He acted surprised to hear that word. Like he hated it or something, and I got worried he was going to be mad.

"That's what you thought?" He shook his head side to side. "Lisbeth, you've got to understand . . ."

"Hey, lover boy! I have a restaurant to run," Buela called from the front.

He looked over his shoulder. Crystal motioned him to hurry.

"We're cool, Lizzy," he said, frustrated. "See you around. Gotta go."

"See you," I said.

Way to keep digging that hole, I thought.

Maybe the Hamptons would be the best thing considering I had no job, Mom was in the hospital, and there was no Jake.

I dialed Tabitha to tell her. She started squealing so loudly I had to hold the phone away from my ear.

"The Hamptons are going to be so much fun!" she said and started squealing again.

50 "Are you sure?" Jess asked, holding her scissors and a hank of my hair. "Just cut."

She poised her scissors a few inches from the tips of my hair.

"Here?" she asked.

"Higher."

"But your hair . . . there's so many other ways you can wear it," she pleaded.

In the cheapie full-length mirror she had propped up against the wall, she could see my expression.

"Even more?" she asked.

"Even more," I said.

Jess sighed. It wasn't like she didn't know how. Jess and her mom could cut any hairstyle on anybody; it's just that in South End not a lot of the big ladies came in asking for pixies or elfin cuts. And though she had been chopping up her own hair for ages and dying it pink or turquoise, she had always admired my long hair, which I had kept that way since grade school.

"You're sure?"

"I'm very sure. All off."

And it began, the first big chunks of my hair dropping to the floor.

Sitting in the middle of Jess's Chinatown loft as her scissors snipped away, I admired what she had done with her apartment. Everything was furnished almost entirely with things she found on the street. It all had a purpose that served her aesthetic and the clothing designs she was working on. You could tell she had spent long nights into early mornings working there. Doodles, drawings and Post-it notes dotted the whitewashed walls. All the scribbles were about one thing and one thing only—her new line of dresses.

The dress designs were sometimes sketched directly on the walls, alongside fabric swatches taped or pinned beside them. Fragments from her journal that she later embroidered on the hems of her dresses were jotted nearby.

Over the entrance to the apartment she had scrawled: *She put on her thinking cap and stumbled through the door but only multiplication tables came to mind.*

And over the bathroom mirror: *When your heart breaks, the pieces shatter. They show up unexpectedly at the bottom of the pit you're digging, or sewn into the stitches of your dress.*

Sitting in the middle of Jess's apartment was like being inside her brain.

"Chin down, please," Jess said, interrupting my thoughts with a poke in the back. "So? I'm sure you've got some kind of new adventure to tell me."

What was it was about getting a haircut that made you want to instantly confess your deepest darkest secrets? Sarrah the nosey-parker girlfriend was gone, just as Jess predicted, so I let it all pour out—the odd meeting at the St. Regis, the creepy image of Robert Francis in his bathrobe holding Morris in the light of the doorway, poker night with ZK and the taxi-cab kiss. I recounted it all. Jess responded with awe and cautious concern.

"My mom says your mom came home," Jess added, snipping away.

"Yeah, they've given her three days to get stronger before they start the approval process for a new liver, if she can qualify at all. But she's in the hospital rehab program and finally going to AA meetings twice a week. Incredible, really," I said.

"And Nan?" she asked, as I watched the last big chunk of hair fall to the floor.

"She's moved out of the manor and is staying in my room, if you can imagine. At least they're talking," I said. "Mom's a tough customer, but so is Nan."

Now that the big chunks were gone, Jess gathered my hair in front of my face and started another round of cutting. I puffed the hair away and she combed it right back—I think she purposefully didn't want me to see what she was doing. It reminded me of the way the Italian barber in *Roman Holiday* cut Audrey's hair. Every Audrey fan knows that the haircut in the barbershop at via della Stamperia next to the Trevi Fountain made Audrey famous forever.

Next to *Breakfast at Tiffany's, Roman Holiday* was my favorite Audrey fix. I had seen it almost as often. I would kill to go to Italy and ride around on a Vespa with a guy like Gregory Peck holding on to my waist. Of course, I would just kill to go to Italy. The movie was Audrey's big break, but as in a lot of showbiz stories you read, the film wasn't written for her. Elizabeth Taylor was slated to play the part, and instead of Gregory Peck, it was supposed to be Cary Grant.

At the time, Audrey was simply an aspiring actress, auditioning for a director she didn't know. I had even seen her screen test for *Roman Holiday* on YouTube. It showed a subdued, dignified Audrey performing an audition scene until the director yelled cut. Luckily the cameraman left the camera rolling and captured Audrey's real personality as she chatted away about the war and ballet dancing to benefit the Resistance during World War II. Film historians have said that the candid footage won her the role.

The most marvelous part of the movie, as far as I was concerned, was the haircut scene. In that scene, before your very eyes, she was transformed from the typically stuffy, boring Hollywood princess to a newly minted screen persona that redefined glamour. As each lock of hair fell to the floor, Audrey's eyes grew round with delight, and her charm, innocence, and waiflike features were revealed. When the barber was finished, Audrey was liberated, and the starlet we've come to know was born.

I didn't have such lofty goals for my haircut. I just felt it was time for me to shed my good-girl image and become something more.

Jess was circling back to shape and refine my hair, completely absorbed in the process. She didn't do anything halfway. She moved around me, nipping with her scissors like a sculptor, forming my hair closely to the shape of my head. Each tiny cut created movement upward, off my neck, and forward, to frame my face.

Through my bangs I could see the open closet where the dresses were hung. There were still dresses of Nan's I hadn't worn. Modified Chanel, Lilli Ann, Chez Ninon, and others. I figured I'd take those with me to the Hamptons.

Alongside Nan's dresses were Designer X's masterpieces. The closet burst with dresses made of sheer materials, like one chiffon dress I could see with a lace underlay. There were lots of floral detailing, ruffles, even sequins. Embroidered full-length gowns were interwoven with delicate knee-length tulle frocks. The dresses were starkly accented here and there with a studded belt or a biker jacket.

I couldn't believe how many dresses she had already finished. I wondered if she ever slept.

"Isak won't stop bothering me about you," I said through the falling hair. I wanted to draw her out on how she felt about her show. "I don't see how I can keep him away. He's even demanding it on my blog. I mean, I don't see why you won't meet him now."

"I'm just not ready," she said.

"And when will you be ready?" I asked.

"I don't know," she said, sounding exhausted. "Maybe when it's perfect. Depends on how the show goes, I guess."

"You're crazy. He *has* to see your show."

"Lisbeth, you don't understand. You only have one chance, and if you're not ready when they see you, they'll never come back," Jess said. "It's like a dress—it's all first impression. If you have depth and talent and skill after that, great, but if the first impression fails, you've failed."

"I'm sure you'll be ready."

"We'll see. Now shut up for a minute while I try to finish your hair."

She cut the sides up around my ears, which was weird because I hadn't felt my ears free of hair for longer than I could remember. The final strokes took away sections from my cherished bangs so they were lighter and shorter. There certainly was no going back now. I admired her work in the mirror: ultrashort, feminine, with a feathery touch.

"This will be great in the Hamptons," I said.

"What?" Jess practically dropped her scissors.

"The Hamptons," I said. "Tabitha invited me for a few days."

"But the show . . ." she trailed off. She seemed tired. "You're going to miss my show." She had the sound of inevitability in her voice.

"No, I'll be back in time," I insisted. "It's not like I'm going to another country." I hadn't expected her reaction.

"I have a bad feeling about this."

"But you don't have a date yet or the space?"

"Not yet, but when we do it will be sudden. It will all happen at once."

"And I'll be there," I added. "Besides, I'm doing all my posting and promotion online. I might make more connections this way. Donna Karan is out there, and everyone else."

"Lisbeth, what's happening? You're not becoming one of them, are you?" she asked, a sad glint in her eye. "You're actually summering in the Hamptons. You'll just get swept away with all of their million-dollar houses, their lives."

"No, I've handled it so far," I said, wondering myself if it sounded true.

"Listen, we'll have to do it like a pop-up show anyway, don't you think? We'll get more attention that way," I added.

"Oh, I don't know that kind of thing; you're the queen of promotion. All I know is that I have two more dresses to finish. I have models to find and audition. I have to do fittings. All before Fashion Week starts. It's too much." She sounded hopeless.

Walking over to the closet, I lifted a few dresses to see how she was doing.

"These are amazing," I said. "You've outdone yourself, Jess." Each and every dress bore her trademark—the lines of her journal sewn into the hems of her designs.

"You've created an entire vision. Oh my god, this one . . ." I picked up a soft orange chiffon dress with the tight blush silk skirt. Like the first patterned black one with the snowflakes, this was a dual dress—fairy-tale chiffon on the outside and sexy satin underneath. The asymmetric hem was gone, and the new color concept was eye-popping.

"This is your signature dress," I said, almost breathlessly. "I've never seen anything like this. You could do this in a thousand different colors and it would work. Isak will love it. Everyone will."

"Yeah, whatever," she said, plopping down on the bed, sounding like she was in too much pain to think about it.

Kicking off my shoes, I stripped down to my underwear. I had to see if it felt the way it looked. I slipped on the tight satin underskirt. It felt sculpted, almost the way Audrey's Givenchy felt that first time. Pulling up the overskirt and blouse, I felt the intimacy of its illusion—body-shaping underneath but a freedom of movement—an absolute perfect construction.

The dress combined two contradictory spirits—floaty and loose on the outside and tight and form-fitting underneath. It exuded sexuality and confidence, beauty and power, simplicity adapted to fabric. I couldn't help wondering why no one else had ever designed such a dress. Its wearability, even with the tight satin skirt underneath, could only have been designed by a woman.

A little smile crossed Jess's face as I twirled before the mirror, but I could see she was fading on me—I had to do something immediately.

"Okay, measurements. Fittings. Plans. I'll stay tonight and try on everything. We'll get a head start right now," I said. "I'll work on the marketing and planning in the Hamptons over the next few days. You'll just have to mend fences with Sarrah enough to get her to wrangle up nine or ten really distinctive models from the school."

"Ugh, God save me," Jess moaned.

"Then I'll come back a few days before and we'll get everything set and make sure my blog followers and Isak are there." She gave me a sideways glance, trying to decide if I was for real.

"Come on, lazy bones, let's do it," I said, walking over to the bed and dragging her up on her feet. Then I went to the stove to make coffee.

That night I tried on everything. One after the other, each dress was spectacular. It was like living a fairy tale or playing princess when we were kids. Everything was cool, feminine, and dazzling.

Jess took notes on adjustments.

We designed the order of the show with the orange chiffon the last, and I put together my first thoughts on a guest list.

A big problem to solve was where the show should be staged. Jess was still waiting to hear about the FIT auditorium. School was in its lighter summer session and she was hoping that one of her teachers would help her get it. But I insisted that it had to be held away from the school. Jess couldn't seem to understand why.

"Because Designer X doesn't go to school," I said. "Designer X needs to appear fully formed out of nowhere and be fiercely fabulous."

"Only there is no Designer X except on your blog," Jess said wearily. "I'm just a freshman fashion student from New Jersey having her first independent show. I am not 'fully formed,' and I don't have any fabulous connections."

"Jess, you're more than that. It's not enough to design a great collection—you have to make a splash to get the right kind of attention." I tried to think of alternatives for a moment.

"Doesn't Sarrah work in an art gallery somewhere?" I asked.

"Please, not more Sarrah," she said, shaking her head.

I hated bringing up Sarrah so much, but I was determined to make Jess's debut incredible, and I knew that Sarrah was so infatuated with Jess that she would help.

"Yeah she works at Below the Line. It's one of those storefront art spaces under the High Line. But can't we worry about that later?" I could see that Jess's eyes were glazing over. She seemed overwhelmed by it all.

"Sarrah has to get permission for you to have the show there," I said. "And it has to be off calendar. Maybe on Fashion's Night Out—that's in five days—when everyone's in town and the press is trying to find a good story. Something new. Can you be ready by then?"

Around the time we were freshman at Montclair High, Anna Wintour of *Vogue* started Fashion's Night Out in New York City. It was the recession, and Anna Wintour hoped to save her industry and to help perk up sales in retail stores in Manhattan.

Almost immediately, it became a huge worldwide event and a prelude to fashion week. All the stores in the city that sell clothes stayed open until midnight, handing out free champagne. It was a great night for happenings and off-beat news stories.

"I don't know," she said, exhausted.

"The actual show is going to take all of a half hour. Promise me you'll ask Sarrah?"

"That's too much. I can't promise anything right now. I'm too tired," she said, collapsing onto the bed. I flopped down next to her. We were both ready to drop off to sleep.

Jess turned to look at me. We stared into each other's eyes, as Jess admired her work on my hair.

"You're the best friend . . . ever," she said.

"No," I began, "I'll never be able to hold a candle to you." But she never heard me.

Jess had fallen asleep.

My Jess. Then I dozed off, too.

The next morning I woke early. I let Jess snooze away. I tiptoed to the closet, stacked a few of Nan's remixed dresses into a clothing bag, and then filled one of Jess's monster bags with shoes and purses. If Tabitha and I partied every night for five days straight, I was ready.

As I was getting ready to leave, I realized that Jess had been watching me the entire time.

"Go back to sleep—you need to rest," I said. But she got out of bed and walked over to the closet. She picked out a dress from her new designs. It was the first one I had tried on, her signature dress, soft orange chiffon with the tight blush silk skirt underneath.

"Take this," she said, unzipping the clothing bag and placing the dress inside. Then she stretched to wake up.

"How can I?" I said.

"It's a great dress. It will be fabulous at a party. Don't try to tell me you're not going to a party out there."

"But it's one of your originals, maybe the most important dress in your collection," I said. "It has to be in the show."

"Exactly why I want you to take it." She poured herself a cup of coffee and sat on the stool I had sat on the night before when she was cutting my hair.

She took a long sip and peered at me over the coffee-mug rim. "Bring it back, okay?"

51 It was a clear blue Thursday morning, and I felt as if I were traveling to another world. I boarded the Hamptons Jitney at Fortieth Street with the summer hoards—urban surfer dudes, preppy boys wearing pink and green, giggling well-groomed tweens carrying Vera Bradley travel bags, and an eighties music fanatic playing "Small Town Girl" so loudly that I could hear every word through his earbuds.

But nothing could disturb the tranquility and excitement of escaping the city to visit the unexplored Eden of the Hamptons. Unexplored by me, anyway.

The Jitney was just a bus, honestly, but it felt like transportation for the privileged classes with attendants serving your needs and offering a choice of muffins or granola bars as well as orange juice, water, and Wi-Fi, the lifeblood of any blogger.

As we reached exit 70, the landscape and air changed. We passed through the towns of Southampton, Water Mill, Bridgehampton, Sagaponack, Wainscott, and East Hampton. Gazing out the Jitney windows, each town seemed more beachy than the one before. Hydrangeas were everywhere. The big blue flowers made me think of little old ladies and churches.

"On way 2 Hamptons. Darling will you be there this weekend ? :)" I texted Isak. I hadn't seen him for a while, and I needed to lock him into Jess's show. I waited for his reply.

"Hello DFC :) I'm off 2 Italie back in NY 4 FW," he replied. Not until Fashion Week? That was unfortunate. But since we didn't know yet exactly when Jess's show would be, there wasn't much I could do.

"Hope you'll b back in time for Designer X ;)" I teased back.

"When ?! When ?! :)"

"Last minute ;) Will let you know."

The Jitney pulled into Amagansett. As I stepped off the bus, the difference between the scented air-freshened Jitney and the beach air was so revitalizing it practically made me giddy.

As the taxi pulled up to the enormous mansion by the dunes, the balmy ocean atmosphere embraced me: clean, salty, with hints of lilac and privet. The clouds in the sterling-blue sky above were full but not threatening.

A stocky woman in a classic black-and-white maid's uniform opened the door holding a barking, squirming Pomeranian— Galileo.

"We are so happy seeing you," she said loudly in a thick Russian accent over Galileo's yapping. "Miss Eden has been anxiously waiting. My name is Zoya. I welcome you." She seemed very excited, but when she glanced down and saw my lonely roller and garment bag, she stopped, alarmed.

"Did they lose bags? You want I call them?" she asked. She seemed upset that I had so few.

"No, no, it's fine," I said, smiling. "These are my bags."

"Really? But what will you wear?" she asked as we walked inside. I laughed. "Ah, maybe you go shopping spree?"

Galileo sniffed and remembered me as I walked into a lively, boisterous houseful of people. Even though Tabitha wasn't there, she had plenty of houseguests. Balty was back, and I had to admit I enjoyed talking to him though he still ogled me. This time it was his sister, Flo, who kept him in line.

"Tabitha told me you'd be here this weekend," Flo said, excitedly. She was wearing a lovely black one-piece swimsuit and huge red floppy straw hat that almost enveloped her entire body in shadow. I could see she had the kind of skin that would sunburn badly.

"I think you'll be very pleased with what I've cooked up for you," she said. "We can talk now if you have a moment." There was a devious sparkle in her eye. I couldn't wait to hear. Until that moment I hadn't realized how much I was counting on her.

Balty soon drifted away, utterly bored, as his sister and I sat by the pool droning on and on about click-throughs, e-book links, RSS aggregators, AdSense, AdWords, lions and tigers and bears, oh my. Bottom line: it would take time, but if we worked together click by click, entry by entry, we could develop an income stream and potentially a worthwhile and profitable "brand" from my little blog. Flo Birkenhead's excitement was utterly infectious.

"This is what I love to do!" she exclaimed, her eyes glowing with excitement beneath her voluminous hat that spread like a flaming mushroom top over her. I could tell it was true. The idea of initially earning three or four thousand dollars a month, which Flo dismissed as negligible, was huge for me. It was at least double what I would have made working at the Hole if I had worked forty hours a week.

We talked for hours while dozens of houseguests milled about the house. They were swimming in the pool, sleeping sunburned on the sectional in the living room, watching the US Open on the flat-screen, and driving quads across the lawn, ripping up the manicured grounds for the gardeners to repair. Tabitha had all the toys—a ten-seat theater, skateboard half-pipe, sunken tennis court, and a complete spa facility. I'd heard there was even a two-lane bowling alley somewhere.

Soon my head was swimming and I needed a rest. Zoya showed me to the guest cottage, which would have been a complete house for some people. After she insisted on hanging up my clothes in the massive walk-in closet, I flopped down on the bed and crashed.

"Are you going to sleep all night?" Tabitha asked and shook my arm as if I were dead.

"Night?" I said groggily, trying to sit up. "Really? I thought it was afternoon."

"It was about four hours ago," she said and took a sip of some chilled mixed alcohol concoction she was holding. "Now it's night. That's the way it always happens. First the afternoon and then the night," she said. "Now it's time to play." She handed me a drink, something with tequila in it.

52

I'm sure there's a difference between an "event," "a benefit," and a flat-out party but I wouldn't be able to tell you what it is. We drove up to an enormous Bridgehampton beachfront house made of wood and glass, parked Tabitha's limo with the valet, and stumbled in with our entourage. Everyone in our group was already hammered.

The entire ocean side of the house was made from oversize mahogany-framed glass sliding walls, which were fully opened to the outdoors. We witnessed the last orange and purple rays of sunshine setting over the nearby bay. A glass bridge crossed the infinity-edged pool reflecting the sunset. Tabitha seemed to know everyone, and it didn't take long for her to be scary drunk. Every direction you turned, there was sushi or a grill or a bar and always lots of people.

The strange thing was that I couldn't tell who was giving the party and whether just anyone could come. There was no hostess or activity that seemed to be the focus, and I suspected Tabitha didn't really know these people as much as they knew her in that celebrity way.

I found myself waving, air kissing, and making empty-headed conversation with a long procession of people I didn't know and who had no idea who I was or wasn't, which didn't seem to bother anyone but was exhausting. I wondered, was this how the other half parties? Eating fabulous food at enormous mansions with people they don't know?

Tabitha couldn't even tell me whose party it was. I developed my own pet theory that the owner was a plastic surgeon, because this particular group seemed to be filled with so many women who had enhanced surgical recontouring. Even the young women had bodies that were anatomically impossible. I felt positively flat, not for the first time, but this was extreme. At least I wouldn't have to contend with random injectables in my body for the rest of my life.

I commented to Tabitha about the over-the-top bodies, and she laughed. She proposed a drinking game where we'd each have to throw back a shot every time we saw a woman with a breast augmentation and two for a Brazilian butt lift. But that was a bad idea because there were too many. She told me about a package deal one cosmetic surgeon she knew in the city offered with unlimited plastic surgical procedures ("within reason," his offer stated), including a Hamptons luxury home rental and a full-time nurse for your recovery, as well as a chauffeur, invites to VIP and celebrity parties (more parties, I assumed, with people you didn't know), and a budget for a new wardrobe (because your new body would need new, slimmer clothes, I assumed). I just hoped that whoever bought the package didn't worry about looking puffy.

We left Bridgehampton for another party in Amagansett not far from Tabitha's. It was a birthday bash for a sixteen-year-old girl who was the daughter of a friend of hers. But you'd never know it was a party for kids.

The adults easily outnumbered the kids and the teenagers were scary. They ran around with a total sense of entitlement and confidence that I assumed only Daddy's trust fund could provide. Watching them intimidated me. The girls, many of them a mere thirteen or fourteen years old, wore tons of makeup, the tightest skin-tight Lycra tube dresses, and high heels just to look older.

It didn't take Tabitha long to nab a teenage boy, Maxwell, and that was the beginning of our problems.

As the evening grew later and later, Tabitha decided to take him along. I wondered whether his mother would be panicked, searching for him. Walking the parking lot, we glided through car porn—Lambos, Masers, Ferraris, Bentleys, Aston Martins—until we reached Tabitha's stretch.

"Where to now?" Maxwell asked, almost giddy arm in arm with Tabitha. You could tell he figured he had lucked out. Drunk pop star, stretch limo, and adults who didn't care about the drinking age or corrupting a minor. How old was he really? Like fifteen?

"Let's stop by the Talkhouse," Tabitha slurred. "It should be picking up about now."

Mocha pulled up in front of a bar and live music joint in Amagansett, Stephen Talkhouse, which resembled somebody's run-down summer cottage. Even though it was almost two in the morning, people were pouring in and out of the club and it seemed like another hot new band was about to go on.

53

Tabitha took the door of the Talkhouse by storm—the big Asian bouncer seemed familiar with her and waved us in. There were too many of us, so they stamped our hands without even counting to get us out of the way. The bartender knew Tabitha and her taste for tequila, so he set up a margarita for her and lined up drinks for us immediately.

A great variety of people were pouring into the club for the next show—some arrived in limos, some on foot. One couple, looking like they just came from a wedding reception, were toasting others in their wedding party, which included the best man and three bridesmaids in identical hideous purple dresses. Others wore sandals and cutoff jeans. It was a totally eclectic mix.

I was surprised to find Chase drinking at the bar across the room. I hadn't seen him since the paparazzi disaster at D&G and his last-minute rescue. He waved, I smiled, and he sauntered over.

Before he reached me, everything fell apart.

Tabitha was already on her second margarita when the Big Asian guy from the door walked over. Someone at the bar must have alerted him, because he headed straight for Maxwell, our noticeably underage stowaway. Maxwell was taking a sip of his drink when the bouncer grabbed his hand to stop him. Maxwell had the guilty expression of someone waiting to be caught. Being a kid of fifteen, he was totally willing to walk away. But Tabitha wasn't.

When the bouncer asked Maxwell for his ID, she went ballistic. Maybe she had forgotten that he was only fifteen, maybe she was just so drunk on the parade of drinks that made a wet, dizzy trail through every party we had attended that she didn't know where she was, or maybe the Princess of Pop was so insecure she needed to impress the little entitled rich kid. Whatever it was, she was indignant.

The Asian guy seemed perfectly capable of handling Tabitha, and it would have just been a drunken rant if a woman at the bar, no less drunk than Tabitha, hadn't thrown her two cents in. It was all too loud, too crowded, and happened too quickly for me to try to calm Tabitha down.

"He's just doing his job," the lady screamed as the Asian dude listened, stone-faced, to Tabitha's tirade.

"Back off, bitch!" Tabitha countered as friends of the lady at the bar tried to pull the lady away. When the lady lost her footing and accidently wavered toward Tabitha, she overreacted. Let's face it, in Tabitha's diminished state a fly buzzing nearby might have made her feel threatened. She, being the totally smashed Princess of Pop, hauled off and punched the woman.

Chaos ensued, and Tabitha, Maxwell, and the lady at the bar were all hustled outside. Mocha had already jumped out of the limo, opened the door, and was ready to hurry her off.

Chase followed me as I trailed Tabitha outside. I didn't know if Maxwell was already inside the limo or not, but as I approached on the street side, Tabitha's window rolled down.

"Come on," she said, "let's get out of here and go to Robert's, where we can do what we want. ZK will be there. He's dying to see you." As I processed that Robert's was Robert Francis's house, I began to panic. At 2 A.M., it was about the last place I wanted to go near.

"Think I'll stay here with Chase," I said as gently as I could.

"Who?" She scrutinized Chase in her drunken haze. "You're the video shooter."

"Yep, that's me," Chase said self-effacingly.

"You're hooking up with a video shooter instead of ZK Northcott?" she asked drunkenly, sneering at me as if I were a lowlife. Chase took an immediate step back. I sensed he was embarrassed and maybe had a different orientation altogether.

"Tabitha, please," I said and wanted to explain we were just friends when Mocha tapped the partition to get her attention. A police car was approaching.

"Suit yourself," she said, silently closing her window as Mocha drove away.

"What's this world coming to when a pop star can't score a drink for an underage booty call?" Chase said as we watched her limo get swallowed up in the night. I assumed Tabitha figured it would be better to explain things to the cops when she wasn't totally plastered.

"Can I buy you a drink?" he asked. "You know, the Talkhouse is a pretty good antidote to the limos and McMansion parties, not that I ever go to those. But you look like you could use a change."

"Sure, why not?" I shrugged. To think I had just arrived that day. Uh, it was 2 A.M. Okay, the day before.

As the East Hampton Police pulled up, we squeezed our way back in the door. Chase grabbed us a couple of beers and found a spot at the corner of the stage on the far left of the club near the soundboard. The flashing red police light reflected intermittently on the windows of the club, but everyone inside seemed to have moved on. The cops appeared content to confine their investigation to people outside. I wondered if they would follow up with Tabitha.

The whole club was so small you could literally step up on the stage if you wanted. It was only a foot or two off the floor and about twenty feet wide and fourteen feet deep. The ceiling was low enough to almost touch on your tiptoes.

Behind the stage was a backdrop, an ancient sepia-toned picture of a stoic man with long black hair, his shirt buttoned at the top with a scarf tied at the neck, holding a walking stick in one hand that almost looked like a rifle but wasn't.

"Who is that?" I asked.

"That's Stephen Talkhouse," Chase told me. "He was one of the last chiefs of the Montaukett Indians. Where we're sitting used to be their land, before the tribes of Laurens and Von Furstenbergs invaded." I laughed.

"And what brings you out here?" I asked.

"I had a gig shooting a charity event that turned into a week-long job," he said. "I thought I'd hang out a little, get some sun, maybe pick up another gig before heading back. And what's your angle out here?"

A seizure of insecurity washed over me, and I wondered if I had already let my guard down with Chase.

"Some family matters to clear up in East Hampton," I lied, hoping to sound superior. "Then back to the city for Fashion Week." His inquisitive brown eyes brightened, and he ran his hands through his tousled auburn hair.

"For Designer X?" he asked with a knowing hipster smile that renewed my fears he was on to me.

"Yes," I said, leaving it at that. He had been following my blog. I worried why. Moments later, the energy inside the steamy club inexplicably ratcheted up as people started to clap in unison. Everyone seemed to know that the band was about to come out.

The first band member onstage was a hot-looking drummer followed by a tall, languid bass player who reminded me of Max from Tabitha's band, then a keyboard player and the lead singer.

"With all these fans, they must be local," Chase said. The lead singer picked up his guitar to wild cheers. I nearly spit my beer.

It was Jake.

He wore the same sky-colored Blue Note Records T-shirt he used to wear at the Hole. He threw a nod to cue the band, and the bassist slid his finger all the way down the neck of his guitar, thumping a low bass-line intro as Jake hammered four chunky power chords, then kicked the distortion pedal. Immediately, everyone was on their feet, dancing and singing along.

It was one of those classic guitar hooks you couldn't forget, a throwback, like the opening to Rick Springfield's "Jessie's Girl." His immediate feedback loop with the audience encircled the room. Preppies and locals were dancing together.

I was awestruck.

He had no idea I was standing a few feet away, and I hoped he wouldn't see me. On the second chorus, Jake allowed the noise of the band and the crowd to build to a crescendo. Watching him move with such grace and power, I found I couldn't swallow or speak or breathe. I could only remember my mistakes, starting with the fact that I just didn't have the confidence to believe that Jake Berns was really interested in me.

I had been right about one thing though. Hearing his yearning, soulful voice opened a hole in my heart. The band joined in with husky harmonies while Jake's distinctively silky lead guitar ripped across the melody. Why couldn't I have confided in him? Why couldn't I have let him know what was going on?

As he stalked across the stage, totally in his element, I had to admit to myself that I had always been hopelessly attracted to him and afraid of what that might mean. Probably like every other girl here, I guessed.

Some chick in a cropped shirt in the front row got up on the other end of the stage and started dancing, and he played off her excitement. The crowd loved it. At the end of the song Jake politely escorted her offstage, and that's when he caught sight of me. He appeared shocked momentarily but recovered immediately, turning away.

I don't think anyone noticed except Chase.

"Do you know him?" he shouted above the music. I shrugged yes, hoping I didn't look as totally undone as I felt.

Jake's whole set was mind-blowing with its emotional anthems and flat-out rockers. I was standing so close that I could almost touch him.

He pretty much avoided looking my way through most of the performance, although he gave me a soft smile near the end. *Just enough to be kind,* I thought. He leapt around the stage with his unassuming charm in the same old tennis shoes he used to wear at the Hole.

The Rockets finished with a rollicking dance song that everyone in the crowd seemed to know by heart. As soon as Jake ripped the last chord, the Talkhouse was on its feet, demanding an encore. After a few moments, the band gave them what they wanted: two more songs.

Still, they asked for more. These were his fans, his following from all walks of life, not just locals. They wouldn't let him go.

They began to cry out for a third encore.

"One night! One night!" they chanted. I didn't know what that meant, but even when the houselights went on, the fans wouldn't let up, they wouldn't stop. Usually when the lights come up people leave, but no one moved an inch.

"One night! One night!" It seemed like a song they had come to expect.

Finally the lights dimmed, but the band didn't come out. Only Jake. The audience quieted down as soon as they saw him.

He plugged the lead to his Sunburst electric into the amp and flicked on the power switch.

"Okay, I wasn't going to sing this one tonight, but I guess I will," he said in his soft, melodic voice. He was looking down at his guitar, adjusting the tuning. "This song is for a friend of mine."

Even though I was standing right next to the stage, what he said didn't register in my mind until he lifted his head and I saw that Jake was looking at me.

"You know when there's someone so awesome and you love her with all your heart and it doesn't work out?" The crowd moaned, but I barely heard them. The room seemed very far away, like I was alone in a tunnel with Jake Berns at the other end.

"Take me, Jake Berns, I'm yours!" someone yelled in the back and everyone laughed, but then got real quiet again.

"This song is for that girl," he said, and I had to look away. I didn't want to see him looking at me. "It's about what *didn't* happen . . . that one night."

With a palm-muted intensity he played the solo rock chords on his guitar and started singing.

One night the look in your eyes was like a light,
It shined so bright that I couldn't see,
That . . . one . . . night,

The whole audience sung along to the chorus as it repeated.

That . . . one . . . night.

Jake poured himself into the song, singing to me as if no one else was in the room. Chase knew—I could tell by the way he was looking at me. The crowd didn't know why Jake was staring off-stage, and they were straining to see who he was looking at. I wanted to run out, run away, but there was nothing I could do.

You know the clothes you wear?
The color in your hair?

You were so damn fine,
That...one...night.

Though muted, Jake rocked through the mournful chords of the bridge. He had everyone in the room completely under his spell.

Hey I was the one,
I was the one with the bird in the hand that let her get away.

His voice went into a dark, haunted place and then rose back up only to plunge again, and everyone was singing along...

That...one...night.

He kicked into the bridge, and the crowd knew every word.

Time heals everything; it truly does.
Time heals everything, but love.

There was a serious key change, and Jake cut off into a sailing riff on the guitar, spinning around onstage until he jumped and landed right in front of me, and somehow they turned the spotlight on us.

We both knew he was singing to me and only to me, driving his muffled guitar down to almost nothing. I was flat-out embarrassed, trying to keep my composure, but I couldn't turn away.

Hey I'm the one,
I'm the one with the bird in the hand that you let get away,
One night,
Just one night,
That one night.

Everyone knew every single word to the song but me.
They were all singing along to a song that was about that night

in the parking lot behind the diner when I ran away. And as Jake sang, I knew the real reason I fled. I thought I was going on an adventure to the Big Apple. I thought I was Being Audrey—and I was—but, more than that, I was afraid of Jake Berns, afraid of how he made me feel and afraid of how he felt about me.

He repeated the chorus one more time.

One night,
Just one night,
That one night.

He allowed the final chord of the bridge to ring out, and it was over. Jake exited offstage, never glancing back.

As soon as the crowd began to leave, I tried to run out. I wanted to get out of there as quickly as possible, but Chase stopped me.

"You have to stay," he said and handed me a handkerchief. I hadn't realized I was crying.

"Why?" I said. "I can't."

"You've got to say hello to the guy," he said. "Whatever you guys had, he put his heart out on the line." Through my tears I nodded no, looking at Chase as if he were crazy. It was too much to ask.

I couldn't handle it, but we stayed as the club goers poured out onto the street. I tried to pull myself together as best I could.

"Here he comes," Chase said. We saw Jake, wearing one of his vintage flannels, enter the wings on the other side of the stage, about to walk our way when someone called him from behind and he turned.

As I feared, the woman from Reilly's, the one in the swag cowboy gear, appeared. She came running up to him, giving him a kiss.

It was more than I could stand.

Even Chase stared in stunned silence.

I ran out of the club as quickly as I could and kept running.

54 The next morning, I slipped out of Tabitha's house before anyone could see me. Zoya was up, but everyone else was snoring away. I hadn't been able to sleep for all the obvious reasons.

Chase had been unbelievably cool about the Talkhouse, especially since I had all sorts of regrets and paranoid fears afterward. I was worried that Chase would be faced with the fact that I'm a fake from New Jersey. I'm not sure he had put that together or cared to.

He had given me a ride home in his equipment van and, to change the subject, pitched a video concept for my blog if I wanted to try it.

"You could be exceptional on camera, totally fierce," he said. "It would be great for your blog and not bad for me, either." I was too messed up to talk about it but promised I would consider it. He was going back to the city soon. He had hoped there'd be more social events to cover in the Hamptons, but he was finding it hard to get into most of them. He promised to check up on me before he went back to the city and gave me his number in case I needed it.

I called Courtney while walking into town. I didn't think she'd even answer that early in the morning, but I needed to hear a familiar voice, even if it was just voice mail. I didn't want to call Jess. There were too many things I hadn't done for her show, and I felt guilty still hanging out in the Hamptons. I was surprised Courtney picked up. Her voice seemed totally different on the phone, totally upbeat.

"How are Mom and Nan getting along?" I asked.

"There have been a few big fights," she said.

"Who's winning?"

"Unclear. But Ryan finished summer school." That alone was remarkable. "Nan says hi. You should call her," Courtney said.

"I will," I said, feeling guilty.

In town I found a coffee shop in one of the stores on Amagansett

Square and tried to regain my focus. In the frenzy of last night, I hadn't noticed a text I received from Jess.

"WE GOT THE GALLERY !! ☺"

I texted back. "For fashion's night out ?! :) :)"

She responded a few minutes later. "Working on that . . ."

Thankfully I had something to think about besides Jake. I'd planned to make a few entries on my blog and prepare an announcement for Designer X's pop-up show. Playing on the flash-mob idea, I hoped I could intrigue my followers to show up spontaneously and make the event something that they all had a part in making happen.

If the gallery would give us Fashion's Night Out, I'd have to get back to the city in three days at the latest. I posted my first tease.

Designer X Unmasked! Exclusive Pop Up Show near the High Line. Your presence required. Details to come!

Then another text from Jess popped up on my phone.

"R u ok?" That simple question gave me pause. Don't ask why, but my gung ho spirit deserted me, and feelings from last night opened up like a trapdoor beneath me. What could I say?

I found myself pathetically googling Jake Berns and his band. Their Web site popped up. The press clippings revealed how far the Rockets had come over the summer. They'd been picked by WFUV's Internet feed as a band to watch and were being mentioned as opening acts to all kinds of great bands. I knew the gigs probably didn't pay much yet. I wondered if Jake still worked at the Hole. It was painful seeing him play for the first time in the Hamptons of all places.

There were a half dozen pictures of the band. I scoured them for any sign of Monica in the background or nearby. She was in two of them. Always wearing that swag country style. She certainly dressed as if she had some serious money.

It was hard to believe I had just arrived in the Hamptons a few days before. It was so fabulous and hopeful when I was sitting with Flo talking about click-throughs. Yesterday morning I could do anything, and now I felt worthless. Closing my eyes, I'd see Jake singing to me and, just a moment later, kissing her.

It was self-torture, but I downloaded "That One Night" from the iTunes store in the Indie Up and Coming section and played it over and over until I felt sick.

Walking back to Tabitha's, I saw an East Hampton Town Police car pulling away. So I assumed the police were following up on the Talkhouse dispute. I wondered if it had hit the local newspapers and New York gossip blogs yet. Mocha, standing guard, nodded as I entered the house and headed toward Tabitha's bedroom.

"You don't want to go in there." I heard someone say. I turned to see ZK.

I was so glad to see him that I threw myself into his arms, hugging him so tightly I almost knocked him down. I could tell he didn't quite know what to do—the man who always knew how to handle everything.

"Oh I missed you," I said.

"Has it been that long?" he said, smiling.

"I don't know. It feels like forever."

"Well I've come to whisk you away."

"I'd like that," I said.

"Where's Tabitha? I need to talk to her first."

"I wouldn't."

"Why?"

"Robert's in there. She called him."

"Oh."

"Don't feel bad. There's nothing you can do. Tabitha's always been this way," he said. "Robert's here to pick up the pieces and get her going again."

"I should have stopped her somehow."

"She would have just punched you instead. Talk to her later, after she's rested. In the meantime, I'm here to entertain you."

"Really? What do you have in mind?"

"Let's see, first I'll have to get you something white."

55

ZK became the antidote to how adrift I felt, not because he was so much more together than me, but because he felt the same way. After I grabbed a white tennis skirt, white socks, white tennis shoes, and a white blouse from the Maidstone Club tennis boutique, ZK showed me to the dressing room. I reappeared dressed for the part, ready to play but without a clue how to even hold a tennis racket.

There is no name for the luscious deep-green of the grass courts in the yellow afternoon sun at the Maidstone Club. A cooling breeze drifted through the trees as ZK diligently tried to teach me how to hit a basic groundstroke. To me the ultraexclusive golf and tennis club seemed like the ideal setting for a glass of wine. Tennis not so much.

On the court farthest away from the clubhouse, at the edge of the hill above the pond, ZK fed me ball after ball. I hit the fuzzy yellow thing everywhere but in the court, several times forcing profuse apologies to those unfortunate people trying to play doubles nearby.

It was more fun when we were the last ones left and the sun was setting. ZK finally abandoned any pretense of actually teaching me the game of tennis, and I just hit the ball whatever goofy way I could. I even hit a few in the court. I concocted a story about how I never learned tennis as a child because of some infantile illness. The story was so elaborate it was pointless.

We ended up in his car, where he kissed me again. It felt so nice to be held by someone who wanted to hold me. Unbelievable, really, that it was none other than ZK Northcott, practically the most eligible bachelor in America. Was I the only one who knew the wayward boy he sheltered inside? He was a good kisser, that boy. I felt bad that I was taking him for granted.

Back at the house, Tabitha was still sleeping so I didn't disturb her. I decided to eek out a day or two more with ZK. I'd still have time to get back to the city for Jess's show. I hoped that I could reach Isak and push my Tumblr and blog following and that we'd put on a pop-up show that could make a splash. I would have invited Tabitha, but there seemed to be a tacit understanding that no one should bother her. I figured I'd save her invite for the last minute before I left.

Flo found me as I headed to my room.

"Lisbeth, I have something for you," she said, reaching into a giant pink straw bag. "It's symbolic really." She pulled out a long blue check. "You'll probably just want to frame it." I think my mouth was open as I read my name across the top line and the amount in the box to the side: $2,987.00. "It's coming together much faster than I expected." She had a mischievous, self-satisfied smile. "This advance is one of our company checks and is simply based on the tracking data. More checks will come later, but I wanted you to have some idea of what we might expect initially. A little pocket change can't hurt, right?"

She happily demurred to my profuse thanks, and we gossiped a bit about Tabitha. In a conspiratorial tone, she told me they had given her something to calm her down and that, as a result, she hadn't come out of her room in days. I told her I was off for an evening with ZK. The mention of his name brought an amused smile to her lips.

"He's such a good boy," she said tactfully. "It's his family I'd be cautious of. I hear the entire Northcott family is unwinding, and that can make one do things one wouldn't do normally. But I'm sure you can handle him."

Her words were still resonating in my ears later that night as ZK and I entered Nick and Toni's for dinner. After our first glass of wine, I noticed people staring at us.

"Is it my imagination, or are we under observation?" I asked. ZK didn't glance up as he cut his steak, but he must have noticed.

"I told you, being a Northcott comes with a fair amount of unwanted attention," he said.

Although it persisted throughout dinner, I didn't mention it again. There was something on ZK's mind, or so it seemed, as he was not as lighthearted as he had been earlier in the day.

The table next to us was occupied by two couples, middle aged, very well dressed, a bit stuffy, and noticeably well-off. I couldn't help observing the wives smirking and whispering. ZK seemed to grow more tense as the night went on, no matter what kind of small talk I made. He asked for the check at last, and I figured that would be the end of it.

As we were leaving, one of the men at the table began talking in a voice that all the tables around us could hear. "His father should pay for the rest of his life—it's despicable," the man said, undeniably making a point.

ZK pivoted, thrust the chairs out of his way, reached across the table, and picked the man up by his collar, shoving him against the wall. Silverware and plates fell to the floor.

"Don't you ever say a word about my father again," ZK said, his teeth clenched. The panic-stricken man's face was turning blue. I thought ZK would choke him or he'd have a heart attack. The maître d' and bartender stepped in, separating them, and I hustled ZK out. It wasn't until we got in the car and drove away that I dared ask him what was going on.

"I apologize for my behavior," he said. I wasn't sure how to ask him about his family, how far to go, and what I should know. But it came spilling out of him anyway.

"My father is in more trouble than we ever thought," ZK said, visibly stiffening, reverting to some schooled behavior. "There are issues now for the whole family." He said he was reluctant to go into the details, but gradually it came pouring out.

Years ago his father had invested with Bernie Madoff and lost most of the family fortune, which was bad enough. But as time passed and many of the investigations took years to complete, it surfaced that Northcott Sr. had not only invested with the Ponzi con man but fronted the fund to many families in his social set for preferred fees in the last days of the scam. He narrowly avoided a prison term by ratting out other people he knew who had done the same thing, ruining their families as a result. The revelations were coming to light after years and years of investigations. As a result, at sixty-eight he earned the animosity of his oldest friends in New York's Social Register.

ZK's mother filed for divorce to protect herself and the other children from further repercussions, and his father had withdrawn to their mansion on Gin Lane, one of the last original houses near Georgica Beach, not far from the famous Grey Gardens.

His father had squandered the remaining family funds to pay his hefty legal fees to avoid jail, failing to pay the bank mortgage. Now the Bank of America—a bank the Northcotts helped found in 1904—had sold the land and begun the process of auctioning the actual house out from under him plank by plank. It was the house in which ZK had spent every summer of his childhood.

56 It was remarkable how dull Tabitha's house had become since she remained sequestered in her room. The houseguests dwindled, including Flo and Balty. Zoya was especially happy I had decided to stay a few days. She told Tabitha, hoping that would motivate her to leave her room, but it didn't.

Occasional reporters would appear outside and try to gain entry, but it seemed that Robert Francis or a PR agent or someone had successfully kept a lid on the incident at the Talkhouse. It made me think that for every LiLo event we heard about on TMZ, there were at least two or three more.

Jess was haggling with the gallery about the date, and, though she was confident they would come through, she was afraid to let me send out my eBlast. Keeping track of days passing was a challenge. Waking up at noon and staying up until four in the morning made it hard to determine where one day ended and another began.

The next night I shared my fanciful pursuit of Donna Karan with ZK. He laughed.

"Lisbeth Dulac has the hottest indie fashion blog and you're not sure you're worthy to meet Donna Karan?" he said. "These are the things that make me wonder whether you arrived here from outer space. Would it help to meet Donna's daughter, Gabby?" he asked. I nodded eagerly.

"So let's go to Tutto," he said. Tutto Il Giorno was this ultracool Italian restaurant in Sag Harbor owned by Donna Karan's daughter, Gabby. True to form, ZK was an old buddy of Gabby's husband, Gianpaolo, who shared ZK's passion for racing Ducati motorcycles. I decided to take my first check and celebrate and, at the same time, make a potential connection for Designer X.

ZK picked me up at Tabitha's on his Ducati 1100 S, and before long we were eating and drinking the night away with Gianpaolo, Gabby, and Maurizio, the restaurant's other owner and chef. Espresso martinis were the drink of choice. Gabby was more than generous in accepting my invitation to the forthcoming Designer X fashion show. She said she would be heading back to the city the next day and would love to attend.

As we closed the restaurant down, the men began to argue about the relative merits of their motorcycles. This turned into a bet, and they decided to race to Sagaponack.

I held on to ZK for my life as we zipped down the back roads of Sag Harbor to Sagaponack. ZK was winning, but I think he pulled back when he noticed my nails digging into his leather jacket. I was holding on in sheer terror. We smoothly pulled into the driveway of an empty ultramodern mansion owned by a Bosnian multimillionaire friend of Maurizio's. After a few touches of the security pad, we were all inside.

Here was an entire nine-bedroom villa fully lit up without a soul in sight. In the Hamptons the locals call these "zombie houses"—kept absolutely dustless, the refrigerator fully stocked, the wine cellar with three hundred bottles chilled exactly at fifty-five degrees, the air-conditioning full blast throughout the house, with not a leaf in the swimming pool in the middle of the summer. It was just one of the thousands of mansions expensively maintained throughout the Hamptons, with landscape lighting illuminating every tree on the property throughout the night as if it were Christmas.

ZK grabbed a twenty-year-old bottle of wine and some glasses as we all drifted through the rooms of the house.

"Here's to being in the Limelight," ZK said to me as we toasted. After a little while, Maurizio and Gianpaolo wandered off and ZK gave me a tour of the trove of modern art displayed throughout the house—artists that ZK knew well and sometimes personally. Artists I didn't have a clue about. I nodded as if I had some awareness of art history, which I did not. Nervously spinning my bracelet about my wrist, I worried once again that I was over my head with ZK. But he was so comfortably inebriated and we were so relaxed in each other's company, I felt reassured.

"We're really just two drifters, you know," ZK said to me. "We should escape! I could start over in L.A. We don't have to stay here. We'd be better off leaving. It would be good for you, too, a new fashion world to conquer." I wondered if he intended to leave everyone he knew and grew up with. More than that, I wondered if he really meant to take me to L.A. with him. The fantasy made my head spin.

We kissed by the pool and kissed in the living room. We kissed again in the kitchen and kissed in bedroom after bedroom after bedroom until we were more than kissing. We stripped off our clothes, letting them fall into puddles on the lacquered oak floors, and fell into the nearest bed.

Before, ZK's kisses would sweep me away, seizing me, engulfing me. But that night we were unhurried and slow, deliberately drowning in each other's arms, soothing each other and losing who we were.

"I'm not Holly. I'm not Lula Mae, either," Audrey said in *Breakfast at Tiffany's*. "I don't know who I am. I'm like Cat here, a no-name slob." Like Audrey pretending to be Lula Mae pretending to be Holly Golightly, I pretended to be somebody I wasn't and ZK was my Fred. His inner life was so secret; who knew who he was pretending to be?

We cuddled in the master bedroom beneath the weight of luxurious comforters overlooking an arbor that glowed in the dark sky. That night the lost lonely little boy inside ZK, not the flawless dashing Kennedyesque fashion darling, made me shiver and melt. It was the man who seemed apart; more so after sharing with me his family's fall from fortune. Resting in his arms, I pulled myself tight against his body.

Somewhere in the middle of the night I woke up with a start and realized ZK was watching me. We kissed again and I curled up into him, trying to hold every part of him close. Comparing this moment to any other moment in my life, I couldn't recall being more content; words didn't come close to truly describing how I felt.

"It's a shame that you fell for someone like me," he said. "I was hoping you wouldn't."

I put my finger to his lips.

"Be quiet. Don't say that," I said and snuggled closer. Someday I would tell him the truth about where I came from, and he would realize how little his father's stature and money mattered to me.

Our naked bodies fit in a tangle of arms and legs like complementary halves, like pieces of a puzzle. It felt so good to feel the texture of his skin and to have him right up against me. I wanted to stay that way forever, holding him until his worries faded and were forgotten.

The next morning I awoke and he was gone. Only a note was left.

My father called. Have business to finish. Meet me at Robert's tonight.—ZK

57   I tore apart the bedsheets.

On my hands and knees, I crawled over every square inch of the bedroom floor. Methodically, I retraced the location of every kiss and embrace, rewinding the entire evening back to the wine cellar, scouring every corner of the villa over and over. Pacing the driveway where the motorcycles were parked, I was dumbfounded and heartbroken as I realized it was gone. Nan's bracelet had disappeared.

ZK had left so mysteriously that it made my stomach churn. I was alone in this strange, empty house, trying to come up with rational reasons that made it okay. Everything about his sudden departure was wrong. I cast about for excuses and picked apart my own behavior. Was I too willing? Had my Jersey pedigree come through and put him off? Did his blue-blood instincts sniff me out? Or was this the reason he was a player and never stayed with anyone for long?

I called Zoya, Tabitha's maid, and she sent Mocha, who arrived in no time. It was good to see his familiar face. As the villa faded from view in the rear window, I thought of Nan, wishing I could call her about the bracelet, but I feared she'd be too worried. My phone buzzed.

"Haven't heard from u. Everything ok ??"

It was Jess.

"Good," I thumbed halfheartedly.

"THEN GET YOUR ASS TO NYC !! WE HAVE A DATE !! FASH NITE OUT LIKE U SAID !! THERE STILL ENUF TIME ?!?"

I couldn't deal with it.

I reread ZK's note instead.

Meet me at Robert's tonight.

The last place I wanted to go, although everyone else seemed perfectly comfortable hanging around him. Speaking to ZK was the only thing I could think about. I couldn't leave for the city without seeing him first.

My thoughts spun like a dreadful merry-go-round, returning to last night, the rowdy dinner with so many fascinating people, the crazy motorcycle race, ZK's museum tour of the art on the villa walls, our endless kisses, our pile of clothes, the fit of our naked bodies.

Then, falling into confusion, I thought of Nan's lost bracelet, the way ZK was awake watching me, his self-deprecating, almost self-pitying comment. I tried to put myself in his place—his family broken by his father's recklessness. People whispering. The grand name that once opened doors dragged through the mud.

My father called. Have business to finish.

Why a sudden call from his father? When had that occurred?

It was still early morning and Tabitha's house was asleep when I returned. The balmy sea breeze rippled through the lush trees, swaying the branches and exposing the underside of their leaves. It was soothingly quiet by the pool.

I kept checking my phone messages, my texts, hoping for something from ZK. I started to text ZK and stopped. I felt like there was a hole where my heart used to be and it was sucking everything inside.

As more time passed, it was becoming difficult not to feel hurt and stupid that I was worried about him. But then I'd feel guilty, fretting that something terrible might have happened to his father and that I was being insensitive.

Unfinished business... what did that mean?

I rose and returned to my room to take a bath and rest and prepare myself for the inevitable visit to Robert's.

58 As soon as the white limo drove up in front of Tabitha's mansion, Zoya and Mocha and the entire house staff were in an upheaval. From the balcony window I saw the flurry of activity in the driveway. A tall, gorgeous man with long black hair stepped out first. His shoulders were so broad, his jaw so chiseled, he looked like Superman.

A rail-thin woman followed and required the aid of the Superman to steady her. She had strawlike bleach-blond hair and wore a floral-print, rose-colored dress that seemed inappropriately short for her advanced age. At the same time, the Peter Pan collar made her appear like a prematurely aged child. Her large, gaudy jewelry, no doubt very expensive, made her bony wrists seem even skinnier.

I heard someone on the staff whisper that this was Tabitha's mother, Eva Eden. Tabitha said she was forty-eight years old. She looked like she was in her sixties.

Downstairs, I found Tabitha outside her bedroom for the first time in days. Already swept up in her mother's sudden arrival, she seemed both terrified and excited.

"Did you hear? Mommy is here! She'll be thrilled to meet you!" Tabitha said, sounding like she was fifteen. "We're having afternoon tea by the pool. You have to join us! Mommy's so British these days. She said she's going to stay long enough to clear up the whole guardian situation. Isn't that wonderful?"

I was speechless, wondering how to react. Not a mention from Tabitha of the fact that she had stayed in her room for two full days or the incident that had caused her confinement. Not a word about Robert and the police.

"You're going to Robert's this evening, aren't you?" she asked excitedly. "You'll come with us in Mommy's tacky white stretch, right?"

"Of course," I said reassuringly. I hadn't seen Tabitha like this for a while, agitated, childlike with an undercurrent of desperation. I wondered if she was afraid that her mother would disappoint her. I wondered how she felt about Robert in the aftermath of her run-in with the East Hampton police.

"Come, Mommy's waiting," Tabitha said. We headed for the pool, where I could see that Zoya had set up a full tea service for the four of us, including Eva's hunk.

"So sorry about the other night," Tabitha confided in a whisper to me as we entered the pool area. "I'm sure with Mother here I can get back on track. Please don't give up on me?"

"Of course not," I said. How bad I felt for Tabitha. It was the only thing that made me forget how bad I felt for myself.

Eva held out her bony hand as I approached. "It's so nice to see that Tabby has a new friend," she said. I held her hand, not knowing whether to shake it or just let it go. It was so fragile I feared it might break.

"Lovely to meet you, Mrs. Eden," I said. Her rag-mop hair spilled over her tiny shoulders chaotically as she gave me a huge gummy smile.

"Call me Eva—everyone does," she said. Up close you could see the wear and tear on her face that no amount of plastic surgery could restore. As we sat, I felt her empty eyes staring at me as if she were seeing me from far away.

"I'm considerably more fun than the rest of the people Tabby hangs out with," she added with an incongruous laugh. Zoya served caviar and toast points along with the tea.

"So tell me about yourself, Lisbeth. What is your family name?" Eva's hand shook unsteadily as she raised her cup of tea.

"Dulac," I said. "Not much to tell, I'm afraid. But I do have to say your daughter has been absolutely wonderful to me." I hoped to move the attention away from myself as quickly as possible while finding anything I could say that might help Tabitha.

"Lisbeth is always too modest," Tabitha chided. "She has a blog that has gone viral and she's the sponsor of a very mysterious clothing designer called Designer X." So that is how my life appeared to someone on the wealthier side. I was "sponsoring" Jess. Wonder what Jess would think of that.

"I hope you'll tell me more," she said. Zoya returned to pour more tea, but Eva covered the top of her cup with her hand. "Make me a vodka martini, dirty with olives," she whispered to Zoya.

"Yes ma'am," the maid said, making a little bow. "Lisbeth and ZK have been very chummy lately," Tabitha added to refocus her mother. The comment made me flinch. It took a moment to realize that Tabitha had no idea what had happened since she disappeared into her room.

"What a lovely boy. ZK is my favorite," Eva said. Zoya arrived with the martini, and Eva's eyes widened as she reached for it. "It's always more fun meeting people over martinis, don't you think?" She took a long swallow and seemed to come alive.

"Mother's here to talk to Robert," Tabitha said. I tried to decipher her expression; she seemed to be trying her hardest to appear calm and assured.

"Oh Tabby, you worry too much about these things. Everything will turn out fine, you'll see. They always do, don't they?" she said and ran her skeletal hand through Tabitha's hair.

Eva Eden totally creeped me out. I couldn't imagine a more terrifying mother, and it wasn't like my mother was easy.

My phone buzzed. When I checked, it was a text from Jess. I used it as a reason to get away.

"I hope you don't mind if I excuse myself," I said, holding up my phone. "This is Designer X now." I rose to leave.

"I hope we talk with you again soon," Eva said.

I smiled and nodded, feeling terrible leaving Tabitha, but it was all more than I could deal with. I swiftly walked toward my room, glancing down at the text message.

"COUNTDOWN HAS STARTED !! WHEN WILL YOU BE HERE ?!"

59 I turned off my phone and threw it on the bed. I couldn't read another text from Jess. I opened the closet door in the guest room and curled up into a ball on the carpeted floor. I remembered all the times I had drifted off in my closet to "Moon River" and the *Breakfast at Tiffany's* DVD looping over and over until I awoke for school.

Jess's show was *the* most important thing, but my head hurt every time I thought about it. I closed my eyes, remembering the empty villa bedroom by bedroom and how I felt before everything went bad.

I couldn't believe how long I slept.

The modified Chanel caught my eye as I sat up. The black dress was embellished with a spray of multicolored jewels, shortened and tightened at the waist. I reached out, taking my silver flats and the dress, and stepped into the bathroom. I washed my face, put on some makeup, and pulled my hair into shape. Checking in the mirror, something felt off. I hardly ever thought about Nan's lucky talisman before, and now my wrist felt bare without it.

I wondered if Tabitha and her mother had already left, but when I checked the driveway from the balcony the white limo was still there. Eva's Superman was flirting with some of the maids.

I walked over to Tabitha's bedroom and heard voices inside arguing. Before I could turn away, the door opened and Tabitha came out looking terrible. She had been crying.

"Are you okay?" I asked.

"I'm fine," she said, closing the door behind her. She seemed anything but fine.

"We have to stay a little longer. I can't go until I work this out with Mother. Robert always charms her," she said.

"I understand," I said as comfortingly as I could. She returned to her room.

Deciding to act as if I wasn't upset, I turned on my phone and texted ZK, as though nothing was wrong.

"See you @ Robert's ;)"

There was no answer. I waited some more and noticed an unread text from Jess.

"I CAN'T W8 TIL U GET BACK. CAN'T DO THIS WITHOUT U !!"

I wondered how I would pull myself away and get back to the city. I couldn't even focus on what I should do. I decided, no matter what, to take the Jitney back in the morning. I couldn't fail Jess. I couldn't stand waiting at Tabitha's either. I marched outside to find Mocha. He was about to leave on an errand and I hitched a ride.

60 Even after Mocha passed through the gates and turned down the driveway, it was a full ten minutes before we caught sight of the looming three-story Tudor-style manor. When I entered, there were two beefy security guards at the door. They nodded as though they knew who I was before I could give them my name.

I passed through doors as thick as bank vaults into the main entrance with its grand matching staircases. Following the other guests into the first-floor library, I ran into Balty and Flo. They had stopped at Robert's on their way back to the city. They were abuzz with the news of Eva Eden's arrival and more than happy to fill me in on the dirt.

Balty took special pleasure in dishing Eva. "Tabitha's mother is a generous longtime charity donor to the Addiction Relief Foundation in the U.K. and the chairwoman for their fund drive," Balty said with a smirk. "At the same time, she has a heroin habit that would kill most people."

"You're so unfair, Balty," Flo said, chastising him, rolling her eyes. Flo was wearing an exquisite black sequined dress and a silver necklace that sparkled with diamonds. Everything she wore was well matched to her supersleek red hair.

"I guess you're right," Balty agreed, laughing. "I mean, they only found eight grams of the lovely white powder and two hundred and fifty milligrams of diazepam in her Rolls when they stopped her." Tabitha's alcohol problem seemed tame by comparison.

I heard a familiar dog yap and turned to see Robert holding Morris on the far side of the room chatting with Dahlia. I don't know why it was surprising to see them talking. Perhaps it was my mood, but there seemed something sinister about those two together. What could they be plotting? And where was ZK? That's what mattered.

I hoped to slip away unnoticed, but Dahlia seemed to have extrasensory perception when it came to knowing I was around. She turned my direction and gave me an icy smile. Managing to smile back for form's sake, I found myself rubbing my wrist where Nan's bracelet used to be. I hadn't realized how many times I had unconsciously reached for that good-luck charm.

Excusing myself from Flo's company, I searched from library to gallery, through the walnut-paneled ballroom, asking for ZK, but nobody had seen him. The nervous feeling in the pit of my stomach was draining all the energy out of me.

I overhead someone say there were twenty-five bedrooms in Robert Francis's mansion; I felt like I had searched half of them.

The mansion was so enormous that I never doubled back on my path.

Passing through room after room, it seemed as though I'd entered a kind of Escher painting of never-ending rooms and staircases. I turned down an unfamiliar hall and noticed that the crowd had thinned out, so I headed back downstairs, where most of the partygoers were gathering.

"Looking for me?" I knew that voice, unfortunately.

Morris barked twice in Robert's arm, the dog's tiny tongue sticking out, panting.

"No, actually," I said.

"Here, let me get you something to drink."

"No thank you. I'd rather not," I said, watching Morris wiggle uncomfortably in Robert's arms.

"Of course not." Did I detect a wounded tone in his voice? "Determined to avoid me, I suppose. Even though I've helped your good friend Tabitha evade arrest and scandal for the umpteenth time."

I glowered at him silently.

"I won't keep you," he said, sounding resigned. "At least let me show you the best view in the house." He led me through a doorway toward two huge bay windows.

The mansion had a view of the churning ocean unlike any I had ever seen before. The lighting from the house illuminated the dunes in sharp waves of light and dark. Chiaroscuro, I think my high school art teacher would have called it. Through the interplay of shadows I could see the Atlantic's explosive white foam, but the windows were so thick that besides the murmurs of partiers elsewhere in the house, the wind, the ocean's waves, and everything outside was unnaturally soundless. All the drama of the crashing waves took place in eerie silence.

I shook myself out of my daze.

"I have to go," I said and turned to leave, but the room was dark and I wasn't sure which way to go.

"Oh come now, Lisbeth, don't be ridiculous." Robert dropped Morris to the floor and closed a large door I hadn't noticed. I felt my neck stiffen, angry to find myself at a disadvantage again.

"Really, dear, I've tried so hard to please you. At least you can talk to me."

"What do you mean?" I asked, steeling myself.

"What possessed you to cut your hair? I preferred it longer," he said and moved behind me, standing close enough I could feel his breathing. I had to buy time and find an exit. "The pixie cut is too boyish for my tastes."

Morris jumped to the footstool, and I saw in the darkness there was a bed. There were so many bedrooms in this house I hadn't realized that we had entered one.

"As you know, I am meeting with Tabitha's mother tonight. My sister Eva always does as I ask. Considering her relationship with the authorities and her mental outlook, she could hardly take care of herself let alone a daughter. Tabitha didn't help her case by picking a fight in a bar over a minor. I have a legal responsibility to her recording label and her trust to retain control." Morris yapped, panting expectantly, and I realized we were facing a mirror. "Of course you could change that," he said. Was every one of the twenty-five bedrooms in this mansion designed for his uses? "If you agree, I'll release Tabitha."

"Agree to what?" I cringed as he ran his fingers through my hair.

"Lisbeth, dear, girls don't run out on me," he said and roughly grabbed my hair in his fist. I gasped, his strength greater than I expected.

"I've helped other girls like you," he said. His other arm gathered around my waist and forcefully dragged me toward his body. As he kissed my neck, I twisted to slip away, but his grip tightened painfully in my hair. His arm was too muscular. His grasp of my hair was too firm.

I couldn't help noticing Morris watching us in the mirror.

There's always a mirror, I thought, remembering how the mutt had dutifully jumped up on the footstool by the bed the last time, yapping at his reflection.

Robert's hand slid upward to my breast, searching for my nipple. I squirmed and tried to twist away. He pulled me closer, grabbing my breast, and I screamed. I kicked him and felt his grip loosen. I squeezed tighter to duck out of his hold, diving forward, but he held on firmly and fell on top of me. I struggled to push him away, and the moment seemed to unwind in still frames; Robert smashing into the mirror, the hundred jigsaw pieces of glass momentarily suspended in air, Robert's stunned expression from the floor, staring up at me in broken agony.

We both seemed stuck there for the longest time. I closed my eyes for a second to recover and then, opening them again, noticed that behind where the mirror had been was a mounted camera inside.

"You were taping me?" Alongside the camera tripod, I spotted a box of DVDs with different labels on them. One had Tabitha's name on it.

We both heard a sharp creaking sound and looked up. There was a long shard of the broken mirror stuck in the top of the frame, wavering suspended—until it dropped—plunging into his leg.

He screamed.

Someone would hear. Someone would be coming. I grabbed as many DVDs as I could, including Tabitha's, and headed for the door.

"You can't just leave me like this," he said, his voice shaking in pain, his hand covering the wound, trying to stop the bleeding.

The door was massive. I had to put the DVDs on the floor and open the door with both hands to get out.

"At least you have to send someone to help me."

But I just grabbed the DVDs from the floor and ran.

61 Lying in bed I stared up at the ceiling of Tabitha's guest room. I glanced at the few spattered drops of blood on the reworked Chanel hanging in the closet, at the DVDs on the vanity, and fell asleep waiting for the darkness outside to turn blue.

Bolting awake, impatient to talk to Tabitha, I threw on a blouse and jeans and tiptoed barefoot through the breezeway in the early morning air to her room, hoping I could wake her, and found the door open.

In the sitting room adjoining the bedroom, Tabitha gazed out the window at the ocean.

"Come in," she said quietly. Cozy in her lush pink robe, Tabitha rested with her legs tucked under, enveloped from her neck to her ankles in pink. I sat as Zoya poured two cups of coffee and retreated.

"Last night, at Robert's . . ." I started, but she held her hand up for me to stop.

"I know," she said, putting a spoonful of sugar in her coffee. She slowly took a sip, holding the cup in both hands. "Robert has been in Southampton Hospital all night."

"And your mother?"

"She left this morning, couldn't deal with it, as usual." Tabitha took another sip of coffee. On her face there was an expression of annoyance and disappointment. Her face was puffy from crying.

"I found these." I placed a few of the DVDs with her name on the table. Tabitha glanced at them. Her eyes narrowed, and her face drained of color.

"What are those?" she muttered in a soft voice almost to herself.

"I know what you've been going through."

"You mean Robert . . ."

I nodded.

Her breathing steadied and she reached for a tissue, but her eyes were dry.

"I should have known. I used to keep count of how many times.

But then he stopped and I forgot about it for a while." Composed, she lifted her cup and took a sip. "I was younger. But it would come up in my mind in flashes at the oddest times. I couldn't control it. He played one of these once, of another girl. So I knew he had a camera. I didn't think he had them of me. So obvious."

"He's your uncle. How long did he . . ."

"Don't. Please." She peered back out at the ocean. The waves rose and fell in a soothing rhythm. After a few moments she gathered herself.

"I was actually jealous at first, of the others," she said and started to laugh, unable to help herself. "There was a girl who had a blog like yours, and Robert started a magazine with her name all over it. She was nothing before Robert. He's invested in plenty of people, you know. It was better for them. I mean, there's nothing wrong with that, is there?"

My stomach felt uneasy.

"Are you saying that's why you sent me to meet with him?" I asked.

"He has a ton of money. I didn't know—maybe you would want his help. It was Robert's idea. And he was willing; he said he was willing to release me from all of his control. I didn't think it through. Really, he made it sound harmless, like a favor." She had a sad, pained expression, like a little girl in trouble.

Could that be true? If I had succumbed to Robert, would I have gained entry into the world of money and privilege I had first encountered that night outside the Met so long ago? Other girls had done so. I could have buried Lizzy from New Jersey forever just by giving myself up to him.

"You should turn these over to someone," I said. "We have to stop him from doing this ever again."

"Stop him?" She stifled a derisive laugh. "From having sex with pretty young girls? It happens all the time, every night, everywhere. I only wanted to stop him from controlling me." She dropped her stirring spoon to the plate, her eyes glassy with tears.

The wind was blowing across the ocean against the waves,

making them higher and crash harder. The airstream above carried a soft white fog, floating in, layering the blue sky. How could it all look so beautiful when I felt so bad?

"What are you going to do?" I asked, wondering if I held her and hugged her, the way Nan hugged me, would it make her feel better. "We have to give these tapes to the police. You have to see someone. You have every right to be free of him."

"You're not from here, are you?" she asked, turning toward me. Her eyes pierced deeply into mine as if she could see everything inside of me, a sharpness to her voice I hadn't heard before. "Why did you have to be the girl in the bathroom who found me? You don't know. You don't know what you're talking about," she said.

Fearful I might reveal something unconsciously, with my eyes or my face, I turned away.

"You should leave," she said and tapped her cup with her stirring spoon. Zoya appeared instantly.

"More coffee."

62 The taxi smelled of cigarettes and mildew as I watched the dunes and scrub pines whizz by. The Hamptons sky was clouding up. A light rain was falling, or was it just fog? I opened all the windows. It felt good on my face.

I checked the Jitney schedule and realized there were only two buses left that could take me back to the city in time for Jess's show. Four days ago I thought the Jitney was special; now they were just buses, glorified Greyhounds.

Too much had happened that I couldn't understand, that I couldn't twist into part of my Being Audrey game. Everything had turned too serious for that.

I arrived at the Jitney stop, and there were dozens of people waiting to get on, part of the mass exodus that happened every weekend in the Hamptons. You could almost hear the sucking sound of people leaving the eastern end of the island. I didn't have a chance. I'd have to wait for the next bus.

My phone buzzed, and I dreaded to check it.

"WHERE R U ?!" It was Jess of course. The little creature inside my stomach woke up, very unhappy.

"We go on at 7 PM!!"

I was trying to calculate how long it would take to get from the tip of Long Island to Chelsea on the west side of New York City and if it was even possible in the Hamptons' summer traffic. I began writing a text, but before I could finish . . .

"R yur ppl coming?"

I deleted my text to begin writing an explanation, trying to find some way to justify myself and why I was late, when I received another text.

"R u comin ?!"

I had to stop and take a breath.

"Yes :)" I thumbed as quickly as I could.

☺ She texted in return.

I sighed, physically and emotionally exhausted, meditating on the smiley face.

On my phone I blogged a new Limelight entry as if I had no worries in the world. I figured it was my one last-minute shot at making Jess's show a success, even if I couldn't be there.

Tonight is the Night! The Designer X Pop Up show only happens if you are there! Style mavens, cynical fashion hipsters, fashion addicts, runway fanatics, designer devotees, loyal followers. See her runway show in person. Show your designer devotion. Satisfy your need for immediate gratification. Come take your pictures. Post them everywhere. Rock your Instagram with pix of Designer X's new looks. Only you can make it happen. #xbelowtheline2nite.

As the fully packed Jitney pulled away onto route 27, my last hope for arriving in time, I madly blasted everyone on my list of followers.

I called Isak, but there was no answer, so I texted him again.

"Designer X . . . Below the Line Gallery 7pm !! Please say you're going !! :)" If Isak made it, I would be okay. I left messages at Flo's office for her and Gabby to come.

I squinted down the street, but the next Jitney was nowhere in sight.

I sat on my roller with my garment bag in my lap and worried. I had to be realistic and think of what I could do other than just break down and sob because that's the only thing I felt like doing. Undone by ZK, I had left everything unfinished. Because I was unhappy, I guaranteed that no one would be happy with me.

I wondered how Jess could forgive me. My Audrey project was coming to an unfavorable end, letting down my best friend, losing ZK, Tabitha, and Jake without a clue what I would do with the rest of my life.

"Hey Lisbeth!" a familiar voice called out. "Need a ride?"

I turned to see Chase in his white van. "I thought I'd drive by just in case. Just a wild hunch, figured I might find you here."

"Tell me you're not some weird stalker?" I asked. Chase laughed, getting out of his van, embarrassed in front of all the other people waiting for the Jitney.

"No. Okay. Yes. I told you I've had you on my radar for a while. Just saw your blog entry, and I figure you needed someone to shoot that fashion show of yours. Am I right?"

I was speechless.

"Well, I'll take that as a yes," he said, grabbing my suitcase and putting it in the back of his van. "Let's hurry. I've got to do some tricky driving while I pull together a crew if we're going to make this happen."

63 There was a succession of texts as Chase madly wove his van through the expressway traffic taking access roads and conduits that I thought for sure would wind up at a dead end.

"It's 6:30 and NOBODY'S HERE :/"

"You promised . . . :*("

I decided not to respond. We were either a half hour away or going to be stuck in traffic forever. I would be there or not.

I had to do a quick inventory of what we needed. Like music. We hadn't even considered that. I figured I might know one person who would be willing to show up at the last second and sent a text. While I was texting, my phone buzzed again.

"We are supposed to start in TEN MINUTES !!"

"Tell her to stall." Chase insisted, looking over my shoulder as we zipped around the line of cars exiting the Midtown Tunnel.

"Will be there soon :)" I texted back. I saw the three dots that meant she was responding when my phone died. I plugged it into Chase's car charger and waited.

"Are we going to make it?" I asked.

"Shouldn't be a problem. Do you want to change?" he asked.

"What do you mean?"

"Designer X—don't you have something of hers to wear?" He was eyeing my garment bag. At Tabitha's I hadn't been able to bring myself to put on Jess's dress.

"I'm supposed to change here in front of you?"

"No!" he said, looking mortified. "Back there, behind the equipment crates."

I crawled my way to the back of the van, out of Chase's line of sight, as it bounced around, and stripped down to my underwear, pulling out Designer X's exquisite signature creation. In the bumpy minivan I stared at it, afraid to put it on.

Slipping on the tight nude satin underskirt, I felt the familiar hug of it and pulled up the rest of the dress, the overskirt and the blouse. It made me feel exactly as it had when I tried it on the first time.

"This is your signature dress," I remembered saying to Jess. *"Isak will love it. Everyone will."*

It's something every woman can tell you—there's one pair of shoes or a sexy bra that makes you feel beautiful and strong in those gut-wrenching moments—like going to a wedding after breaking up with your boyfriend or to some terrible high school reunion.

I guess guys have their lucky underwear or shirts, like Jake and his flannels. Jess's dress gave me that sensation. It communicated through the fabric, cut, and texture. The van came to a stop.

As I put on my heels, I peered out the tiny dirty window in the back of the van. I could make out two other vans that seemed as though it might be Chase's crew already unpacking. I saw Sarrah and a man I assumed was the gallery owner on the street screaming at each other. That couldn't be good. Squinting, I could see Jess on the sidewalk, totally stressed, surrounded by her models sitting on fire hydrants, leaning against streetlights, sitting on flattened cardboard boxes on the curb in her finest designs.

I tried to open the van door from the inside but it wouldn't budge, so I pounded on the window. When the door opened I almost fell on my face.

"Sorry about that," Chase said. "Gotta get that fixed."

As soon as Jess saw me, she let out a scream and ran over. She was wearing one of her self-made tiered iridescent skirts and her vintage Sonic Youth T-shirt tied at the waist. Over her shoulder she carried the ever-present monster bag filled with all kinds of emergency makeup, hair spray, and sewing stuff.

We both screamed and hugged.

"I'm sorry I'm so late," I said.

"It's okay, it's okay, but what are we going to do?" she said.

"I don't know. Why are all the models outside?"

"What?! You don't know? I texted you." My cell phone was still connected to the car charger.

"Know what?"

"There's no room!" she shouted.

I took in the whole scene for the first time and almost fell into shock. Serious apoplectic shock. There were literally hundreds of people everywhere. The tiny gallery was crammed with them. And really cool people, I might add. Hundreds of fashionable people had converged on the Below the Line Gallery, proof that the posting and e-mail blasts worked. These were at least some of the fashionistas who followed my blog. I wanted to stop and examine each and every one of them—how they were dressed, their ages, their style. But there was no time.

"I guarantee you, they were not here twenty minutes ago," Jess said. "It just happened."

Chase sauntered over. "You're the promotional genius," he said, giving me a smirk. "Where are we setting up?" People were clogging the street. Cars were honking, having trouble getting by.

"There's not enough room," I said, stunned.

"Gee, you just figured that out?" Chase asked. He eyed Jess. "This could take awhile."

"Well, we'll just have to go up there." I pointed to the elevated highway above us. "Have you ever shot up there?" I asked. Chase acted like he was afraid of me, as though I might bite him.

"Do you mean—the High Line?"

The High Line is an official New York City park built on the rusty remains of a derelict elevated railway that used to wind down the West Side Highway. It is now filled with walkways, plantings, seating areas, and little amphitheaters. Jess and I would walk up there every time we went to the stores in the Meatpacking District. There were happenings and events staged up there every day. Jess and I had talked about it, but never in our wildest dreams did we think we'd have the chance to do a fashion show there.

"Yeah," Chase said. "I've shot a bunch of times for Tommy

Hilfinger after he waited about three months to get a thousand permits from the mayor's office."

"Can we do it on the fly? It's a pop-up, right?'"

Chase grinned. I could see he was into it.

"Okay, boss, it's your show." Chase whistled to his crew, and they sprinted ahead with all of their equipment and lights.

"Have all the models come with us. I'm sure everyone else will follow," I said. Jess and I began marching straight down Ninth Avenue, just ahead of our entourage of provocative models in their dazzling dresses and a horde of gawking fashionistas gathered behind us. It felt like a movable party. It felt like we could take these people anywhere.

"There are no chairs and no stage," Jess said to me as we walked. "Where will the important people be?"

"With everyone else," I said. "Who knows who's the most important person in this crowd anyway? They all could be."

As the crowd snapped pictures with every conceivable camera and phone, we made our way to the High Line stairs at Fourteenth Street. They would post these pictures on their Instagram and Twitter accounts, but we had to make sure that the runway was the show they'd remember.

Walking into the covered Chelsea Passage, where the High Line cuts through the Chelsea Market building, we encountered a sea of cool blue fluorescent light that bathed the tunnel columns mingling the High Line's industrial architecture with the cityscape around us.

Chase had already set a backdrop curtain, and we took the models behind there. Massive concert speakers and a DJ deck already had been set up on either side of the runway, and there was my friend Bennie doing a last-second tech check.

"Lisbeth baby! I knew you'd call me!" Curly-haired Bennie, wearing a funky pinstripe suit and shades like some tripped-out mobster, was scratching an electronic turntable. He had gotten my text. Jess and I felt like the littlest kids at the biggest party of our lives.

"You've got about thirty minutes, I figure, before the cops shut us down, so we have to start right away," Chase yelled over the rising din of people settling in. "Good luck."

Everything in Jess's monster bag came out. We lined up the girls, touched up their makeup and hair, straightened the lines of the dresses, pinning anything back that didn't look right. Then, abruptly, the lights went out and the whole area was dark, muted, and quiet. In hushed whispers, Jess reordered the models at the last second.

A spotlight snapped on, and Bennie kicked up the music, cranking the volume. An infectious beat reverberated, turning the cavernous space into a giant stereo speaker.

"Go! Go!" Jess yelled, pushing the first model onto the stage.

Bright flashes lit up the architecture as a wall of fans with iPhones and photographers fired their shutters. The models had to walk toward that blinding spotlight just concentrating on keeping their heads up and putting one foot in front of the next while trying to look natural. I'm not sure they could see anything in the extreme contrast of dark and light.

I slipped out from behind the backdrop to see the show and the audience from the wings. Jess's last-minute sequence ordered the dresses by color, and it was a revelation.

The show opened with a series of white looks that quickly evolved. Sea-foam green was followed by solar yellow and honey orange. Little by little the bolder colors emerged, illuminating the chiffon dresses and the layered skirts within skirts.

The dresses came to life with attractive details—a ripple of sequins, a plunging neckline, a backless dress, a cuff—offering new energetic concepts of style and design. The shimmering blues were the most stunning. They had an almost stellar depth.

No ordinary models, Sarrah's friends were an entire show unto themselves. They were as lithe and lovely as any girl who had ever hit the runway. But these were massively tattooed, slash-and-burn, hardcore, multiracial beauties with some seriously hairalicious hairstyles.

One girl had the words BROKEN DREAMS tattooed across her chest in goth lettering. And of course the most ravishing, purest one of all was Jannush, a tranny friend of Sarrah's who strutted down the stage in mile-high stilettos. Truthfully, the models were the perfect contrast to the dresses themselves, and the tattoos were a counterpoint to Jess's lyrical inscriptions.

Sarrah had contributed in other ways as well. She had taken some of Jess's journal entries, the ones stitched into the hems of the dresses, put them on a loop on her computer, and projected them across the ceiling above the models. The audience ahhh'd and oooh'd at each one, loving it.

VIP spotting turned up some surprising people. I waved to Flo, who had brought Rachel Zoe with her. Flo gave me the proudest smile and a thumbs-up. I scanned the crowd and thought I spotted Gabby but wasn't sure. There was a lady in a strange lavender outfit who seemed important. And then Betsey Johnson and Isak! Where had he been? Thank God he was here. He threw me a kiss.

The lighting was austere and dramatic. The music was shamelessly danceable. It was an instant pop-up fashion event for Designer X beyond our fondest hopes, but the dresses and looks warranted all the attention.

As Jess told me before, a dress had only one chance to make an impression, and after that it had to deliver on the cut, the style, and fabric. The first opportunity was the only opportunity, and this was it.

Sarrah's model friends were a big hit, too, and I'd never thought girls that tough would blush and giggle, but they did. And Jess . . . what can I say about the best friend a girl could ever have? She had already made me seem to be someone way more sophisticated than I could ever have seemed myself. At the same time, she was the kind of friend who never stopped laying it on the line. While never wavering in her support of my crazy ideas, she kept me centered and honest even when I was telling the biggest lies of my life.

And me? I was just glad that I didn't let her down.

The girls did three passes, switching dresses furiously in the back. After Jess and I had finished the last turnaround, we held hands as the models made their walks for the finale.

After the last model had made her turn, a chant went up: "X, X, X!" Soon everyone was chanting, "X, X, X!" It was time for Designer X to take a bow, only Jess was seized with stage fright.

"You've got to go, and you know it," I said. "Come on, step out in front for once."

"No. It's your moment. You created Designer X. You drove me to do this crazy thing, and you invented a name for it, dragging me into it until I had to do the best work I could possibly do."

"It's the designer who ends the show," I said, but I could see the wheels turning in her head before I finished speaking.

"Not when you're wearing my best dress."

All the models had taken the stage and joined the audience in clapping and chanting. Bennie dropped a totally ecstatic pop beat that sounded like little musical bubbles colliding. As everyone chanted "X, X, X," Designer X and I held hands and took the runway triumphant. I did a spin in Jess's finest dress, and we both took a bow.

It was over almost as soon as it started. Apparently the cops had been there for the last ten minutes but were nice enough not to shut us down. Chase was tearing the whole thing apart as fast as he put it up.

Bloggers, tweeters, and the like swamped us from all sides with cameras, microphones, and smartphones.

When I introduced Isak to Jess, they bonded immediately, instant best friends and colleagues. As more and more people gathered around Jess, I slipped away. I found a bottle of water and a quiet corner and tried to bring my heartbeat down to a normal level. Finally I could catch my breath.

"That's quite a show you pulled off, Lisbeth," a voice said from the shadows.

"Who is that?" I said and turned to see ZK emerging into the light.

"No. You can't just show up like this."

"I'm sorry," he said, holding out his open hand. "More sorry than you will ever believe. Can we talk?"

"I don't know," I said, stepping away from him.

He was dressed in a tux, his dark wavy hair slicked back the way it was when we first met. The gold flecks in his green eyes reflected the last of the lights from the fashion show.

"I know it's hard but there are things you need to know," he said.

"Are you okay?" I asked him.

"Me? I'm fine. It's about the bracelet."

"Why did you take it?"

"I can't talk here. Will you come with me?"

"Hey Lisbeth!" Chase called. I turned. "We're going out to celebrate. You're joining us, right?"

"Yes. Text me where. I need to do something first," I said, trying not to look behind me.

"Are you talking to someone?" Chase asked.

I turned back to ZK and saw he was hiding in the shadows.

"No, but I'll catch up with you soon," I said.

"You're sure?"

I nodded and he left.

"Follow me," ZK said, half his face in shadow. And I did.

64 The stretch limo pulled away almost as soon as the door closed. In the darkness I hadn't realized anyone else was there.

"Nice of you to join us, Lisbeth," Dahlia said, neatly tucked away in the back corner of her limo. Wearing a silver metallic Cavalli minidress with a plunging neckline and a broad silver cuff, she was provocative and intimidating at the same time. "ZK is lovely as always, isn't he?"

ZK watched impassively.

"What do you want?" I asked.

"I think men are so much more attractive when they're depressed, don't you?" She examined ZK's profile as if he were a curiosity in a store that she might buy. "They have this deep, brooding, desperate look when they're disheartened, like trapped creatures. I think it's sexy. What do you think, Lisbeth?"

"I think you're a monster."

"Oh now I'm a monster. That's flattering," she said as if it was the funniest joke in the world. Holding out her champagne glass, she waited for ZK to get the message. He filled her glass from a nearby bottle.

"We enjoyed your little fashion show, didn't we, ZK?" A glaze had settled in ZK's eyes, which locked in a long-suffering expression of his that was familiar to me. "Join me in a toast to Designer X," she said, holding up her glass, "and an end to the little pretend life you've been living." Her laser-focused eyes bored into mine so intensely I felt like I would evaporate into nothing.

"ZK, if you had any decency you'd stop this," I pleaded.

Dahlia threw back her head and laughed.

"Decency?" she said, barely glancing at ZK. "I think that word left the family crest ages ago. Besides, ZK showed me this exquisite bracelet of yours." She pulled Nan's inscribed platinum band out of her silver clutch and waved it in front of me.

"Give it back."

"That wouldn't be much fun, would it?" She slipped the bracelet on and off her slender wrist. "That's the problem with you, Lisbeth. You're not much fun, and I like my friends to be more fun."

"I can see that I have deeply offended you, and I am sorry. But, please, I will never bother you again, please give me the bracelet and I will go away."

It was hard to describe the expression on her face. It was like the look of a cat pinning its claw down on a mouse's tail. My begging delighted her.

"You don't *bother* me, Lisbeth. You're not fun, but you're enter-
taining." Dahlia placed the bracelet back in her clutch and snapped
it shut. "So tell us about your Nan? She sounds like a fascinating
person," Dahlia began, gazing into my eyes with mock seriousness.
"Dulac—that's her last name, isn't it? Just like yours." She laughed
again, more of a cackle, really.

"You couldn't possibly understand anything about my grandmother. Nan is a wonderful person, with more grace and style than
you or anyone you know," I answered.

"Oh really? Then I assume you are aware she's also a tad notori-
ous. Not to mention your grandfather—Sammy G—'hardened
criminals,' I think, is the term they use."

"You've got it wrong. His name wasn't Sammy. My grandfather's
name was Frank and he was just a construction worker."

Dahlia could hardly contain her pleasure.

"So you grew up thinking he was a construction worker?
What's that expression they have where you come from? Fuhged-
dahbouddit!"

"Okay, stop it now, Dahlia," ZK spoke up. "You're being ridiculous."

"Take it easy, lover boy," she replied. "We'll be done soon enough."
She ran her hands through his hair like he was a pet. His eyes
haunted, he looked horribly humiliated.

"Poor ZK," Dahlia said, studying his profile. "Even though the
whole affair was my idea, I think he actually fell in love with you."

ZK shoved Dahlia's hand away.

"Stop the car!" he yelled, and the limo pulled to the curb. ZK
opened the door and stormed out. The steam from a manhole cover
rose up in the street. We had driven uptown, but I couldn't see
where.

"Lisbeth, please get out of the car," he said. Dahlia didn't seem
to care, so I slipped from the limo, relieved to be outside but concerned about the platinum band in Dahlia's clutch. She watched
the scene unfold as if she were viewing a play.

"Lisbeth, this is the truth, and you might as well know because Dahlia is going to expose it," ZK said. "Dahlia put a private detective on your case as soon as she met you. She pushed me to invite you to Soho House that night. The man who you thought was your grandfather is the Sammy G who gave that bracelet to your grandmother. He was a Mafia boss who had been in hiding for almost forty years until he died. He married a society girl named Simon Fleurice Dulac—your grandmother—who vanished mysteriously decades ago."

"I don't believe you," I said. "None of this makes any sense. How can *you* be part of this with *her*? Why should I believe any of what you are saying?"

"I know," ZK said, as his whole body seemed to slump like a marionette whose strings had been cut. "You're so different, Lisbeth. Wherever you came from, whoever you are. Everything is new to you, filled with possibilities. I have none, never have had any. In my world I don't stand a chance," he answered. "I had hoped you wouldn't take me seriously, but you did. And the more I grew to appreciate you, the more I knew I would be bad for you. I made another shameful Northcott bargain in a history of bad bargains. My family was at stake. It was the only way."

I turned to Dahlia, who was enjoying the drama.

"Dahlia, your private detective has simply mixed my Nan up with someone else," I said. "Please just give me back the bracelet. I'll do whatever you want. I'll disappear. Just leave Nan alone."

She paused, seeming to savor the situation. I thought for a moment that she might be gratified by how utterly devastated I was, how broken ZK seemed, and return Nan's bracelet.

"I can't dear, sweet girl; it's federal evidence. When we discovered the truth, I was obliged to consult the district attorney, an old friend of my father's. There's nothing I can do now. Oh, I forgot, I've been talking to a delightful *New York Post* reporter about you; he's done quite a bit of digging, which was very helpful, including a certain Page Six photo."

Page Six. Those words felt like a punch in the stomach.

"You've had your moment, ZK. I must admit, it was a moving performance, almost seemed like you meant it," she said with a smirk. "It's time to go."

His feet seemed glued to the street. Dahlia's eyes hardened. "If you'd like me to hold up my end of the deal, do come along," she said, and the limo driver closed her door.

ZK walked around the limo almost as if his body had no choice. He barely glanced up as he ducked inside. But I saw in that mere instant his pleading eyes, the lost boy in all his agony.

Dahlia lowered her window.

"My dear, I think you can assume your life is ruined. I wish I knew how to make one of those evil supervillain laughs. This would be the time for it, don't you think?"

65 With every step it felt like I was leaving behind some part of myself. I compulsively moved forward, staring down at the sidewalk in that determined way people walk in the city where no one dares talk to you. I found myself at Central Park by Columbus Circle and realized I was only a few blocks from Tiffany's.

Even though the evening was winding down, the carriages and their sad horses were still escorting tourists through the park. Turning down Fifth, I saw the seamless glass box that was the Apple store glistening in the moonlight.

Yellow taxis sped by as I approached the street corner at 57th. For the first time, it felt sad to peer up and see the familiar chiseled logo. Not at all like the times Jess and I, as so many girls, would bring our breakfast to eat in front of Tiffany's windows.

I gazed down Fifth Avenue.

In a few hours, at dawn, the streetlights would still be on when

Holly would arrive by taxi. Gazing up at the Tiffany logo, she'll release an almost imperceptible sigh from her shoulders. Wearing her sunglasses in the morning twilight, she'll float on tiny steps to the jewelry-showcase window and delicately take a cruller from a white bag with her long black gloves. She'll gingerly remove the plastic top of her deli coffee cup and let it tumble into the paper bag, not spilling a drop.

Without a soul in sight, she'll examine the stunning display of diamond bracelets and miniature chandeliers, tilting her head ever so slightly, contemplating their elegance and beauty.

I could see her standing before me in her fragile splendor. I had always assumed she was an early-bird window-shopper with an intimate knowledge of diamonds and pearls returning from some fabulous party.

Now I realized she was outside staring in. She came to Tiffany's because she needed to make herself feel better. She was endlessly searching for what she never had, sad for whatever she was missing. Just like me.

She went to Tiffany's that morning to feel safe. She must have been somewhere unsafe that night.

Although it's hard to find anything bad about Audrey, there must have been a dark side in her life that people don't talk about. After all, she was a heavy smoker who liked a glass of bourbon. Rumors of affairs with married men and anorexia have been around forever—Audrey's own version of the mean reds—but she kept her problems discretely hidden in a Givenchy dress where no one would see. I wished we could talk, Audrey and I, and she could tell me if she ever made it feel all right.

It was time to go back to New Jersey.

66 I should have told them right away. Nan, Mom, Courtney, and Ryan were all sitting there waiting for me. I couldn't imagine how unbelievably fast Dahlia had put her plan into action.

"Pinched Givenchy!" was the headline on the front page of *The New York Post* lying on the kitchen table in front of them.

My face was on the cover.

I was wearing the dress.

And the tiara.

They had cropped out ZK and Dahlia.

"I've done something terrible," I said, which at the time seemed like a massive understatement. I waited for Nan or Mom's reaction, but there wasn't one.

When the NYPD detectives picked me up for interrogation, they asked if I had a lawyer. I knew we couldn't afford one, so I was given a public defender, who seemed even younger than me, like he was just out of law school. He seemed more terrified than I was of the press and was no help at all.

Without any prior criminal record (I hadn't even had one day of high school detention) and my name and face plastered on tabloids, I wasn't considered a flight risk, so they sent me home to Jersey. After all, they didn't have formal charges—yet.

I had read the article on the PATH train home. *The Post* gave me the full tabloid treatment, I guess because it was a slow news day in a slow news week, and because their venerable Page Six had been victimized as part of the fraud.

Dahlia slipped the whole story to some intrepid society reporter for *The New York Post*, who did his best to uncover the sordid details about me and Nan. It hadn't taken long to search through their photo archive. I should have known that evidence of my Givenchy napping would surface.

Pretty much everything in the article was true: how I had faked and photobombed my way among the Upper East Siders, freeload-

ing in their world of conspicuous consumption—limousines, personal shoppers, weekends in the Hamptons—passing as one of them when I was a wannabe South Ender from Jersey.

It featured a teary-eyed Tabitha Eden with a quote beneath her picture: "I felt devastated and betrayed. She wormed and manipulated her way into every aspect of my life. I regret every moment I knew her." I assumed someone had written that line for her, but it made me sad regardless. How Dahlia persuaded Tabitha to be in the article I'll never understand. The reporter discreetly kept Dahlia's name out. No one would have known she arranged the whole thing.

Back home in the kitchen everyone seemed stunned, except smart-ass, smirking Ryan. All the color drained out of Nan's face when I got to the part about Sammy. And when I admitted how I let the bracelet get taken away from me, I couldn't stop sobbing and threw myself at Nan's feet. I hugged her legs, hoping she wouldn't hate me, afraid to meet her eyes.

"Wow," Courtney finally said over my sobbing, "and I thought I was the bad girl in the family. Totally beats me." Everyone laughed a little at that.

"So is it true about Dad?" Mom asked, turning to Nan.

Nan ran her hands through my hair. Her head trembled a little as she spoke.

"I knew they would find out eventually," Nan said almost in a whisper. "I'm just glad Sammy's not around to see it."

"Can I tell my friends at school?" Ryan asked. Mom laughed a little.

"Typical Ryan," she said. "Just keep a lid on it, okay?" Then she turned to me.

"Come here, Lisbeth," she said. When I got up, I was surprised to see that she was holding out her arms for me. We hugged and I just kept sobbing. I don't think my mom and I had hugged since I was tiny. Her arms were kind of flabby because she had lost so much weight, but her skin hadn't shrunk. It felt good to feel close to

her. I couldn't help thinking that for the first time she didn't smell
of cigarettes and booze.

There's nothing like having your personal problems and the
worst situation you've ever been in in your life put on national me-
dia for everyone to slice, dice, and dissect. As soon as *The Post* article
came out, *that very day,* we clocked at least twenty-six threats on
our phone at home. Unsurprisingly, my e-mail and phone number
leaked out pretty quickly, but it took a little longer for them to find
Lisbeth Dulac's Facebook. The mere success of my blog, Limelight,
was my undoing. And it happened almost instantly.

Trolls are angry monsters who live under a bridge and eat goats
by snapping their necks and drinking their blood while venting
their inner rage on Instagram, Tumblr, and Facebook. I shut off my
phone and stopped opening my e-mail account, but Limelight was
a mess.

"Liar," "Fraud," "Poseur," "Hoax," and the most troubling,
"Con Artist," were just some of the non-four-letter words I was
called in the various news outlets, although liar and hoax *do* count,
if you're being technical. On the blog the words were much worse,
the kind of sexually violent, unprintable words that only anonymous commenters can get away with.

Misogynists, stalkers, serial harassers, and cyberbullies came to
the site in waves. I learned the art of triage and skimmed to find
out if there was any actual personally threatening data or just your
normal everyday nasty invective. When our address on Pine Street
popped up, I knew we were in deeper trouble and stopped looking.

We changed our number a bunch of times, but stuff just happened. Someone using a falsified Uber account thought it was
funny to send twelve limos to show up at our house all at the same
time between 11:30 P.M. and 2:00 in the morning.

It was raining the morning the police, wearing blue raid jackets,
stood outside our house.

"We're here to execute a search warrant," the agent said as Mom
let them inside. The search warrant gave the government authori-

zation to seize "fruits of a possible crime," even though I hadn't been charged with anything. It made me wonder what the "fruits of my crime" were.

Wearing blue nitrile gloves, they basically ransacked my bedroom and seemed pretty happy when they found my closet and all the Audrey Hepburn posters. They neatly rolled up the posters as evidence, tagged them, and put them in big plastic bags. I couldn't help thinking what Jess would have said about their curatorial techniques. They took my computer and all my VHS and DVD copies of *Breakfast at Tiffany's, Roman Holiday,* and the other Audrey Hepburn movies. I have to admit, I wouldn't have been able to watch them anyway.

News trucks and reporters started crowding up the streets as another group of agents arrived and Mom let them in. What else was she supposed to do?

When a woman wearing a dark blue business suit and dark blue blouse flashed her FBI medallion, we all knew they were here for Nan.

Nan asked permission to use the bathroom, and they made a big show of checking out the downstairs bathroom before she entered, even stationing an agent outside the little window and ventilation fan in the back with another agent in front of the door. As if at eighty-one she was going to make a mad dash for freedom. Nan just wanted to tidy up her makeup and look nice for when they took her away. She didn't even try to avoid the cameras as the feds walked her out of the house in handcuffs, head held high and smiling as bright as ever, wearing her patented double strand of white pearls.

I couldn't believe I had caused all these horrible things to rain down on my family.

I climbed back upstairs, crawled into my empty closet, and cried.

67

"Lisbeth was the quiet one," Mrs. Walker, my biology teacher from Montclair High, was quoted saying in a *New York* magazine piece. The article compared me to JT Leroy, the literary hoaxer who famously fooled Carrie Fisher and Asia Argento, and to Esther Reed, a con artist with multiple identities, both of whom were caught for masquerading as someone they weren't for fame and profit. "I would hardly have ever expected her to steal a world-famous dress," Mrs. Walker added condescendingly. I think they talk the same way about serial murderers.

The piece went on to assume that I was the latest example of social anxiety disorder, appropriately abbreviated as SAD in the DSM-5, where psychiatrists catalog all forms of mental illness. Also known as social phobia, it is considered the most common anxiety disorder: 12 percent of Americans have experienced it in their lifetime. It's also a disorder that is frequently associated with crime. They analyzed me as being withdrawn, introverted, and characterized by intense social fear, theorizing that I lashed out at society by pretending to be someone else. I was kind of insulted by their theory.

The article made Mom consider moving away, and I think we would have if Nan weren't still under threat of a federal indictment. And then what happened to Mom made it impossible.

She woke up vomiting, and if Courtney and I hadn't rushed to Mom's bedroom and turned her on her side, Mom would have drowned in her own puke. Stuff was up in her nose and everything. It scared the shit out of us. Even after we turned her over, she still wasn't breathing, so I stuck my fingers down her throat and desperately tried to clear her airway. Finally Mom coughed up more stuff, and I got her to sit up while Courtney called an ambulance.

At the hospital, her liver tests were alarming: ALP—186, GGT—455, MCV—111, and a platelet count over 96,000. I didn't really know what all that meant—even though the doctors and

nurses kept talking about it. Finally I found Dr. Newton to find out what was going on.

"Her liver isn't functioning," he said. "We can stabilize her for a while, but we're not sure what we can do at this point."

"But she stopped drinking," I said, feeling hopeless.

"Which is a good development, but the damage was already there," he said.

"What about a transplant?" Courtney piped up. "She's on the list, right?"

"We've already moved her to the top of the list. And we'll even go outside our designated area, but there are no guarantees that an organ will be available or that your mom will be able to endure the long hours of surgery," he said.

Courtney and I silently held hands in the waiting area, alone with the ferns and the rows of mauve chairs with the endless, repetitive voices of cable news filling up the empty space.

After Mom's condition stabilized, we were allowed to visit her. Every nurse, doctor, and orderly watched as we came in. I couldn't help feeling that their opinions about me had changed, as if I had caused this terrible thing to happen to my mother. I certainly didn't feel like the good girl anymore.

"Your lovely daughters are here," Nurse Brynner said. She was just as warm as ever. Unlike my mother, she seemed healthier than before. As we entered, she whispered to me, "Maybe you can talk some sense into her." I had no idea what she was talking about.

When she saw us walking in together holding hands, Mom looked pleased. We sat down by her bed. She seemed to be resting well and no longer in pain.

"It's mostly just dehydration," she said, as if that was an explanation for her condition. "I'll get back on my feet soon."

"Dr. Newton doesn't think so," I said. I guess I had lost all my reticence in talking to Mom the way I used to. Courtney was horrified.

"Don't speak to her that way," she said.

"I'm just saying there's more going on than that," I responded, defending myself.

"Well, you don't have to talk about it now!" she demanded. I thought she might start screaming at me, and I winced a little. I could see Mom knew what was going on. It was like she always knew what went down between Courtney and me but was just so messed up in her own life she couldn't acknowledge it.

"No Court, sorry. Lisbeth is right," she said. "There is something we need to talk about." I braced myself, terrified at what she might say next.

"I told the doctors and the nurses and everybody that I don't want a transplant."

"Are you crazy?" Courtney said. Now she was really angry.

"I don't deserve it, Court. They shouldn't waste an organ on me." I could tell she had been thinking about it for a long time. "A transplant isn't like other operations. I've seen the patients that need them and how difficult the surgery is. There's a terrible shortage of organs, and many people who are a lot more worthy than me are waiting for them. I'll just do the best I can."

The wind seemed to go out of Courtney. I was devastated, too. We didn't know what to say. I listened to the various medical monitors beep and whirr, making a symphony of sadness in the room.

Slowly, I found myself trying to unravel the logic of what Mom was saying. I knew she was trying to do something noble. It seemed selfish of me, but I was starting to get mad that she was bailing on us. Sure, it was the "good nurse" in Mom who was trying to do the right thing, but she was giving up on us, too.

"It's not fair," I said determinedly. "You're saying that *we're* not worthy. I know I fucked up royally. But I need you more than ever—Courtney and Ryan, too. Nan for that matter, not that you ever think of her."

Mom looked at me astounded. Courtney didn't know what to

make of it. I'm not sure Court understood what I was trying to say. She was so used to being left behind, and although she was always mad about it, in some way she expected it.

"I can't sit here with you," I said. "If this is the way it's going to be, I've got to go."

68

I expected Jess, but I hadn't dreamed that Jake would show up with her.

I mean, Jake was an effin' rock star practically. I was surprised that the press wasn't following *him*. Of course, by now my story had been replaced with other headlines, like the one about Kim Kardashian dancing with Kanye at a Miami disco even though she's eight months pregnant with another baby. The TV news vans and reporters' cars were no longer hanging outside the house.

Jess and Jake sat down on the couch in the living room. I couldn't help realizing that when I was younger we never sat in the living room. I never spent any time downstairs if I could help it.

Jess was wearing all black. Since the runway show, she had dropped out of FIT and become even more devoted to her fashion line, if that was possible. Judging by her clothes she had definitely made the transition to being a city dweller. After all, in New York City black is always the new black.

Jake wore his usual jeans and flannels, which kind of pegged him as dated, in a Seattle grunge kind of way. But it suited him. With his dark hair and smoky eyes he seemed different, too, even more "Jake," his presence bigger somehow. I guess that's what happens when you get to quit being a waiter at a cheapo diner and dedicate your life to your music. My friends Jake and Jess were moving on with their lives, as opposed to you know who.

"How's Nan?" Jess asked.

"She's more upset about how angry Grandpa would have been

that the bracelet he gave her is sitting in a federal lockup somewhere than anything else," I said. "On the plus side, an old NYPD sergeant in the precinct where they questioned her said that she had the nicest smile he'd ever seen from someone not high on something and asked her for a date." Jess and Jake laughed.

It felt unbelievable to be sitting so close to Jake again, watching him. I kept flashing back to the Talkhouse, where he leapt around the stage like a panther, ripping the music out of his guitar like it was a screaming beast. That song of his started repeating in my mind.

"Is she here?" Jess asked. "It'd be so cool to see her."

"Nah, she's at the hospital with Mom," I said.

"And your mom?" Jake piped up. He caught me looking at him, but I averted my eyes, worried I'd fall apart if I actually met his glance.

"She hates that she's crossed over to the other side of the bed rails. I think the problem is that she's flat-out scared of all the stuff that can go wrong in surgery. She keeps telling us these horror stories from her years on the ward, about catheters that kink, wrong medicines being prescribed. She's a mess basically."

Jake just sat there staring down at his shoes, pretty quiet. I didn't know what else to talk about. I was starting to feel really pathetic.

"Thanks for getting me fired at the Met, by the way," Jess said.

"I'm sorry. I kind of screwed things up for everybody."

"Just kidding, actually. I was going to quit anyway. I think they transferred Myers to the Met Museum Design Store at Newark International Airport, Terminal C," she said, smiling. "So what's next for you?"

"Just waiting to see what the court does. Pretty much being at the hospital all the time, seeing if Mom gets a transplant and cooperates, trying to make things up to Nan. Thinking about college, I guess."

Jess gave me a woeful look and I could see Jake fidgeting.

"You know, Lizzy," Jake said finally, as if he were lifting a heavy weight. "I asked to come along with Jess to see you because I wanted to say that I know you're in all this trouble for what you did but I think it was actually pretty cool. You lived your dream. It's got to count for something."

Same old Jake—sincere, earnest, heartfelt—but I couldn't stand it. He was being supportive like always, but I couldn't look at him. After all, I blew it. I didn't see how to put a good spin on that. I wanted to ask him how Monica was. That would have been the civil thing to do, but I couldn't.

"Thanks," I finally stuttered out. "So how's the big-rock-star tour going?"

Jake excitedly went on about the cities they were hitting and everything about the tour bus and the band. I didn't really hear any of it.

For some reason I couldn't help thinking about the final scene in *Roman Holiday*, when Audrey faces the reporters and she and Gregory Peck share that unspoken feeling between them. They shake hands, pretending as if they never met, even though he's been the love of her life, and then she leaves him alone standing at the rope, gazing at the empty spot where she was last. After everyone is gone, he leaves, taking the long, endless walk out of the palace hall, contemplating what might have been if life were different.

But life isn't different. And there I was, still thinking that everything in my life was like a scene from an Audrey Hepburn movie.

I realized Jake had stopped talking moments ago, and I felt awkward. Jess piped up to fill in the uncomfortable space.

"Have you checked Limelight recently?"

I shook my head no.

"I haven't even turned on my phone," I said.

"Well you should, where is it?" Jess asked.

I went to the kitchen. My phone had been on the counter, sitting there for ages. I didn't even know if it had any power. I was too depressed to turn it on, so I just gave it to Jess. She powered it up and handed it to me.

In my hand it kept buzzing as one after another voice message kept showing up. Lots of random phone numbers and texts, lots from Jess, even a few from Jake and lots and lots of calls from Isak.

And in my hands, at that very moment, it started to ring.

Isak was calling.

69

"You better hurry or you'll be late," Jess called as I slipped on a floral top and Designer X's first pair of jeans—still in prototype actually. Her coated skinny jeans felt so wonderful, they made you want to dance.

A light evening breeze was flowing through the open window in the guest room. As I snapped the window latch shut, I noticed the yellowed front page of *The New York Post* tucked in a shelf in the corner. I couldn't believe Jess still had a copy.

Throwing a few things in one of Jess's monster bags, I dashed out of her West Village apartment to catch the PATH train at Christopher Street for my nightly reverse commute.

Truthfully, all the notoriety didn't hurt my blogger following. After a while the fan mail came back. You can't win an argument with a troll, so I never tried, and slowly they faded to the bottom of the comments list.

"I have more than a grudging admiration for you," one commenter wrote. "Fabulously brazen," another said. Flo stood by me, thankfully. She didn't mind how my fraudulent behavior exploded our "brand." Honestly, my brand was very much in keeping with who I was. Even if I wasn't who I said I was. As you can guess my clicks and visits skyrocketed—everyone had to check it out.

I gunned the Purple Beast and drove out of the parking lot by the Grove Street PATH station and made my way down the parkway, just as I had done every night for the last few weeks. One more time and I could take a break.

The New York district attorney's office examined my case and determined that I hadn't gained any money or valuables from the hoax. In fact, I had even managed to *lose* a valuable bracelet. So I hadn't actually committed a prosecutable crime. I fell back on Nan's advice and apologized like mad, promising to never, ever do it again.

The investigation was much harder on Nan. She's forgiven me over and over, but I couldn't stop feeling terrible about it. If Dahlia hadn't hired the private detective to investigate me, I don't think Nan would have ever told us her secret.

Everybody was astounded that the little ole lady in apartment 5A of Montclair Manor had been a major fugitive all that time. Only Betty claimed that she had been suspicious. She told channel 2 news that she knew Nan was hiding something. One or two of the other blue-haired ladies complained that she was a card shark and cheated at bingo.

Turns out, Grandpa was a well-known member of Cosa Nostra from the fifties who mysteriously dropped out of sight. Frank Wachowicz, aka Sammy Graziano, was known as the Gentleman Gangster, famous for dressing well and carrying his gun in a paper bag so that when he walked down the street, it looked like he was bringing you a sandwich.

The feds were so embarrassed that he had been living across the river in plain sight they claimed he was a secret witness under protection who sang like a canary.

"Grandpa was too honorable for that," Nan told me. It was the only time I had ever seen her angry. "My Sammy quit the mob for me, so we could have a normal life. Sure, there was a rule, the omertà, but, like a lot of rules, it was made to be broken. Your grandpa just knew how to make it work."

The New York Post reporter dug up some astonishing black-and-white pictures I had never seen of Nan and Grandpa at the Stork Club and the El Morroco, out on the town in the late fifties. Jess and

I would sit around with the photos and pick out the actual dresses we had redone.

In those pictures you could see what Nan was really like in her younger days. Sitting with Ida Lupino, Josephine Baker, Diana Vreeland, and an occasional Kennedy, she was one of those exquisite creatures whose intelligence was as impressive as her surpassing elegance. She wasn't just hanging passively on Grandpa's arm. You could see her active engagement with everyone around her.

Judge Ruston gave Nan a mere slap on the wrist, despite Dahlia's district attorney friend and the efforts of the DOJ's finest prosecutors. It was nearly impossible to prosecute her with Grandpa gone.

I overshot the parking space as usual, screeching on the brakes. I still couldn't control the Purple Beast. One tire was up on the parking block, but it was only one. I had to hurry; the band was already near the end of their set.

"I'm impressed with how you've utterly messed everything up," Isak said when we finally got together. I was so happy to see him that all I could do was agree.

"Seems like you have some fabulous shoes to fill," quipped Isak, referring to Nan's glamorous past. Even so, I apologized to Isak for being such a phony. He was utterly dismissive.

"Sure you're a phony," he said. "But you're a real phony. Not like all the phonies these days. I find it absolutely exciting that there are still people in the world who manage to have these thrilling, preposterous adventures. Besides, you know, we're all fakes."

The outrage and publicity hadn't affected Jess at all. Her Designer X line began to thrive immediately. It certainly helped that she had Isak Guerrere as her partner.

Mom is still a worry. She was the most emotional one about the whole Mafia thing, finally coming to grips with how terrified she had been as a child. They had to keep moving from house to house in the middle of the night, and she had to change schools all the time. She knew something was wrong, but no one would talk about it.

There was a waterfall of tears the night at the hospital when Mom and Nan had the heart-to-heart they should have had decades ago. Nan hugged Mom to tell her how sorry she was that she put her through so much and never told her why. That night, it felt like some big thing in the world had changed. A missing connection had been restored that made us a family again. Now she just had to get through the operation.

I slipped by the guys at the door, who didn't even bother to ask— they were used to me showing up late.

Courtney was the first one to tell me about Monica and Jake. Turns out Monica frequented Harris's Riverside Bar and Grill. That's where Courtney bartends. Monica would come in there on weekends with her two kids and her computer-nerd husband for brunch. She was married and lived in Weehawken. Courtney and Monica had struck up a friendship. Monica talked about this hot band she represented and what a hunk the lead singer was. It took a while for Courtney to put two and two together. The cowboy thing was an act for her music-management business, which she was devoted to almost as much as she was to her husband and two kids. She was actually a typical Jersey soccer mom wearing black-framed glasses and sweatpants.

The band had already finished the set by the time I made my way inside. The packed crowd was asking for another encore.

The truth is that I never felt like myself until I put on the Givenchy. It seems crazy that I had to go to such lengths to find out who I really was. But I guess something had to change. Something had to lift me up to get me out of where I had been.

"Sometimes good things aren't always so great," as Nan used to say, "and bad things often turn out to be good for you." I never understood that when I was a kid, but I certainly do after all that has happened.

As I wormed my way through the crowd to the corner of the stage by the soundboard, Jake came out by himself, plugged into his amp, and gave me a wink as he started to sing.

One night the look in your eyes was like a light.
It shined so bright that I couldn't see,
That . . . one . . . night.

The whole audience sang along to the chorus as it repeated.

That . . . one . . . night.

The NYPD took a long time to finalize their report on the investigation, and here's what I learned: if you pretend to be another real person it's fraud. And if you pretend to be a doctor and treat someone it's a crime. But if you pretend to be Audrey Hepburn, there's no law against that.

You know the clothes you wear?
The color in your hair?
You were so damn fine,
That . . . one . . . night.

Jake grabbed me and pulled me up on the stage, in front of the whole crowd at Reilly's, as the rest of the band came out and played the last verse, that strand of black hair falling across his face as he leaned over to kiss me.

It was a condition of our reconciliation. I had to be there every night for the encore at his last gig at Reilly's to make up for, well, you know. Can't say I minded at all.

Time heals everything; it truly does.
Time heals everything, but love.

I held on to him even after the song stopped, his heart still beating fast from the show. His whole body was warm. The audience felt so far away.

"So Lizzy, you ready to take off?" he whispered in that soft Jersey voice as the audience shouted.

I nodded.

We were taking Jake's '76 BMW and going for a little road trip, stopping wherever and whenever we wanted to.

Just me and Jake.

And his guitar of course.

I wondered if he could play "Moon River."

Acknowledgments

To say I owe a debt to Truman Capote is like saying a flea owes a debt to a dog. As a young disaffected writer from the South I read Capote with awe and wonder. It may be obvious that I am beholden to the author who created Holly Golightly and wrote the novella *Breakfast at Tiffany's,* as well as to screenwriter George Axelrod and director Blake Edwards, who adapted Capote's literary work for film. Discerning readers who know the novella and the movie adaptation well will find a multitude of allusions, references, homages, tributes, and deliberate echoes of those works and other movies from Audrey Hepburn's career woven into the scenes and dialogue of this book. I'm grateful to the bloggers and online fans for their inspiration in culling the most intriguing aspects of Audrey Hepburn's career.

I would also like to acknowledge the support of a number of generous people who I am lucky to have known and benefited from: novelist Jean Craighead George, my sole source of encouragement for decades; *New Yorker* fiction editor Veronica Geng, who early on helped me find a writing voice that it has taken a lifetime to recover; my editor, Brendan Deneen, who gave me a cupful of commas and told me to write three more chapters—I'm grateful for his faith in my abilities and his naive belief that I would finish on time; Barbara Marcus, publisher of the Children's Division at Random House, whom I was fortunate to have found during a brief window in her extraordinary career—her warmth, encouragement, and expertise were crucial to my efforts; Carla Riccio, former Dial Press editor, who worked almost as hard on this manuscript as I did and pointed me down the path toward that "sensuous journey with words" so many people talk about, which I was stumbling around, hoping to find; the *Southampton Review* editor Lou Ann Walker, who taught me the ropes in this and many other literary and life endeavors; costume designer Lisa Lederer, whose joie de vivre and original take on fashion has informed this book throughout; Amy Berkower at Writers House, Ken Wright, now publisher of Penguin Children's Books, and Nichole Sohl at St. Martin's, all of whom launched me on my way and carried me through the storm; Jan Kroeze, lighting designer and director of photography, and Michele Pietra, fashion stylist and couture expert, who gave me invaluable insider advice; Gloria Henn, who came into my life to help me build an empire and made me realize my job was to tear one down instead; Fred Perkins and Henry Guberman, who enabled me to find the room to do so and write again; Anne Richards, who has always been a compass from our earliest days working together; and film and stage director Mike Nichols, who likely has no idea who I am or where we met but who, in a casual conversation, mentioned a bit of advice that he used to try to help his children understand, which I couldn't stop thinking about and became instrumental to the story of this novel; and finally my kids, Mac, Jake, and Tess, whom I adore—if it weren't for their lively, wonderful lives and their endless needling and condescension, I wouldn't have worked so hard to succeed. Without the help of these wonderful people, this book would not have been possible.

Finally, the entire book attests to the enduring legacy of Audrey Hepburn, who intuitively and through her own self-design became the first movie star and actress of the poststudio age. Her personal transformation—the Pygmalion Effect, some call it—stands as a model for everyone, especially those young women living in the gray suburbs and forgotten inner cities aspiring to become something better and happier, intent upon the dangerous work of reinventing oneself despite whatever troubled origins they may have. Audrey Hepburn represents nothing less than the creative transformation of self and will always be an icon for others more for that reason than for her compelling talents as an actress, her advocacy for the world's children, or her sense of style.

DATE DUE
